INSHA

To Emma

love

Ays

# INSHALLAH

by

Alys Einion

HONNO MODERN FICTION

First published by Honno

'Ailsa Craig', Heol y Cawl, Dinas Powys, Wales, CF64 4AH

1 2 3 4 5 6 7 8 9 10

Paperback ISBN 978-1-909983-08-3

Ebook ISBN 978-1-909983-16-8

Published with the financial support of the Welsh Books Council.

Cover design: Rhys Huws

Text design: Elaine Sharples

Printed by Gomer Press

*This book is dedicated to the women in my life,
who have taught me so much.*

## ACKNOWLEDGEMENTS

I am blessed to be loved and cherished by some wonderful people, but this book would never have existed without the support of my doctoral supervisors, Tiffany Atkinson and Louise Holmwood-Marshall. Thanks both, you were a great team.

More than anyone else, I would like to thank Claire, for believing in me.

## Baraa

Today, I will marry the man who raped me.

A free woman never plans an escape route. I made this choice freely, the sun and the stars and the adolescent dreams of a girl grown up before her time notwithstanding. The weight in my hands belies the softness of the fabric that I lift, watching my face in the small bathroom mirror. My hands are covered in swathes of soft, black, silky stuff. This is the third time I've tried to do this. My eyes are huge in my face, with dark shadows under them. For the third time, I raise the headscarf and attempt to drape it correctly, folding the fabric around my head, across my shoulders, and securing it with pins around my face. Tight, tight, tighter, and the last part, the fold that covers my face, leaving only my eyes visible. This is me, invisible, on my wedding day.

At least I don't have anyone expecting me to wear white. No bridesmaids, no hen party, no bevy of friends and family in false formality, just me and my husband to be, in this shabby student house, and the open door to the future. No need to escape, because this is my choice, isn't it?

"Amanda?"

"Muhammed."

For such a slight man, he has an amazing presence, filling the room from his place in the doorway. A warmth fills me, flooding my senses. I've been here before, alone, taking stock, thinking of my choices and their consequences. The veil drops from my face, leaving it exposed, framed by the black scarf. Turning, I smooth the fabric of my dress over my body, but there is no tell-tale bulge.

"You look lovely," he says softly, his coal black eyes intense, shadowed. I want to keep looking into their depths,

1

into the mysteries of his feelings for me. He says he loves me. It should be enough.

"Thanks. And thanks for the dress." Thank you for paying for it, for recognising that even as hurried and low key as this formality is, a girl still wants a new dress on her wedding day.

This is the last day of my old life. I'll emerge from the mosque today a Muslim wife, soon to be the mother of his children. Then he will take me away to a new world, a new life where I can begin again.

It is a long journey. With twins, I suppose it seems longer than it would for the unencumbered. Five month old twins, my sweet boys. Abdullah with his placid nature and Shahid, who never seems to sleep or feel the lack of it. As we near Riyadh, I see the few women on the flight putting on veils to cover their faces, and some even covering their eyes. I can't bring myself to do it. How can they see, or breathe, with their entire heads covered like this? The interior of the plane is hot, and with the headscarf on, it feels hotter. I feel sweat forming across my forehead. Muhammed picks up the *niqab* and pushes it into my hand. "Put it on," he says, and I do so. My breath is hot on the inside of the fabric, and I want to hyperventilate, to pant, to tear it off. But the eyes of those around me are no longer following my every move. I have become invisible.

All the long miles here I have been wondering, questioning, but it was too late, too late, the plane already in the air, the seatbelts fastened, my choices made beyond any chance of return. Will they hate me for these choices, my children, or will they be glad I gave them the life I felt they needed? I dare not question too closely. I am a naïve Welsh woman and my husband is taking me home to his family in Saudi Arabia and I don't really know how it got this far. I am glad of the veil now. It means no one can see my face and the lingering doubts that claw at me.

Stepping off the plane is like stepping into the closeness of a sauna. Hot air like the intimate breath of a lover. Unrelenting. Two heavy babies and a carry-on bag, and all around me signs in the Arabic I have been struggling to learn to read and understand. We enter the terminal building, and the blessed relief of air conditioning. Muhammed strides forward, tall and proud in his white *thobe,* seeming larger and more powerful here than he did in Western dress back home. "Wait here," he says, none too gently, over his shoulder as I juggle the twins, Shahid grizzling loudly on my lap as I sit on a small bench, Abdullah asleep on my shoulder. I am tall and gangling, much taller than the few other women I see and many of the men. At least sitting down I am not so noticeable.

Muhammed speaks swiftly with the uniformed guards in customs, showing my passport. A female guard in *abaya* and veil is summoned as I wait, seated, in a small room. I take off the *niqab.* My identity checked, we proceed, with my face once more covered.

"Look down," he tells me, watching my behaviour closely. "Don't look people in the face. Don't raise your eyes to meet them." But my tallness, my towering presence, makes this demure stance ludicrous. I am downcast and still lofty. We move towards the baggage reclaim area, and Muhammed leads us to the right belt, then fetches a trolley. I am still holding both babies, and as the belt begins to move, I look desperately for the buggy.

Abdullah wakes, and starts to cry, and I lift him up and try to talk and laugh him into quietness, but his eyes widen as he looks at my face, and he turns red and screams even louder. Of course, he has never seen me like this, with my face covered by black, only my eyes showing. To him I must seem like a stranger. This is my fault. I should have worn a veil before, regularly, so he would get used to it. Shahid wakes and joins his brother. They make an impressive noise.

Muhammed stands with the trolley, and I point to each bag as it finally appears. The buggy is here, and I unfold it and settle the boys in it. Abdullah stops crying, but Shahid still screams his protest.

"Come on," Muhammed orders, and we leave, him with the trolley piled high with my mismatched luggage, me with the babies. I feel awkward and uncomfortable, and the scarf blocks my peripheral vision. It is hard to remember to keep my eyes downcast.

Outside in the crowded arrivals area, Muhammed waves and calls to someone.

"Muhammed." It is a man a little taller than Muhammed, but very similar to him in features. Long white robe, and a scarf on his head. Like the men in the airport. They hug, chattering rapidly in a cascade of Arabic.

"Amanda, this is my brother, Ahmed," Muhammed says. Am I supposed to look at him or not? I don't know. How should I greet him? But Ahmed only nods at me, and gestures towards the exit, still speaking rapidly to Muhammed.

The doors open, and the heat hits me like a blow, and the brightness of the sun immediately makes my head ache. The smell of heat and exhaust, and something else, an almost spicy, organic smell, all suffocate me in the burning air. My mouth dries instantly. The heat closes in around me, like a vice, the air too hot to breathe, burning down my throat into my lungs. Panic rises, and I breathe slowly and try to calm myself. No one else seems bothered, but

4

the children are crying. Breathing shallow, quick breaths, I murmur reassurances to them, try to calm them. The black fabric of my scarf and clothes heats immediately, and the light is blinding white and too bright to allow me to see properly at first. My eyes adjust at last, as shapes coalesce into recognisable forms.

The airport is a cluster of buildings, there is a lot of traffic noise, and a lot of people. Blindly, I follow the two men until we reach a car, and climb in with the babies. As Ahmed puts the buggy in the boot, I hear questions in his voice, even if I don't understand the words. Muhammed answers, liquid language spilling forth, and I wish I could understand.

Too tired now to do anything but close my eyes and lean my head against the seat. The car smells of cigarettes and of the air outside, thick with the hot, strange smell. The boys are alert on my lap, looking out of the window with big, wide eyes. Shahid bangs on my chest as the car pulls out. Sweat is running down my back, my chest, and my neck. My mouth is so dry. I need water, and somewhere to lie down.

"Amanda," Muhammed speaks over his shoulder, from the passenger seat in front of me. I look up. I must have nodded off. My mouth tastes foul, and the fabric of my clothes is hot and damp. Both boys are red-faced and sweaty, still looking around in wonder. Muhammed gestures to me to get out of the car. "Come on," he says in a low, stern voice.

It is time. We have arrived. The sunlight blinds me again as I unfold myself from the seat and step out to greet his family.

A house, pale and sandy coloured. A big square house with small windows and a dark door, and then inside, welcome shadows, and cooler air, cool, cold, but scented with food smells and something else, something like incense. The sweat on my body chills suddenly as I stand on hard tiles in a dark hallway. Doors around me. Too tired, too tired, and the light and the smells are strange and wrong. Hot coffee and more spices and a sweet smell, like smoke.

"Muhammed…" I turn, but he is gone, and there are people around me, men and women and children. The boys are lifted from my arms. A small, wrinkled woman is standing before me, looking up at me with a fierce expression. I pull off the veil, and the headscarf.

"Hello," I say, and smile.

"You call her *Khala*," says a young woman appearing from a doorway to my left. "Hello Amanda, I am Layla. I am Muhammed's sister, and your sister, now," she smiles warmly. Huge brown eyes, and thick, long, chocolate brown hair, and soft, smooth cheeks and skin the colour of dark honey. A full, pink mouth. She's beautiful. And I am sweaty and red in the face, and I know my hair is a mess, and there are shadows under my eyes. What are they thinking of me now?

"Khala," she says again, gesturing to the older woman. "This is my mother. You should call her Khala. It means… auntie."

"*Khala*." I say experimentally, trying to make the 'kh' sound like she does, a liquid, throaty noise. "I'm very pleased to meet you both." Fall back on good, British politeness, good manners. My mother always said manners make up for a great deal. "I'm sorry, I don't speak any Arabic at all."

Khala opens her mouth and a torrent of words pours forth. I shake my head. Tears threaten, I want to rest, please. Please let me rest.

6

"This way," Layla says. She takes me to a quiet room, with a low couch like a sofa and thick rugs on the floor. The windows are curtained. It is dim and cool and welcoming after the heat and light, the colours muted. The boys are there, with a girl of about nine or ten. She looks like Layla, but her face is fuller, softer, and her eyes have a glint of something calculating as she looks me up and down.

"This is my sister, Gadria," Layla says. "She is very pleased to meet her nephews at last, as am I."

"Your English is very good."

"Thank you. It is not so good, not all the time. But I have been practising, in school, ready for you to come."

Khala appears, tiny, dark and swathed in a black dress that seems more menacing on her as the backdrop to her fierce expression. She wears a headscarf fastened tightly around her wrinkled, brown face. She moves fast, full of energy. She sets down a tray of a hot, dark drink in small glasses; the air is suddenly thick with a hot, steamy mint smell. My mouth waters. She hands me a glass of hot, mint tea. Why do they serve a hot drink in a hot country? But the drink cools me immediately. Layla pours me another glass.

More words I can't understand. Khala picks up Shahid, who stares at her in fascination.

"My mother says, which is this one please?"

"This is Shahid," I say. She hugs him, strokes his hair, and his cheek, kisses him, and croons at him, all the while talking in Arabic. After a moment, he smiles.

Layla is smiling too.

"And this is Abdullah, then." Layla picks him up, ignoring Gadria's complaints, and her mother sits down and takes him on her lap beside Shahid.

"Good, strong boys, she says," Layla remarks, sitting beside her mother. "They are big, yes?"

"Yes, very big, they eat a lot!"

"But my brother said they…came early, not at the time they should?"

Khala is looking at me. Suspicion. She's had twelve babies, for heaven's sake, she would know. I told him this would happen.

"Yes, they were early, but they did very well, in the hospital, and afterwards, and they feed well, I think they have caught up."

Suddenly Khala grabs my wrist, pulling it towards her, then my other, then shakes both my hands, raising her voice, shouting at me.

"What, what?" I look at Layla in confusion.

"You have not your wedding gold?"

"I don't know, what do you mean, I have my ring." I show Khala the ring, but she bats my hand away, still shouting. Layla hurries from the room, then returns.

"Muhammed did warn us, so my mother had these ready, but I think she expected you would have some, at least, yes?"

I have no idea what she is talking about.

Still gripping one of my arms, Khala takes a pile of gold bangles from Layla, and starts to try to force them over my knuckles and onto my wrists.

"Oh, please, no, don't, thank you, I mean, thank you for the gift, but I really don't like to wear bangles, I don't like anything on my wrists."

All three of them are staring at me. Layla translates, or at least, I hope she does.

Khala continues shoving the bracelet onto my wrist.

"Please, stop, I really hate having anything on my arms at all."

"But you must," Layla sounds upset. "You must, please, it is very important."

"Why?"

"You are married."

I stop fighting, and Khala relinquishes my hand. Layla helps me put the gold bracelets on. "Why must I wear them?"

"Oh, a bride, a woman, she marries and then…the next day, the morning after, the…"

She stops speaking, and her colour darkens. Blushing.

"Yes, ok, so after she is married, she has to wear bracelets?"

"Yes, it is a shame if you do not. If you do not, it is like you are not married. You do not…look married, to other people. It means shame."

"Right. Like a wedding ring."

She nods.

The metal is cold but warms immediately. It feels hard and bulky on my wrists, and my skin crawls. A shudder, suddenly, someone walking over my grave. The bracelets ring sibilantly when I move, a constant constriction on my flesh.

"Didn't you have gold at your wedding?" Layla asks.

"No. It was a small wedding. I think Muhammed felt that there was no need."

Pause. Translation. Response. Am I imagining that Khala sounds so annoyed?

"My mother will buy your dowry gold," Layla says then. She is smiling. "She says, you must have your dowry gold as soon as possible. I can see you don't understand so I will tell you more about it. When a bride is married, she has a dowry, this is her price, her worth, yes? It shows how important, how valuable she is, to her husband and his family, and to everyone else. Special gold jewellery is put on. This is the sign of her dowry. My mother will buy this for you."

9

I know this is a gift, a kindness, really, but it seems more like she is saving face. Is it my fault I don't know about these things?

"Please tell her, thank you. That is very kind."

Waves of fatigue rush over me. "The babies fed recently, they will want to sleep," I say to Layla. "And I am very, very tired. Is there somewhere I can go and rest?"

She looks worried. Then nods. "Yes, I will show your room."

I pick up Shahid, and she takes Abdullah. I can't distinguish one word from the conversation between her, Gadria and Khala. They don't seem to pause anywhere. How does anyone learn to understand this language?

"This is your room," Layla opens a door on the first floor. A large room, painted white, with closed blinds and a big, wide bed and a large white cot next to it. Abdullah is already drooping, and settles immediately. Shahid, for a wonder, starts to close his eyes too.

"Thank you Layla. Can you show me where the bathroom is, please?"

"Yes." She shows me a room. "This is women's bathroom. No men come here. The men's bathroom is there."

"Thank you for your help."

She smiles, and when I come out of the bathroom, she is gone.

The bangles irritate my wrists as I lie down, sliding one hand under the pillow as I always do. The thin bands of metal press into my skin, an unpleasant feeling. The world spins away, and I know sleep is coming, at last.

In the dream the light is blinding me, and I can't see, and vague shapes are beyond me, many shapes, all clad in strange colours, all faceless, shouting at me in a language I don't recognise. Too many shapes, people pulling at me, someone is tying my wrists, shackling me, holding me, I can't get away, let me go, let me go.

In the dream I am pinned. I am trapped, in a small place. I cannot get out.

Walking from the bedroom, down shadowed stairs, across echoing tile and shadow into a small room with closed blinds. Blinds, blinding, the sun glaring. In here the shadows. No one rushes, no urgency in step or voice or attitude of body. In their dresses Muhammed's sisters seem like patchwork pieces against the colour of the room, contrasting and yet fitting. Belonging. In my denim skirt and peasant blouse I feel unfit for any of this. The street sounds are muted by shutters and drapes, the light too dim. I am lost in the shadows.

Layla appears, looking friendly. Gold combs hold her hair back, and her fresh face is eager.

"You are well? You are rested?"

"Where are the twins? And Muhammed?" I have no time for pleasantries. While I was sleeping someone has taken the babies from their cot, taken them who knows where.

"Our mother took them," Layla explains. "She and Muhammed have taken them to see our father."

"Taken them? Where?"

"Into the family room," Layla explains kindly, but she looks alarmed. Yes, I think, you may speak English but you do not understand me.

Layla leads me through doors and past a carved wooden screen in the hallway, into a large room at the front of the house. It is lighter, and a large television stands in one corner, tuned to an Arabic news channel. The pitiful smattering of Arabic I had half-heartedly tried to learn is of no apparent use. The relentless linguistic stream is a thread of unintelligible syllables and unfamiliar sounds. How on earth am I ever to understand it?

Muhammed sits on one of the low couches. The relief at seeing his familiar face is like a rush of cool air.

"Muhammed," I cross the room to him. He does not rise, or kiss me, or even hold out his hand to me as he would at home. Is this some cultural issue? But there is a faint smile as he looks at me, a smile I choose to interpret as kind. Perhaps he understands. "You slept a little?" he asks.

"Yes. Thank you."

Rugs and cushions cover the floor. I smell coffee and cooking and cigarette smoke and other, indefinable smells. It is warm inside, but not hot. My babies are being handled by Muhammed's father, who nods at me, and his mother, whose sharp voice spits out Arabic invective as I reach for Shahid.

"She says he is ok to stay with her," Muhammed offers. "You can rest now." I wait for him to reach out, to touch me, or to come and sit beside me as we sat, back home, sharing space, our bodies connecting. But he doesn't.

"I'll take him now," I insist, reaching for Shahid, and for the moment she relents. I could have anticipated this, I suppose, the family wanting to monopolise the babies.

"You are feeling better?" Muhammed asks softly as I settle Shahid against my hip. He is eager to feed.

"I'm rested. I woke up, and the children were gone."

He shrugs. "You're with my family now. They are happy to help. You don't have to do things by yourself now."

"That's good." I try to swallow my unease and smile. "Should I feed them upstairs?" I ask him. Layla hovers in the doorway. Unspoken communication passes between them, and then Khala interrupts with another torrent of Arabic.

12

"You can use the…" Layla says a word in Arabic, it sounds like "gorfer fire" and I am led back to the small, shadowed room beyond the screen.

"This is…" she pauses, "a room for women. Do you understand?"

I nod. "Could you bring Abdullah to me? I expect he will want to feed too."

"Yes, if you wish." She leaves, and I settle Shahid to my breast, letting the blouse fall so that my flesh is not exposed. Layla returns, holding a sleepy Abdullah. On the low couch, I balance him under my arm and he latches on to the breast as if he hasn't fed for a week.

"No men will disturb you here," Layla says as I cover myself again, as modestly as possible with two babies at the breast.

"Thank you."

She stays while I feed them. I feel at a loss, the pressure to make conversation growing between us.

"You have a big family?" she asks me at last.

"Just my mother, father, two sisters."

"Two sisters, that is good. Are they married too?"

"My older sister is married, she has two children. I don't see them much. They don't live near."

"Yes, sisters often move away," Layla agrees. "My older sister lives with her husband in…" she says a word I don't understand – maybe it is a place name. "And your other sister?"

"Oh, well, she lives with my parents." I have no desire to try to explain her limitations to my new sister-in-law. Layla continues to sit with me, but I have run out of conversation.

Both babies sleep after their feed, and following Layla's suggestion, I lie them on floor cushions and cover them with the light cotton sheet she brings.

"It is time to cook the meal," Layla says then. She walks away.

Am I to follow? It seems so. But in the hallway I run into Khala, who starts chattering at me, but it all sounds like "yik, yik yik". Layla has disappeared. Khala starts trying to turn me around, her arms full of black cloth. She is shoving the clothes at me. "*El bisi, el bisi!*"

"What do you want me to do?" I shout at last, annoyed.

Layla sticks her head out of the kitchen door. "She wants you to put those clothes on."

"Oh." I take the things. The black dress or coat thing that the women wear is long but not long enough. A good three inches of ankle show below the hem. Khala tuts and fusses around me, and somehow I get the scarf fastened. Then a veil, over my head, completely obscuring my face. I can hardly see.

"*El basee a kibba, see, shukti?*"

"This is ridiculous," I say, lifting the veil. She yanks it down again. I pull it up. Like some old comedy film, we could go on like this forever.

"Amanda, you must learn to wear these things, my mother is showing you what the women wear here." It's Muhammed. He is resplendent in a long white robe, with a red and white headscarf held in place by a thick black ring of fabric. He looks so very different in this outfit, it's as if I don't know him. "It is not so difficult. My mother is trying to help you."

"Ok, ok," I say, pulling the veil down again. "But I can't see anything, Muhammed! Muhammed?"

But it seems he's gone again.

The kitchen is brightly lit and filled with modern equipment. Khala stands at a long counter, and with abrupt gestures I am put to work chopping onions and tomatoes.

Large pans cover the stove, and the smell of hot oil and onions makes me feel disjointed. Layla, Gadria and Khala move in unconscious harmony.

At last, Layla says, "Amanda, why are you wearing these in here?" She pulls at the veil.

"Your mum told me to put them on."

She bursts out laughing, as does Gadria. I feel hot and bothered, as I take off the yards of black fabric.

"She only wanted you to try it on. Hang it in the hall," Layla says, still laughing.

I do so, blushing furiously, feeling foolish and awkward. I have to try. I have to do this. I have nowhere else to go. My children need this, a father, family, a sense of place and security. All the things I fear I cannot give them alone. So despite my embarrassment I slip back through the shadowy hallway and into the brighter kitchen. The windows are frosted glass, and I feel strange as I keep trying to look out. Like some insect drawn to the light, my eyes return to the windows over and over again, rebuffed by the opaqueness.

"Can we not open the window?" I ask Layla as I help with the dishes piled up in the sink.

"We do not open the windows," Layla says. "Has Muhammed not explained? Women must not be seen."

"Oh." Why didn't he tell me?

I turn to Khala, trying to make conversation, a connection. "There is so much I don't know. I hope you can help me learn how you do things here."

Layla translates. Khala says something and turns away. Layla shrugs at me. "She is sad to have missed your wedding. That is not how we do things here. A wedding without family, it is a... Oh, I don't know the word."

I think I can guess it. Shameful. Muhammed was wrong. We haven't fooled anyone.

15

Khala doesn't like me. She speaks her anger though short, impatient gestures, darting looks and a determination to ignore me. Perhaps she is justified – I am an unknown quantity, untested, and essentially alien. I run and jump and move, answering to her shoves and gestures, tears pricking at my eyelids, bewildered. There are smells of spices, and the heat from the stove, and vegetables that look unfamiliar to my eyes, bigger and brighter and strange in shape and texture. At last she gestures me to the sink again, where I wash dishes and pots and knives, greasy bowls and spoons.

In a flurry of activity she serves the meal, gesturing me to follow her into another room, where the food is laid out on big platters on the floor. I am about to sit, when Layla says, "Amanda, we must wash first." I follow her and go into the bathroom to wash my hands. When I come out, she points back to the other room.

Everyone sits around the cloth. I fold myself awkwardly onto the floor.

The lamb stew is unfamiliar, chewy and spiced, greasy and sour. I take pains not to eat with my left hand, remembering what Muhammed told me about Muslim customs. I try to copy Layla, who takes pieces of bread, folds them around the meat and vegetables, and eats in quick, economic movements. I feel clumsy and awkward.

Gadria watches me during the meal. I stop eating. I can understand her being curious, but why is she staring so much? I smile at her. Her expression doesn't change.

"Amanda, we must help to clean up," Layla says afterwards.

"I am going to see to the children," I say, rising. Khala starts saying something, but I walk away. It's too much. The voices follow me down the hall, raised, angry maybe? I'm so tired still. I don't understand what is happening. In the other room, I watch the boys sleeping and try not to cry, but the hot tears come. When they wake, I feed them again, until they start fussing and crying and chattering. Layla appears, smiling. "Let me take them, yes? Then you can rest?"

"Thank you."

"My brother says you should go and lie down, maybe, if you are not so well." I nod. Yes, a sleep would help perhaps. In the dim bedroom I drift in and out for hours, not noticing when someone puts the twins to bed in the big cot, until I wake, my body attuned to a different diurnal rhythm, to find Muhammed sleeping next to me.

In the warm darkness I listen to my sons breathing and wait for sleep. Minutes inch by, and I cannot relax or close my eyes. Muhammed sleeps next to me, unaware, snoring a little. I feel tense, stretched thin and tight like wire about to snap.

Then it comes, from inside me, starting down in my belly, in the place where the skin has tightened back to almost normal. It is a scream, a rabid, wild thing of a scream, and it builds and grows and rushes through me. But I stop it at the last moment, trap it with lips and teeth and will. I have come here to be what I must be. This is my life now.

A hand reaches for me in the darkness, and the scream retreats, secretes itself. The hand is on my breasts, then my belly, then clasping my hand and guiding it to Muhammed's erection. With practised fingers I encourage him, and he seizes me, all hot breath and sudden sweat. I open for him, wanting to feel him inside me. Roughly, he enters, but I feel nothing, only his body heat and weight on top of my body. I sink into the too-soft mattress, and disappear.

## *Hawā*

The dark before dawn. An eerie sound permeates the room, distant yet insistent, penetrating. Men's voices, ululating and exhorting. It is the *adhan*, the call to prayer. This is the first prayer of the day, the dawn prayer, I remember. I perform the necessary cleansing, trying to remember the right order of things. I kneel and stand and kneel, and mumble my way through the Arabic words. The babies wake too, and their whimpering escalates until I can stop and pick them up. Khala appears as if by magic, and sweeps up Abdullah into her arms, gesturing for me to follow with Shahid. In the bathroom she starts to strip them off and wash them with brisk efficiency.

Suddenly, a shout, a strange, *lalalala* type noise, like a wail, bursts from her, and she is shouting in my face again. She looks at both boys, shouting at me, gesticulating.

"What the hell is wrong?" I demand, frightened now. What's the matter? Why is she so upset?

Layla appears, looking sleepy, in a long robe. "What is it, Umma?" Then she stops on the threshold, and looks aghast. "Oh, oh," she looks at me. "They are not…you have not…" She gestures to the boys.

"Oh, yes, they're not circumcised. I never got around to it. I didn't know where to go or who to ask. I assumed Muhammed would sort it out once we got here."

Khala is shouting again, and the boys are crying now in the confusion. Their grandmother ignores the screams, and has them dressed and bundled up within a few minutes, but she doesn't stop shouting.

"Please, tell her I am sorry, but how was I supposed to know? Muhammed just left me there on my own with the babies, and no one told me what to do!"

18

Layla translates, looking upset, but her mother storms off down the corridor. I can hear the ranting continue all the way down the stairs. Other doors in the house start to open. We've woken the entire household.

"I'm sorry," I tell Layla.

"She's upset," she replies, and hurries after her mother.

I wish I could talk to Khala. Settled into the women's salon with a cup of strong tea, I feed the twins and long to speak to someone, anyone. To whom can I go to for advice about this great task of motherhood? I want to know if I should start weaning them, and how. What foods should I start with? They are over five months old now, and the time is surely coming when I should start? How can I communicate my concerns to her? But she has brought up seven children, and given birth to twelve, or so Muhammed said. Surely she is the best person to ask?

I stroke Abdullah's soft hair and look into his huge, dark eyes. His skin is the colour of my tea; brown, but milky, softened, diluted. His hair, and Shahid's, is thick and dark. He looks like no one in my family. I play with both of them, gently, fingers and toes, and elicit smiles that are a great relief after so many tears. Will they adjust to all the noise here? Again, I question my decision. I want desperately to go home. But I have nowhere else to go. I have to make this work.

No sign of Muhammed. He was gone when I got dressed and he hasn't come into this room where I feed the boys. Layla said it was a room for women. Does that mean he will never come in here? I settle Abdullah on the floor again, and carry Shahid with me on my hip as I explore my new home, in search of my husband.

It seems there are two areas to the house. There is the

public area, in which the men sit, in a large, long room filled with light. The windows in every room are frosted glass, and thick curtains cover them, especially at night. During the day the curtains are drawn back, to show net curtains and to let in light. This is the family room, where the men sit and watch television, and talk when there are visitors. In the central hallway, a screen divides the public area of the house from the rooms which the women inhabit. Behind this, I move between the women's sitting room, with its small television and perpetually covered windows, and the kitchen. Between the kitchen and the men's room is the dining room, with doors at either end. Muhammed is nowhere to be seen. Where has he gone?

In the kitchen, I offer to help. Khala's small, black eyes look me up and down, and she barks instructions at me. Layla translates.

"Chop onion," she says. I obey. "Wash these," she says. I do as I'm told. Layla holds Shahid and croons at him in Arabic. He watches her distrustfully, then, for some unknown reason, relaxes, and cuddles in to her body. She smiles down at him. Layla is fifteen, and unmarried. She is still at school. When she looks at Shahid, her whole face softens. I stir pots which smell savoury and spicy, and strangely sweet, and wonder what on earth it is I am cooking.

Breakfast is an unfamiliar combination of a dish with onions and tomatoes, and some sort of porridgey, yoghurty thing with fruit and nuts in it. It is sweet, and has a strange texture, but smells appealing with cinnamon and other spices. I am hungry enough to eat almost anything. The ritual of the meal is mystifying. First, Khala takes a long sheet of plastic from a roll in the kitchen, and lays it out on the floor, spreading it flat. Then she places a large white tablecloth on top of it. Flat bread on a plate is set down, and the large platters of food. Spoons are placed around the centre.

Sometime during the cooking the men have all appeared. "Muhammed," I say when I see him, waiting for some gesture from him. He smiles but looks distant. "What is it?"

"I…" I don't know what to say. Khala says something to him, and he nods. "You are helping my mother, yes?"

"Yes."

"Good."

The men sit, then after some discussion, the women join them. We use the bread to dip up food with our fingers, or just our fingers. Again I find this all very difficult, and envy the ease with which they scoop and eat, with an innate grace. I eat a little, Abdullah on my lap, Shahid on Layla's lap.

Khala starts the questions again, as soon as the meal is finished.

"When were they born?" she asks, and again I give her the date we had agreed on, to make it seem that they were conceived after we were married. There is some discussion amongst the family. It gets quite heated. I watch their faces, trying to divine somehow what they are talking about. At last, responding to an order from her mother, Layla turns to me.

"They are planning a wedding for you. Our mother says that there must be some sort of celebration, to welcome you, and so our family can meet you."

"Is that really necessary? It's been over a year now, and we already have children."

Layla translates. I don't need to understand the words to get the meaning of Khala's response. She is emphatic and her vituperative response alarms me. Abdullah starts crying on my lap.

"You will need to be introduced to the family," Layla insists.

"I can understand that, but we are already married. It seems stupid to have another wedding. Muhammed," I turn to him, "Can you just explain that I don't see any reason to have a wedding?"

The raised voices and shouting are disturbing, and Abdullah continues to cry. I stand, awkwardly, and try to leave the room, but Khala rises too, and hurries up to me, almost spitting the words at me. She takes Abdullah, and holds him up to her shoulder, patting his back, and then turns her back to me. She returns to her seat, her staccato gestures and invective continuing.

"Why is everyone so angry?" I demand of Muhammed, who seems to be ignoring the interaction.

"What?" He looks at his mother. "No one's angry."

"But everyone is shouting."

He shrugs. "They're just talking."

"Well, let them know that I do not want a wedding, and as far as I'm concerned, there won't be one."

"Amanda, this is my family. These are traditions for us."

"I know. But we are married, we have children, if she wants to do something can't she just have a party for us or something!"

"You don't understand."

"I don't. Not at all. But I am not going to be put on display so she can hang more bloody gold on me and make me a spectacle!"

"You should not be so ungrateful."

"I am not ungrateful, Muhammed." My voice softens. "I am very grateful and glad to make a new start with you here. I am glad that my sons will have your family around and I am happy to be here with you. Please just explain to your mother that I don't like being the centre of attention and there's no need to go to such expense, ok?"

"I will tell her," he says, but his face has darkened and I know he is not happy to have to deny his mother her wishes. The conversation which follows between them is unfathomable to me, so I go back into the women's room with Shahid, and set him down. Soon he is rolling on the floor and playing with his toes. He smiles at me. I tickle him and then pick him up. He laughs, and that makes me laugh too. Back on the floor he lies content, eyes starting to close.

Back in the dining room I fold myself back onto the floor. Abdullah reaches for the piece of bread I pick up, so I give it to him, and he starts gumming it enthusiastically. The food has cooled a lot, and the sweet thing is almost pleasant. I have a few more mouthfuls. Then I realise Khala is speaking to me.

"What does she want?" I ask Layla. There is more Arabic.

"We have to make the tea," Layla says. "Come, I will show you. Leave Abdullah here."

Back in the kitchen, we make sweet tea with mint, and bring it into the dining room with small, clear glass cups on a tray. Then Layla instructs me to clear the dishes, and then orders me around the kitchen. She watches while I do most of the cleaning up, using Arabic phrases and then translating them, trying to get me to understand. "I am going to school now," she says, finally. She leaves without another word. I feel lost. What do I do now? Should I clean the stove, or clean something else? What do I do with the food waste?

Soon enough, Khala comes back in, and starts on me

again, pointing, pushing, and shouting the words in Arabic. Slowly I figure out what she wants me to do, but obviously not well enough or fast enough for her. She pushes me out of the way frequently to demonstrate how she wants things done. "*Nubthathee!*" she says, again, and again, as I wipe surfaces, wash dishes, sweep and mop the floor. "*Nubthathee.*" I think it means clean.

At last, exhausted and confused, some time alone with the boys in the women's room. Muhammed has gone out, somewhere. He didn't even bother to say goodbye. The twins want to play, and when I turn the TV on, I find with relief that alongside the Arabic channel you can get an American news channel. It is a pleasure to listen to English.

The *adhan* sounds, mid-morning, I think. Khala communicates her wish that I should pray with her. First, she instructs me in how to carry out the ritualised cleansing, and which parts of the body should be washed, in what order, and I follow, corrected constantly. Then the praying. She indicates the direction, and I follow her lead, and kneel and stand and prostrate myself as she does, mumbling the words I have learned. I can't find the calm centre that I reached when praying alone. Again, I feel awkward, ill-prepared, an ill-fitting garment. Nothing I do is as it should be done. I stumble over the words, start to stand when I should be kneeling, kneel when I should be forward on my face. She is judging everything about me, it seems, and in every respect, I fall short of what she would expect in a daughter-in-law.

Just when I start to relax, there she is again, my diminutive mother-in-law, shouting and gesticulating and physically pushing me around until I do what she wants. I help with washing, hanging the clothes to dry in a small courtyard. The boys start to cry, I can hear them in the little

24

sitting room, their howls escalating in volume. I run to fetch them, but as I leave, she grabs me and shakes her hand in my face. I pull away. She marches off.

I make up two bottles, determined to carry on mixing the feeding and moving towards weaning them, but when I bring them into the women's room, where Shahid has been screaming as loud as he can for the last ten minutes, she is there, with her blouse lifted up, bringing him to her breast. Abdullah has quieted, and is watching them both with his big, dark eyes.

"What are you doing?" I ask, in English, of course. She looks at me. She doesn't understand my shock. I reach for him, and pull him away. "Don't do that!"

This is followed by another stream of Arabic. I think she is telling me how to calm the baby down, or maybe that she was happy to do it. Or maybe she is saying that she has had twelve babies and is a much better mother than me. I don't know. But I do have two babies to feed. So I hand her one of the bottles and give Shahid back to her, then pick up Abdullah, and hold him close, offering him the other bottle.

After this feed, it is time to cook again. In the absence of an interpreter, I stand, non-plussed, after the boys are set down on the floor cushions, sleepy and complacent. In a stream of language, with some prodding and poking, Khala herds me back to the kitchen.

I wash my hands, and she begins showing me how to cook. "*Bhusal*," she says, handing me a large white onion. I take it. She gestures to a chopping board. Ok. So far so good.

"*Sikeen*," Khala says then, and hands me a knife.

Right...

"*Ghuttee!*" she orders, gesturing to the knife and the

onion. Not so difficult. But I slice the onion and she wants it chopped, so she shows me, nearly taking my finger off in the process. She hands me more, and I chop them, feeling slow and clumsy. The onions go into the big pan on the stove. The sharp, onion smell fills my senses, and my eyes start to water.

"*Dhomatt*," she shows me a bowl of tomatoes. "*Ghutee!*"

"Like this?" I say, making neat slices. She smacks my hand away, and shows me again. I follow her lead.

And so it goes on.

"*Dijaj*". Chicken.

"*Zate*." Oil.

"*Shai*." Tea.

"*Ghara*." Coffee.

"*Tsuckra*." Sugar.

My head aches with trying to remember the words. It feels like we are cooking for an army, the quantities are so large.

Chicken, cooked with spices that I must grind in a mortar and pestle first. Rice. Salad. Round flat breads. She tells me the name of each dish several times as we cook. The chicken dish is *Al-Kabsa*. The counters are too low for me. The pots she uses are huge. The fat she uses for frying comes out of a plastic bucket. The great big pot she puts the rice in is too heavy for me to lift, but she hefts it easily from the sink and places it on the stove. The burning spice smell makes my nose itch; the onions keep my eyes watering. She says a lot of things to me, none of which I understand. I feel tired, and out of sorts. I want to sit down, and I feel hot and bothered and irritated. But she doesn't stop, taking out odd-looking dark lumps which smell vaguely of citrus, shoving them at me, and then stirring the rice. "*Laymun aswad*," Khala says, pointing at the black lumps. I nod. She makes a salad, ordering me to do most of the chopping. I am surprised at such a meal in the middle of the day.

A glance at the clock tells me it is just after two. A short while later Layla reappears, home from school, and Gadria with her. Layla takes off her *abaya* and veil and comes into the kitchen, looking around for what needs to be done. Her mother immediately starts a rapid torrent of conversation, which she returns. Then she turns to me. "She wants to ask you if you have any other clothes."

"Of course I have other clothes," I say, feeling myself blush. Layla looks at me curiously. "I just wore this because the skirt is long and Muhammed said…"

"She will take you to the dressmaker," Layla says. "The dressmaker will fit you with clothes." Gadria glances at me too. A hot blush rises from my neck to my eyebrows.

"Muhammed said that I would need to get clothes once I was here," I reply. "I know that the clothes you wear here are different to at home. I would appreciate being able to get some new things – I haven't really bought anything new since the boys were born."

Layla translates, or at least, she turns to her mother and speaks. Both women look me up and down.

"And she has spoken to Muhammed about the circumcision. We will take them to the Imam soon."

"Oh."

I know it has to be done. And it's a minor operation, surely? I wish I could talk to her about this. I need to know more, to know what's involved.

"Layla, how is it done?" I ask her. She shakes her head. "Muhammed will tell you, I'm sure."

"But I need to know. I mean, what do you do, afterwards? How do you take care of them?"

27

Layla shrugs. "Yes, my mother will show you. She knows what to do."

The ritual of the meal starts again, the plastic on the floor, the tablecloth (I wonder if I should call it a floor cloth?) Then as I stand looking at the boys, asleep in the women's room, I hear voices beyond the screen. Layla comes in, carrying a sleeping baby, and sets it down "My father has brought a friend home with him, and our sister Fatima is here, with her husband. Do not go into the dining room. You must not be seen by the men who are not your family. The women…" she pauses, listening to the conversation in the rest of the house. "Men eat first," she says, and hurries away

After a short while, Khala opens the kitchen door into the dining room, and we take in the mint tea. She ushers me back into the kitchen, then goes back and knocks once on the door that leads to the men's room. Then quick as a bat in flight she darts back and closes the kitchen door behind her, joined by another woman so similar to Layla that I know she is yet another sister. In the kitchen, we drink tea ourselves.

"This is Fatima," Layla says. "My sister. She lives with her husband's family. She has two children – the baby you saw, and her older child, Suleiman, is with the men in the men's room."

"*Salaam alaykum,*" I say, feeling self-conscious. She gives the usual response, and then says, in English, "Muhammed is lucky, an English woman for a wife, and two sons immediately."

"You speak English as well?" The relief is so great that it is only then I realise how tense I have been, how excluded and stressed I have felt.

"Most of us do," she says. "We learn in school, it is

28

compulsory. English is the language of business, is it not?" Although her tone is mild, I sense a deeper meaning to what she says. Is she mocking me? Or criticising my Empire heritage?

She turns away, dismissing me now, and starts a conversation with her mother and sister. I sip my tea, feeling my stomach rumble. After so much cooking, I'm starving. Then I hear Shahid calling out for me, on his way to crying already. I hurry into the room, pick him up and put him to the breast, but after only a few minutes, he turns away and starts fussing. "Ok, I'll get you a bottle." I'm not surprised – my breasts feel less full now, and I think my milk may be drying up. Back in the kitchen, Shahid is passed to his aunt for inspection and admiration. The room is hot and stuffy with the lingering cooking smells. Layla takes over feeding Shahid, and tells me to do the dishes while we wait to eat. I wash the pots and pans, clean up the stove again, and watch the women talking. Fatima fetches the baby back in, and there is more discussion.

At last, we hear a knock on the dining room door. Khala waits a few moments, then opens the door. The men have eaten more than half of the food. Before sitting down, I check on Abdullah, but he is still fast asleep. Shahid is sitting contentedly with his grandmother. The women start eating. The food is barely warm now, but none of them seem bothered. Silence falls. As soon as we have eaten, it is time to make the coffee. I clear the dishes as I am bidden, and Layla makes the coffee, instructing me as we go along.

"First, you grind the coffee beans, and the spices," she shows me. The spices smell strong; cardamom, I think.

"Then you boil the water and the ground coffee together." She gestures to me to wash the platters while she works. I want to seem eager, interested, willing to learn. But

29

my head feels thick, and it is all so strange. Nothing even smells right.

"Amanda, look," Layla orders, an echo of her mother. "Now we strain the coffee, and then we add the spices, and boil it again." She shows me, pouring the coffee through a muslin cloth and sieve into a second pot, which she places back on the heat. The smell is bitter and yet perfumed. I start to feel a little sick.

Khala carries the coffee through, after handing Shahid back to me. I sense from this some sort of pecking order of tasks. Again the knock on the door, and the retreat. We take our coffee in the women's room, and I sit, playing with the boys on the floor, listening to the conversation with utter incomprehension. I don't want to be here. I wish I could be alone, just me and the boys. I'm tired and empty and I feel a bit sick. I ate very little food, partly because the chicken and rice was not hot, and it was greasy and hard to manage; partly because I found myself with no appetite when at last we were able to eat. Facing the dishes, half empty, picked-over, made me feel as if I was eating leftovers from someone else's plate. Perhaps this is what is making me queasy.

The boys are tired. As soon as I have finished the dishes, I take them up to the bedroom and put them in the big cot, settling them both down. Abdullah falls asleep within moments, but Shahid takes longer, refusing to settle without songs and a lot of attention. I stroke his nose gently to make him close his eyes, and eventually he stops resisting.

My body sinks into the soft bed. It is shaded and shadowed in this room, with the thick curtains drawn, but light spilling over the top and under the bottom to break up the darkness. A wave of dizziness makes me close my eyes. Jet lag. That is what they call this. I feel heavy, then

30

light, as if I am floating away. I can hear the voices downstairs, just faintly, the women's voices, the wail of a baby. What are they saying about me? They weren't unkind, just distant. They didn't ask any questions. I was expecting them to at least ask why. Why did I marry Muhammed? Why did I want to come to Saudi Arabia? Perhaps they don't want to know. Perhaps they don't care. Perhaps all I am is a burden to them, a problem that needs to be solved, or overcome. Does it matter? I am here now, and I can't go home.

So tired now. Too tired to keep my eyes open. The bed seems to be swaying underneath me. I can hear the babies breathing, a soft sound. I can hardly feel my own limbs, or the rise and fall of my own chest. But I can feel my head against the pillow, and I can smell the sourness of my sweaty body. And I can feel, deep in my body, the thrum, thrum of my heart beating. My mind chases itself in every decreasing circles, the words repeating in my head, *dijaj, laymun, nabthathee, nabthathee!* I am trapped behind glass and I can see no way out. Memories of my mother, telling me not to marry Muhammed, my friends on my wedding day, begging me not to do it. No one could understand. No one knew my history. How could I explain to them, really, that it was meant to be, that this is what I am *supposed* to be doing? Few of them have the same belief in fate. As I lie exhausted, the memories return, and I can't escape them, segueing into dreams that take me back to where it all began.

At sixteen I was like every other girl in my community, heading for a life of marriage, pregnancy, babies, and family. That's what life is like in the South Wales valleys. In the late eighties, in the aftermath of the miner's strike, I was offered no ambition other than to be somebody's wife. I had no choice about staying on in school either, although I loved books and had an interest in literature. I thought of maybe becoming a teacher, but it seemed a dream that was very far away with little possibility of realisation. Practicalities ruled. At sixteen I was supposed to leave school, get a job in a factory, and find a husband (or boyfriend).

So I did. Lots of women worked in factories, the camaraderie of the production line providing them with a life outside of the home. There was work, home, family, bingo on a Wednesday, the club on a Sunday afternoon, and the husbands working and tolerating their wives working, as long as tea was on the table when they got in. In the narrow cleft of my home valley, even after the mines started to close, there was still the Phurnacite plant, a vast Dantean hell of glowing reds and noxious fumes, like our own version of Mordor, spewing out poisoned water and air and turning the hillsides black. Winters were cold, and the long school holidays spent on hillsides playing in makeshift dens, or picking winberries in the summer sun, running screaming from flying ants' nests and chasing friends and siblings. My sister was too much older than me to be happy to have me tagging along, and would run away from me to meet with her friends, all practising their disco moves and putting Farah Fawcett flicks in their hair.

On cold days, low cloud days, the valley would fill with a thick yellow smog smelling strongly of sulphur, so thick it caught in your throat and nose and robbed the flavour from food. Washing could not be hung outside to dry, windows were closed, and children coughed and wheezed from one end of the village to the other. The mountainside by the plant was black, deadened, littered with the coal-black stumps and trunks of trees on which green shoots would grow each spring, only to be choked to death before summer. We lived in row upon row of council houses, played in streets paved with concrete, ran wild in the scrappy patches of green and trees, or in dilapidated parks and playgrounds.

Green, black, brown, gold, the colours of the world as I grew up, the colours a backdrop to school, home, friends of my own, and a growth into womanhood that brought the boys flocking round. My parents held themselves apart from most of the families on the street, the ones out of work, the ones who would never work, the wife-beaters and drinkers and the women who sold themselves to other men for the price of a bag of shopping. We were brought up to be middle class, even though money was tight. My father worked in the plant and brought home a wage, but there was little left over for luxuries.

My parents were preoccupied with Jan, my sister who would never leave home, and would always need care, simple and sunny as she was. Most of the time. She had her black moods but we loved her. Karen, my older sister, left home when I was twelve, and she was sixteen, to live with her boyfriend and work full time in a bank. She married him two years later. She followed the script. It was no wonder that I would end up doing the same, no matter how hard I tried not to.

I wake, confused, to find the twins gone again. Following the sound of voices down the stairs, I find them in the family room with their grandparents. There is some heated discussion amongst the men. Gadria is reading a book, lying on the floor in front of the television. Layla is in the hall, talking on the telephone, painting her toenails at the same time. Khala is playing with Shahid, laughing and tickling him. Abdullah is on Muhammed's knee, and his father, Abdelaziz senior, whom they call Baba, is talking to the baby, perhaps telling some kind of story, punctuated with gestures and hand shapes. I watch from the doorway. It seems I wasn't missed.

I sit down on the sofa, though it's not really a sofa, I think. It's more like a set of low boxes covered in fabric, with cushions on top, around three walls of the room. Or benches perhaps. Gadria stares over the top of her book at me for a while, then she returns to the page. Abdullah laughs suddenly at his grandfather, and I smile too. Khala says something to Muhammed, and he replies. I wish I could understand them. No one pays any attention to me. No one bothers to translate. I sit. What should I do? Should I ask them to translate? Should I try to start a conversation? I don't know. Would it be rude to interrupt? Paralysed by uncertainty, I just sit there. Muhammed gets up. I rise too. He leaves the room, and following him, I hurry into the cool hallway.

"What do you want?" he says as I join him.

"Where are you going?"

"Out. I'm going to meet Ahmed."

"Oh. What are you going to be doing?"

His stare is unfathomable. I don't understand. "I will be back later," he says.

"Muhammed, please, you can't just leave me here, I don't understand anyone."

"Amanda, don't be silly. They all speak English."

"Your mother doesn't."

"The others will help you."

"I know but you can't just keep leaving me here with them. I thought you and I would have time together too."

His face darkens. "This is my family. I know you have a

lot to get used to. But they have welcomed you and they will take care of you. You are part of my family now. I will be home later, then we can be together."

I don't know what else to say. "Ok, fine."

"I will see you later." He kisses me on the cheek, and is gone.

The family room again. Seated in the corner, I watch them playing with the twins. Layla sweeps in, says something to her sister, and then the pair of them rush out again. The phone rings, and Khala answers it, Shahid on her hip. The spaces in the room close around me. The light is dim, filtered by heavy curtains drawn across the windows. Shadows everywhere, and then the sudden scent of coffee, and Khala in the doorway, shouting at me and beckoning me to come.

In the kitchen, coffee and dates, a large tray. Then a knock at the door. Guests. No one speaks to me. I finish setting out the tray, Khala takes it, and hurries off. Women in veils disappear into the smaller sitting room. Khala passes me again, says something. I shake my head. Then she reappears with the twins, and, ignoring me, disappears into the room with the women.

Should I go in? Do these women speak English? Who are they? No sign of Layla to translate. What to do? I approach the door. Women talking rapidly, gesticulating, beautiful women in stylish clothes, their perfect hair and make-up shocking after the veils and scarves and great black draping coats. There are stains on my blouse, from cooking, and my skirt is creased. I feel scruffy and unkempt. My hair is brushed, but it's not styled. I'm not wearing make-up. The twins are being passed from woman to woman, admired it seems. They look happy. There's only one place for me to go. I climb the stairs to the bedroom, turn on the air conditioning, and sit down. What am I to do with myself? I lie back, letting fatigue claim me.

I can hear the boys down in the rooms below, but they sound happy. Muhammed is right. It's good to be able to let someone else help for a change. Their baby sounds follow me into sleep, where I sit, unfathomably, in a library, trying to find the right book on raising a child as a Muslim. Every book I open is blank. When I look around, the shelves stretch endlessly, and when I call for help, nobody comes.

Waking, I feel Muhammed's hands upon me. He takes advantage of his masculine physiology and pulls me to him, still asleep, and enters me from behind. I wake to the feeling of him thrusting into me, the pushing against my buttocks, his hand on my breast, clutching and pressing. When he is done, he leaves the bed, and the bedroom, and I roll onto my back. I can hear voices in the rest of the house, traffic noise from outside, and one of the children starting to wake. This prompts me to drag myself out of bed. The bathroom first. I dash in, and although I hear Shahid starting his usual morning protest, I take a shower, emerging to realise I do not know which towel to use. I take a clean one from a stack on a shelf. I dry myself, put on my nightdress, and hurry back to the babies. Shahid is wet, Abdullah is stinking and starting to squirm. I change them both, wrap up the nappies, then dress myself while they lie in the middle of the bed, playing with their own feet. The voices from downstairs continue. Layla is calling me. With a baby in each arm I make my way to the kitchen.

"I need to feed the boys," I tell Layla as she beckons me in.

"You must help with breakfast," she insists. "I will feed them."

"No." I shake my head. "I will feed them. I'll help when they are finished."

36

Gadria looks up at this, taking her gaze from the pot she is stirring. Khala protests in Arabic.

In the women's sitting room, I settle one on each breast, and then Khala comes running in, shouting, waving her arms, communicating by gestures her annoyance and her insistence that I should be helping with the food. I shrug, as best I can with the boys across my lap. She leaves, and I hear voices in the kitchen. Is it normal to talk like this? I wish I could understand what she is saying.

Tears flow down my face. The rhythmic sucking at both breasts starts, stops, starts again, as both boys feed. Shahid holds my breast between his two hands, possessive. "UmmShahid," Layla says, from the doorway, Gadria standing behind her and peeking around at me. UmmShahid means mother of Shahid. It is supposed to denote respect. "Breakfast is ready." Does she notice the tears? I feel so alone. I miss home. But this is my home now.

## Bil-_g_aibi

"You have much to do here, with the babies, and the housework." Layla looks at me earnestly. "UmmShahid, you must, how can I say it? You must help, like me, with the … the cooking, and to keep the house clean…"

"Ok, I understand." Well, it is no different than keeping my own home clean. And here it won't be just me.

"So, I must explain to you…"

Ah, so that is what the rapid discussion at breakfast was about. Khala was giving Layla her instructions before going shopping. With the boys asleep, Layla takes me about the house.

"Here is the place to keep the cleaning materials," she says, pointing to a cupboard in the room beyond the kitchen. "This is where to do the laundry." She shows me how to use the machine, the dryer. I fetch a load of the boys' clothes, and we start a wash.

Back to the kitchen. "We clean, every day, all of this," she points to the stove, the sink, the surfaces, shows me the places where the food is stored. "And we sweep here, and clean the floor." The tiled hall, the stairs leading up to the first floor.

In and out of every room, she instructs me in the cleaning that must be done. Sweep here, clean that. There are three bathrooms, one downstairs, two upstairs. "Bathroom for the men," she says, in the downstairs one, which is tiled in light cream tiles, and features a hole in the floor, and a long hose in the wall with something like a shower head attachment. "Women do not use."

"Right." I try to pay attention. I still feel tired, fuzzy, not quite connected to the world, or to myself. When will the jet lag dissipate?

"This is the formal room, the men come here, but we all sit here when it is just family. We sweep, vacuum, clean here. Make it neat."

"Ok."

"Here, dining room." We enter through a door from the front room, and then leave through another door which opens into the hall.

We go through each bedroom, the two bathrooms upstairs. At last we are back downstairs, where both twins still sleep stretched out on cushions in the smaller sitting room. I wish I could join them. The sheer size of the house is daunting.

"Thank you," I say to Layla. "I am happy to help. This is my home now."

"Where are you going to start?" she asks.

"Oh!" I wasn't expecting this. "Well, I suppose, while the boys are asleep, I'll clean the kitchen, maybe, sweep the hall."

Layla nods. I hurry to the kitchen, find what I need, and start cleaning. She doesn't follow me. I don't know where she is, but I suppose she is doing whatever it is teenage girls do when they get some time to themselves. My back aches. I'm tired and starting to feel hungry, but I don't feel as if I can just help myself to food.

When Shahid wakes and starts yelling in protest at my absence, I have already cleaned the kitchen, the laundry room, the entrance hall, and the downstairs bathroom. My back aches, and my hands are wrinkled and red from the cleaning products and the hot water. I pick up Shahid, who quiets as soon as he sees me, and return to the hall. Layla is still nowhere to be seen. Should I call her?

Shahid likes to be on my hip. I can manage to tidy up, and vacuum, though it is awkward with him there. At last

I have to stop, sit down in the smaller room with my boys. I fall asleep with Shahid on my lap. Layla wakes me. The *adhan* is sounding. "Amanda, you must pray," she says. "My mother is home. You must then help with the cooking."

"Yes, of course." But I am dizzy with fatigue and sleep, and feeling a little sick. I push myself upwards, climb the stairs to the bathroom to get ready for prayers. I just want to lie down, lose myself in sleep. A longing for something else, something familiar, rises in me, but I push it down.

"Amanda?"

It is Muhammed, appearing from nowhere as I return to the bedroom to put away clean clothes.

"Muhammed." I let the pleasure and love show in my voice, my face.

"You have been helping, today?"

"Yes, I have. I have done cleaning, and laundry, and cooking …" I look for approval from him, for praise. He smiles, and a flood of relief washes through me. "I said to my mother you were a good wife, good at looking after yourself."

"I don't think your mother likes me." He opens his arms and I move close to him. He smells of sunshine, dust, and sweat, and that unfathomable smell on the air that greeted me when I first arrived.

"She will get to know you. She doesn't dislike you, but you have to admit, it's not easy for her to have you here."

"I suppose not."

"So be patient, you will learn how things are done, and get to know everyone. Ok?" He drops a kiss on the top of my head. Everything feels right again, like when we were first together, first married, sharing most of each day with each other. We had to get to know each other then, too.

"Ok."

"Well, hurry now as I know my mother needs you to help with the dinner."

The sickness starts, early in the morning, with nausea that rises at the smell of the food cooking. I realise my tiredness and the feeling of never having enough sleep is not jet lag. My period is four weeks late. I know I am pregnant but I don't want to think about it. The memories of last time are still too fresh. My mother said I would forget, but I have forgotten little about the birth, and the discomfort of late pregnancy. I can't imagine coping with another baby with the twins still so young. Still, I know what will be will be. I can only accept.

Breakfast. My boys sit on the floor with us. Ahmed, Baba and Muhammed have eaten. Ahmed is waiting to take the girls to school. We sit around on the floor, and Khala tempts both boys with a soft, milky rice dish. They smack their lips enthusiastically, and open their mouths for more.

I manage the sickness in the morning, throwing myself at what needs to be done and trying to keep up with the demands of my mother in law. I am learning Arabic words, enough to understand what I am being told to do, but not enough to start having anything like a conversation with anyone. Layla has been helping me, as has her sister-in law, when she visits with her daughters, which is, seemingly, every other day. Contrary to Saudi tradition, Muhammed's brother Abdullah lives with his wife and children, not with his parents, but in a large house several streets away. It is bigger than this one and has a swimming pool. Abdullah works in some kind of company connected to the oil trade. That is how anyone who has money makes their money, here. Abdullah is very successful. He also does some teaching in America, as does his wife. Ahmed works with his father; they import, sell and fix cars. Muhammed is working with them too, now. I have managed to learn this much.

I feel weak, and still a little nauseated, but I make myself eat some of the sweet dish, and some bread. There is a perfumed taste to the food, some spice or herb maybe. It doesn't taste right. As soon as I stop eating, Khala gesticulates to me to start clearing up.

I jump to my feet, and take out some plates, then start washing up. Gadria and Layla leave for school. When I return to the dining room, Khala has disappeared with the twins, and left the rest of the dishes. My knees ache as I squat down to start clearing up.

"What is this?" I ask Khala. We are in the kitchen, preparing the main meal. The onions are chopped, the flatbread kneaded and prepared (with much poking, prodding and incomprehensible criticism), and I'm chopping peppers and tomatoes. Khala is putting spices into a huge pan, larger than I would have ever imagined using at home. I am curious about a large pile of pale, odd-looking stuff that she has brought out. "What kind of meat is it?"

She shrugs at me. She tosses spices and oil into the pan, then points at the whitish grey stuff. "Ghuttee!" she orders. I take the stuff; it feels greasy but tough, and has an odd smell. My stomach churns. I chop it as directed, then Khala puts it into the pan. The smell that rises is awful, and I run from the kitchen, up the stairs, and into the bathroom, just making it in time.

I feel weak. I clean up the toilet before returning downstairs, trying to breathe through my mouth. Khala grabs my arm, and pushes me towards the pan, making stirring motions. I shake my head. "I can't. Please, let me just go and sit down. The smell is making me feel sick."

42

She pushes me towards the stove again.

"Sick!" I raise my voice. I make retching motions. She gestures me towards another pot, but the smell from the big pan is so disgusting, I can't bear to stay in the kitchen. Unable to make her understand, I walk away, go into the little sitting room, and shut the door.

"UmmShahid," Layla hurries in. How long have I been sitting here? The boys are gone, presumably removed by Khala. "What is wrong? Are you ill? My mother says you wouldn't help her with the dinner."

"Layla, can you please call me by my name."

"If you prefer, I suppose I can," she says. "But you should be helping."

"Yes, I know, I know I'm supposed to help with everything, but I feel sick. What on earth is she cooking? It smells like something died."

"It is a stew." Layla looks bewildered. "I don't know the word, it is a meat stew." She disappears, then reappears with a dictionary. "Ah, yes, it is meat from the... intestine?"

Tripe. She is cooking tripe. No wonder it smells so bad. It smells like curried dog shit.

"I can't stand the smell," I say to Layla, who still looks perplexed. "I really can't."

"Have you finished the cleaning?" she asks.

"No."

"Well, perhaps you should do some now, and we will call you when dinner is ready."

"I'm sorry," I say. She looks just like her mother now, disapproving. I've let them down. "I can't help it. We don't eat tripe at home."

"There is rice, salad and bread as well," she says. "You don't have to eat it if you don't want to."

"Where are the boys?"

"Gadria is playing with them in the front room. She said you didn't wake when she came in. You seem very tired. Are you unwell?"

Should I tell her? I haven't mentioned it to Muhammed yet. "I think I am pregnant. Expecting another baby."

"Oh, that is good news." All smiles now, she hurries from the room, to tell her mother, no doubt. I pull myself to my feet, and follow her out, to find some task I can bear to do. But the smell of the tripe stew permeates the house, and I hurry upstairs to clean the bedrooms, wondering if I can ever get away from the stench.

Dear Mum,

*Thank you for your letter, it was good to hear how things are. I hope Jan is enjoying the new day centre, and Dad is getting used to being retired. I didn't realise he was going to be leaving the factory so soon.*

*I hope you are well too. Karen hasn't written to me yet, though I was hoping she might. I feel so far away. Everything is so different here, from what I eat to what I wear. I'm still struggling with the language, but I'm starting to understand a few more words.*

*You asked me to tell you about the family. Muhammed's family is vast. He has two sisters living at home: Layla and Gadria, and three married sisters, Fatima who has a baby boy two months younger than the twins, and lives nearby, and Nadia, who lives with her husband's family in a town near Mecca. Aliya lives in Jedda and is married to Nasuf. We see Fatima quite frequently. The daughters all speak some English, which helps. He has four brothers: Abdullah, who is married to Jahira and lives about three miles away, and works in the oil industry – they visit the USA where they both do visiting lecturing; Ahmed, who lives nearby and works with his father, and Abdelaziz, who seems to have a job of some kind but I'm not sure what it is, and who spends a lot of time away from home. Then there is Ali, another brother. He's in prison. I don't know why. There seem to be a vast range of cousins and uncles and aunts as well, but I don't really know who they all are, and it will take me ages, I think, to sort out all the relationships.*

*They are kind to me, Mum, really, and they are all trying to help me to settle in.*

*The boys are thriving. I get lots of help with them from Muhammed's sisters. They are both starting to eat solids, and they are alert, and active. Shahid has started crawling, and he's like a crab, scuttling about as fast as he can. Abdullah sits and watches him, it's really funny. They are growing so fast. Thank you for the clothes you sent, that's really kind. And thanks for sending me some books. I have read all the ones I brought with me. But don't feel that you have to send us things all the time, I know it is expensive.*

*I want to describe Riyadh to you, but I haven't really seen that much of it. I don't go out very much – there's no need. Khala, Muhammed's mother, does the shopping. (Khala's not her name, it means sister of my mother, but it's what I'm supposed to call her). It's too hot to go for walks, and women don't go out alone here. We have been to visit Fatima, who lives in a lovely house, and to visit Muhammed's brother Abdullah, but other than that, I haven't really been anywhere yet. It is hot here, hotter than the hottest day in summer, and the sun is blinding white. There is no grass anywhere, and the streets are dusty and sandy. But there are huge date palms growing everywhere, so there is some green. Everything is different.*

*I do have some news. I'm pregnant again. It's due in July. I'm feeling ok, though I've had some sickness. But everything*

45

*seems fine so far. I've been to the doctor, had a scan and blood tests. As far as I can tell, it's all ok.*

*I hope you are all well. I miss you all. Give my love to dad, and Jan, and Karen. Tell Karen to write to me.*

*All my love.*

*Amanda.*

I know she won't write back. I can send these missives regularly, chatty little updates about life here, but my mother will have no time to reply, even though I've included clear instructions about the return address and air mail envelopes and postage. Ever since I was six years old, when Jan came along, Mum's life has been set on one course, love and duty defining her response, her daily tasks. In many ways I am glad I am here, so I am no longer a burden to her. Too far to visit, I am safely put aside and dealt with, married off. No doubt she would like me nearer, as I know she misses the boys. But away from her there is no added pressure to be involved, and she can stay in her routine with Jan and my dad and the house.

She was good to me though when the babies came. I couldn't have asked for more support than she gave.

Muhammed had gone. A white plane climbing the sky carried him away. Outside the airport I looked up and imagined myself beside him, carried into the low cloud in the belly of a fantastical beast. And in my belly rode the twin lives I carried. We had spent the summer together, Muhammed and I, doing simple, tourist things. Walks on the beach, shopping in town, family dinners. He had been solicitous. Polite. Charming, with his overly formal manners and courtly broken English. At night he was caring and tender, and as I retreated further and further into my own body awareness, he seemed to be the perfect knight protector. He had plans for us, a home to make back in his country, a future to build. I trusted him and did not once speak out against him leaving me before the babies came.

With him gone the enormity of this pregnancy hit me. At five months, I looked three times my usual width. Fear and uncertainty added to the weight of pregnancy to slow me down, make me sluggish and at times freeze me still, for days on end, rendering me incapable of action. Muhammed was gone, and I was married to a Muslim but I had no one to teach me how to be one myself. Muhammed would not leave until I moved back to be with my parents. So I shared a room with my sister Jan and spent my nights tossing and turning and trying to get comfortable in a narrow single bed that, as usual, was too short for my length, and in which the increasing size of the hard lump that bisected me found no support.

I counted away the hours and the days. In some months, Muhammed would come back for us, me and the babies. I knew that I would travel with him, and meet his family and bring his children up the way he believes is right. He told me of the words to say at the birth, but he was to be back by then. He promised me he would be back for the birth. I waited for him, instructed by my mother in motherhood, managing nappies and feeds. It was hard to know what to buy: too much, and it would be left behind when we left; too little, and I may find myself wanting, lacking some essential item. I watched the other expectant mothers in Mothercare and Boots, so excited, buying rack after rack of clothes, great parcels of equipment, blankets, sheets, bottles, sterilisers and toys. All the paraphernalia of babies, but I couldn't understand them, or why they needed so many things. Clothes, yes, they will need clothes, but surely not so many? Blankets – wouldn't two sets each be enough, one wash, one wear? Cots, carry cots, prams, pushchairs, why all of these things? I looked at everything with a critical eye, wondering if this or that is suitable, if anything I buy will be deemed inadequate or inappropriate by his family. I knew so little about them, except that Saudi mothers expect their daughters-in-law to care for their husbands, to be good wives and mothers. How this was to be achieved, and with what tools and materials, I could not determine. I would have to wait and find out. This is what seemed to signify pregnancy, for me. Waiting.

# Qaul

The new *abaya* covers everything. Its very plainness is surprising. It covers every part of me. Looking at myself in a mirror reveals my face; the veil then covers it. I am reduced to, first, a face, stark in its sudden appearance, unadorned, and then, to nothing. Is this my choice then, to become nothing? Don't ask me why I am doing this. I can't even give myself an answer. Instead I remove the veil and *abaya* and prepare for my day.

Opening the shutters and the window, I look out into a walled garden space, but there is no sign of greenery. The white-yellow of the sky is blinding. The heat is like a malign energy, sucking the last ounce of moisture out of everything, taking my breath away. Here inside, shadows and light collide. I am heavy and lumbering, and I don't want to move or to do anything. I shut the window quickly against the force of the heat from outside.

I can see slanting shadows like bars across the faces of my two sons. They sleep better now. After the circumcision, Khala showed me the little cups used to keep the penis from rubbing against the nappy, they cried and cried, and wouldn't sleep, not for weeks, not even after the soreness was all gone. I imagine that the psychological insult will take longer to heal. But they have fallen back into their old sleeping patterns, and I am glad.

The sickness is growing – every day it is longer, it seems. Nausea, fatigue, the inability to move or act. A few hours of alertness late morning to early afternoon, then a deepening spiral into lassitude. I put on the *abaya* to go out, briefly, to visit Fatima, because Khala insists we all go. It's almost as if she doesn't want to leave me here alone. But it's too much effort, and I unwind the

49

headcovering, cast aside the black *abaya* and cloak, and return to my bed.

This pregnancy is different. I've tried to explain it to Muhammed when he questions my increasing disability. Something is wrong. There is an unease within me, as if this child is unhappy, as if it will never be comfortable within me. Each movement seems a protest, each day a battle of wills, his against mine, his body sucking the strength and life from within me. Already I am as big as with the twins at this stage, but something just doesn't feel right. I can hear the twins playing, Shahid starting to fret, but I am so tired, so tired. All I seem to do these days is yearn for rest and sleep. Sleep carries me away, chasing me down a long corridor to the accompanying hum of the air conditioning, and I can lose myself in dreams of green leaves and cool breezes.

It was different last time. When the woman doing the scan told me I was carrying twins, I laughed.

"You've got to be joking."

"It's true. See, here, one twin, and another."

I stared at the monitor in disbelief, but I felt no negativity. Instead it seemed as if something inside me hardened, coalesced, became stronger and even more determined. Was this the challenge that Allah had set for me, then? Not just to be a mother but the mother of twins? It was frightening. Still, the fear of the unknown was tempered by the deep and certain faith that I must see everything as ordained, as something that was designed for me, a test of my will and my ability to submit. It had been this way from the beginning.

When it came I wasn't ready. In the weeks of scans and visits, of hands that pressed my abdomen and shared concerned looks, I had become immune to the prescience of imminent change. My body acted out of concert with my mind, accomplished at what it must do, acting on deep instinct and natural inclination. While I was sleeping, my body had begun the work.

I woke racked with pain. I struggled to control it, or to control my reactions to it. It was the grip of a giant fist, relentless, too strong to draw breath. And then it was gone. I breathed, moved, stood, slipped softly from the bedroom and down the stairs to the living room. At the foot of the stairs it came again – the tightening, the pain, the giant's relentless grip. Breathe, I told myself, breathe and relax. That is what the midwife told you.

But this could not be me, this alien, heaving thing. I was trapped by the fist and by the unwanted pain. I walked, then crawled, then curled around my vast belly, thinking, 'Call the midwife, call the midwife.' But I couldn't seem to breathe and move and think at the same time. The fear robbed me of volition.

"Amanda?" It was my mother, small and pale in the light from the hall. Her hair was in curlers, skin shiny from the night cream she uses.

"Mum!" It's all I could say, to tell the story of the pain and the suddenness of the change.

"I'll phone the hospital," she said without preamble. I knelt against the edge of the sofa, shooting pain arriving from every direction, from my back and belly, scoring down my thighs, deep into my groin. My babies, I tried to remind myself. This is it. It's time.

Time was a circle of seconds ticking around the clock, the same minute repeated. The contractions came thick and fast, and all I knew was the pain. The midwife was short, plump and pink-cheeked, with long curly hair tied back, and glasses that reflected my own face back at me.

"Amanda," she said to me, a firm hand on mine, steel in her voice. "Amanda, breathe with the pain. Breathe, in, and out, and relax, relax, relax. Let it go, now. Let that one go, and rest before the next one. That's it, just rest now."

"It's starting again!" I wailed, as the pain ebbed and then returned, and the fist gripped around me and inside me and pushed, and squeezed, and there was a great pain in between my legs, deep inside me. Was this my first child, fighting its way out of me? "God, get me something for the pain!"

"The ambulance is coming," said the midwife. I could see my mother, dressed now, hair hastily brushed, checking bags ready to leave, my dad, grumpy and tired, hovering in the background.

"Please, make it stop," I heard my own voice begging, over and over.

"You have to let it come," said the midwife. "Don't fight the contractions, don't be afraid. Let them come. Every one means your babies are one step closer to being born. Come on now, Amanda, breathe with me, that's right, deep breath in, and out, and relax, relax, relax." I tried, and for a few moments a blessed relief, as the fist released me. "Oh holy Jesus God!" I moaned.

"I thought she was a Muslim," I heard the midwife say to my mother.

"She is."

I'm not, wailed the voice inside my head, because if I was, I wouldn't care about this, and I wouldn't be so afraid. *Inshallah, inshallah, inshallah. Allah hu akbar!* Why was I born a woman if this was always to be my destiny, this pain, this great, great pain?

Hours passed, a bumpy, swaying, sickening ride with strangers who were at once kind and impersonal. Hospital doors opened and closed, and there were machines, and the sound of two heartbeats, and there were needles and lines and fluids, and voices telling me to breathe, and relax, and more needles. I floated on a sea of half-pain, somewhere above myself.

"What's wrong with her?" My mother's voice came from far away. She sounded so tired, so anxious, I wanted to reach out and comfort her. She shouldn't be upset.

"That's the pethidine working," said the midwife, a different one, in a different uniform, young, thin, blonde, with sharp eyes and a sharper voice. "She should calm down now."

"My babies," I roused myself enough to say.

"They're fine, we've got two heartbeats on the monitor."

A haze of pain and faces and voices, and hands touching me. "We just need to check how far along you are," said the sharp-voiced midwife. I wanted the other one back, the soft, gentle one. A man's voice, thick and dark, and insistent.

"Open your legs now, we need to find out if you are dilating."

Hands on my thighs, my knees, forcing my legs open.

"No, no!" I tried to fight, but my body was no longer my own, my arms and legs wouldn't do what I wanted them to.

"Amanda, do what they say," urged my mother. Still that strain in her voice.

"Come on now," ordered the midwife, her hands on my knees, holding my legs apart.

"No!" I cried, but it didn't stop. Cold fluid on my vulva, hands holding me down, holding my wrists, my knees. I couldn't get away, because the pain had me pinned to the bed with its gravity. Then fingers, rubbery fingers probing inside me, inside my vagina, painful, searching, piercing.

53

"Stop, please stop!" I sobbed, begging to be released. "Please, don't, please."

"Can't you stop that?" my mother said, and she was crying. *I'm sorry, Mum, I'm sorry. Sorry to put you through this. I'm sorry. I'll be good.*

I stopped fighting, let go, let them force their way into me. The fist of pain pushed down from the inside, the doctor's hand pushed up from the outside, they met inside me, in the place that was no longer my own.

"Ow!" I cried out, despite my passivity. A sudden pressure, sharp and unanticipated, a huge bulging feeling, and then a balloon burst within me with a huge gush of hot fluid.

"What's happening?"

The sharp fingers were withdrawn, and the voices changed.

"Good," said the doctor's voice. "Five to six centimetres, and the membranes have ruptured."

"Clear liquor," said the sharp-voiced midwife. "Good FH."

"Just carry on," said the doctor. "VE again in an hour. And double check the lie."

"I'll bring the scanner in."

"I'll come back in ten minutes. Put up a drip if progress slows."

"Yes, doctor."

This made no sense to me. I was fighting with the fist again, this time sharper and more resolute than before, and new pains inside me, in my hips, in my groin.

"Come on Amanda, breathe the gas now." A mouthpiece, a dry breath in, yes, yes, I can do this, breathe, breathe, fight the fist, fight the clenching and the squeezing, and out, breathe out, let go, lie back, pain gone.

The gaps between the pains lengthened a little, and I dozed in between, aware only peripherally of my mother, sponging my face with a flannel. It smelled of the soap she always used. The doctor and midwife wandered in and out. Hours passed. I breathed the gas, did as I was told, and when the pain reached its apex, each time, begged for release. I prayed, to every god I knew, old and new, to Jesus and Mary and God and Allah and Mohammed the Prophet and anyone else who might be listening. Make it stop! Make it stop.

After a long time, the energy in the room changed. Night had fallen, and outside the shaded windows, the sky was dark. I felt the fist coming again, and at the same time the pressure down in my backside, and the sudden, overwhelming, inescapable urge to bear down, to push.

"I've got to push," I gasped, grunting now when the fist came. I can't stop it, can't help it. I have to push.

"No, don't push yet, I have to check," said the sharp voice. "Pant and breathe through the contraction."

"I CAN'T!" I shouted, still pushing.

The hands were on me again, legs pulled apart, feet flailing against the bed. Then my feet were lifted and placed in stirrups, and the fingers probed inside me, searching. Less painful now, but still unwanted.

"She's fully," said the voice. "Push the call bell."

People rushed into the room, doctors, midwives, others – I didn't know who they were, why they might be there. I was high in the air on a bed, legs held high and wide, fully exposed, in a room full of strangers, all talking, all looking, and I was pushing, pushing, pushing.

Beep of machinery, hiss of gases, more words. "Paediatric resus trolley, find me a laryngoscope, did you check the time, is she term?"

Meaningless babble, only one voice made sense now, my mother. "Push Amanda, push away, that's a good girl, push now!"

Push, push, push, pain and pressure and I was being broken open from the inside, but my baby was coming, and I could feel it coming, coming, filling me, rushing from me. Head out, the rush, the sudden release and gush and…

"It's a boy." The indignant yell from my firstborn's lungs cut across the room, and I laughed, and cried, and I could focus on my mother now, and the tears in her eyes, and the joy. A stranger leaned over me, heavy, hard hands on my stomach. "What are you doing?"

"Um, stabilizing the lie, so your second baby comes out the right way," said the stranger, a young man in a white coat.

The pressure was unpleasant, but I tried to ignore it as he kept his position, pushing on me. Poor baby, I thought, poor little one, being squashed like that. I struggled to draw in a deep breath, to come back to myself.

"Is the baby ok?" I looked for him through the crowd of people. He was crying so much. *Bring him back to me, please.* Minutes later he was returned, wrapped in blanket, with a hat on. I looked down into his milky eyes, his coffee-cream skin, the close-curled dark hair. He yelled at me, indignant, and I laughed.

"Abdullah," I said, knowing that he must be named by a man, knowing there were things that must be done. But there was no Muslim male nearby to do them. Muhammed said he would come back, but he's not here, and it hardly seems so important now. I said the words in his ear, as Muhammed taught me. It would have to be enough.

Another flurry, the scanner probe pressing on my belly, more drugs, more voices, and the fist was back, and more pushing, and out rushed my second son, screaming as well.

Shahid. He was a mirror image of his brother. More hands, more needles, pressure and a sudden hot release of afterbirth. I reached for the second baby, brought him close to me, and whispered the profession of faith. Exhaustion flooded me, a cold wave, like sleep. The midwife took the babies, to check them, to dress them.

"Well done, lovely," said my mother, kissing me. "I'm going to phone your father, and I'll see you later."

I clung to her hand, which had been in mine the whole day and half of the night, and then let go. "Thank you," I whispered, hoping she heard me, hoping she knew what it meant.

Khala is making the tripe stew again. The raised voices and abrasive chatter blend into one noise. The stench is unbearable, and only the urge to vomit is strong enough to rouse me from my bed. Wretched, I heave over the latrine, sweating and alone. The rainy season is close; the air is heavy and humid and every noise an irritant.

"UmmShahid, will you come and help?" Layla is outside the bathroom. I cannot rise, but stay on the tiled floor, gasping.

"UmmShahid? Amanda?"

My sister-in-law enters, cautiously, and sees me white faced and still heaving.

"You are ill?"

"Something's not right," I tell her.

"I fetch my mother."

"No," I protest, but she is gone. Khala comes in a staccato of hurrying feet. Saying nothing, she touches my face, presses my belly, my back, barks a few words to Layla.

It is then that my waters break.

I am only seven months pregnant. It is too early.

"It's too early," I say, but am ignored.

The fist is back, awful in its sudden return. How blissful the forgetting, the anodyne of time passed. It is so different this time. I don't want this, I never wanted this, the relentlessness of this continued possession. It will be over soon. So early, will I have the baby here or get to the hospital?

Khala is short and efficient with me. I feel unwell. Vomit rises again, more water gushes from me, pools in the folds of my ruined nightdress. I see blood.

There's a confusion, of noise, light and movement, a compression of time, voices and pain. The giant fist is crueller this time, with fewer pauses between the gripping and the tearing. A hospital bed, lights and white coats and Arabic injunctions to bring the doctor, bring the doctor! Who is that writhing, heaving demon on the narrow bed? Why are they holding her down?

In the sudden silence, the gushing release, there is no cry. No child's voice. A collectively held breath is not released, and my flaccid belly lies empty as its former occupant is whisked from the room.

I rouse to hear the mutterings of a doctor who will not look at me.

It's a boy.

This same doctor moves toward me, and I feel touch, violation, weakness. Pain.

Am I dying?

A fullness and a pressure, his hand is deep inside me, pain like I never imagined, his face turned slightly away, eyes distant. Now I want to return to my earlier disassociation. I am impaled on his fist while his other hand presses on my empty abdomen, and I can't breathe. Make it stop now, make it stop.

Bleeding. I am bleeding. The heat flows from me with

the blood, and cold settles, a shivering, aching cold. Am I dying now? Will I die with my legs high in stirrups and a stranger's fist thrust far inside me? Turning my face to the wall, I think of my children, and my mother, and of rain, and grey skies, and green grass. It was raining when the twins were born. Cool now, air-conditioned hospital, and I'm getting colder.

Is this what it feels like? This drifting away, the great weight of tiredness? Darkness and letting go? I can do this, I can let go.

Waking to a dim room, to the sound of babies crying, I feel a sullen, lingering ache. There is an intravenous line in my arm, fluid dripping regular as a heartbeat. Narrow bed. My toes are numb from pressure against the footboard. The baby. Where is the baby?

A veiled nurse walks by.

"Please, where is my baby?" She stops and gives me a look of pity. The ward is filled with women and their female relatives, with babies and families. There is no sign of my mother-in-law or my sister-in-law. And no sign of Muhammed, which means there is no one to translate or take care of me.

"My baby," I insist, slurring the Arabic. "Where?"

At last she understands me, nods, and walks away. What is happening? Struggling to sit up, a great weakness and lassitude steals my will.

"Your son is in the neonatal unit," says another nurse. English. Someone speaking English, not music to my ears, no time for that.

"Can I see him?"

"You have lost a lot of blood."

"Please, I want to see him."

"You must rest."

I don't want to rest. I want to see my son.

He looks tiny in the huge incubator, wires and tubes and monitors beeping and hissing. I stand unsteadily, dizzy and sick, veiled, wearing a *niqab* with a slit for my eyes. My baby. His eyes are shut, they look sealed, like they will never open again. Poor little baby.

The room turns black around me, and darkness takes me again. I wake back in my own bed.

"You had a blood transfusion," the doctor informs me. He speaks English. Thank Allah. "You will be with us for a few days, then go home."

In my bed, I sleep and wake and sleep again. Women fill the other beds, female relatives come and go. No one visits me. Day and night and day blend into each other. On the third day, Khala appears, with Layla. They pack up my things, swiftly, whisk me out to the car. Ahmed is waiting. I can't wait to get home and see my boys.

The Arab news runs constantly on the television. I long for an English channel, Eastenders, Neighbours, not this. The alternative is CNN, when I get the chance to watch it. Khala sits in front of the screen, watching the twins play on the rug. Shahid piles bricks on top of each other, Abdullah crawls along with his wooden cars, pushing them under the feet of his grandmother. My back aches constantly these days, whether from the lingering effects of the pregnancy or from standing at counters that are too low for me, I don't know. Floods of memories accompany my halting progress around the house. Laundry takes me back to my mother – the sharp scent of washing powder, her overall with its front pocket full of pegs, her hands red and damp. The smell of washing drying in a crisp breeze. Here the laundry dries rapidly, but the dust is a problem.

"Amanda."

I turn from my place in the doorway, towards the darkness of the hall, the shape waiting for me.

"Muhammed."

"Why have you left the children with my mother again?" His white *thobe* is spotless, his eyes are glittering in the shadows of his face. Maybe the heat and the blood loss are getting to me. My mind is wandering. I want to be with my youngest son, but Muhammed shows no sign of being ready to take me.

"I need to go to the hospital."

He turns away.

"Muhammed, I need to go to the hospital! I need to see how Mahmood is today, how they're treating him."

"*Inshallah*," he says in that offhand, assumptive way. A wall. The simple argument of faith, except there is no argument. It is there, and insurmountable.

"Look," I hiss, aware that Khala is watching us now, disapproving. Raised voices don't matter here, they are par for the course, but that soft menace is unacceptable, "I'm going to that hospital. He hasn't been feeding well, and I'm sure they're not looking after him properly. I need to be there. Now, are you going to take me there or do I have to go on my own?"

His face darkens. I step back. I know that tension of his body, the twining fingers.

"Don't push me, woman."

A burst of Arabic from his mother draws him away.

"Don't you push me," I persist. "My child is alone in that hospital, and I am going to be with him and take care of him."

"You were there all day yesterday," Muhammed barks against the background of his mother's rapid-fire interjections, and the agitated voices on the TV news. I catch some of it. Khala's grandsons will be better off with her and her daughters. Let the English woman go to the hospital.

Iraq is interfering with Kuwait, an act of aggression. War is coming.

There is an ache inside me that has nothing to do with the birth. Looking at Abdullah and Shahid, I see them with new eyes. Their coffee-coloured skin and dark chocolate hair. Their Arabic chatter, some words, but mostly babble, babble in the accent and cadence of this place, these people. The gestures of their fat little hands, even the turn of their heads, and their posture. Alien. But all of this is my family now. This is familiar.

I can't be mother to them without letting go, somehow. And Mahmood needs me the most at this moment.

Muhammed doesn't understand my concern, I can see that. *Inshallah*. As Allah wills it. Mahmood will live or die, weaken or thrive, and we must simply accept. If Mahmood dies, Allah takes him, and he waits at the gates of heaven for me, calling me on to glory. He is my son, and the place within my body where he lay still resonates with an echo of the nurturing, the cradling, the growing of his person. His cells are still those created by me, from my body. My son. My self in miniature, a bud broken from the stem too early. And now that he is forever separate, my love of him must become a conscious act.

Muhammed glowers at me. "Put on your headscarf," he orders. He wants no trouble with the *mutaween*. An unbiddable wife roaming the streets alone is too much.

Caught between breaths, I trip over this image of myself, uncovered, unaccompanied. Unaccustomed. Perhaps this is my new title. The unaccustomed wife.

With practised fingers, I settle the scarf around my face, one tuck here, a fold there, and I am framed and covered. My eyes are huge, and in the tiny mirror, I see steel in them. I seize my *abaya*, cloak myself, close the buttons.

Is she swearing at me in Arabic? Khala seizes me, frees a fold of the scarf, and rearranges me so that my face is also covered, only my eyes, barely visible through a slit in the black fabric.

"Stop it." I push her away. The fabric is hot with my breath. As we leave the house and the heat of outside slams into me, I unhinge the veil and let myself breathe more easily. Within seconds, my hair becomes heavy with sweat.

"Cover your face," Muhammed says.

"No," I reply. "I am going straight to the hospital. I'm with you. If we get stopped, I'll cover my face."

As the car reaches the hospital, Muhammed seizes my wrist before I can leave the car. His grip tightens slowly. Pain shoots from my wrist to my elbow as he twists.

"Don't defy me," he says softly. His face is so close, I can smell his breath – sour, with a reek of alcohol. This early in the morning? Or left over from last night?

Frozen, I say nothing, locked in place by the pain and the menace. The moment passes. Muhammed walks me to the door of the neonatal unit, then leaves without a word. I do not know how long I have here, or when he will be back.

Pushing through the door. The noise and the smells surround me and draw me in. Beeps, alarms, heart monitors. The hiss of oxygen. Iron cots and women in *abayas* around the babies, or holding babies. Relatives moving around. I look for Mahmood. He was in the transitional cot yesterday, a plastic bowl with a cover and an oxygen line. There he is. From here I can see that he is screaming.

I am across the room before I know it, without knowing how I arrived here. Opening the cot, my tiny, red-faced baby turns outraged eyes to me. It's as if those eyes convey how lost, confused and hurt he is. He is freezing in my arms, soaking wet, stinking of urine and faeces. The hospital gown he wears is saturated with his own waste.

I seize a passing nurse. "Where are my son's clothes? The clothes I brought in yesterday? Why hasn't he been changed? Why isn't anyone looking after him?"

A blank look. I try to repeat the question in Arabic. She shrugs.

"He's freezing! His skin is blue." I'm screaming. "He's sick, look at him!" Thrusting Mahmood into her arms, I rummage through the cupboard next to the cot. All the clothes I brought in the previous day are gone. I find a dry blanket, a nappy, then turn back to the nurse to find she is gone, and Mahmood is back in the wet cot.

"I need clean clothes," I yell after her.

An avenging angel in black stalks the ward, screaming in English, a baby clutched to her chest, and surprised Saudi women melt from her path. Clothes appear, hands offer blankets, comfort, understanding. Another woman leads me back to the cot, another mother, and takes him from me, and together we change him and wrap him warmly. I thank her with my eyes – words have left me.

He is starving. My breasts ache, and I go looking for the feeding room, clutching him to my chest. On the way I realise how ill he is, and when another nurse appears, I seize her arm. "My son is sick." His breathing is laboured, nostrils flaring, fighting to inhale. "Get a doctor."

Feeding him is difficult as he gasps for breath. I take the oxygen tube and place it under his nose. After half an hour I seize another nurse. "Doctor!" I yell at her.

It takes another half an hour for a doctor to come. Mahmood's lips are blue. Am I losing him? Is a hungry god even now waiting to take him away beyond my reach? He is so small and passive in my arms. Fragile.

I look at the darkening bruises on my wrists. I look at Mahmood's tiny chest, rising with such effort.

"Mrs…" An English speaking doctor approaches me with deference.

"Doctor, my baby's been left in wet clothes, wrapped in a single sheet, for I don't know how long. His breathing…"

"Let me take a look at him." Gently, Mahmood is lifted from me. Without a word, this doctor moves into the intensive care room, places Mahmood under a warmer, turns on the oxygen. No one speaks to me. I am a tall shadow across the cot, a dark shape, a face hovering mid-air.

Stroking Mahmood's cheek I watch him change, lips pinking a little, a calm flooding through him.

More doctors, more nurses, IV lines, and drugs. I watch from my place, unmoving. Around me the flow and ebb of staff and procedures continues.

The English speaking doctor returns. "Is your husband here?"

"What's wrong with my son?"

"Is your husband coming soon?"

"I don't know. Please, what's wrong?" My hands are shaking. I want to sit down.

"Pneumonia," he says, and turns away.

Pneumonia. Mahmood is too small for such a big word. Drugs and drips and wires and lines, bandages and dressings and underneath it all, the shrinking flesh of my flesh. This is my fault. I let go of him too soon.

Unlike Mahmood, the twins were born at full term, six pounds eight and seven pounds one ounces. They were loud and demanding from the moment they entered the world, and every moment was filled with meeting their needs. It was hard at home, too much for Jan who needed her routine, including sleep. I was rehoused in a council flat a week after the birth, a tired, used space in a featureless enclave of mean, brick buildings surrounding a central courtyard covered in tarmac. Outside were rows of rotating washing lines, and doorless sheds that housed wheelie bins and rotting furniture and old pushchairs. Inside I had a living room, a bedroom for me, an even smaller one for the babies, a bathroom, and a kitchen the size of a cupboard. Muhammed had not returned. His absence was recorded as abandonment by the woman at the social. To outside eyes I was just another single mother, but I had no interest in standing around in the communal yard, smoking, while the babies sat in a pram, gossiping and complaining like the other mothers in the block. I had a husband. I just had to figure out where he was, and when he was coming back.

Allah, I said in my head, you are testing me again. This is another challenge. Can I do this? Can I be mother and father to the boys until he returns? Two months since he had gone, and all I had had was one phone call. My father paid to have a phone put in the flat, and my mother visited once a week. Other than that I was on my own.

Hours pass. No feeds, milk in a syringe fed through a tube that runs from his nose to his stomach. A nurse hovers. Why did he have to get so sick to receive the proper care?

How long have I been standing here, counting every breath? My legs and back are aching, my feet feel bruised. The smells of food invade my consciousness. Other mothers

66

share food with their families, but no one is here for me. At last I unfreeze my limbs, find a chair, sit down. Stand, change Mahmood's nappy. Sit again. Around me the tide of activity and time advances and recedes.

Hunger inside me is the only sign that I still live. I am reduced to a simple state. Watching. Waiting. Guarding.

I look up, and Muhammed is watching me.

I hate to put Mahmood down, relinquish him, tiny, into the great space of the incubator, where he shrinks and becomes nothing, a wizened face peeping out from the great machine. When I do, Muhammed turns and walks away. I am expected to follow. I look at the baby. A nurse walks by, smiles at me and the sleeping baby. I hurry after Muhammed. But I am torn, and it seems as if, as I leave the ward, entering a different kind of light and noise as we pass through the corridors, that a ghost of myself is left behind, hovering watchfully over the cot. I hope this can be true, I hope they can feel it, the nurses who left him alone so long, the presence, not just watchful, but wrathful. Perhaps this will make a difference. Perhaps in the darkness of the quieter night time, those same nurses will sense me, and pay him more attention.

My heart is in my mouth as Muhammed pulls out into the chaos that constitutes Riyadh traffic, and I can smell the alcohol, and another smell, sour, on his breath. His driving is dangerous, erratic. I hang onto my seat.

"Why are you so late?" I ask him.

Slap. He reaches again to strike me a second time, and I lean away. "Stop! What are you doing?"

"Don't ask me questions. I have been working, what a man does is not for a woman to know. I must work now, I have three children. I must go to work and you must take care of the children."

"I know this. I'm grateful to you, I really am, I know you are a good father."

"You spend too much time at the hospital."

"Mahmood is sick. If I hadn't been there today, he might have died."

The lack of emotional responses from him is like a brick wall, and I just keep on butting my head against it, time and time again. Why doesn't he care? He must care, they are his children.

As we arrive back inside the gates of his parents' house, he stops the car and shakes his fist in my face. "You will not shame me, Amanda. You must be a good mother, good wife."

"I know Muhammed. I am trying. I'm doing my best."

He's gone, and I sit shaking for a moment in the car. Then the door opens and he drags me out, the heat seizing me too in its fiery grip, before I am thrust back into the cooler shadows of the house. In the kitchen doorway, Khala is waiting for me. "What did she say?" I ask Muhammed.

"She says the boys have been fine today, they have played a lot, eaten well."

I smile my thanks, and she nods at me, turning back into the kitchen. Without having to ask, I know I must follow her tiny form. The gold on her wrists flashes as she directs me to start cutting up the meat and vegetables and I roll up my sleeves and set about the task.

The hospital again. Mahmood has been moved into the nursery ready for discharge, and in a few days I will bring him home. I have an appointment with the obstetrician to get checked out. I sit on a hard plastic chair in the waiting room, draped and veiled and tired, thinking about the twins and Muhammed and the last few weeks of going back and forth and trying to spend time with the twins and with Mahmood both.

And dealing with Muhammed and his drinking. Since Ali his brother has come out of prison, they have been drinking and going out more, and leaving me at the mercy of his family, where I cook, clean, snatch time with my sons, and hide in my room for long hours of the night, wondering when Muhammed will return and renew his assault upon my body. The bleeding stopped some weeks ago, and we are back in the old routine – his demands, my responses, automatic now. More and more often I must coax him into sufficient hardness to perform. If I fail to manage it, he gets violent. That usually works where my ministrations fail.

A nurse approaches, folders in hand, and asks me a question. I can't understand her, and ask her to speak more slowly. She does, impatiently. Still, I can't understand her.

"Do you mind if I help?" asks a soft, female voice with an American accent. The other occupant of the waiting room is a short, slightly plump woman whose *abaya* is well cut and whose eyes twinkle at me over the *niqab*.

"Uh, no, please, go ahead."

There follows an interchange of rapid Arabic which loses me after the first few words.

"She wants to know if you have started menstruating again after the birth," says the American.

"Oh, uh, yes. Just once."

More Arabic. I answer a few more questions, then the nurse retreats again.

"Grace," says Grace, leaning forward to bridge the distance between us. A hand appears from under the long black cloak, and seeks out mine, to hold it briefly, rather than shake it. I see her light coloured fingers, feel warm flesh, soft skin, and catch a breath of perfume.

"Amanda," I reply, awkwardly.

"You too?" She nods at the scarf. "Married a Saudi?"

"Yes, two years ago." Even as I say it, the weight of that much time hits me, all at once. "I have three children," I explain.

"Ah." She is grinning, under the veil, I can tell by the crinkles at the corners of her eyes, the sound of her voice. My own shyness surprises me. "I have five, now that's an achievement!"

Grace laughs, and I smile with her.

"So you've just had your third…?"

"Yes, he was early, you know, and he's been in the special care unit for a while. We're taking him home soon. I had twins first."

She grins. "I've twins too, just the one set. A boy, a girl, then the twins, also boys, and my last was a girl. That's enough, I think. I'm here to make sure of it."

"Oh." I pick absently at the rough cloth of my *abaya*, which is the same one I have been wearing for weeks. I can't remember the last time I took care over my appearance. When did I last wash my hair? Most of the pregnancy weight is long gone, and I feel thin and fragile and inadequate.

"Five, that's a lot to handle," I say absently. Three is bad enough.

"Oh yes, but they're good children. Very good. And a blessing, too, really, all of them healthy."

"How did you find it, having them here?"

"I had them all here, so I can't compare really. It was ok, no worse than I expected. You?"

"I had the twins back home," I explain. "Not much different, but at least I could make myself understood."

Grace nods.

I hear my name being called, and start to rise.

"Here," Grace stops me. "Take my phone number, and give me yours. We should have coffee some time, the kids can play together."

"That would be lovely," I reply, and she fishes in her bag, and writes her number on a piece of paper, and I do the same. As we exchange numbers, our fingers touch, and for the first time, perhaps since arriving here, I feel a connection with someone. Someone who has no obligation to care for me, or accommodate me. Someone who might want to know me for myself.

"Ah, my grandson, my grandson," Khala croons over Mahmood, as soon as I take him home. My mouth is dry from the hot air, and I am drained and limp from the heat outside, but I am mobbed by the twins as soon as I get in. Mahmood is whisked away rapidly, passed from relative to relative with glee. In the women's salon, I sit with the twins climbing all over me, and Layla brings in the mint tea, and smiles at me.

"He looks strong, even if he is small" she remarks as she sets down the glass cup. The smell is reassuring, familiar. Hot, sweet and refreshing, I can see why they drink it so much, because it soothes the throat much more than a cold drink. Muhammed appears in the doorway.

"My mother says she will look after the boys if you need a rest."

"Thank you."

He looks at me, and there seems to be a touch of the old tenderness there. Have I pleased him then, bringing Mahmood home at last, healthy and ready to be accepted into the family? For a moment, I relax. Yes, I can rest. It is good to have others around who can help with the babies. I close my eyes, and let go.

*Dear Mum,*

*Well, I said I would write more often, so here we go. All is well here.*

No, this is a lie. All is not well. I miss you, and Dad, and my sisters. I miss clouds, rain, fresh air, and people speaking English. I can understand people now, what they say, what they mean, at least some of the time. I would never have believed, before I came here, how much can be conveyed by one slight shake of the head, a raised eyebrow, a brief movement of one shoulder. There is a language of women here, and it is mostly silent, filling the spaces between words.

Understanding Arabic is only half the battle. Understanding women, their codes and expectations, the subtlety of their communications, their intimate looks that assume shared meaning, this continues to elude me. I have to be alert, on guard, always sensitive, and questioning.

*I am getting on well with Muhammed's family, and they are taking good care of me and the twins.*

They are such passionate people, so quick to shout, argue, remonstrate. It's just their way, a real antithesis to British reserve. You get used to the raised voices, the sudden outpourings, the emotional tides that run high and fast and sweep through the house many times daily.

*There's a lot to learn here, but I'm doing well, listening to my husband and my new sisters and parents-in-law.*

I miss you. I miss home. I miss roast beef dinners, and cheddar cheese. Tomato ketchup and baked beans. Plain old white bread. I miss feeling hungry, and I miss sitting and enjoying a meal. That is what the men do. They sit and relax and talk, as we rush back and forth, bringing tea, food, coffee. Collecting errant children and empty plates. Sharing the women's dance of service, and then later, we eat, when

72

the guests are fed, and we have a few precious moments for ourselves. Then we are up and dancing again, dishes, cleaning, children, more coffee. It is easier when there are no guests. But these are such hospitable people. They are kind, and I am well taken care of. The house is large enough, the children are loved, if differently.

*I want to tell you so much about life here, about how warm and kind the people are. It is nothing like home. I want to tell you about the city, Riyadh, which is big, and strange, and full of markets called souks, which sell all kinds of things, gold, silver, meat, spices.*

There are so many things to tell you. Yes, it's different here, but when I weigh things up, it's a good life, and as long as I remember the rules, I get by. I miss English roads, because there are rules I understand, and people obey them. Here, crossing the road is like some medieval test of courage, littered with booby traps. Taking the boys out is hard enough, with the need to not be on the streets alone, to always be covered, to behave properly, but negotiating the roads is nothing to negotiating the culture. I'm learning.

*I hope you are well, and Dad, and Jan. My new little son is still in the hospital, but they say he will be home with me soon. I go to see him every day. I will send photos when I can. I wish you could see him. He's beautiful.*

I hope to see you sometime soon, when I can get permission to visit with the children. When we can afford it. With the war imminent, I would rather be at home with you. They say the Middle East is at boiling point. But maybe it will pass us by.

*Give my love to everyone, and write soon.*
*Amanda.*

I have been asleep, briefly, in the women's salon, and the children are nowhere to be seen. I move through the shadows to the rest of the house, following the sounds of voices. A cry of fear, a baby's cry, breaks the silence, and I hurry towards the kitchen. Muhammed is there, holding the baby.

Seeing Mahmood in his arms, I want to snatch him away, as he staggers drunkenly around the kitchen. My baby, small, precious, my little one, not big and tough and laughing like the twins as they tumble around on the floor, oblivious. Or maybe not oblivious, not really, for they have already learned to avoid their father's feet and hands, and stay well out of his way, always aware of his presence, where he stands and how he moves. So they have grown already, and are being formed in the knowledge of his instability. Like me, they have learned to be watchful.

My arms ache to reach for Mahmood, to take him back into their comforting protection and shelter. Shelter from his father, a raging thunder of words and unchecked power. He could crush that tiny body within his fists, I know this. There are pots boiling on the stove, and I have placed myself between them and Muhammed as he drunkenly dangles the baby at the end of his reach.

"My son!" he slurs, "another son, praise Allah." He mumbles on, incoherent Arabic that I cannot follow, even now. I see it happening as if in slow motion. The baby held high, screaming in terror, and Muhammed's foot slipping on the hard, wet tile. My son, falling towards the floor and I can't move, because if I even reach for him, Muhammed will turn on me and I have two other sons to bring up and protect. I cannot hold them all in my arms at once.

Just before the baby reaches the floor, his father catches him, laughing, and the malice and uncaring in his eyes

74

when he looks at me chills me far more than the fear of Mahmood hitting the hard floor.

"Allah doesn't want to take him yet, it seems," he says, his eyes on mine.

He knows, he knows! He sees me unmasked, naked emotion on my face. Is this why the Arabs veil their women, so that they cannot display the hatred and fear that consume them, day by day? Does every other woman feel as I do, fear as I do, hate as I do? They cannot. All men cannot be like this. He must be the exception, surely?

For a moment he stops, as if checked by a blow, and then the laughter bursts from him, as he carries Mahmood away, still screaming. Khala takes him, soothes him, and I scoop up the twins and hurry back to the family room, heart pounding. Khala brings a bottle, and for once I don't regret that I couldn't breastfeed this one.

Steel in my spine, steel in my heart, encasing the love and joy and wonder of my children. Steel in my eyes as I enter the room, set the twins down to play, and take Mahmood from Khala, kissing him and holding him against me as gently as I can. His crying calms as he takes his feed. His heart beats against my chest and I feel the steel spreading throughout me, as if freezing me in time, in this one moment, when I realise that I cannot stay here, cannot stay with this man who cares so little for my children. Someone has paused the playback of my life, and I step outside it and see myself as a statue, frozen, and know that when time moves on again, I will still be here, this statue, holding this moment, forever.

## *Hāsib*

The trip to Dammam was arranged without my knowledge. Still, excited by the prospect of the city, I find a stirring of affection for Muhammed within myself. At last we are going somewhere together. Away from his mother, father, sisters and brothers, we can be a family in our own right.

Then he tells me that the children are not to come. Apparently Muhammed has male guests arriving while we are in Dammam, staying in the home of some distant relatives who are away making a pilgrimage to Mecca. So I understand the reason he is bringing me along with him – he needs a woman to take care of his needs, to establish and underline his status as a married man. It is a business trip. This will be my first exercise in behaving as a proper Saudi wife, away from the protection and guidance of my mother-in-law, sisters, cousin, who by constant, if often silent, checks on my behaviour, keep me in line.

I am aghast at the thought of leaving the boys. So much of every day is caught up in them, so many things to do for them. So easy to lose myself in them and their needs, to ignore the awareness of that other me, the woman-that-was, before the mother that is.

"Why can't we bring the children?" I ask Muhammed as he outlines his plans for the trip.

"There is no need to take them, it is only for a few days."

"Who are these friends of yours?"

"A man I know, from business." He turns away, and I continue with the task of packing. What kind of business? I want to ask. What kind of work? Will they help you set up your own business, now, instead of working for yourself, trying to save enough to open your own garage? Where does your money come from, these days, to pay for trips to the city? But I don't ask these things. Without disturbance, the days slide by, weeks and months blurring into one another without notice, with few signifiers of either time passing or of my own state. Subsumed in this, I have become all that I appear to be. I aspire to be nothing more, only the proper Muslim woman, praying to Allah to give me strength of endurance, to give me guidance in the many small decisions of my life. As long as I am obedient, as long as I submit, then Allah will help me. He will guide me, surely, as long as I can find the proper questions to ask.

I pack my own clothes, the tight, fitted dresses in bright colours, edges thick with embroidery, the *abayas* and scarves and veils for my face. Male guests. I will spend my days chiefly swathed and shadowed then, it seems.

After Muhammed leaves, I examine my own face in the mirror. It looks older, a stranger's face regarding me, the eyes knowing. The extreme pallor strikes me first, and strongest, a washed-out parody of flesh, bloodless, almost featureless. My unaccustomed face, which rarely sees the sun unshrouded. Wandering fingers on my own cheeks, savouring softness, the yielding surface somehow unlike skin, but more pliable, like dough. Only the lips, a dark pink, reddening at their junction where my nervous teeth catch and bite and worry. Reddening lips, high, dark eyebrows, white, bloodless, yielding skin. Who is this creature? Is this the face my children see?

I check the bag, add a few items, then slip downstairs again to check on the boys, but in my mind I am already relinquishing them to their grandmother's care. She will feed them, change them, scold them when they fall and cry for comfort. Perhaps they are better off with her and their grandfather, learning how to be boys and men here, in this place. A lesson I can never teach them.

Dammam is a long, dusty car journey characterised by the constant need to drink, and then to urinate. Muhammed has no sympathy with my repeated requests for a rest stop, for safe places to uncover necessarily and relieve myself. There is nothing to do but watch the desert roll by, the sandy, stony, and avoid the other crazy Saudi drivers who follow no road rules. Muhammed tells me to be quiet almost as soon as we get into the car, so I watch the sand and hills roll by. Occasionally we pass a bulldozer, moving sand away. In the distance a dark yellow cloud looms.

"Sandstorm," Muhammed mutters when I point it out to him. "It is far away. It may not reach us."

The cars pass at incredible speed, and when the sandstorm hits, we are lost in a world of whirling brown and yellow, with very little visibility. Fear rises like bile and I feel as if I can't breathe.

"Can't we pull off, wait it out?" I ask him as he weaves around yet another car and increases his speed.

"Don't be bloody stupid, it's about fifty degrees out there. We just keep going. Now be quiet and let me drive."

I shut up and cling to my seat, praying that I make it through alive. When the storm passes, the sand sits like snow on the car and along the roadsides. Muhammed has to swerve to avoid drifts of it.

Dammam – all busy-ness, noise and smells, traffic, people, food. It smells different here, being so near the sea. I wish we could go to the sea, but Muhammed wants to get us to the house as soon as possible. The noise when we stop at the souk is like the roar in a football stadium, or some gladiatorial event, and the pressing throngs of men in white, and women in black, are frightening in their vastness. Everywhere a sea of faces and black veils. I feel tiny, lost, threatened. I am not used to being outside, not now.

Muhammed tells me where he will pick me up. I savour for the first time the fact that I am alone and doing this shopping myself. In the vegetable souk, I haggle with the vendors, keeping my eyes down, remembering the words that Khala uses, ignoring the curious looks.

The house we are staying in belongs to someone he knows. I cannot work out the relationship, but it is some cousin or other. It is small, only the two rooms and kitchen and bathroom downstairs, and two bedrooms and a bathroom upstairs. I put my things in the bedroom.

Muhammed is out, out, out, I don't really know where. He left without ceremony, without explanation. His friend was here, Yusuf, and so I couldn't question Muhammed about where he is going, what time I should expect him back, if I should make dinner, and if so, for how many. This is what trust in a marriage must be, trusting in him, that he will come back, will not abandon me here, powerless, with no liberty to choose even to go home to my children. Trust and belief. I believe he will come back to me, or at least come back for me, to continue my work as his wife and the albeit errant mother of his children. Errant. Aberrant, deviating from the line of compliance that drives through the centre of our joined lives.

Dutifully, I turn to the kitchen and prepare a meal. For the first time, uncertainty. Never before have I prepared these dishes alone, without the presence or the oversight of his mother, his sisters, the guardians of female sensibility, of the secret and arcane rituals of the kitchen and the women's salon. The kitchen is unfamiliar, and it takes time to find the things I need. I stop, suddenly, in the middle of an automatic process of heat, chop, stir and season, to question myself. Am I doing this right? How much salt, how many onions and tomatoes, for three of us? Should I make enough for four, or more? Do I put the lamb in now, or later? Have I remembered it right? In the measured dance of the kitchen, I have forgotten the steps, or at least, for the first time in months, have come to notice them, and stumble. This point shows me how very far I have come, how I have come to wear the uniform of my Saudi life with increasing ease. It has become habitual.

I watch my hands fly, chopping, mixing, shaping, as if they belong to someone else. Soft caress of flour under my fingers, cool water, sticky dough. Sharp scents and the sting of spices in my nose, and heat, heat, always the heat, and the sticky heaviness of my clothes and the hair on my neck. Long, long days in the same steps of the dance. And I'm tired, so tired. And I miss my boys.

Food prepared, I wander through the rest of the house, touching walls and door frames, safe behind heavily curtained windows, unveiled to myself, but unwitnessed. I could dance naked from room to room, lie down and pleasure myself on the rugs that cover the floor. Slowly, I remove the head scarf, and lift the damp mass of hair away from my neck, shaking it free. Then comes the *abaya*, cast aside as I stand, bared, between these four walls, with no other to see the uncloaking of the woman that I am. The cotton of my dress is damp as I trace my own outline with my hands, wonderingly. Little trace of the pregnancy weight remains; only the puckered skin of my belly gives testament to motherhood, and the heavier weight of my breasts.

I remember what it was like after the last time, how my body had changed so much, a sudden change after the gradual swelling of pregnancy. And how it was when Muhammed finally came to fetch me.

80

The twins were five months old, and heavy to carry. They slept for longer periods, but still not all night. And Muhammed had finally got in touch, by phone, to say he was coming back.

He arrived, a flurry of noise at the door. He was smaller than I remembered, and his eyes were sharper, casting piercing looks at me, as I opened the door and ushered him into the flat.

"Muhammed," I waited for a greeting, an embrace. He dropped his case in the living room, and shed his coat.

"Can I get you a drink, coffee maybe?"

"Yes." He didn't look at me, but around at the walls and doors of the flat.

I went into the kitchen, and while the kettle boiled, listened to him moving around. I had expected a hug, a kiss, an embrace. Why wouldn't he touch me? I put the mugs in the living room, where he was walking around examining everything. He picked up each baby in turn, held it for a moment, then returned it to me.

"Boys," he says, nodding. "Two boys is a great blessing."

I nodded. "I am so glad you are back. I've missed you. You've missed so much of them growing up already. But I have photos."

He grunted. I settled both boys into their playpen, surrounded by soft, bright toys.

Then we were busy with the coffee, and the meal I had waiting. I stopped eating as soon as the boys got restive, and instead fed them at the breast, one each side, sitting on the sofa. I could see Muhammed watching me. He was quiet. How strange to have to try to make conversation with my own husband.

"How was your flight?"

He shrugged. "Ok. We are booked to return next Saturday."

81

"Right."

"Is there much that you will need to get before we leave?" he asked. His manner was distant, almost formal. "No, just luggage," I said. "I don't have enough suitcases."

"We can get some tomorrow." He was watching me again. I felt uneasy.

Dinner cleared away, I bathed the twins, read them a story, and settled them into bed. Muhammed showed no interest in their routine, and when I offered him to help, he shook his head and went into the kitchen to have a cigarette. At last, I could return to the living room. I felt nervous, excited. How would it be between us, after months apart? He felt like a stranger again, not a husband or a lover.

The curtains were closed, even though it was summer and still light outside. He had closed them. The room felt stuffy and dark. Muhammed was sitting on the sofa, leaning back, watching me through half-lidded eyes, his third can of beer in his hand.

"Stop there," he said to me. Standing in the middle of the room, I watched him. He looked me up and down, then approached me, kissed me. I leaned into his embrace, welcoming the warmth, the touch, the connection.

"I've missed you," I murmured.

He leaned forward, and there was something about the look on his face that stopped me saying anything else. His hands were urgent on my body, and the memories flooded back of how often he had touched me like this. My response was almost automatic. As I unbuttoned my blouse and stepped out of my skirt, he said, "I want to see you, to see what having these babies has done to you, to your body."

My clothes fell to the floor, garment by garment. The air was cold, and soon I was covered in goosebumps.

Muhammed said nothing, but looked me up and down, again, very slowly. With a gesture, he ordered me to turn around. Slowly, I rotated on the spot. The carpet was rough on my bare feet.

"Have you been with another man?" He asked.

"What the...?" The words shocked me, and a chill flooded my body. "What on earth do you mean?"

"The marks, on your...your arse", he growled. "You have a lover, you have been with another man."

"I bloody well haven't been with anybody else! There is no one else, and I haven't been outside this house without the twins since they were born."

His expression was dark, thunderous. Fear stabbed into my belly. "They're stretch marks!" I said, as loud as I dare. "From the babies. Having twins put a lot of strain on my body. I put on a lot of weight. They're the same as the ones on my stomach."

"Stretchmarks here are from the babies," he said, jabbing at my stomach, and he was spitting in anger as I cowered away from the open handed slaps.

"What on earth do you think the marks are?"

"You like this, when we make love, you like me to scratch you, to dig my nails in!"

"Yes, I do. But these are not the marks of someone scratching me."

He calmed down enough for me to explain, to rationalise. Eventually, I took his hand and traced his fingers first over the indentations of the livid marks on my belly, and then over the ones on my buttocks.

"See, they are the same. Someone as thin as me can't carry twins and not get stretchmarks everywhere."

He grunted. I couldn't tell if he was agreeing with me, or if he had accepted this. But in the end, it was enough.

He unzipped his jeans, and did it – there, on the carpet, me on my back, him pressing down on me. It was the first time since the birth of the babies. I gripped hard with the muscles of my vagina, holding them tight, tight, tight, with every thrust. I had been practising, afraid of what he might say if I was too changed, if I felt too different. Afraid he wouldn't want me.

He grunted again, satisfaction, completion, and rolled off. Cold air on me again, and I was stiff like an old woman as I stood, slowly, put on my clothes, and went into the kitchen to do the washing up.

Later still, he was on the phone to his mother. A heated discussion in Arabic. I closed the door to the hall, afraid he would wake the babies. Eventually he called me in.

"My mother says this can be true," he gestured at my body. "That women can have marks like this, not just on the stomach."

"Women can get stretch marks in all sorts of places," I said. He shrugged. The matter was closed.

Day wears away into evening, and I straighten my clothes, brush my hair, put on a little make-up and some more of the gold jewellery Muhammed's mother gave me. I tidy up after my earlier moments of abandon, don the *abaya* and drape the scarf over my shoulders. I start the coffee, put the soup on. This soup is like a stew, with small, flat circles of dough, like flatbreads, layered into it once the stock is boiling. It is like, but yet not really like, stew with dumplings. It is a spiced sauce that thickens as the dumplings cook – if I have done it right.

On with the rice now, thick, sticky rice, and then the lamb dish, with its acrid, oniony scent. It should be enough, more than enough, for four, or five or six even. Muhammed mentioned his friend bringing a woman with him. What will she think of me, tall and white and awkward? This is the reason for the make-up, the extra effort. The Saudi women are always so well-presented, so proud of their appearance.

At last, the door opens. I seize the scarf, and bring it over my hair, bring up one corner and tuck it in on the opposite side, to cover my face but leave my eyes exposed.

"Amanda," Muhammed speaks from the hall. I hurry in.

"Coffee?" I suggest, unnecessarily.

Muhammed nods, then, "This is Yusuf, the cousin of the wife of Fatima's husband's uncle."

Is everyone here related to each other? Still, it is kind of him to introduce the stranger to me, to remember my Western sensibilities. I nod, withdraw, arrange the coffee and dates on a tray. When I return, I see the bottle of whisky on the floor next to Muhammed. Where do they get it from?

There is little to do, everything is ready, but I busy myself in the kitchen, making the homely noises of the dutiful wife. The soup in the big tureen with spoons. The large serving platter for the lamb and rice. Mint tea ready to be poured, for after the meal.

The call to prayer penetrates the walls and frosted windows. I retreat to the smaller room, and carry out my prayers. Rhythmically stand, kneel, press of carpet and hard floor against my knees, my hands. Every repetition makes the floor harder. After the last, when I kneel back on my heels and look up, Muhammed is there.

"We will eat now," he says.

As I pass him, I smell the whisky on his breath.

The meal is placed on a tablecloth in the centre of the room. I rise to leave, my stomach rumbling, retreat behind

85

the screen. Women's country. Alone in this new landscape, I miss the boys, the noise of their chatter, and the warmth of their hands and bodies. My arms feel empty, my body barren and lifeless, cold. Today, tonight, I am untouched, because they are not here with me. What we are doing here remains a mystery that Muhammed has not revealed to me, except that it is to do with business. Why his "friend" has not brought his wife with him has not been explained. If he has a wife. He is still quite young, and with bride prices the way they are, it is likely he is still unmarried.

Laughter, voices getting even louder in the dining room. I tidy the kitchen, wash up the pots and pans, and when I hear Muhammed and Yusuf finally leave, return to the dining room. The lamb and rice are cold now, the soup lukewarm. I eat a little. It isn't the same as his mother's cooking. Then I clear away and finish my chores.

"Amanda." Muhammed leans against the kitchen doorframe, eyes flashing, cheeks flushed and dark.

"Was everything ok with the meal?" I ask him. "Was there enough food?"

"It was…ok." He is watching me intensely. Hot eyes like coals, it seems, and I still myself, and wait.

"Come here."

I obey. Close to him, I smell sweat and food, cigarettes, alcohol. His breathing, heavy and fast, alerts me to his mood. Slowly, I raise my eyes to his. With one hand, he removes the veil from my face; with the other, cups a breast and squeezes until I gasp. He kisses me until I respond to him. He leads me into the main room, and wordlessly offers me the whisky.

It has been years – far too long – since I've tasted alcohol, especially strong spirits. It burns, a shockingly familiar heat, which starts in my throat runs, like fear, through the heart

86

of me, until there is no air let to breathe. Muhammed's "guest" eyes me with hunger, and something else. I am still unsure of the unspoken, the silent language of gesture and expression. Even after these years of residence and obedience, I am an outsider. I cannot begin to know what his facial expression means, but I have never seen a Saudi man look at a Saudi woman like that.

"I promised Yusuf I would find him a woman while he was here," Muhammed says, slurring his words a little. "It wasn't possible. You will go to him instead."

"Muhammed?" I turn to him. The lust in his eyes arouses me. My body responds, accustomed to answering his needs, his every command. Thus stimulated, I walk into the bedroom, and begin to remove my clothes. Each layer falls from me like skin, like flesh, until, raw and exposed, my nerves sing and sigh at the slightest sensation. Cold of air conditioning has become ice and fire and freezing. Rasp of carpet is abrasive wire wool on the soles of my feet. The cotton sheets are like rough, newly-cut wood. But my skin remains whole, and unmarked, for the time being. Muhammed watches from the doorway, and I wait. Is this what he wants from me? What kind of test is this? Am I supposed to obey, or resist.

"I don't want to do this," I say quietly. He crosses the room and strikes me, hard, across the face. My head thuds against the bed and dizziness engulfs me. "I am your husband. You will do as I say." I see. It is a demonstration of his control over me. I wait under the covers as he leaves the room.

Now I am bloodless and nerveless. Yusuf enters the room. Eagerness and hunger, and still that indefinable "something" that sets this interchange apart for me. As if that is the only thing.

Is it rape if I say yes? My body says yes because it has learned to obey, on some primal, fleshly level. He stands before me, naked, smelling of male sweat and sex, already partly erect. There are no clear thoughts in my mind, only the compulsion.

Full and hard, his penis throbs. He thrusts my body back onto the bed, seizes it with his hands, and settles between the open legs. Enter, thrust, withdraw. Enter, thrust, withdraw. His mouth does not seek lips or skin, but hands knead breasts firmly. Then hands, hands on shoulders, and the repeating piston. Hips rise to meet him, my hips, my body, my skin, his weight and the garlicky, whisky sourness of his breath. Hard, hard enough to hurt, inside and outside, pain, and this I understand. As he reaches his climax I glance over his shoulder. Muhammed is standing in the doorway, watching.

The journey from Dammam is a long, dusty drive home under the hot sun. I look out at the desert. Browns and grayish sandy stone, and sand in drifting dunes. Rising and undulating, shapes and shadows, valleys and hills. Stone cliffs and the dusty surface of the tarmac, the drumming thrumming hum of the tyres on the road. Muhammed doesn't speak to me. He listens to the radio, drums his fingers on the steering wheel. I sit beside him in the front of the truck, wearing sunglasses against the glare. I want to say something to him. Has it made him happy, that I did what he wanted? Am I a good wife? Has he finally accepted that I will do what he asks, whatever he asks?

The sun sets behind us, a golden disc in the rear-view mirror, turning slowly to bronze, then orange, and then disappears beyond the horizon. We drive on into the night, towards the lights of Riyadh in the distance.

I miss my boys. I miss the family too, sharing tasks with his sisters, having women to talk to. He hasn't mentioned them once. I think about what I have done. A hot flush rises, and something else. Shame. Not at what I have done, not really, but because in the end, I didn't fight it. I summoned the same responses I give to my husband, as if I enjoyed it. Muhammed hit me and then he did it to me too. Was he watching for a similar response? I did everything he asked, but he has hardly spoken to me since.

I want to get home, now. I want to see my children, and I want to sleep in my own bed. But the swift desert night is falling, and there are still many miles to go. The brownish yellow sands turn grey and colourless as the light fades, and the air cools perceptibly. I watch the landscape disappear into blackness and remember.

It was easy, in the beginning, to believe that we were just another couple. We went out to cafés and restaurants, nothing exotic or expensive, and we visited my family, and visited friends. The pregnancy had very little effect on me in the first few months. The midwife told me it was because I was tall, and that I would show soon enough. Muhammed seemed to notice little difference, except that my breasts grew fuller and more defined.

"You are much firmer, much more rounded," he said one night as we lay naked, his hands all over my body as usual. I enjoyed the feeling of him, pressed up against me. He wanted sex all the time, it seemed, from the moment he got in from college to the moment he fell asleep, often moments after his final climax. I didn't complain. The closeness felt so good. Being wanted felt amazing. When he walked in the door, his dark brown eyes would flash with desire and I felt powerful. It was me having that effect on him. There was no one else, just us, language no barrier as his English improved, enough for him to say that he wanted me. After the first time, every time after was better. It didn't matter than he didn't talk much about his home, or his culture, I was reading about Saudi Arabia in books. His body spoke to mine, and that was all the language we needed.

"Mama!" Abdullah meets me as I run downstairs. I overslept. Khala must have got the twins up, and the baby. I sweep him up into a hug. "Hello, my love, I missed you." He wriggles and smiles in my arms. "Come on, where are your brothers?"

Khala is in the family room, with Mahmood on her lap. Shahid is playing with plastic toys, lying on the rug on the floor. He laughs when he sees me. I can't help but smile. I lower myself to the floor to play with him. "Shahid, my little man, what are you playing with? Trucks? Are you going to be a mechanic like your uncle?" I tickle him and he giggles.

"Leave the children, you are late, you need to start the cleaning," Khala says in Arabic. I can understand her – she speaks slowly to make sure.

"I haven't seen my babies for four days," I say in English. Then in Arabic, I manage the words for no, babies, and time. God, this is awful. It's all very well understanding her, but knowing what to say in reply is another matter.

"Go, I am with the children. You must do the cleaning." Her face is set. She calls out to Muhammed, who is somewhere in the house. When he appears he looks angry at being summoned. She chatters at him, and he shrugs. "Amanda, she says you must do the cleaning now. You have not been here for some days, and you overslept this morning. There is much to do."

"But Muhammed, I haven't seen the boys for four days. I just want to spend some time with them before I start on the housework."

His face darkens. Then he slaps me, hard, in the face. One hand on my cheek, I look from him to Khala, who is watching. She shows no outrage at this treatment, makes no protest.

"You are lucky to be here," he says to me. "My mother pays for everything, your clothes, your food, the children's needs. You have a home here. You should be grateful. You should work and repay their generosity."

How can he just walk away like that? There are tears in my eyes, but I won't let Khala see. I pull myself to my feet, and stumble out into the kitchen. The breakfast dishes are waiting for me.

Full dark. In the lamplight of our bedroom, I sit at the edge of the bed, putting moisturiser on my face.

He climbs into bed and looks at me. I put down the pot of moisturiser and remove my nightdress, closing my eyes as his hands reach for me and push me onto my back. In my mind I can see Yusuf, and Muhammed behind him, watching us.

"Who is the better lover?" he hisses. "I am, I am better." He slams into me. I can tell he's been drinking again. "You enjoyed it with him," slap, slap. "You wanted him." A hand on my throat, gripping, bruising. He twists my nipples painfully, until I cry out. "You wanted another man. You are not a good wife to me."

"I was only doing what you told me to do! I thought it was what you wanted!"

Slap!

"Please, Muhammed, you'll wake the children!"

He finishes quickly, rolls off me, and disappears into the bathroom. The bed sways underneath me. My face burns where he slapped me, my neck throbs with pain. He returns, and says nothing, just lies with his back to me.

I have been lying awake for hours, listening to Muhammed breathe, snore, and sigh. The temptation grows in me. A pillow, a simple thing, shut off the breath and the life. But there will be signs, and evidence, and I can't leave my children motherless. This is where I find myself, lying in the dark with the ache in the secret places of my body, and the vivid memories too bright in my mind. A drip, drip, drip of fear and anger is wearing away at the stone of my compliance, and further, further the channel cuts through the strata of my self. Here the sandstone of my outer self gives way to the granite that lies under it – and beneath, the diamond hardness that makes me a mother, and a survivor. A cave of crystal pierced for the first time with the light of knowledge, or the beginnings of new vision. A secret chamber of the self, and out fly the shadows that have lain, unnamed, since its formation. In one, I see my shadow self, my dark twin, and the cold stone face is not stone but hot lava and blood boiling with pain and shame and secret pleasure. I know now what it is to feel inside my body, and my shame is also my secret triumph – that I can endure. He can dominate, and I can submit. I can rise and meet each challenge, and I can conquer through the giving, the yielding, the knowledge of my flesh under his hands.

Seven a.m. Prayers and the children to be seen to, breakfast to make, greetings to Layla, Gadria and Khala, and the small rituals of the day are a tide that carries me along. It is a relief, to fall into these patterns. I drink coffee and feed Mahmood, discuss the war that is coming with

Khala, and sympathise with her anti-American sentiment. I wonder what the papers and the news at home are saying, about this supposed war's supposed justification. I wish I could have a real conversation, not a stilted question and answer session, hampered by my poor Arabic.

Housework – the children underfoot. Layla talking about her future marriage, her husband-to-be's family. He has four brothers, two are unmarried. She will miss her mother, she says, folding clothes dried inside the house. No point putting them outside – the dust of summer would settle on the clean laundry, and within minutes it would need washing again. I help Layla with the sheets, pile up the twins' clothes and Mahmood's tiny things, and carry the basket upstairs, thinking about the recent invitation from Grace, the American woman I met at the hospital.

Footsteps behind me.

"Muhammed," I turn and face him, mind still on my day.

"I'm going out soon," he says, watching me fold his clothes away. "I can take you to your friend's house on the way. I just wanted you to know I have arranged a flat for us to live in."

A smile, genuine, born of real pleasure, spreads across my face. "That's wonderful! Thank you!" My arms are around him before I realise it, just thinking of being alone, myself...

He remains stiff, not acceding to the embrace, but for a moment, not rejecting it either. For a moment I wonder, is this really good news? Perhaps I am safer here, where his mother and sisters help me overcome my ignorance, and save me from the social and cultural ineptitude which here could lead to consequences so severe as to be almost unimaginable.

Or maybe he thinks that this will make me happy. Maybe he is doing this for me.

The burning pain of hope and the unfreezing of some small part of my emotions makes me shrink away, denying the good for fear I will be disappointed. But there is the temptation of freedom, of being able to order my own day, spread my time over and through activities other than this still-alien routine.

"That's really great," I tell him. "It would be good for us, to be just us, together, in our own place."

"It is a small flat," he warns, but not coldly. Instead he smiles. "But big enough for us."

"Thank you," I say again, and this time, his arms reach for me and he kisses me, gently, like a first kiss. Like a beginning. Maybe this is what we need, to be ourselves again, the way we were before. Ok, there are the children now, but they sleep well enough now and we could have private time back. Maybe this is all we need.

"You need to do something with your time." Grace says. The boys play in her family room with her children. I can hear my twins laughing. Mahmood rests in my lap, sleeping. He still feels like a stranger. Seated in Grace's beautiful house, I feel grubby and awkward.

"I'd like to do something that takes me out of the house," I confess. "All day long, with the curtains drawn, I forget which day it is. Sometimes weeks go by without me noticing."

Grace nods. She hands me a coffee, American style, not Arabic, and this taste takes me back into myself.

"Were you already a convert?" she asks. The coffee cups are white china, thin, with flaring scalloped edges and thick handles. The heated surface presses against my knuckles, a small pain.

"No, not really. I was…interested, I suppose, especially in the mystical side of things, the dervishes, the slavish devotion of those who do believe. I…" But I can't say it. I can't explain it, even to myself. I've never said it aloud. I was pregnant, and it seemed that this was what I was supposed to do. I don't say the words, but they are there in the air, an invisible billboard advertising the kind of woman I really am.

"I can't get a job," I say to Grace, "what would I do?"

"Plenty of women work," she replies. "Think about it."

I think of working in a women's mall, in a shop, and the headless, faceless dress forms displaying clothes.

"I suppose so."

"Now that mine are in school most of the week, I can spend more time doing the things I want to. I feel freer. But I have plenty to keep me occupied. You need that too."

"Suleiman works for his father's company?"

"Yes, but his father works in another office."

"What are they like with you, being Western?"

It's the question I've been waiting to ask since we first met. Through the bitter taste of the coffee – I have grown used to the sugar and spices the Saudis add – I relish the question in my mouth, and relish even more the depth of her answer.

"They were kind, and tolerant, especially at first. I must have made a heap of terrible blunders and offended everyone. There was some distrust, wariness, I suppose. I can't blame them. I would be the same, I guess, if the boot was on the other foot!"

I nod, remembering.

"Now, well, there are still times when they treat me like a naughty kid, correct me, or shake their heads slightly, all meaningful. And Mimi likes me to keep my hair covered, even at home."

There are other questions I long to ask, but just speaking and hearing English is overwhelming me. The gestures – when she speaks English she is all Western, with proper eye contact, wry smiles, laughter.

"Umma…" It is Gaffar, her oldest son, speaking in Arabic, explaining that the children are getting very noisy and making a mess in the other room.

Grace answers him in Arabic, and in an instant, as if speaking the language was her cue, her body language follows. She brings her scarf forward in that sweeping, unconscious gesture, a gesture of all women. I know I do it too. Just as I check my coverings automatically when I see another woman, covered and veiled and proper in every respect.

Gafar runs back into the large family room.

"I should check on the boys…"

"They're ok." Grace lays a hand on my arm. I stay put. Apart from the sounds of the children playing, it is very peaceful here. The nagging unease I feel is because I am unused to this, sitting and drinking coffee with a woman friend. And then I realise what else is missing.

"Where's the rest of the family?"

"Suleiman won't get back for another few hours."

"No, I mean your mother-in-law, brothers, sisters…?"

Grace laughs. "That crowd? Heavens, Amanda, did you think I would put up with sharing my kitchen with my husband's mother? Oh," she adds, correctly interpreting my expression, "I know that's not how it's done, and we started off there, with all those in-laws around about. It was mighty useful when the kids were just babies, but I couldn't stand it for very long. That was part of the deal, from the beginning, that we would have our own place."

"Doesn't it make it harder for you – childcare, the household, you know?"

"No, no, I manage just fine, just fine. We have a maid, you see. The family insisted." She laughs. "They're in and out pretty much every day, we're over there on a Friday, of course, after going to the Mosque. It works out great. I read scandalous Western literature in peace, and I get Suleiman to myself more. Else he's out with his brothers and brothers-in-law, and I can speak English to the kids and teach them more about the world than they get in school."

The *adhan* sounds, the call to prayer, eerily echoing around the house, a faint but urgent summons. I rise, and wait for Grace to do the same.

"Where are you going?" She smiles. "Sit down, sit down. Honey, that's the other reason I like my own place better. There's no one to see or judge."

"The children…"

"Sometimes they remember, sometimes they don't."

As Grace lets her scarf fall back again, I notice the thick embroidery that frames the cloth, and the richness of her clothes, and her carefully applied make-up.

"You need to get that husband of yours to part with some money and take you shopping," she smiles. "Suleiman is very good in that way, you know. I can't complain."

"It wouldn't make much difference if we did," I sigh.

"No, it wouldn't. It is what it is." Grace rises. "More coffee?"

"No, thanks. I suppose I should get back."

"No, stay a while. Tell me more about yourself. I've been yakking on about me all afternoon."

Her story perhaps is as strange as mine, and as inevitable. Another Red Riding hood who took the path through the woods, but when the wolf got her, she went enthusiastically.

"You seem so settled, like nothing bothers you." I say, almost protesting.

97

"Oh, I don't say it isn't hard sometimes, what with the laws and the way I get looked at. But Suleiman is worth all of that, and the children…"

She is happy, I realise. This is happiness. She is content, in her lovely house with its rich furnishings, her husband who loves her, five children who converse as easily in English as in Arabic. Mistress of her domain. The behavioural code is a small price to pay.

"You must be happy?" she says, when I give voice to some of these thoughts.

How to answer? Am I happy? Here, now, I am content, and have slaked my thirst for friendship and conversation. As Muhammed's wife I am looked after, included, cemented into the mosaic of family life. I see and feel through the eyes of the woman I am supposed to be. And so I suppose that woman is happy with her situation, which must mean I am happy too.

"I do well enough," I say to Grace, who nods. She accepts my answer for what it is, as much as I can give at this moment in time.

"How is Mahmood's health?" She asks, a careful subject change.

"Better. I think the climate suits him. If we were back home in the UK with all the rain and cold, he might not do so well."

Mahmood, Mahmood, my small son, fighting for life from the very beginning. Too eager to be born, and then too stubborn to die. He wheezes a lot, catches cold easily. He's susceptible to every bug that goes around. Weaning him is a nightmare. But still he hangs on, holding on to me, because I love him too much to let him go.

Being with my children. Yes, these are the times I touch again what happiness might be.

"I'm pregnant," I told him as he hovered in my doorway. The shared student house in which we lived offered little privacy, and I had thought he might have guessed by now, as I'd been throwing up for the last week. As he looked away, I told myself it doesn't matter. I had contemplated not telling him, wondering whether I should tell him at all. I could go home, reconcile with my parents, become a single mother and learn to live a different life.

Fear, a cold emotion, a freezing of thought and action, flooding through me. The reality of pregnancy was a great fear, and I was frozen in place. There was an awaiting momentum, a deadline towards which I had to make my own way. No escape, I was fettered from within.

"Are you sure?" Muhammed came into my room, his hair and moustache clean and neat, his white shirt pristine, his eyes bright. From inside me a tendril of feeling stretched towards him. It was hope.

I couldn't divine his feelings, his reactions. Then he smiled, and said something in Arabic. "You are sure. I see. Then I will marry you. We will be married and my child will be brought up Muslim."

Shock was replaced by something else, almost as if I was waiting for this to happen.

"Don't I have to convert to Islam to marry you?"

Muhammed was standing now. "Yes. Of course."

"Well, I'm not sure I want to, I don't know enough about it. I can't just make that kind of decision in an instant. Islam doesn't seem to be a religion that does a lot for women."

"Be careful what you say," he warned as he sits beside me. "You are right, you know very little about Islam. Women are revered in our culture, in our faith. A woman is the heart of the home, the mother of a man's children. All women are held in high esteem, and are protected."

"As long as they toe the line, follow the rules." There was bitterness in my voice. I did not recognise it until the words came.

"Islam is a religion of love," Muhammed insisted. His hand on my arm was heavy, warm. "You are carrying my child. We must be married. And we must not tell anyone that we have already slept together."

"What do I have to do, to convert?"

"It is very simple. To begin with, the *shahada*, the profession of faith is all that you must do. Eventually you must follow the Five Pillars of Islam: *salah, shahada, sawm, zakat* and *hajj*. Then you are a Muslim."

"The profession of faith?"

"*La ilaha illa Allah wa-Muhammad rasul Allah.* I bear witness that there is no god but Allah and that Muhammad is his prophet."

The tone of his words as he spoke was unfamiliar to me. It seemed grounded in certainty. An ache of longing grew, a response to his conviction. I pressed my arms across the emptiness in my stomach, remembering its source. "Do you really want to marry me?"

He cupped my face with his hand.

"You are the mother of my child. It is a sign from Allah, it is the will of Allah. We must marry."

He had been good to me those past weeks. He had made food for me, he had spoken to me, he had touched me gently. I felt better when he was in the house.

"Tell me what to say." I got up off the bed. "Do I have to go to the mosque or anything?"

"Not for this. We will have to see the Imam when we marry. But to become a Muslim you can begin at any time."

He said the words, and I repeated them. Then he left,

momentarily. When he returned he was holding a long, black and white patterned cotton scarf.

"This will do, for now."

"For what?"

"You must cover your head when you leave the house."

"Now wait a minute, who says so?"

"It is in the Qu'ran."

"I thought women only had to be modest," I protested. I learned that much in my comparative religions course. "And I will be. I'm not wearing a headscarf."

"You must get used to it. When we return home, you will wear it all the time."

"Home?"

"To Saudi Arabia. We will return there after we are married."

"Oh. I thought..." What did I think? That we would settle down like a nice suburban couple somewhere in England? That we would live here until he finished his studies? I had never considered this.

"Do you have a house there?" I asked. Or a tent? Or a palace, in marble and gold?

"My family has a large house there. We will live with them. Sons stay with their families, daughters go to their husbands' families. It will be good for you to have my family to look after you and help you when the child comes."

Simple words. When the child comes. I knew myself to be trapped by this, trapped by my body. My body and its reproductive urges had decided my fate.

"I hadn't imagined living somewhere else. What is it like?"

"It is a desert country, hot and filled with sunlight," Mohammed said. I glanced at the grey sky and threatening rain. The wallpaper was faded in the small kitchen, and the air was stale with cigarette smoke and yesterday's cooking. We shared this place with three other students. The emptiness inside me only partly came from morning sickness. It had been growing for months in this dull, drab house, between the moments of insight gleaned in lectures, a thin, pale shoot of uncertainty.

Perhaps I was ready for something new.

"You will have to keep your head covered there," he warned me. "My mother will teach you all you need to know to be a good Muslim woman. My sisters will help you too – some of them speak some English." I imagined a host of brown-skinned, veiled women, waiting with open arms, and thought of my own mother and her perpetually tired, burdened face. But it was my own face I saw, lined and creased with worry like my mother's. He was offering comfort. He has sisters, a large family. They will help me. His hand reached for mine, a soft squeeze of reassurance. There was no other choice to make.

It is Khala who tells me I am pregnant again. During the preparation for the move, the conversations, the planning, the borrowing and buying of extra furniture, I find myself suddenly worse for wear, tired, heavy and lethargic in the mornings. My appetite, sparse at best, has dwindled to almost nothing, except for a constant desire for hot, strong tea with a little milk. I am not aware of sickness or nausea, but everything seems to be a much greater effort than I had imagined. There is much discussion amongst the family. I do some quick calculations. It has been a long time since I kept track of every monthly change. Fatima informs me of her mother's conclusion during a visit one afternoon.

"She says you will have a child." Is it disapproval which

colours her voice, or jealousy? All children are a gift of Allah. But here, during pregnancy, people don't discuss pregnancies in the same way as we do at home. I know that at home, when I first got pregnant, everyone wanted to talk about it, happily and perhaps wilfully blind to the fear and the threat of death that comes with it. It is all different here. Khala simply acknowledges the pregnancy. I am not sure how far along I am, but it makes no difference to her. She remembers, it seems, my last period better than I do. She makes a pronouncement of the projected due date, which makes me about three months along.

Three months. I sit with Mahmood on my lap, watching him reach for my hair. Three months. Three months ago we were in Dammam.

The thought keeps me sleepless. Muhammed has been informed, not by me, but by his mother. If he has done the same calculations I have, then I may be in trouble. But maybe he doesn't understand, or doesn't care. Whatever happens, the baby will be his. It belongs to him, now, and always. As does the body in which it now resides, feeding and growing. I dream at last, in brief snatches, of deserts and sandstorms and the moonless orange city sky at night, but in the dream, the orange underglow is the smoky fire of torches, a mob with torches, and they are coming for me.

## *Shān*

"So hot!" I realise I have spoken aloud. Fatima smiles at me. A family outing to the desert, after the rains, the brief desert flowers in bloom, but no sign left of the short flood that brought them into being. Food packed in cool bags, bottled water, blankets and umbrellas to keep off the sun. Sand too hot for bare feet. The boys run like puppies, tumbling over each other and laughing.

Laughing too, I settle beside my sisters-in-law, fanning myself with my head scarf.

"Do you think you will ever get used to the heat?" Fatima asks, slowly, in Arabic, and then in English.

"No." I say in English, and smile to soften the response. "I grew up in cold weather. It is never as hot as this, not even in the hottest summer. Few British people would even understand this kind of heat."

Heat so dry it sucks the moisture from the mouth as soon as you speak, the sun a hungry animal, drawing from me every ounce of wetness, of fluid. I have learned to breathe with my mouth closed, and to use short, rapid sentences. To conserve the sweet liquid inside me. Around me, the family are unperturbed. For them, this is pleasant, almost cool.

"You start your job soon," Fatima says, "at the school."

"Yes, I am really looking forward to it."

She raises an eyebrow. This idiom, like so many others, does not translate.

"It will be very pleasant," I say. "The boys are growing up, the twins will soon be ready for school themselves."

"And Khala will keep Mahmood with her?"

"Yes," I nod, watching him stumble and fall into his brothers, playing some game that involves a lot of running and shouting.

104

"Your friend, Grace, she works at the same school?"

"Yes."

"But you are pregnant again, why are you starting to work now?"

"I can work while I'm pregnant, and that means I'll have a job to go to when the new baby is old enough."

It is enough. I smile again, to myself. Change has come, like the sudden rains in the desert, and next month my new job begins. It was so easy, far easier than I imagined. It seems Saudis are snobs about who teaches their children to speak English, and native English speakers are considered second to none. No matter that I have no qualifications to speak of, no references except a recommendation from Grace. I am "English", and so the school can boast of my expertise and the quality of teaching the children will get. I am looking forward to it.

Since our return from Dammam, Muhammed has become, paradoxically, more distant and more demanding. It doesn't bother me as much as it should. A kernel of something – resentment, maybe, or something else – stirs within me. As with the planned new home, perhaps he is, really, trying to please me, in his own small way. Perhaps he does care for me, and guesses at the kinds of differences and restrictions that will still plague me, here, in his country.

Perhaps not. Perhaps he seeks to separate me from his family, who are too protective, too knowing. I will be outside that safety net. Perhaps he thinks that in a place of our own we can regain some of the tentative intimacy from those months in England, getting to know each other. Who can tell? Do men ever think of such things? More and more I see men as babies, living in the here and now, wanting every need satisfied as soon as it arises, and relentless in every new desire and demand. Always wanting, only temporarily satisfied by the pacifying breast.

Sitting on the sand, I see Muhammed in every one of my three boys, like a ghost beneath the skin, possessing their very being. The set of Abdullah's head, the way Shahid stands and looks down at his brothers, Mahmood's all-seeing eyes which turn towards me every minute or two, to check I am still where he left me. Is this my curse, to love most what has come from him? Looking at them, I know that no matter what I do, I will never be free of him. They have his skin tone, hair colour, eyes and attitude. So he will always be with me. When I look at them, my heart fills with love, but it feels like desperation.

Khala calls a halt when she has had enough, which is not soon enough for me by any measure. She is of desert stock, only one generation removed from the nomadic life, shrugging off this kind of heat as nothing unusual. I, on the other hand, have gone beyond wilting.

After the walk and the drive home, I leave the children sleeping in the women's salon, and return to our rooms to pack. There is surprisingly little – a few suitcases, the twins' things in boxes. Muhammed will move the furniture tomorrow; some male relative or other will help. The flat is a mile or so away, an apartment in a block nearer to the school and the centre of town. Nearer to Grace. This is pure luck, and more than anything, I am simply eager to be alone, to be free of the endless need to dress up, visit relatives, make vast mountains of food endlessly for family and guests. Time, years of time, have slipped past me unmarked. No birthday celebrations, no Christmas, none of the familiar signposts of years turning and passing. At *Eid* I buy gifts for the boys, and pretend it's like Christmas. But I have been completely submerged in the pattern of someone else's days. At least in my own home I will have some control, some space to set my own pace and change the small things.

The bleeding comes suddenly, in the night. Pain in my abdomen, and the hot, gushing blood. I stagger to the bathroom, and for the first time feel sick, so sick it seems I cannot stand up, cannot draw free breath. After vomiting so hard I am sure I will faint, I sit on the toilet, feeling the rush and heat of the pregnancy pouring out of me. It is over, remarkably quickly. Shaking and weak, I clean myself up, and for just one moment, regard the tiny, barely formed body, before flushing it away. I clean up the bathroom, and, returning to our bedroom, leave the door open to the hall, to give me a light to see by.

Back in bed, Muhammed stirs, turns over, and throws one heavy hand over my abdomen. I lie there, feeling the cramping pains, but nothing else. I should be sad. I should mourn the loss of a child, the loss of hope. I wait for the pain and grief to surface. It never comes.

*Dear Mum,*

*How are you? How are Dad, and Jan? Is Karen still having problems with her husband? Did you get over that bout of 'flu ok?*

*Life goes on here much the same. The boys are growing fast. The twins are walking, or should I say, running. They're into everything, and starting to talk. I try to get them to talk English, but they're better with Arabic. They hear it all the time, after all.*

*Mahmood is growing too, and he seems well enough, though he does catch things so easily. But he is doing well, and always trying to go after his brothers.*

*Thank you for the gifts for the boys' third birthdays. They don't celebrate birthdays here, really. But the presents were great. Shahid loves the big blue dinosaur, and Abdullah thinks the cars are great. The clothes fit them too.*

*So, what news have I got for you? I'm getting a job, in a school, teaching English. It's a small, private primary school. Grace, my friend, works there. I'm looking forward to it. Khala will have Mahmood during the day. The twins can come with me. And we've moved, as you can see from the address at the top of this letter. We have our own flat now. It's small, well, at least by Saudi standards, but I like it. It's great to have my own place at last. Maybe you could even come and visit some day?*

*I miss you, I really do. I wish we could come home for a visit. We are so far away. I hope you and Dad keep well. Tell Jan I'm well, and happy, and the boys can't wait to come and see their auntie some day.*

*Love from all of us*
*Amanda*

"How is the new apartment?" Grace asks, handing me coffee made just the way I like it. Our collective children tumble like kittens on the floor.

"It's…ok." I don't want to lie. It's very basic, but I have already made it my own in small ways. "I have lots of plans, to make it nicer."

Grace nods. "I know. It takes time. But it's so much better, isn't it, to be on your own?"

"Yes, though the boys miss their grandparents and aunts and uncles. I take them over to visit as often as I can. But I love having my own place. I made a roast beef dinner yesterday. It was almost as good as being at home."

"Do you miss it very much?" Grace sips her coffee and arches her perfectly shaped eyebrows at me.

"Only sometimes. I miss my family the most, I suppose. Especially my mum, although I didn't expect to. We've never really been close, so it seems odd to miss her so much. But I have so many worries about the children – I keep wishing I could go to her for advice. Don't you miss home?"

"Not often," Grace smiles. "I try not to look back. My life is here, now, with my kids. I'm happy enough. I think, after living here, that if I went back, I wouldn't feel like I fitted in there either."

I take one of the cakes on the plate she has brought, and pick at the pastry. Oil coats my fingertips.

"I think I miss the little things. Like now, I want some new curtains, but I have to wait to get them until Muhammed says I can."

"I can pick you up in my car, with my driver, if you like. It's no trouble." Grace touches my arm. The touch is like a blow, not in terms of force, but impact. The touch is gentle. It does not exactly hurt, but beneath the cotton sleeve hide the bruises of the previous night, when Muhammed, drunk as he is so often now, held me down too hard. I tell myself he does not mean to hurt and mark me like this. Still, Grace's touch sends a frisson through me, tenderness, gentle concern stirring me more than the rough handling of my husband. Warm and soothing, a caress, a touch of sisterhood. Perhaps she does know. Perhaps it is this way for all of us.

"Nura spoke to me last week, about the start of school. I gave her your new address, as you asked." Grace devours a pastry. "Have you started preparing for your classes?"

"As much as I can. I'm a bit nervous."

"It's easy," Grace reassures. "The children are still young. I'm going to enjoy working with you every day."

"Me too. I am really looking forward to working, to having my own money."

"Except it's not, really, is it?" We share a grim smile.

Grace is the only person I know who speaks openly of the restrictions that the Kingdom places on women. She's right. The money is not mine. It belongs to my husband, because I belong to him, body and— No, my soul belongs to Allah. But there it is, palpable in the air between us. We have sold our very selves and done so willingly.

"If I had known…" I say to Grace, wondering.

"Can you honestly say you would have done differently?" She rises to refresh our coffee cups.

"I could have refused to come," I insist. "In the UK, he couldn't have forced me!"

"Really?" She nods as I follow her into the kitchen, away from the children. "And what about your children? "Something would have happened to bring you here. There would have been a visit, an urgent call home. Or else, maybe you would have woken one day to find him – and them – gone. He would have got you here somehow. A man's sons are too important."

"I know." How can she understand the nature of my sacrifice? She came here happily, in full knowledge of the culture and of the law.

"Oh Amanda," she sighs, as if reading my thoughts. "I thought I knew. I thought I understood. But I didn't, not really. I don't think anyone who has not been here can. I talked to people I knew who had worked here, as nurses, but they lived sheltered lives, inside 'Western' compounds, restricted in their movements, yes, and having to wear the *hijab*, but still at more liberty than any Saudi woman can dream of. They were always outsiders, visitors. All they had to do was play by the rules, do their work, and earn the big bucks. They had no idea what it is really like, for you, and for me."

"How could you come, though, knowing as much as you did?"

"I love my husband," she replies. "It's a simple thing, really. To be with him, I had to be with him here. And... here I feel protected. As long as I play along, act the part, I feel safer than I ever did back home. And he is sympathetic, he tries to understand how it makes me feel. Which is why I have a job. It's the same with Muhammed, I'm sure, or he wouldn't let you go out to work."

"Maybe." Maybe it is. Can I trust this small act of compassion? The new apartment, the job, it all seems too good to be true.

"Has Khala adjusted to the move?"

"As far as I can tell, yes." It is, no doubt, a relief, not to have the awkwardness of my presence when guests arrive. I'm sure she misses my work though. Too often it has felt like I was doing the lion's share, while she and her daughters left the chores to me so they could get ready to go out visiting one family member or another. Having only a small flat to clean and a small number to cook for seems like heaven.

After an easy afternoon of gossip with Grace, her car brings me and the boys back to the apartment. With the door closed, behind the frosted glass of the windows, I breathe deeply, feeling as if I am filling, inhabiting this space with all of my being. It is *my* space, the furniture where I put it, the small, homely touches mine, mimicking Grace's graceful style.

Dinner is already prepared; all I have to do is turn the heat on under the vegetable sauce and start browning the chicken. As I sit on the low cushions, Mahmood climbs into my lap, burrowing into my body like a hungry kitten. Abdullah and Shahid follow, clambering over each other for

111

a space. I hold them close, the twins on either side of me, Mahmood against my chest, and feel the warmth and press of their young, male bodies.

"Story, Mama," says Abdullah, in Arabic. Haltingly, I begin.

"Once upon a time, there was a princess called Rapunzel, who lived in a high tower, kept prisoner by a wicked prince who loved her, but was so jealous he would let no other man see her. All alone in her tower, she spent her time cleaning and cooking and waiting for her prince to come home. And when he did, he was sometimes nice, and sometimes he was stern and cruel. For ten years he kept her locked away, until her hair grew so long it reached the ground when she hung it out of the window."

I pause, seeing their eyes closing, feeling their breathing deepening towards sleep.

"Then what happens, Mama?" Abdullah murmurs. "Does she cut off her hair and make a rope and run away?"

"Maybe." I watch his eyes close too. "Maybe she does."

Bright as the sun is, searing hot, I long to cast aside the veil and feel it on my bare skin. This morning has been a long one, cleaning, ironing, and now shopping, with two toddlers at my feet and the restrictions of being out in public. Shrouded in black, I catch my reflection in the polished surfaces of the cold units, the shelves that hold washing powder and bleach and kitchen equipment. Voices around me no longer hold me mystified, I can pick out the words, the language, the cadence of women's voices speaking to children or to each other.

Abdullah and Shahid run between the aisles, and I turn this way and that to follow them, cursing my limited vision, the folds of the veil that restrict my arms and the long skirt of the *abaya* which hampers my legs. Air conditioning makes the supermarket cooler, but I cannot appreciate it, apart from the cold chill of sweat on my back and neck.

"Amanda," Layla says. "Here." We load our trolleys, Mahmood sitting in the baby seat and reaching for everything as I put it in. I pick over the goods the way that she does, weighing them up, checking them. Next stop the spice souk: out into the heat again, haggling with the vendors, all men, who do not look at our veiled eyes, but whose gazes linger on my length, my concealed shape. They must know I am Western, from my accent, from my appearance. I have not learned to move the way that my sisters do, the way that the other Saudi women do. Even fully covered, I am not the same. We walk through the vegetable souk. "Do you want to get some *sambousa*?" Layla asks as we pass a vendor. "*Sambousa*, Mama!" shouts Sahid. I buy them some of the hot, fried pasties, and get one for Mahmood, though he won't really eat it, just gum the pastry. Then sweet *muttabaq*, stuffed with bananas and honey. All three devour the sweet sticky treats as we walk along.

The car meets us at the edge of the market, and we load the children and the shopping into it, then return through the noisy, traffic-filled streets. Exhausted, I remove the veil from my face, slip back the headscarf and scratch my sweaty scalp. Layla looks surprised, but says nothing. I wonder if she can ever understand this struggle that happens to me now and then. For days on end I forget, and this covering has become habit, habitual, accustomed. I would feel naked without the scarf, the long, concealing *abaya*. But at times I want to scream from the weight and the wearing of the thing, and from the constant noise of the nylon against my ears that muffles hearing. Or maybe the weight comes from the heat, like some monstrous creature that has enveloped me and now forcibly squeezes the life out of me.

The car stops at a junction, and glancing outside I see workmen laying kerbstones beside the road. Dust hangs in a cloud in the air, and the long *thobes* of the men moving around within it are like ghosts. One stands holding a spade, leaning on it, like any workman in the world, but his black eyes meet mine, and he grins lasciviously, and beckons with his hand. "Come, pretty mama," he smiles, still beckoning. Layla notices, and draws me away from the window, wordlessly handing me the headscarf and veil again. I cast the scarf over my head, tuck the ends under one cheek, and slide the veil over the top.

"Not even in the car."

"Not even in the car," she echoes my sigh, but I know she does not understand it. Abdullah climbs into my lap, his brown fingers tugging at the veil, tracing my eyebrows and touching my eyes above the black fabric. I hold his wriggling body for a moment, stroking his hair, but he pulls away from the caress. Shahid is on his aunt's lap, watching the traffic outside the window. A family of four races past on a motorbike, a goat balanced on the handlebars. The man drives; behind him a black veiled woman holds a toddler in her lap, while an older child perches behind her. This too has become commonplace. A donkey cart plods past next, piled high with mangoes and melons. The driver's *ghutra* flaps in the breeze of the traffic speeding around him.

"UmmShahid."

Layla's voice rouses me. I wish she would use my real name. Abdullah is asleep in my lap, and I lift him, heavily, into my arms and carry him into the house. Layla brings Mahmood, with Shahid toddling sleepily behind.

114

Muhammed is in the men's room, with two strangers, and I curse. Now I have to keep the damned veil on inside the house as well. The smells of food, mint tea and thick, spiced coffee greet me.

I set about helping with the food, rolling dough into shape for bread and setting out the serving plates. Khala makes more tea and takes it, on a tray, into the men's salon. I follow, with the cups, and Muhammed meets my eye. There is a hint of approval. I play the part of the demure wife. If my eyes could tell the resentment that is boiling inside me as I set down the cups... Not one of the other men has even glanced in our direction. Muhammed tastes the tea without pausing in conversation, and we withdraw, knowing he is satisfied, for the time being.

I slide between the sheets alone, and lie awake until he joins me, rips them back again, enters my body with his, and savages my skin with hands and teeth. Late into the dark hours I lie there, skin burning, while he snores beside me.

This is how it happened. We entered the mosque, a plain building, but lush inside, rich with colours and thick carpets and gold leaf. The last waves of nausea from the morning routine were passing, and the day was brightening towards noon. The Imam welcomed Muhammed, but said nothing to me. His eyes did not meet mine, and my consent was not asked for. Instead, Mohammed was asked if he would take me as his wife. The Arabic words flowed over and around me, a mystery.

There was some discussion, which grew quite heated. Muhammed translated for me; the Imam required permission from my father for me to marry. I explained to him about my family, that they are not Muslim.

The Imam asked about the dowry, how much it was, had it been paid to me? Muhammed said yes, that the dowry was two hundred pounds, and that I would receive it within a few days. There was more discussion, from which I was excluded. But something Muhammed said reassured him, and discussions ceased.

Muhammed signed a piece of paper. I signed as well. And it was done.

It was done with so little ceremony that I did not feel married. We sat in a small café drinking coffee, Muhammed smiling. His dark eyes were warm.

"We're married," he said, and grinned. I couldn't help but grin back.

"It feels strange," I admitted. "I never expected to marry this young."

"You should have told your parents," he said, stirring the greyish coffee in his cup. "I wish you had told them."

"It's better this way. They have enough to deal with, they always have. I told you, their whole lives have always been focused on taking care of my sister. I've always taken care of myself."

"I don't understand it, how your family can be so distant." His hand lay beside mine on the table. I wanted him to touch me, to hold my hand, to make that connection that comes when we are physically close. I'd forgotten how much I longed to be touched. But he didn't. The small gold rings on our fingers looked too new, too bright, against the smudged grey surface of the table.

"It's their way. My mum would be there if I needed her. But I can't add to their stress, their burden."

"It will be different with my family."

"I know. I'm glad. It's all a bit scary, really."

116

He covered my hand with his, then, and the warmth flooded through me, feeding me in some subtle, secret way.

At home, he took me into his bedroom, where a large bed dominated the space, covered in a white quilt.

"This much I know," he murmured as he kisses me, his hands on my body. "It's not a real marriage until we..."

I nodded, and smiled at his kisses, and laughed when he tipped me onto the bed to finish taking my clothes off. Already my breasts felt full and tender, but he was gentle with me, at first. I could close my eyes and forget how this all began. Only later, deep in the night while he snores heavily beside me, did I crawl out and follow my questing mind's direction.

I found the passage in the Qu'ran quite quickly, the one that tells Muslims that Allah has a mate for them, a spouse, someone they are meant to be with. This is the first explanation for his actions, at least for the decisions he had made about marrying me. It makes sense. Faith and certainty.

"Will you inform the college you are leaving?" Muhammed asked the next day as I made coffee and toast in the small kitchen.

"Mmm." The disturbed night had left me tired. I ached in secret places, but they brought back the memory of touching and of being touched. It was a good feeling. "Yes. I suppose. I can't really stay."

"Ring them today. We should get organised now, before the babies come. I need to make plans for our future."

As he left, he kissed my cheek. It felt like love.

I withdrew from all my classes, but kept using the library. I stopped working in the restaurant at Muhammed's request.

He paid my rent and covered all the bills. We slept in the same bed and ate together each night. I was in a relationship without knowing quite how I had ended up there. As long as I kept busy, I felt no need to question it.

Muhammed was happy to discuss religion with me from time to time, but he tired of my constant questions. Perhaps growing up in a faith makes it harder to explain to outsiders. To him, things just were the way they were.

"But if the Prophet Mohammed had a wife in whom he confided," I asked one day, "and who was considered a great scholar, why are women not given the same opportunities today?"

Muhammed looked at me in exasperation at yet another of my questions. "It is different now. She was a witness to his…" he searched for the right words, "to the holy words. It was a different time. The teachings of the Qu'ran, the Hadith, all of this, tells us how men and women should live."

I know he didn't understand what it is I was questioning. Maybe I simply couldn't phrase it properly.

Books gave me some answers. Days closed in around me, and I read, sometimes from morning until evening, books about the life of the Prophet Mohammed, and about Islam and the rules of faith, and the beliefs. I forgot to eat, but sat, arms crossed over my belly, devouring words and savouring their effects on me.

"You should not stay indoors all the time," Muhammed said one morning as I sat at the table, sipping tea and reading. "Get dressed, go out somewhere."

"Maybe," I replied. The dishes needed doing, and the floor needed sweeping. I rose to busy myself with the household tasks. When he left I returned to the book, ignoring the grey windows, the beckoning door. But the framing window called to me at last, and I stood for a while, half hidden, looking out onto the untidy, untended back garden.

A wet spring morning gave way to sudden sun, and the green of the trees, leaves glowing like jewels, almost took my breath away. Joy, love, some kind of aching longing filled me, filled my chest, my veins, as if I was about to burst. I didn't recognise this feeling, not in myself. It had been a long time since I felt anything so strongly. Bright sunlight on the leaves in the garden, and here, by the kitchen window, the dirty glass disappeared, and it seemed as if I was one with the trees, feeling the kiss of the sun, and the boundless possibilities of spring. The book I was reading, a biography of the Prophet, fell open to the page about the foundations of Islamic faith. Allah reached and understood through nature. Muhammed found God in nature.

At that moment, so did I. Here was something greater than myself, greater than the scurrying rat-maze of my mind. Here was the unnameable, the unknowable, made tangible. I opened the window, and the faint breeze was scented, not with the city smells, but the ozone tang of earth after rain. I could almost hear the trees growing.

I felt bruised, and tender, moving tentatively around the kitchen, making myself a cup of tea, eyes still returning to the green of the trees, and the patch of blue sky above them. I had not felt emotion, or sensation, or whatever it is I was feeling, for so long. Months, years maybe. All those months I had lived alone, empty, uncertain, wrapped in a shroud of non-feeling. It was easier not to feel the hollowness. Being alone became a habit. I had forgotten this rush, the dizzying climb of emotion, the swooping drop of its aftermath. Tears on my cheeks, turning cold in the air that slides around the edge of the open window. Why was I crying? Was I happy, or sad? Was this faith? I understood some of what I had been reading, but was this the dimension that could not be written down? I could feel something. There was a greatness, and I was touched by it. The surge of feeling, of wonder, began to recede but I could feel again. The sound of the radio upstairs was louder, Madonna singing *Papa Don't Preach,* the feel of the cool tiles on my bare feet was more noticeable. There was a grain in the tiles, like wood. My feet were like searching fingers, testing out the surface like a blind woman. My body was awake, aware, and suddenly I felt a flutter, a flitter, the stirrings of something that was not me, in the newly awakened flesh that I had been ignoring. Catching my breath, I stopped moving, mug in hand, wondering. It stopped. Then, yes, there it was again. And the tears came again, my legs weak as I collapsed into a chair. I cradled my belly in both hands. There was life in there. Fear and love and joy and dread, and other feelings, crowded in, filling the void, overwhelming me. And I prayed, wanting to believe that this was it, the connection between me and God, or Allah, or whoever. Wanting to believe. Needing to believe. Needing to give thanks, it seems, for this, this spark within me, and my sudden awakening.

## *Maknūn*

Khala comes from a desert tribe, from nomadic traders who bred large families and kept to strict cultural codes. I hear this in the words that spill forth in invectives against the Americans, who are waging a war for oil and for power. "They wish to stamp the American foot on the people of Saudi Arabia!" she cries, rocking Mahmood vigorously. She is a small woman, but like all my Arabic family, her voice carries through the house. It has become like background music, the rapid Arabic, the strident tones.

Muhammed's brother Ali is back in prison, for selling illegal drugs and alcohol. This makes me laugh. It is little different here to the UK, despite the religious police everywhere. Alcohol is passed freely from hand to hand and Muhammed comes home with dilated pupils, smelling of smoke and whisky. He says he is working all day, in his father's business, selling car parts and imported motoring goods. He gives me some money for food, for clothes for the children, so I assume he is working. But he says nothing of his day, instead berating me for the children not being quiet, for me encouraging them to speak English.

Talking to my mother on the phone, which Muhammed allows about once a month, she asks, "How big are the twins now? Will they go to school soon?"

"There is a school nearby," I say, and she asks me to repeat myself. I realise I have replied in Arabic. "Sorry." The word feels awkward on my tongue. "Either they will come with me, when I start work, or there's a school near here. They will go with their..." I want to say cousins, but for a moment, I forget it, forget the sound and the shape of it in English. I can only say, "Muhammed's brother's children."

"Their cousins?" My mother asks, and there it is, the

right word. This is not the only time this has happened. What can I do? I read books I brought from home, and my mother sends me gifts, when she can, of paperback novels. When we go to into the city, I buy the English newspaper, heavily censored as it is, just to keep up to date with what is happening in the world outside, to remind me that there is a world outside. But I am losing the words in English, for the simple things, because I just never use them.

I've grown accustomed to the veil, the concealing *niqab*. But I'm no different underneath. I stand and kneel at prayers, and feel nothing. Was it all an illusion? What I do feel, following the rules, is restrained, controlled, dominated. Just as Muhammed holds me down in bed, so this culture bears down upon me in daily life, pinning my spirit beneath its weight and the draperies that hide my shape from everyone, including myself. I find myself seeking for that feeling, the golden harmony that was, as it is called, my epiphany. I know it exists, I remember. The ghost of it lingers in my mind, but now, I cannot recall it from the past, from the woman that was, before she became the woman that is.

The boys, in their child-sized *ghutras* and *thobes*, running and playing and laughing. When I laugh, my eyes tell the tale. But around me the eyes of the Saudi women betray little. Is it a matter of pride to them, to be thus unchanging? Unremarkable? Or is it fear? They do not seem afraid, or accepting. They simply are.

Yes, I see pride. Vanity, in the quality and style of their *abaya*s, still the required plain black, but edged with embroidery, tailored, garnished, it seems, with what subtle adornments are permitted. The quality of the fabric – cotton, silk, layered veils, rich with abstract designs, all black. I have learned to discern the differences. To see the disdain of my simple *abaya* and scarf, my face too often exposed. Shops with shapeless, headless mannequins display clothes to be worn, tops and skirts and dresses. Why should I care about clothes? It's not as if anyone sees them, or cares what I am wearing. What I am like underneath. Who I am, now.

Wife. Mother. Daughter-in-law, sister-in-law. Muslim.

Woman. Like all of my sisters here, and how different are they, under the veil? I had thought I would feel changed by this, but I do not. I am a piece of wood, planed and sanded and shaped and made uniform, but the grain, laid down over time from the moment of my birth, is unaffected by the surface.

The children are at Khala's for the day. Grace insisted I come to one of her parties. She holds them regularly, to get her friends together, in the afternoon, to relax, share a little time without the children. There is quite a mix of women, Western and Saudi, and Grace is kept busy running between the two groups, who are at opposite ends of her large family room, each keeping themselves to themselves. Inside this light, warm space, the women sit around the edges on cushions, but Grace has laid out trays of food around the room, so everyone can eat, and drink the hot peppermint tea. I am in one camp, with the ex-pats. We talk English. It feels good.

"Where are your boys?" This is Paula, a friend of Grace's, whom I've met for the first time tonight. "Grace says you have three."

"Yes, twins and a younger son. They're staying with my husband's family."

"Three already? I only have the one, that's enough. Now Mary over there, she has six! Would you believe it?"

"I can't imagine it," I agree, my eyes on the women at the other end of the room. They are fascinating.

The music gets louder as Grace laughs with her Saudi guests. One by one the women around the room, the Saudi women, with their perfect make-up, their gold and their designer clothes, stand up and start to dance.

They are so well dressed, these women, some in rich colours, others in jeans and sleeveless blouses. One, her name is Aliya, wears a low slung skirt of thick green linen, embroidered with flowers, and a short, green silk blouse that displays her midriff. Her skin is like dark cream, smooth and soft, reflecting the light as she moves. She is laughing, and they are dancing in a circle, the Saudi women, bright with gold, arrayed in their best, bare feet moving across the rug, dancing and laughing and teasing.

One of them dances towards me, noting my gaze, and shakes her body, forward and back. As she comes forward, I can see the deep well between her breasts, and the round firm shape of them, visible through the thin white silk top she is wearing. A heat rises in me, a sudden flush, and she laughs again. She doesn't realise that she hasn't embarrassed me. It's something else, a kind of hot awareness. I'm not used to seeing women like this, with so much skin on display, totally relaxed.

"Come on girls, let's dance." Grace teases the rest of them, but at first, none of them get up. Then Paula gets to her feet, and starts to move, and the others follow her.

"Come on, Amanda." Grace grins at me, holding out her hand. She looks beautiful with her curly blonde hair loose, her lips full and red, her eyes sparkling. I shrug, and get to my feet, and her arm rests loosely around my waist. She is warm, but not hot. Her body is firm. We move together, back and forth, swaying with the throb and beat of the

124

music, and I'm laughing, and dancing, and holding her hands, and moving my hips, and it feels good. I feel free.

"You're Amanda, aren't you?" says the woman in the green.

"Yes, and you?"

"Sara." She dances around me, then back to another woman, shorter than her, with very dark, very straight hair and big dark eyes, wearing black jeans and a red blouse. They clasp hands and dance, in and out, smiling at each other.

"Sara dances really well," I say to Paula as we draw near to each other.

"Yes, she does," Paula agrees. "That's Daliya with her." She grins and winks. When I don't get the hint, she adds, "They're special friends."

What does she mean? She laughs at my confusion and dances away.

Grace is dancing with Sheena, who is also American, a taller, stocky woman with cropped, spiky hair. Sheena is wearing blue jeans and a plain white t-shirt, and she dances with great enthusiasm. I wander over, a little out of breath.

"Hey, Amanda, you remember Sheena, right? She's a nurse at the hospital."

"Yeah, we met before. How are you?"

"Oh, fine, yeah, fine. Glad to get out of the house though."

"Me too."

Grace excuses herself, and fetches another jug of cold fruit punch. Savouring the drink, I stand by one wall and watch the women. Sheena is dancing with Daliya now, grinding her hips and teasing. It's almost like being at home, in some club somewhere, except for the absence of men.

"Amanda, you're not dancing." Sheena sashays over to me. I laugh.

"No, I can't keep it up for long."

"Whooee, no, me either, though I used to dance all night, back home." Leaning against one wall, she hooks her thumb into the belt loop of her jeans. "So, are you staying or going?"

"What?"

"The war."

"Yeah, but…"

"Oh, come on, Manda! It's inevitable, it's going to happen. Saddam's not going to let up, and the US needs that oil. The UK too, we both know it."

"Will you leave?"

"Only if I have to," Sheena shrugs. "And you?"

"Oh, Muhammed won't leave, so I'll stay. It might not happen, anyway."

"It will. Just, be ready, won't you? If you need to get out, make sure you can." She's serious now. "Keep your passports handy."

War is coming. The government advises us to prepare by sealing the windows with tape, in case of gas or chemical attack. Khala rants as she directs me from one pane to the next, my height making it easy for me, and for her. What good will this do? I have to ask. She is beyond discussion. We stop going out. Guarded and secret, I have lived between these walls for so long. I am never unaccompanied. Not only the children, not just Muhammed, when he is here, but one or other of the many women who act as my guards and gaolers, in their homes or when visiting my own. Yet I know the fate they are guarding me from is double-edged. The freedom I dream of does not exist – not in this country. I sacrifice one form of bondage for another, one imprisonment for another. The veil and the danger on one hand, one knife edge walked in two minds – quiescent and angry – and the walls and the windows of frosted glass on the other. It's like eating camel meat. Once you become accustomed to it, you no longer really notice any difference.

I dream of things beyond my reach. I dream of rain – hard, heavy, cold rain, wet rain in a British summer, like a gift to earth and grass. I dream of green, of grass and trees and leaves in spring with the sunlight caught in them, that translucent, almost neon green as the earth yearns towards summer. Sometimes I dream of cold, wet cold, dry, crisp cold. I dream I am high on a mountainside, and the wind is blowing, and for a while I think I might fly off. That my body is dry and desiccated, paper-thin and light, and I can be caught up in that wind and tossed high, carried far away. Or a leaf at autumn's end, browned and shrivelled, tossed endlessly on the eddies of wind, from end of the world to the other.

Muhammed is on the roof. For days now the failed attempts at air raid warnings have continued – sirens that no one can hear, radio vans circulating the streets to no avail, because we are all encased in our brick houses, safely behind closed doors and opaque windows. The air conditioner rattles loudly, and the sound of the television, CNN with Arabic subtitles, eliminates all other noises, even those designed to save our lives.

Sheena knows a woman who is married to a man on the American base. She hears first when the air raids are due. Saddam is bombing us in retaliation. For what? For accepting American aid in protecting this country? For accepting American weapons and troops onto Saudi soil? The Americans are only interested in safeguarding the oil, not saving us. There is a base just half a mile away, down our road, with a patriot battery. Too close for comfort, or else a source of comfort, those great batteries of guns, set there to protect, and we come under the umbrella.

I don't feel protected. Sheena gets the call, and calls the network of women, wives and mothers all, who then call others – and so on. Grace is part of this network. She links me in, connects me, even though I spend a lot of time at Khala's house now, back in the safety of the family home.

Grace calls me. Air raid. I go to our designated "safe place", which is the bathroom. Cushions and quilts, the boys grumpy as I take them from their beds and settle them here. And Muhammed goes to the roof, drunk again, with his friend Musharaf, swords in their hands, dancing a war dance, swearing and cursing at the planes as they roar overhead.

I hear the rumble starting, then the drone, and I remember the day the planes first came. We went out onto the streets. Everyone came out, filling the road, the women black shapes with eyes skyward, the men in brilliant white, splashes of colour from their *ghutras* as they too stared upwards. There was none of the chanting, shouting and dancing that usually accompanied such gatherings. Silence. A great crowd standing absolutely still, all eyes turned upwards, as a black cloud crossed the sky, wave after wave of planes, phalanx after phalanx of black invaders, obscuring the infinite blue. The noise, a roaring of antediluvian beasts let loose across the sky, terrifying in their order.

This eerie stillness, and the drone of the planes, comes back to me now as we hear the bang and feel the concussion. The anti-aircraft battery on the base hammers its response. The boys wail, and I gather them onto my lap, Shahid on one leg, Abdullah on the other, Mahmood against my chest. Fear clogs my voice, my throat. I want to comfort them, but can't. I can barely get my arms around them. I cannot speak, but just hold them, fear like a hand over my mouth, silencing and suffocating. Muhammed is somewhere above us, dancing his defiance, while I sit, waiting, waiting, waiting for the bomb to fall.

Sometime later the phone rings, just one ring, then quiet. This is the signal that the raid is over. The boys are asleep, heavy and hot against me. My eyes are closing. I let the sleep come, and trust to Allah that I will live to wake the next morning. I open my eyes to a hot, stuffy room, one leg wet where the baby's nappy has leaked on me. Abdullah is curled against my side, deeply asleep, while Shahid sprawls like a puppy, on his back, arms and legs flung out, tangled in a sheet. There is quiet, no sound of guns, no engines. Stiff, aching, I move away from the children, and set Mahmood, still sleeping, between his brothers. The breakfast needs to be made. The house hasn't fallen down around us. We are all still alive.

Muhammed and Musharaf have gone out again. I luxuriate in being alone. The children are restless, another evening punctuated by the CNN broadcasts. Khala and the family came round earlier, drank tea, talked about the war. She still curses the Americans. I don't understand her logic. The Americans caused this war? I know from CNN why this war was supposed to have started, but I don't believe the party line. It is all about oil, and fear.

With the boys in bed, I watch the tv. The phone network no longer exists – the government has decided to shut down the phonelines when an air raid is imminent. Instead, we watch tv. When the screen turns red, it's time to go. Except there is nowhere to go. The screen turns red. I walk into the bedroom, pick up Mahmood, carry him back into the family room. I return, and pick up Shahid, who wakes with

129

a wail, and try to quiet him. He settles on the floor cushions, staring with wide, dark eyes at the red tv screen. Then Abdullah, heavy and sleepy, who hardly stirs. Sitting and waiting, the tv resumes its broadcast. I turn the sound down low, and I wait. Muhammed is out there, out in the night. The guns start their drumbeat, but I hear no impact. No bombs fall.

Lying here with the children, breathing in their smell, the sweet saltiness of them, I let myself drift, imagining. I imagine a stray bomb finding the exact spot where Muhammed and Musharaf are doing whatever it is they do. I imagine the news coming back, via the community grapevine, or via the police. Your husband is dead. Fear mixed with hope. Perhaps...but no, I can't go there. This is here, this is real, this is what I must deal with. I escape into the corridors of my internal landscape, because the boys need me here.

The guns burst out again.

Then the rumble and thud, louder than ever. The ground shakes underneath me. Glass rattles in the windows. I clutch Mahmood, who is nearest, and try to remember to breathe. The house stops moving, but I cannot stop the pounding in my chest. Shahid wakes and cries, Abdullah starts screaming. I calm Shahid, tickle Mahmood, and carry Abdullah out into the hall. Peering around the front door, I hear noise and see clouds of dust. The bomb has fallen nearby. Abdullah still screams. I go into the kitchen and make some warm milk. Abdullah falls quiet, and the house is suddenly silent.

When Muhammed bursts through the door, the boys are back in bed.

"What's wrong?" I say, as he runs to the cupboard where

he hides his home brew, and scoops himself a glass of the murky liquid.

"Musharaf and I," he says, "were nearly hit by a bomb."

His *thobe* is dusty, his *ghutra* awry.

"We were on the street. The guns were firing. Then we saw it. That one is coming for us, I said to Musharaf. Where should we go? He said. You run this way, I will run that way. One of us will make it. So I ran. I don't know where Musharaf is."

He goes into the bathroom. I take myself to bed. So close. In the bedroom, he strips, and his naked body is a shadow against the deeper night. I turn over, onto my back, ready for when he will reach for my body and take comfort in it. The guns have quieted. When he hurts me, I bite my lip and refuse to make a sound. His breath is rank with alcohol, and the weight of him on top of me is hot, heavy, suffocating. But when he enters me, hard, I welcome the sensation. My heart quiets. I am alive.

Muhammed rises early. I feel the shift and sudden lightness when he leaves the bed, as if a weight has been lifted from me, and I am part of the soft mattress, part of the furniture, and there is release when he is gone. In the absence of his mother and father, he is not so religious about prayers, and I find him at last, dressed to go out. "Do you want breakfast?" He barely looks at me.

"No, I am going out to find Musharaf."

"What is it you're doing when you go out with him, during the air raids?" I can't help asking, even though questions are dangerous.

"We're looking for shrapnel," he replies. "To sell. Someone will want to buy it."

He leaves, and I start the breakfast. The smell of the

131

cinnamon and other spices rises. The boys are not awake yet.

The phone rings. It is Grace.

"Elena rang me," she says. "Mina's husband's cousin Jameela was killed last night. Well, the cousin wasn't killed. She killed herself."

"What?"

"Jameela was living with her husband's family. She had three children, all boys. Her husband's brother lived with them. The bomb that landed in your district last night hit her house. Everyone was killed but her. They pulled her out of the wreckage of the house, alive. But, so Elena says, when she found out that they were all dead, she killed herself."

"How?" Why do I have to ask?

"She hanged herself at the hospital. The official story is that the whole family died in the house. They don't want the story getting out. But Mina was so upset, she rang Elena, and of course, Elena rang me." Of course. Everyone in our network of women friends knows Grace. Everyone talks to her.

"Is Mina ok?"

"You know these women." She means these Saudi women. *Inshallah*. But I feel something, inside me, cold and hard, a frozen spirit being, thawing slightly, and aching.

After the phonecall, I turn off the breakfast and sit in the sitting room, alone. The boys still sleep, worn out from yet another disturbed night. I think of them and their smiles, and the grasping, needy hands of Mahmood. I think of Muhammed, and my fantasies last night, and the near miss. If I believed in magic and the ability of people to influence the world just by wishing, I would think it was my fault, that I had wished it to be so, and that, at the last minute, Muhammed evaded his fate, and the hungry monster of the

132

bomb sought out another victim, one which might punish me in other ways.

Mahmood starts to wail. I rise, straighten my tunic and skirt, and go to see to him. Muhammed doesn't return until the afternoon meal. He brings Musharaf with him, relegating me to the rooms which are the province of women again. I serve rewarmed *fulmedames*, chicken and vegetables and soup and bread. I serve tea and coffee with dates. I follow the proper protocol. The boys play happily. I watch the news, the progress of the war, the propaganda on both sides. I think of guns and of bodies torn apart. Mahmood looks up at me trustingly as I feed him.

The day passes on. I clean the house, play with the boys. The children eat, and are put to bed. The phone is silent. I watch the news. The screen does not go red. At last I go to bed. Only then, only when I am lost and formless in the darkness, made more complete by the blackout curtains, do I feel it. The scream again, a beast uncurling and stretching within me, dragging sharp claws across the tender skin of my heart. To wake and have lost everything, to find your children dead, and your husband. Everyone dead. Nowhere to go, no one to turn to. No man to claim and protect and take responsibility. No home. Are there places in this society for women to go to, women like that? The assumption is always that she would have some family who would take her in. But maybe she didn't. Maybe she woke and grieved, and that grief was too great. No bevy of female relatives to mourn with her, to close ranks around her and wail and raise their arms to Allah. Only the cold, hard knowledge that her whole world was gone.

Tears come. They pour like hot rain down my face, where I lie in the darkness. It is a long time before sleep comes. The darkness does not lift. The tears do not stop.

133

When the planes pass overhead, and the guns start, I stay in bed. I fall asleep to the staccato beat of the guns.

The guns permeate my dream. I am standing against a blank backdrop, a wall plastered in white. Faceless people run past, in dark uniforms. The guns fire, too close, too close. I am covered in sweat, panting, I have been running away, running away, but I have forgotten something.

The children. I can't leave the children behind! I turn, run back, towards the gunfire, the flashes in the night, the smell of gunpowder, a smoky haze in the air, like fireworks night back home, but these aren't fireworks, these are real. I run through the haze, through the fleeing forms, all going the other way, calling for my sons. The guns ring out, and I fall, and disappear into the black and orange night.

"Amanda, did you hear about Sophia?"

Fatima, my sister-in-law leans conspiratorially close to me as we make drinks in the kitchen. Although I am a guest now, I still find myself here, in the kitchen, making the tea and getting cold drinks for the boys. "What about Sophia?" Sophia is one of her friends' older sisters, one of the panoply of women I have met, briefly, at some social gathering or other, perhaps a wedding, and still cannot place.

"She was one of those women the police picked up, for driving a car!"

I smile. I have never driven a car, never felt inclined to, never had the money. Here, it seemed no more than an oddity to me, women are not allowed to drive. And then, when the Americans came, there were female soldiers, and they drove cars and jeeps, and the scandal and gossip circled around and around. Other women argued that they should be allowed to drive as well. Some of them had gone ahead and started driving. Mostly these were women who had spent some time abroad, in America, Europe or the UK, who knew how to drive.

"Sophia was at school in America, yes?" Fatima goes on, as I load up the tray ready to take the tea to the men. Khala has been flitting in and out, holding Mahmood in her arms, fussing over him. I can hear the boys' high voices somewhere else in the house.

Fatima is waiting. I make the obligatory response.

"Yes?"

"And she wanted to go to the clothing souk, to the women's mall, and the driver wasn't available, so she drove herself. She said, if the American women can drive in this country, I can as well."

"Was she arrested?"

"She was stopped, and they told her husband, and she was warned not to do it again."

Fatima relishes each part of this retelling, as she relishes every other tiny piece of news and gossip she imparts as we engage in the usual women's activities. Muhammed and his brother Abdullah are with their father in the men's room, and as we enter, we fall silent. None of the men look at us. I set down my tray, and notice that my two older boys are mimicking the men, talking to their uncle, ignoring us. Moments ago they were clinging to me, clinging to my lap, asking me questions, and I was stroking their hair and letting the dark silkiness of it run through my fingers, over and over again. Now I am as nothing, a servant. I retreat, and beckon the boys to come with me. "Let them stay," my father-in-law says in Arabic. I find myself in the hall, shaking. They are only three and a half, but it seems that already they are not mine, they belong in the parts of the world I am not allowed to access.

I retreat to the women's salon, and sit talking nonsense

to Mahmood, and attempting to teach him English, which he resists. Still he looks at me adoringly and, eventually, cuddles up against me, burrowing into me like some small, wild thing seeking safety and comfort. I think about driving, and the women soldiers at the base, such a short walk away. What if I was to pick up the boys now, and walk down the road, and beg them to take me home, take me away, save me? Would they answer? Would they help?

They would likely be of no more use than the soldier at the British Embassy had been, when the war broke out. They were evacuating all the people who could leave. I heard through the women's grapevine that they were giving out gas masks at the British Embassy. When I arrived, the place was in chaos, and I had to remove the veil before I could get the soldier at the gate to listen to me. I showed him my passport, and those of the twins, and said I had come to get gas masks for my family.

"You should have left already," he said pointedly. "All the British women and children are supposed to be shipped out. Why haven't you gone?"

"My husband is Saudi," I replied. "He does not wish me to leave." It was true, Muhammed saw no point in me leaving, and would not hear of me taking the boys with me.

"Gas masks that way," the soldier said, finally, and I went to another room where there were trestle tables and boxes and boxes of WWII gas masks. Another soldier asked me to take off my veil so I could be fitted properly with the mask.

"Where are the children's masks?" I asked as he did so. "I have three, two three year olds and a two year old."

"We don't have any masks for children," he replied. "All children should be evacuated."

I hated explaining it again, hated the look on his face as

I did so, and the closed, blank expression as he told me there were no gas masks for children, none at all, and neither could I have one for my husband, because he wasn't a British citizen.

"So I'm supposed to sit there with a mask on and watch my husband and sons die?" I demanded.

His impassivity infuriated me. I threw the mask back at him. "Thanks for nothing," was all I could say, and I left the embassy in a rage, belatedly remembering to replace my veil. I went back the next day, though, with Mahmood's birth details, my birth certificate, passport, and marriage certificate. It took me days to get him a British passport, Muhammed complaining all the while that I was wasting my time. It had frightened me, speaking to them at the Embassy, because if I had to leave, if I didn't have a British passport for Mahmood, I would have to leave him behind. By the time I did get one, it was too late. Muhammed would not let me out of his sight, and insisted that his sister accompany me on all shopping trips, and that he drive me and pick me up. It was as if he had suddenly become aware of the possibility that I might leave.

The war becomes commonplace. I wake and fall asleep to the repeated sounds of the guns, thudding through the floors and walls. We hurry about any task that takes us outside. We undertake only necessary journeys. I rarely see Grace, and I find myself chafing at the restriction. The phones are unreliable too, which limits our ability to speak to each other. I become fractious with her and the children, frustrated at never really getting her to myself. She however is patience itself, and retains her cool, calm manner regardless of the state of the war or the impact on our lives. It is only then that I realise how important my friendship with her has become. At night, when the ground shakes the dust into low clouds, when the walls rattle and the guns chatter, I fight the fear and hold my boys close to me, and it is Grace I think of. I model myself on her unflappable fortitude. When I wake each morning and find we are still alive, I thank Allah for my sons and for Grace and for the chance to live another day with her in the world.

## *Munkar*

The war is over. The television is full of it, the radio is full of it, the men are singing and chanting and dancing their war dances in the streets, waving guns and swords and swaying *en masse*. I see my sons doing the war dances too. I try not to think about it. The guns have stopped. The fear has retreated. Life can go back to normal. The Americans have left in huge numbers, depopulating the bases. School has started again, and so my job begins.

It's a new routine. Nura runs the school, and there are six other teachers, two of us who teach English; Grace and me. I teach English to different classes, simple lessons in vocabulary and pronunciation. I rise early in the morning, get the boys ready, get the breakfast, get myself ready. Muhammed sometimes surfaces, sometimes doesn't. I would prefer it if he didn't, except when he stays in bed after I am gone, he gets more irate when I get home, and tends to shout a lot and storm out, upsetting the boys. It washes over me, most of the time, but the boys get home tired and fretful and hungry, and I have to start the dinner straight away, and Muhammed's griping slows me down and slows them down and makes it even harder for me to get things done. Nothing else changes. I clean, I do the laundry, I play with the boys a little, although they are very good at looking after themselves. I usually drop Mahmood off in the morning, on my way, and pick him up on the way back. Sometimes, when I go to fetch him, they are out, and I have to go home and wait for Muhammed to go and fetch him. At the point when all I want to do is lie down, I have to make dinner and deal with the children and sometimes, sometimes, I wonder why I keep doing this.

Grace is why. Grace picks me up in the morning, smiling

in the back of the car behind the tinted glass. She talks to me, she even makes eye contact. All during the day, during the journey home, I absorb as much of her as I can, savouring her presence, the conversation, the scent that fills the car, light and sweet, surrounding myself in her like some psychic talisman against what will happen at home. Grace laughs at my woes, kindly, making light of them, and that means I can too. Around her I feel softer, younger, less gangling and awkward. I copy her easy grace. I smile a lot, and even laugh. She regales me with stories about the other teachers, about Haneefa, who is divorced, whose husband took another wife only six months after they were married. She divorced him and got a job teaching, because she is the niece of the school's owner. She is scandalous, an unmarried woman, but, Grace warns me, it is hard for any woman to re-marry once she has been divorced. There were no children, *mashallah,* though children might have proved her worth, at least.

Yet Haneefa seems perfectly happy, lacking nothing. She has a driver who is yet another cousin, who takes her to work, takes her shopping. She has her job at the school. She has her friends and family. Still, I feel, like my Saudi sisters, the slight sense of wrongness about her.

The school has a small library, which we all take some time each day to put in order. The classrooms are a lot like any classrooms, anywhere. I mark the written work of the older children, sitting at my desk, feeling like a fraud, like a child in a grown up's clothes, playing at working. There are two versions of me. There is the one who is doing all of these things, the working and the talking, so much talking, every day, I am almost drunk on it, after so long alone. And then there is the other me, the one who seems to sit and watch, not believing that any of this is real, or permanent. Warning me not to get too comfortable.

Inside the classroom, I can remove the *abaya*, tuck the scarf in neatly, and almost forget where I am as I tell stories in English, sound out the words, teach the letters, mark the grammar. Other times, when the *adhan* sounds, or when we hear sirens and shouting in the street outside, I remember where and what I am. Grace might wander in while I am teaching, carrying a mug of coffee, to nod and join in and help me. She gives me ideas for homework for the children. We talk in rapid English while the children work, and later, in the staff room, we discuss things like our home lives, and the plans we have, and books we liked, films we both saw, in the time before this. I find myself watching Grace's face, fixating on her mouth, the movement of her lips, the appearance and disappearance of the dimples in her cheeks. The rounded softness to her is fascinating. I want to slip the tip of my finger into the deepest dimple, on the left side of her mouth, and sample the texture of that fraction of secret skin. I can't stop watching her, hungry for every moment with her, feeling empty when she is not around.

I wonder what Grace sees in me. I am not stylish, or interesting. I have none of her easy grace, her ability to talk to anyone on any level. I envy her this. I envy the ease with which she slips into character – one moment, the demure, efficient Saudi lady, the next, the easy American, laughing and sitting cross-legged on the floor.

At school, it is the same. I watch her as she glides into her classroom, and the children sit up immediately, and pay attention. Today, I will stand before my class, and have to shout to call them to order. I have never heard Grace raise her voice. Today is a tough day. There are bruises on my thighs which make sitting painful. Standing too long makes my back ache. But I think of Grace and the pain fades, and a smile dances around my lips as I plough through my day.

I am working through a series of nursery rhymes with the children. This is harder than I first thought. Every rhyme is hazardous, laced with potential danger. Pictures of animals to represent letters could be considered idolatry, Nura warns me. I show the children the pictures, have them copy the words, say the rhymes. Then we recite, practising the pronunciation. Instead of complying, they ask questions. "Why are we singing about Mary?" "Is it Mary from the Qu'ran?" "Why does she grow girls in her garden?"

Too much is lost in translation.

After the class, Grace walks with me to the classroom, carrying a pile of books, mirroring my own burden.

"I should do these now," I say, looking at the pile.

"Have a coffee," Grace smiles, holding the door open. "Do them later."

"I have so much to do!" I reply. My voice sounds flat. I have to mark them here. Later will be cooking, laundry, housework, the boys. Later will be Muhammed and his demands.

I sip my coffee while I mark the pages, laughing sometimes at the mistakes. My red pen is powerful, crossing out, correcting, moulding and shaping the childish handwriting.

Grace is chatting to Nura, who is in a state about something. One of the other teachers, Mounia, is causing problems. I don't know Mounia very well, she is young, and connected with Nura in some distant, familial way. I half listen, curious, as I continue to make corrections with my red pen. Good. Fair. Poor. I remember my primary teachers inscribing the same comments in my book, though not in the cramped, crabbed Arabic which is the best I can produce. But what happened in secondary school? I can't remember. There were marks, of course, out of ten, twenty

142

five, fifty, a hundred. There must have been comments too. I can't remember. The holes in my memory bother me. I keep losing parts of myself.

Grace meets me in the hall, after lessons.

"Will you ride home with me, or is Muhammed coming?"

"I don't know, I'll check outside."

"I'll wait then." She settles her headscarf and pulls the veil over her face, fastening it firmly. I mimic her actions, and step out into the baking heat. My hair is instantly hot and heavy on my neck. My lips pucker as I breathe, and I close my mouth. The heat is terrible. The noise of the streets engulfs me, a devouring roar.

There is no sign, amongst the crush of rushing traffic, of Muhammed's pick-up truck.

"No, he's not here," I tell Grace, who has the twins by the hand, standing by her car, one of them pulling faces at the driver.

"Then come with us." We pile in, and the doors shut. Behind tinted windows I remove the veil and breathe deeply. Already the air is cooling. Grace hoists Shahid onto her lap, and I do the same for Abdullah. Both boys are hot and heavy and tired.

"Where to?" Grace asks.

"Better take me to Khala's, so I can get Mahmood. One of them will take us home."

Grace is watching me, too closely. "It's ok, I'll wait while you get Mahmood."

She rests one hand lightly on my arm. I feel it acutely. Her fingers are soft, and cool, not roughened like mine.

"You could come in for coffee, if you like," I offer.

"Thanks. Martine will have the children, anyway, so there's no need for me to rush back."

143

I envy Grace her Filipina maid. I won't let myself think about all the other reasons I envy her.

Shrouded in the *abaya* and veil, I rush from the car to the house, and stop. Muhammed's truck is parked nearby.

"Grace, Muhammed is here," I say, ducking my head back into the car. She smiles, a small smile, and nods.

"Come on, boys," I say in Arabic. They climb over Grace, out onto the tarmac, scuffing through the eddies of dust and sand on the roadside.

"See you tomorrow," Grace says, as I say goodbye. She holds my gaze for a moment too long. I can only smile back. Then she is gone and emptiness rushes in to fill the space where she was.

A wall of Arabic, male and female voices, the sound of the tv, the chatter of the boys, greets me. Mahmood is playing on the floor with a pile of cushions, making mountains and then destroying them with the power of a tyrant.

"Amanda," Layla greets me, and I take off the *abaya*, and hang it on the hook on the wall near the kitchen. My feet ache. My back aches. A smell insinuates itself into my awareness, and my stomach turns over. Tripe stew.

In the kitchen, I accept a cup of mint tea, and take up my customary place by the sink. The late afternoon sunlight, filtered through the frosted glass and net curtains, is a yellowish, washed out glow. The skin on my hands looks sallow as I start washing dishes.

"And so, Mimi said she had not heard a word since." Layla continues a conversation with her sister. "Reem had everything planned, and everyone knew that it was a love match!"

"And her family agreed?" Fatima adds spices to the stew. The smell intensifies as she lifts the lid of the large pan. I try not to breathe it in.

"Yes, but there was only her mother, and her uncle. Her uncle said it was a good match. They are both the same."

By this, I take it to mean her friend and her fiancée are the same class. I still don't understand all the tiers of society here in Riyadh, it is more complex than the British class system, and I can only tell the difference when people point it out to me.

"And so she waited for him to come back from America, and when he did, he brought a wife with him!"

The shocked exclamations make me smile. Despite the language, they sound like any young women, anywhere.

"But had they…" Fatima asks, softly.

Layla shrugs. "They were betrothed, who knows? But Reem says she won't be a second wife. So it is all over, and her uncle is threatening to send her away. Mimi thinks he is going to marry her off quickly, if he can."

"If he can…" Fatima lets the sentence hang in the air.

"She should have married him quickly, and gone with him to America."

"Would that have stopped him?"

Muhammed is late coming home. I have left him a plate of chicken and *jareesh*. The boys have been in bed for hours. I have marked the homework and exercises that my students handed in today. The books sit in a neat pile beside me. I have taken a bath, and the hot water on my bruises has helped. I am tired, but I can't sleep.

Then Muhammed is there. He tosses his keys onto the kitchen shelf, then comes into the family room. He is drunk, and maybe stoned as well. His pupils are pinpricks, his face dark.

I rise, my eyes never leaving his.

"Strip," he says. I obey. For some time he explores my

145

body, roughly, hungrily. Then he slaps me, hard, and a cry escapes my lips. My hands reach for him, and then he is on top of me, pushing me to the floor, and immediately inside me, holding me down with one hand, his upper body straining away from me. Dissatisfied, for some reason, he seizes my legs and pushes them upward, forcing them up, and wide, tilting my hips. Now he is deeply inside me, thrusting hard and long, and it hurts. His body slams into mine, into the bruises, until I can only feel pain. Pain in my hips and my joints, stretching and tearing. Pain in my thighs, a repeated pounding. Pain deep inside, piercing and relentless.

It is over. I lie cold on the floor. He is calmer now, moving slowly about the flat. I hear water running in the bathroom. Soon, he takes himself to bed.

In the morning, he wakes me early, before the alarm. He is already on top of me, spreading my legs. He enters, and again, the slap, across my face. I respond as if eager, or aroused. Within minutes, it is over. I rise and wash and make the breakfast. I get the children up, and dressed. I pack my bag for the day. We say prayers. Muhammed drives us to school, talking about this brother's business, and the new car he wants to buy.

Grace is there when I enter the staff room.

"Did you get home ok?" she asks.

"Oh yes," I reply, dropping my book bag onto the floor. "In the end."

# *Bāl*

Days are melting into each other. Morning, noon and night are hot, dark shadows. Bright days of work, and Grace, are like splashes of light and colour. The colour and the light spill over into home when, in the hot afternoons, Grace brings us back, and we sit and drink tea and talk, and Muhammed is out, or else relegated to a different room, while the children sleep. Mostly Muhammed is out, "working" with his brother. These days, he gives me less and less money, but what I get from the school is now enough for me and the children, for food and clothes and the occasional treat.

I lose track of days, and weeks, and months, and sometimes I can't remember how long I've been here. School is finished. I have so much to do. Grace has dropped us off with her usual smile. I hurry the boys upstairs. I have started taking Mahmood to school with me. It makes the days easier to manage, although he complains he misses his grandmother and his aunts. He is tired now, and I have to pick him up and carry him the last flight of stairs. Shahid is making his usual noise as we approach the door. Then the neighbours' door opens.

"Hi," she says. It is an English woman I've seen before. "You look hot and tired."

I nod.

"I've just made tea. Would you like to come in for some? I have some cakes and lemonade as well," and she looks at my boys, and grins.

I know it is not how it is done here, but I am so tired, and her pale, freckled face is so friendly.

"Thanks."

The twins rush into the flat ahead of us, and I hear the sudden, loud chatter of many children.

"I'm Kath," says my hostess. "Come on in."

"Amanda," I reply. "Is your husband home?"

A gaggle of curly-haired, brown-skinned children rush past, with my twins amongst them. Mahmood wriggles, and I let him go. He runs to join the others.

"No, he'll be at work for a few more hours."

I nod. Good. I can avoid the veil.

Kath leads me into a clean, light family room, with sofas and floor cushions. It's cluttered with toys, and a piano stands in one corner, open, with music haphazardly strewn across the top.

"Are these all your children?" I say, trying to count heads as they run from room to room.

"Sort of," Kath laughs. "Shall I bring some tea?"

In no time at all, I am ensconced with a mug of strong, English tea with milk, and glasses of lemonade appear for the children, along with a plate of sticky Arabic cakes and sweets.

"You teach at a school, don't you?" Kath says. She sits beside me, and picks up her own tea. Then she loosens the hair grips holding her scarf on, and pulls it off, shaking out thick, blonde hair. "That's better!" she laughs. "Go ahead."

I copy her, smiling. "Yes, I do teach."

"Thought so." She leans back. "I don't work. Too many children."

I've counted six already that aren't mine. "You look too young."

"I am. Only two of these are mine. I'm a second wife."

She is watching my reaction, still smiling.

"Ok," I can't help but smile back. "How does that work?"

Kath laughs again. She is so at ease. I feel myself relaxing.

"It's great."

"Where are you from?"

148

"Surrey. I'm a nurse, or at least I was. Omar is a doctor, an obstetrician. We met in Africa, when I was doing VSO. He's from Kenya. We both had converted to Islam. We agreed to marry. Then I had to go home for a while. While I was away he wrote and told me he had met another woman and wanted to marry her. I agreed, and when I came back, we were also married. We moved here so he could continue his research."

"Wow." What can I say?

"Don't worry, other Westerners I know have trouble with it. But in Islam…it makes sense. It's not as hard as you might think. We work around our problems. And Omar is a good husband, a good father. I'm happy here."

"I can see that." The children, all of them, look at her and speak to her with love and respect.

"How long have you been here?" Kath asks me.

"Four years." As I say it, I realise how long that is. Four years. Four winters, springs and summers, four golden scented autumns that I have missed. Four searing, dry summers here, four steamy rainy seasons. Four *Ramadans*, four *Eids*. I hardly noticed.

"He's Saudi, your husband?"

"Yes. We met in the UK though."

"Ah. And you converted?"

"Yes."

It's refreshing, but it feels strange, now, to have someone look me in the face, full in the face, and communicate with their eyes like this. The only other person who looks at me like this is Grace.

"How do you find it here?" I ask.

"Well, it is what it is," she smiles. "It is easier to be a Muslim here, that's for sure!"

I laugh my agreement.

149

"But it is hard, sometimes, when I miss my home."

"Do you visit your family much?" I feel myself relaxing as we talk.

"No, they have nothing to do with me. I have other siblings, they have other grandchildren. They don't understand my life, my choices. You know how it is. Working class attitudes. I think most of them are inherently racist, though they wouldn't admit it."

"That must be hard."

"We're so far away, and life is so busy, I don't have time to get sad about it." Kath shrugs. "What about you?"

"Oh, well, we couldn't afford a trip home, but I talk to my mother every month on the phone, and I write letters. She's busy too. She doesn't understand but she's glad I'm married and settled."

"Even if it is to a Muslim?"

"I don't think we ever discussed it. We're not that kind of family."

The tea is soothing, a strong, bitter comfort. I feel some of the tensions I have carried home with me slipping away. But I have to get on. I say as much as I drain my cup.

"Leave your boys here for a while, if you like," Kath says. "I don't mind."

"Thank you."

"Mishal, the first wife," she chuckles, "will be home soon, and will be glad I've spoken to you. We've both remarked on how you manage so well, and how beautiful your children are."

"Thank you." I can't think of anything else to say.

"Come and get them when you're ready." She hands me my scarf and veil. I cross the landing, and let myself into the cool, quiet flat.

Dinner is quick to prepare, without the boys running to

150

and fro, or fighting over toys, or demanding one thing or another. I make a chicken pie, an old favourite, with thick, shortcrust pastry that turns out well, but not quite as good as if I could have used lard, with steamed vegetables and roast potatoes. I make gravy too. This means we have to use knives and forks, and plates. I'm hungry for it before it even starts cooking.

Muhammed comes home, and goes straight to the bucket in the bathroom where he makes his home brew. I can smell it on him he comes back with a glass full of the murky stuff.

"Where are the children?" he asks, in Arabic.

"Next door," I reply, in the process of setting out the rugs and cloth and plastic sheets in the front room. The flat is too small for a separate dining room. But if we get visitors I can retreat to the back room if necessary.

"Next door?"

"I met our neighbour," I explain, setting out knives and forks. "They seem like a nice family, and they have a lot of kids. Kath invited me in for tea, and the boys were playing…"

Bang. The blow arrives from nowhere.

"Have you been showing yourself to other men?"

"No, no! Her husband isn't home yet! It was just her, and the children, and they're all very young!"

His hand cups my face. His eyes are close, unfocused. His fingers press the tender area along my jawbone.

"If you are lying," he hisses, then strides across the hall and hammers on the door.

I stand, holding my breath. But Kath answers, fully veiled, and when Muhammed demands that the boys come home now, she fetches them without a word or inappropriate look. As the children run across the hall, she

151

looks at me, and I try to tell her with my eyes. She blinks once, slowly. I hope she has understood.

The boys, who were so excited before, instantly sober and become quiet and withdrawn in the presence of their father in such a mood. I haven't noticed this before. Muhammed leaves soon afterwards, without dinner. I put the pie and vegetables aside for tomorrow, and make some sandwiches for the boys. I have no desire for food.

Morning again. The room lightens as the day emerges from darkness. I feel no change in myself. As the call to prayer sounds, Muhammed rolls over and quickly penetrates me, from behind. I am dry, but in only a few thrusts he is done, gripping me tightly and pulling me against him. Semen runs down the back of my thigh in a cooling stream as he gets up swiftly. The noises he makes in the bathroom wake the boys. In an instant I am upright. Breakfast for the boys and Muhammed. I cannot eat anything. I make coffee, black and bitter, no sugar and spices, and drink it while I work. I stand at the kitchen window, mug in hand, but the glass is frosted, and I am staring out into nothing.

Muhammed has woken up in a virtuous mood. He is going to the mosque, with his father and brothers. He argues when I ask to stay home. I hold my ground. Going too will mean spending the day at his mother's house, cooking, cleaning, socialising.

"I don't want to go!" I insist, clearing the breakfast dishes off the kitchen table.

"But my mother will want to see the boys."

"Then take them with you!"

"Don't argue with me, woman!" He raises his hand, then lowers it, slowly.

"Yes, I will take the twins," he says.

"And Mahmood will need his pram, and his changing bag," I say, following him out into the hall.

"No, I'm not taking the baby. Just the boys."

Within a short time he is gone, taking Shahid and Abdullah with him. Alone with Mahmood, I hear faint noises from the apartment above us. There is no change in the air in the room, the background hum of the air conditioning. Mahmood is in a climbing mood, scrambling on and off our big bed, thumping onto the floor in a heap, then scrambling back up. I leave the door open and wander the apartment, half-listening in case his burbling turns to sounds of pain or fright.

I don't know what to do. The kitchen is clean, breakfast dishes done, floor cleaned, yesterday's food is ready for dinner. The apartment is tidy. The laundry is clean, dry and put away. I stand in the kitchen doorway, looking into the neat, ordered rooms. I have already gathered up the toys and tidied them away, the beds don't need changing. I have nothing to do. I am a victim of my own efficiency.

A thud and a yell. In the bedroom, Mahmood calms with only a brief hug. Again I leave, while he rolls in the pillows upon the bed, playing some imaginary game with total absorption. In the family room, I sit, listless. I can't relax. The sofa that I insisted on is bare, uninviting. The walls are bare. The carpet is clean. The toy boxes are stacked neatly behind the sofa. After a while, a thought arises in my mind. "I don't know who I am." Or is that, "I don't know where I am?" None of this seems familiar.

I go to my work bag. Nothing draws me or invites me to action. My lessons are all prepared for next week. I sit again, cupping my elbows in my hands. Emptiness. Stillness.

A quick check on Mahmood. He has fallen asleep in the middle of the big bed. I pick through my books on the bookshelf, but I have read them all at least twice. I could phone Grace – but not on a Friday morning. She will be busy with her family. I pick up my translation of the Qu'ran, and start to read, odd verses, flipping randomly from page to page, Surah to Surah.

Surah 6 Al An'am vs 97.
*It is he who makes the stars (as beacons) for you.*
*That ye may guide yourselves,*
*With their help,*
*Through the dark spaces*
*Of land and sea.*
*We detail our signs*
*For People who know.*

When was the last time I stood outside at night, and looked up at the stars? Have I ever done it here? Are the stars very different here? They must be. We know what stars are. Were they placed there by some divine hand? Everything that is, from the universe down to the smallest atom, everything is ordered. That is what it seems to me. Everything ordered. To order, put in order, logical placement. To order – to command. I am commanded to be in my ordered place. Is this my place?

In the reflection in the opaque glass, I do not see myself. I see a tall, thin woman with prematurely graying hair. I see four walls and a floor, and sparse furniture. It means nothing. I feel no attachment to any of it, the woman, the walls, the grey Dralon sofa and chrome-and-glass coffee table.

I feel a sudden yearning to stand outside in a rainstorm, or feel wind on my face, or stand in a lonely space and look up at the night and the stars. Then I think of the nights

154

back home, and the terrors in the dark, and the feeling leaves me.

It was Jane who had introduced me to Khadija, a Muslim woman from her feminist book group. Khadija was from Bangladesh – she never really told me about her background other than that she had come to Wales to study at university. We met over coffee in the kitchen, Jane having invited her over when a book group meeting was cancelled. She was short, about five feet tall, and quite wide, wearing full *hijab,* the first woman I had ever spoken to who dressed like that. She seemed so alien.

"Amanda, this is Khadija," Jane said, as she bustled about with the kettle.

"Hello, Amanda," said this voice from behind the veil. All I could see were dark eyes outlined in black.

"Khadija, you can take that off here. None of the boys are home."

"Thanks, Jane." She removed the veil covering her face, and smiled at me. It was a round face, her eyes jolly. She always seemed to be smiling. She had a loud voice, not strident, but enthusiastic, and she never seemed to stop talking.

"I am so glad to meet you; Jane told me a lot about you Amanda. I was talking to her about the book we are reading, and we started talking about Islam, and she said you were looking at Islamic theology as part of your studies."

I loved her voice, the accent thick but not too thick, placing heavy emphasis on certain consonants, a strange inflection here and there. It was musical, beautiful.

"I am interested, how is it you see my faith."

"Oh, I am not sure, but so far I have read the Qu'ran, and it seems very beautiful. I don't understand it. You are the first female Muslim I have met."

"Yes, I hear you share a house with a Muslim man."

"Muhammed. He's from Saudi Arabia."

"Ah. Well, I am from Bangladesh, and we are a different country to theirs. Not so much culture, no so much telling us the laws. Muslim and religion and Muslim and culture – two different things, yes?"

I didn't quite follow, and told her so.

"Well, I am Muslim, my family is Muslim, we live life a certain way because we want to live a good life, in the eyes of Allah, of God. Some Muslim, culture, customs, traditions, like in Saudi Arabia, is not about faith, about Allah, it is about tribes, laws, control. So there is a split, you see? A difference."

"What does it mean, then, to be a Muslim?"

"To believe in one God, with Muhammad as his prophet, and to try to follow the guidance on how to live a good life." Khadija sipped the coffee that Jane gave her. "Thank you, Jane, thank you."

"I knew you two would get along," Jane said happily.

"Yes, I am always happy to talk about my religion." Khadija grinned. "Tell me to shut up if I am boring you. There is so much to tell, not many Westerners want to listen, but I am happy to talk. Islam, it is love, yes, it is not about war or even about the control of women."

"If it isn't, if women aren't oppressed, why do you wear all that?" I asked, gesturing to the veil and headscarf.

"Islam calls for women to be modest. This is a good thing, yes? We choose to wear what we wear as a sign to Allah that we are being modest. Sometimes it is more important than others. No one is telling me to wear these things, not even my husband. I wear them because I want to wear them."

"You're married?"

156

"Oh yes, I have four daughters. My husband works here as a doctor. I myself was studying medicine until I had the children. My husband sees me as an equal, you know, there is no oppression. I chose motherhood and I am glad I did. But in Islam, women and mothers are honoured, respected."

"But there are no female Imams."

"There are female spiritual leaders. I know I am breaking away from tradition, but there have always been women who taught the faith of Islam, many of whom were respected highly, such as the wives of the Prophet, peace be upon him. I am named for his first wife. I am not an expert, I just have faith."

"Khadija was telling me today she is going away next week, to do *umrah*."

"What's that?"

"I am going to Mecca." Khadija grinned. "My whole family is going. You have heard of *hajj,* yes?"

"Yes, the pilgrimage to Mecca, but don't you do that in Ramadan?"

"Yes, but if you visit Mecca to make pilgrimage at another time, that is *umrah.* I am so excited, I cannot wait to be there, my family is excited too. My daughters, it is a great experience. It is a great thing. We must be pure, you know, clean in our thoughts. We must not hurt anything, or anyone, once we start our journey. We must think positive and clean thoughts. I have been before, myself, twice, but my children have not."

I could see the faith burning in her eyes, the simplicity of it, its utter centrality in her mind.

"It sounds wonderful. I am pleased for you."

She laid a hand on my arm, soft, warm, inviting me into female confidences. "Amanda, it is not an easy journey, the people there, there are lots of them, making crowds, people get injured, crushed, but I must be careful not to hurt anyone. We will have to be careful of the heat."

"I can't imagine it."

"My mother is coming too. We stay in a hotel very close to the *Kaaba*, not far to walk. It costs more but makes it easier for us. I am so happy, I cannot wait to make *tawaf*, to share this with my daughters." She was still grinning. "So, Jane, the book group want me to give a talk, when I come back, about my experiences. Well, at least some of them do."

"Yes." Jane gave me a wry look. "But some of the women there, good feminists as they are, think that Khadija cannot be a feminist because she wears *hijab* and is a Muslim."

"They are wrong," she said firmly, but still with that smiling lilt. "I am of course a feminist. To be Muslim is to honour women. It's about time more people understood that women should be respected, honoured, for everything they do. There is no family, no home, without women. Muslim men understand this. We are the sacred heart of the home."

I stared at her for a long time, watching her talk to Jane. It was a revelation, a brief opening into a vast vista of new understanding. When she left I wished her luck with her pilgrimage, and she wished me happiness in my life. I wished I could be half as happy and content as she was.

Feet on the stairs in the hall, and the front door opens, with the sudden noise as the boys spill into the apartment, Shahid noisiest as usual. Muhammed follows them, smiling. For a moment, I feel love, for the boys, and for him, even, for bringing them back to me.

And then they rush past me, the small crowd they make

parting to pass me by as they race for the front room, and the meal I have prepared. Mahmood wakes at the sudden noise, and impatient, he appears, sleepy-eyed, hair tousled, to chase after his big brothers. Their voices echo around the plain walls, thick, piping Arabic, dense, mostly unintelligible.

Excluded, I boil the water for coffee, then make my way into the small front room, and join the boys, who are scooping pie straight out of the dish with spoons, ignoring the knives and forks, and picking up vegetables with their fingers. Mahmood, perched on his father's knee, is chewing happily on a piece of pastry and babbling at him. I sit back, against the wall, where the light from the window does not reach, and watch them eat. I have no appetite. The emptiness and the hollow feeling cave in on themselves, and I feel as if I am fading away, diminishing, disappearing. I cling to this feeling.

Ramadan. At school, I have extra classes, because Nura has gone on *hajj*. In the flat, I catch images of it on the news, the great mass of pilgrims, swathed in white, circling the *Kaaba*. My heart aches to be there too, to feel the ecstasy of *hajj*. Muhammed won't hear of me going when the boys are still small. He has done *hajj*, though it means little to him, an obligation only. At night I lie awake and think of the thousands of Muslims all joined in one purpose, and how powerful that must be. Here I can only make my own devotions, follow the rules of Ramadan, and hope to be a better Muslim. My thoughts are not clean and pure. My dreams are sullied with regret, resentment, anger and negativity. I do not deserve *hajj*.

We fast, sunrise to sunset. At times the need for water overwhelms me, and I can't move with the desire for it. The children are oblivious. I am transfixed by the water in a glass as I put out drinks for them, or distracted by the condensation on the outside of the tap. Like the natives, I sleep the afternoons away, hot and weak and empty. The empty feeling doesn't bother me, but the need for water does. It becomes my obsession, and the moment I can drink, I do so, greedily and single-mindedly.

Muhammed doesn't touch me during the holy month. He doesn't hit me, or hold me down, or conquer my body with his own, filling me, again and again, with his seed. It is a quiet time. While he spends nights away, with his family, or out somewhere with his brothers, my body heals, my bruises fade, and in the hours of darkness I settle the boys and then linger in the shadows of the rooms, silent, relishing the nights alone.

On the eighth night, Kath, the neighbour, knocks our door.

"Would you and the boys like to break fast with us tonight?"

I glance at the clock, and the light in the sky. No sign yet of Muhammed.

"Yes, that would be lovely."

The boys are boisterous, needing to run off steam after a long siesta this afternoon. They disappear, and I am introduced to Mishal, the first wife.

"Where is Omar?" I ask, settling into a comfy chair.

"Oh, at the hospital," Kath answers, bringing in the tea things. She hovers over the tray, glancing out of the window, and as the *adhan* rings out, she smiles, and pours tea.

"Water?"

"I nod, and take the glass, dripping moisture as it is, ice cubes melting like jewels in the blessed liquid. Blissful coolness, wet on my tongue, a tiny river running down into the darkest parts of me.

"I can't get used to it either," Kath says, confidentially. "Even after years of it. It's good for us, I know, but so hard. Harder for us women, I think, because we still have to shop, and feed the children, and make the meals." She hands me a cup of tea.

"Yes. It's not so much the food – I never have much of an appetite during the day anyway. But I get so thirsty! And I miss my tea, more than I thought I would."

"It certainly reminds us of our duty to Allah," Kath says, topping up my tea cup from a large china pot. It reminds me of the ones they had in school, when sixth-form girls were allowed into the canteen for morning break, to drink strong, milky tea and eat rubbery, buttery toast.

"Yes, though sometimes…"

She looks at me for a long moment.

"It's not easy, here, is it?" She nods as if I have replied. "There are no lessons, no real services, no guidance other than the holy books. Not that I don't see the benefit of finding your own way through the teachings, but…for us, for women like us – unless you have a helpful husband… no, it's not easy."

"How do you manage it? You seem very…devout."

"Ah, I am one of the lucky ones. And I read a lot. Of course, Omar discusses everything with me. When we were in Mecca…"

"You were?"

"Oh yes, we lived there for two years. While we were there, one of his friends was an imam he had known in London. He was happy to talk to us mere women as frankly and openly as the men. I learned a lot from him."

"You're lucky. Usually I'm so busy, I don't have time to think much. But when I do have time, there are no… answers."

Her hand rests on my arm. Her touch is heavy, warm, nothing like Grace's. But it penetrates the thick shell around my mind, the numbness that I no longer notice. The sounds of the children playing fade into the distance. The pounding of my heart is painful. I can't draw a full breath into my lungs. The frank sympathy in her face, in her eyes, in her touch, is silent, and it overwhelms me.

"Is it very hard for you here?" She says softly. She is so close to me, I can feel the solid heat radiating from her body.

I can't answer her. No words can capture it, can pin down the greatness, and the emptiness, can come near to expressing all of it. I am still hungry for that sense of rightness and faith that drove me to marry Muhammed. I say something similar to Kath.

"I don't know. Coming here, the most Muslim country in the world, I thought, well, maybe I was stupid, but I thought it would be full of very spiritual people. Religious people. But it's not."

"Ah," says Kath, nodding sagely. "Yes, it is a shock. Here we are, where the greatest Muslim holy place can be found, and yet the people do not seem to value their faith. I think this is a great lesson to learn, Amanda, that there is Muslim faith, and there is Arabic culture. Here you see the culture of the Arabic tribes mixed with interpretations of Muslim doctrine enshrined as laws. It's all about interpretation. But I know that my faith is such that I would never countenance a woman arrested for being found in public with a man who is not related to her."

"I just can't make sense of it. Muhammed doesn't even pray when we are at home, though his mother is very devout, and he prays when he is around his family. It seems like he is going through the motions."

Kath straightens the cushions on the sofa as she considers

her next comment. "I think, if I can be honest with you, that there is a great difference between being brought up in a Muslim country, and really having a deep faith. I think faith comes to us through moments of insight, of crisis, when religion brings meaning into our lives. And for some people, there is not that spiritual dimension."

I have to agree with her. "I think you're right. But I don't understand how people can take a set of beliefs and bend it to their own will, their own purpose, like that."

She laughs. "Look at Christianity! Jesus taught a doctrine of love, tolerance, equality, and respect. And look at the Christian Church! Holy wars, torture, the Inquisition, oppression – you need look no further to find the systematic disempowering and disrespect of women. All done in the name of God."

I sigh. "I know. It makes me question, is my faith real?"

She puts a hand on my arm. "It is for you, my dear."

Misha enters, carrying white cloths for the floor. I feel as if I am waking up. I am alert suddenly, to the tableau we must make, so close on the sofa. Misha notices nothing, but smiles as she lays out the cloths ready for the late meal. "Kath, can you make sure the children are washed before dinner? Amanda, my husband will not be home tonight, you can relax, but your husband…

"Oh, he will be out late, if he comes home at all."

"Good, then let's eat."

She whisks in and out of the room, laying out platter after platter, Saudi food and English, rice and vegetables, chicken and mutton, flat bread, soup and dumplings, salad, couscous, and a plate of sweet cakes.

"This looks wonderful." The smells are amazing – I feel hungry for the first time in ages.

The children rush in, five girls, six boys. Kath reappears

carrying a plump, brown baby. I go and wash my hands, and join the meal, which is unusually loud with mingled conversation and laughter. "Ah, that feels so good," Mishal says, biting into a flatbread wrapped around spiced chicken breast.

"It amazes me how the Saudis can manage, in this heat, to go without water all day," Kath says.

"My mother-in-law told me about that," I say. "The desert people, they don't drink much water, at any time. This means they don't miss it, when they are fasting. It started in the desert, because they might go days, or longer, between places with water. And whatever water they were carrying would be for the animals. So, they rarely drank water. Fasting or going without water wasn't such a problem for them. It wasn't until she told me that, that I realised I've never seen her drink water, and she only ever has a small glass of tea, and then only sometimes."

"So, tell us about you," Kath says, taking the baby from Misha and offering him a sticky lump of rice to chew.

We talk. The evening passes. I feel myself breathing out more, letting go of all the tensed muscles that have been holding me together for so long. At last, Mishal starts carrying the children off to bed. Mahmood is asleep on my lap. Abdullah and Shahid are drooping like flowers. Kath helps me get them across to the flat.

"Come over again," she says, as I open the door. The quiet, plain rooms seem empty and dull, after her apartment. "Soon."

"I will. And…" I want to make the same offer to her, but I can't.

"Don't worry," she says, waving as she turns away. I haven't told her much about it, but already she understands. I wonder, as I get the boys washed and changed and into bed, how much she might have heard through the adjoining walls, and how much of her sympathy stems from this.

It started as something and nothing. After the first time, every time there was an element of something dangerous, or something that bordered on the edges of what I thought was usual sex. But it felt like a game, and if it hurt occasionally, it didn't really matter. He liked me to submit to him, and I thought we were just playing, that this was a role he wanted me to assume in bed. There were bruises, occasionally, and sometimes sore muscles. But nothing violent. Perhaps it was the pregnancy that stopped him, the sign from Allah. Or perhaps it was knowing that there, in the UK, there were places I could go to if he got too rough. I couldn't tell. All I knew was that him touching and taking me was the only thing that made me feel real most of the time.

The last day of Ramadan. Night falls, and fireworks light the sky. Muhammed comes home late, to find me sitting in the dark, watching the haze of coloured lights through the frosted glass of the family room window. He brings the smell of gunpowder and alcohol into the room. He is alone, for which I am grateful. I don't ask him where he has been. I don't say anything.

"Come here," he demands. I go. He lifts my skirt and fumbles with my underclothes. I put my hands on him and coax him into enough of an erection to do what he must. He falls asleep soon afterwards. I listen to his snores and I wonder when it stopped feeling good.

*Dear Mum*

*I know it's been a while since my last letter, but life just seems to run on here and before I know it, weeks have passed. I was sorry to hear about Dad's bronchitis. I hope he did as he was told and rested – though knowing him I doubt he did, or at least not without a lot of complaining. How is Jan now after the day centre closed? Is it harder to get to the new place? I know it's further away but I wasn't sure what the buses might be like. It's a shame she has to get used to new people, but I hope she's enjoying it there.*

*The boys are all very well. Shahid and Abdullah are happy in school, and Mahmood is growing well. His appetite still isn't brilliant but he's doing well. He's so much quieter than the twins!*

*My work is going well at the school. I'm really enjoying it. I always thought I might end up teaching, but I never guessed it would be somewhere like this. It's not hard work, but the children take a lot of energy! I miss you and Dad and Jan. If you have time, write me a postcard or something. I feel further and further away from you all. How are Karen and the children?*

*I will try to ring sometime next week. I have to be careful with the phone bill now. Muhammed's work is not very reliable, so I just have to manage the money as best I can. You know how it is with a young family.*

*Give my love to Dad, Jan and Karen*
*Amanda*

## *Zikrun*

Nura is in a panic when I arrive at school. "Is Asha here, have you seen her?"

I shake my head, then say, "No, not at all."

Grace appears at my elbow.

"Nura, calm down, what is wrong?" She takes hold of Nura's arm and leads her back into the staff room. "Asha will be in, I'm sure, she won't be long."

"It's not that," Nura wails, wringing her hands and pacing. She twitches a curtain aside and peers out into the street, looking up and own. A four by four with tinted windows rolls past, slowly, and Nura draws back. "Did you see any of the *mutaween* outside?"

"No," Grace is looking unsurprised. "What has happened?"

Asha, it turns out, is in a lot of trouble. It seems that she has been having a clandestine affair. Here, in the school. In the library, no less.

Grace may not be shocked, but I am. How can this be? How could she manage it? And how could none of us have known about it?

In this, I realise, I am mistaken. Grace is not surprised, because she already knows. She knows.

"How long has it been going on?" I ask her, as she makes Nura a cup of coffee.

"Three or four months."

"How have they managed it?"

"Nura knew about it."

Asha is divorced. The man she loves is not allowed to marry her. There was no other way they could meet, no other place, no other camouflage for them. So they used the school as their meeting place. Unsanctioned love, risking more than simple social exclusion or disapproval. Here, Asha could lose more than her reputation.

The children sound noisy in their classrooms.

"I'll go and sort the classrooms out," I tell Grace and Nura, who still looks scared.

After the first round of classes, Grace finally explains.

"Nura had a letter telling her that Asha's family had found out about the affair. She had a warning that the religious police had been informed."

"How had they found out?"

"Nobody knows. Maybe one of the parents, or one of her family. It doesn't matter."

"Any sign of her yet?"

"None at all. Nura rang her brother's house, but they just said she was not there.

"What will happen to her?"

Grace looks at me. There is no fear in her eyes, but a terrible sadness fills them.

"It's best not to think about it." She turns away. As she does so, her headscarf slips, and a bright edge of shining, curling hair peeks out. "Best to forget about her."

How can I forget? How can I erase her existence from my mind, from my memory? How can she be gone?

"Grace," I follow her, unable to let it go. "Grace, tell me, what will happen."

"She has committed adultery. If she had a husband who would speak for her, maybe things would be different. But without that, she will be imprisoned, and she could be stoned."

"No! That's barbaric! It doesn't really happen, does it?"

She shrugs. She looks like a grieving angel, a black-veiled Madonna mourning for something great and wonderful that has been lost to a world of evil and corruption. "Like I said, best not to think about it."

I go through the motions, collecting the children, riding home in Grace's car, carefully avoiding the subject. We dare not speak of it in front of the children, hers or mine. On the way home, we pick up her son, Gaffar, who goes to Islamic school. As we pull up to the pavement in front of the school, I cannot pick him out from the crowd of *thobe*-clad boys, running on the pavement, kicking a football, shouting, like boys do everywhere, I suppose. Gaffar emerges from this throng, a frown on his face, his skullcap perfectly centred. Confirming his mother is in the car, he enters, and then looks at me, a cold look on his face. Grace has covered her face.

Gaffar ignores me. More than that, he avoids me. The car weaves in and out of the traffic, and Gaffar talks to his mother in rapid Arabic, his whole body angling away from me, and my presence in the car.

At last Grace leans towards me, and touches me on the arm in that way she has, that seems to wake every nerve in my skin, and by a neurological osmosis, it seems, every nerve in my body. "Cover your face, Amanda dear," she murmurs. "Gaffar is feeling his masculinity rather strongly today."

Because she has asked me, I do it. Because she has confirmed, has even anticipated this, I can follow her lead. I taste something in my mouth. I have clenched my jaws tightly and bitten into my own cheek. There is blood on my tongue. Gaffar no longer faces away from me. Instead, he engages Shahid in a conversation about football. He has relaxed.

At home, I am alone, for a while. I spare a few thoughts for Muhammed, wondering when he might be home, and what will happen when he does. I think of hard floors, and his fist on my body, and of putting the children to bed first.

169

I carry out prayers with the children. There is a knock at the door.

It is Khala, with Fatima and my father-in-law Abdelaziz. I welcome them, settle them in the family room, and go into the kitchen to make tea. Fatima joins me. I can hear Khala with the children, chattering away non-stop. Fatima talks of her home, her husband's family. It strikes me again how different things are here. Carrying in the tea, the room seems too small, with so many people in it.

"Mama!" Shahid calls as I come in, "Umma is telling us a story!"

"That's nice." Of course, the conversation is in Arabic. I can't think to phrase anything else I might want to say, so I serve the tea, and retreat again to see to the dinner. I had planned chicken sandwiches and soup. Now I must make something else. I make a spiced rice dish, vegetables chopped and diced, rice, stock, and put the chicken in, chopped, so it will go further. I fry spices in the small pan, and stir them in to the liquid. I can hear what Khala is saying, hear her talking about her family, telling stories from her past. I can't understand much of what she is saying. Something about her grandfather, who was a slave trader, and her grandmother, who lived with the tribe, and who was married at the age of nine to a man ten years older than her. He disappeared for ten years, trading, and she had a child soon after he left. She ran the family farm and raised the child alone within the tribe, never knowing what had happened and if he would ever come back to her. When he returned, he expected to have his wife look after him as normal, but she was angry, and told him that she would divorce him if he did not return more frequently. She bore him fourteen children, of which eleven lived to adulthood. Khala was the eleventh, the last living child. She describes the desert at night as a magical landscape, alive with *djinn* and unnameable forces. She talks of weeks moving from place to place, oasis to oasis, and wet seasons when the *wadis* flooded and they had to scramble to high ground. Her voice is full of emotion, and my boys sit, rapt, engrossed, fascinated by the world she creates for them.

When she looks up and sees me listening, she smiles, a shared confidence, mother to mother. I smile back, amazed. I had no idea her life was so hard.

The two younger daughters arrive. Gadria is talking about getting engaged. At thirteen, she wants to be like Layla, wants to be promised. I add more rice to the pot, more water, more seasoning. I put out more glasses for tea. Fatima stays with her family, no one helps me. There is no sign of Muhammed. I go into the room, lay out the cloth and plastic on the floor, shoo the children out to wash before dinner, and invite my guests to do the same. Here, as everywhere, there are two bathrooms, but I don't have a dining room. With them out of the way, I tidy up, and then return to the kitchen to make a salad.

When I serve the food, we all eat together, except I can't eat. I hover. I clean up in the kitchen. No one comments on Muhammed's absence.

The phone rings.

"Amanda?"

"Dad." I can tell by his voice there is a problem. "What's wrong?"

"I've got some bad news, love. It's your mum. She has breast cancer."

I sink to the floor, the cold tile bruising my knees. "What? What does that mean?"

"She had surgery, Amanda, a few weeks ago, and

171

chemotherapy. We're hopeful, but, well, the doctors say they can slow it down, but not stop it."

"How is she?" I say, from my heap on the floor, tears streaming down my face.

Someone has noticed me crying out in the hallway. Fatima comes out and sees me. "Amanda, what's wrong? Are you unwell?"

I welcome her speaking to me in English. I can't think in Arabic now.

"Amanda? Amanda! Are you there?" My dad's voice, flat and distant, comes from the receiver in my limp hand.

"Yes." I pull myself together. "Yes. What do I need to do?"

"I think you should come home, soon, if you…"

"If I want to see her, you mean."

"Yes. Like I said, we've got some hope, but…" The crack in his voice threatens to break me, then and there. He is crying. My dad shouldn't be crying, not like this, not to me. I've only seen him cry once, when his brother died. I was fifteen. I walked in on him, and it was like seeing him naked. It was something I knew that I, his daughter, should not be seeing.

"Oh, Dad, I'll sort it out. I'll call you when I know the details. Can I stay with you?"

"Of course. Your mother is in the General, Greenwood ward. You can ring if you want, they'll give her a message for you."

"Ok."

Fatima waits as I set the receiver back. "What has happened?" she asks, as I drag myself to my feet.

"My mother is very ill. Cancer. I have to go home."

"I see."

"I don't know what to do."

172

"When Muhammed comes home, he will deal with it."

I stare at her. Does she even know her brother? How can she not realise how useless he is? I run this household, not him.

"He will have to do this," she says. "You cannot leave the country without his permission. He will have to arrange travel for you, and sign a paper at the airport when you leave."

"Right."

I go back to the kitchen, switch the kettle on, make myself tea, good, English tea in my big, blue mug, and drink it standing, staring out, as if I can see, through the bright frosted glass of the kitchen window. I can hear the boys' voices. It's probably time to clear up after the meal. The tea tastes bitter. I want to cry, I should cry, but I have no tears. My mother, my mother is sick, my mother is dying. Is she in pain? Is she afraid? Is she suffering?

"Amanda." Khala appears. "You must visit your mother, you must go. The boys will stay with us, and you can go."

She speaks slowly, so I can understand her Arabic.

"No, I want to take the children with me!" I insist, pushing myself away from the counter where I have been leaning. "The boys need to see her, they don't know her, they'll have no memory of her."

She follows me as I clear the dishes, start washing up, her voice beating at my brain like blows from a fist, over and over. The boys must stay here, the journey is too long, I won't be able to cope with looking after them and looking after my mother. The boys must stay here. In the end, I stop arguing with her, just let her talk. When Muhammed arrives, I hand him the food I have set aside, tell him what has happened. Khala starts her harangue all over again. Muhammed agrees with her.

173

"No," I tell Muhammed," I want the children to come with me."

"They should stay here!" Khala repeats. I am sick of the sound of her voice now, and something stirs in me, something strange, hot, and quick.

"We'll discuss this later," I tell both of them.

The family are gone. The first slap comes out of the blue, the moment the boys are down for the night. My face burns and immediately begins to throb. This is my punishment for defying him in front of his family. The second follows soon after.

"If I say you do not go, then you do not go!" he hisses into my face. His hand grips my wrist, painfully.

"Muhammed, my mother is very sick. She will die soon. I have to go."

"Then go without the children."

"They have a right to see their family, their other grandmother. How can you be so cruel?"

He twists my arm. The scream that bursts from my mouth surprises the both of us. Then his free hand is on my mouth.

"No noise, no noise from you!" he says, crushing my face. I can't breathe. Then he throws me aside, and storms out.

Darkness. Alone in the bed, I hear him in the room. He pulls back the sheet, turns me over, pushes my legs open. Like a blind man, hands all over me, mapping my body with hard probing fingers. He is on me, pushing, pulling, pinching, and then inside me. I can't move, he is pinning me down with his weight. I can't draw breath. He is heavier than he used to be. I can't respond. He punches me once in the face, then in the breast, once, twice, three times. I start

174

to thrash, lights popping in front of my eyes as I struggle to breathe. His hand across my throat, pressing, pressing, choking me.

Darkness.

Morning. Light from the window cast across the bed, across my lids, penetrating. Pain, bruises, bleeding, a cut on my cheek, another in my groin, and my throat is tender and sore. In the mirror, my face is pale, there are purplish marks of fingers on my neck. Was he trying to kill me? I don't know. I ache a lot, all over.

Breakfast is a slow affair. I stir eggs, and scramble them, the warm smell rising, earthy and thick, hot butter and the smell of warming flatbread, slow fingers fumbling with the cutlery, the spoon, the kettle. Brown tea, white milk, my left wrist will not take the weight of the mug. Two hands, shaking, to bring the mug to my lips.

Muhammed is behind me, in the kitchen.

"I am sorry," he says, in his broken English, in that oddly formal way that first endeared him to me. "I am sorry. I think that you should go, and take the twins with you. The twins will remember her. If they see her, and spend some time with her, they might remember. But Mahmood, you should leave him here, with my mother. He is too young, he wouldn't remember her anyway. And the three of them, on your own…"

"You're not coming, then?"

"No, I have to work, and it will cost less, if I stay. I am better here."

"Right, so I can go, and take Abdullah and Shahid?"

"Yes." He nods. I wonder if he has taken advice from someone on how to handle me. His father perhaps, or his friend. Either way, he has compromised. He has said I can go. I cling to that. I can hold on to that. But I won't believe

175

it yet, not until I am on the plane, with the twins beside me, and that plane takes off. Not until he cannot call me back.

"Oh, Amanda." Grace envelops me in a fragrant embrace as soon as I tell her. I want to stay within the circle of her arms and never let go. "So, will Muhammed let you go home?"

"Yes, but only if I leave Mahmood behind." The brief, emphatic closing of her eyes says it all.

She is still holding me close. A faint blush on her skin, she radiates warmth and concern. One hand strokes little circles on my back, stirring something deep inside me, a knot of feeling that uncoils, like a snake that has been twisted around itself for too long. It is painful, and for the first time since the phone call from my father, I feel tears pricking at my eyelids. It all comes out in a rush, and I am crying, sobbing, and Grace is holding me, and I am clinging to her, too tightly. Gently she disentangles me, like a mother detaching a child, and leads me to a chair. The staffroom, mercifully, is empty.

"I'm sorry, I hadn't, I couldn't, I couldn't cry, you see, I had to hold it together. And Muhammed…" Wordlessly I unfold the tight headscarf and show her the marks on my neck.

"Oh, Amanda!" she says again. I cover myself, ashamed.

"You know, they are not all like that?" Grace says.

"What do you mean?"

"Men. And Muslim men, especially. They are kind, and caring, and most love and respect their wives, and take great care of them. It has nothing to do with Islam, it's just him. You know that, don't you?"

I nod. "But he…" I can't find the right words. "He's

176

ashamed of me. At first, he seemed proud, proud that I am English, proud of our children. But now he seems ashamed, and angry all the time. Angry at me."

"It's hard for them," she sighs. "This culture – men as young as he is almost never marry. They cannot pay a dowry. Often, they are in their thirties or forties, and of course, their wives are much younger. And the expectations of them are so different. Men and women here move in different spheres."

"I had noticed."

"I think, if you must know, that he just doesn't know how to handle the responsibility. And because you don't behave like a typical Saudi wife, he feels he has to control you somehow. That doesn't make it ok," she adds swiftly, seeing the look on my face.

I shake my head. "If I had known…"

She smiles. "No one can though, not really. We'll always be incomers, and never really belong." After a pause, she adds, "He must be very unhappy."

Only Grace could say something like that, to me.

My tears have stopped. I feel cold, and then sudden heat as I realise I am wishing she still had her arms around me.

"Come on," Grace urges. "Let's get to work. And be glad he has only held one of them hostage, rather than all of them."

As I start my class off, reading "Little House on the Prairie", I realise she's right. He is holding Mahmood ransom, to make sure I come back. He has realised how much danger he is in of losing everything, but why then, is he letting me go in the first place? If it is true that he has to give me permission, then why is he letting me go?

On the way home, Grace asks her driver to stop at the mosque near her flat. "Go," she says to me, "I'll take the twins with me, and send the car for you in an hour. Take some time to yourself."

I cover my face, and slip from the car. It isn't prayer time, and a few men are in the mosque. I take a place in the women's room, having left my shoes at door and performed the ritual cleansing, kneel down, and begin to pray. Kneel, bow, stand, kneel. I let the rhythm of the chanting prayers, and the repetitive movements take me, and lose myself in the cadence of the prayers. On my knees, brow to the floor, I pour out my heart, to Allah, asking for…for something I cannot name. Guidance? Strength? Strength for what?

To cope with what is to come.

Strength to go and to come back.

Strength to endure, to keep on going, to take every blow and still protect my children.

There are no trumpets, no voice of God speaking, loud or quiet, but after a time I stand and find my shoes, and go to the door to look for Grace's car. I feel a sense of peace. I am ready.

It is Grace who helps me make the arrangements, and it is my money which pays for the tickets. Grace finds someone to cover my teaching, and takes the boys for hours at a time while I pack, make arrangements, prepare for the journey. But it is Muhammed who drives us to the airport, and deals with check in, and signs the papers that allow us to board the plane. The boys are excited, running around, fighting, and ignoring my attempts to engage them with books and games. I look around absently, and realise I am checking where Mahmood is. But Mahmood is with his grandmother. He didn't cry when I said goodbye. He seemed happy there.

At the last, as Muhammed stands at the desk, pen in

hand, he looks back at me. I cannot read his expression. My heart is in my mouth. Will he stop me now? Or stop me taking the twins, now, when the choice would have to be made swiftly, and finally?

But no, it is done, and then we're at the gate, and he doesn't embrace me, or kiss me. Instead, he ruffles the boys' hair, and says goodbye to them in a hoarse voice. We pass through onto the plane.

The hours pass. The boys are distracted by a long, complex film in Arabic that I cannot follow or figure out. There are swords, horses, camels, and desert scenes. Shahid is particularly engrossed, which is a blessing.

I open my eyes; the air hostess is offering me tea, and Shahid is asleep.

"An hour to go," she informs me, in English. She wears a navy blue headscarf, neatly pinned and tucked, and subtle make-up that enhances her huge eyes.

There is movement around me, like giant birds flapping and disappearing. All around me, women are removing their *abaya*s, tucking in their headscarves, and showing their faces. At once the cabin is a riot of colour, and designer clothes, perfect make-up. I haven't the energy to do the same. I sip the tiny cup of tea, and wish I could have five more. My legs ache, and my sinuses throb.

As the plane descends, I wake the boys, and take them to the toilet, and tidy up our things. I look out of the window as we drop below the clouds. The green, the intense green, and the blue-grey of the heaving sea, they hurt my eyes.

"Mama, Mama!" Shahid bounces up and down in his seat, pointing. "Look, look! What is it?"

"Grass, and trees, and the sea." I tell him. I repeat the

words in English, and Arabic, and English again. He sits back, big brown eyes wide.

It is a rush, getting off the plane, herding the boys along, and then I smell it. Cold air. Rain. Rain on tarmac. Lovely, lovely rain, and the light, the light is so different. Inside the terminal, the signs are all in English. How strange. I feel naked with my face exposed. The boys fight to ride on the trolley with the baggage. I feel cold, too cold, and the boys do too, shivering in the jackets I brought for them. I will have to buy some thicker clothes while we are here.

It all looks wrong to my eyes now. The light is wrong, the sound is wrong, the voices, English sounds foreign, somehow. I find myself translating the English announcements into Arabic in my head. Parts of me ache as I try to manage the trolley – my left wrist is still weak and painful.

Outside. The colours seem all wrong, greys from the low cloud, darker wet grey pavements, grey stone buildings, concrete and dirt and pigeons and the smell of the cars. The air is thin and bitter, not thick and rich like back in Saudi. Crowds press around me, and my hand raises automatically to cover my face, then I remember. I let my arm drop. Rain on my face, light, soft, cold rain. Shockingly soft, a caress.

The twins fall silent, wide-eyed as I hail a taxi, driven by a man. I fish for the English money I changed at the airport. Cool air. Breathe it in, thin and cold and wet, and I'm shivering now, and like the twins. I put their jumpers on in the taxi. Train station, English voices, English faces, English tea and cakes while we wait for the train. Everything tastes strange. The tea and the milk and the thick, doughy cakes. I try to ignore the stares, the open hostility, and the frequent comments. Hard plastic surfaces – chairs tables, barriers, doors. Shahid is quiet, then suddenly questioning, what's this, what's that? I answer him, and the newness affects me. The familiar is strange to me too.

On the train, I take off the *abaya* at last. Around me are "normal" people, bright, colourful, different. Pale skin, red hair, blue eyes, blonde hair. A visual cacophony. Voices loud as they talk to each other, women with too much flesh visible, men in jeans that look odd to me now.

I bought the boys colouring books and comics at the station. Now they sit, turning the pages, pointing things out to each other. Several times I have to remind them to read from the front to the back.

Another station, this one familiar, a Victorian edifice of red brick, gone tired and old now, dirty and dark in the corners. Signs in Welsh and English. I spot Dad straight away. He looks old, really old, hair fully grey, face grey too, and lined, and shadowed. The boys are overtired now, withdrawn, resentful.

"This is your grandpa," I say to them. Dad hugs me quickly. "Mandy. Good to see you. Good to have you back, love."

He stoops down, and shakes hands with both boys. "Hello Shahid, hello Abdullah. I'm your Grandpa."

The boys cling to me, little cold hands in mine, bodies pressed against my legs.

"Give them time," Dad says.

"Jan," I say. My flat faced, doe-eyed sister smiles at me. I hug her. I remember her body, the way it feels, short and wide and lumpy, and how she doesn't react to hugs, just lets them happen. Still I know she likes to be held sometimes.

"Manda," she says, in her thick voice. "We're going to see Mum in the hospital."

"Yes, love."

"You've been on holiday."

"Sort of. Boys, this is your Auntie Jan. *Khala* Jan." They stare up at her. I know why. It's not her special difference, the one the adults notice. She is a woman, unveiled and uncovered.

"Come on. The car's in the car park." Dad leads the way out.

I stumble along, stiff and old and tired. Into the car, piled into the back, the boys still quiet. Then the hospital, the long corridors, and Mum in her bed, shrunken, not looking like my mother at all. Her eyes meet mine, and there is a faint smile on her face.

I hold her hand. When did she get so thin? She appears diminished, propped on her pillows. Tubes and lines connect her to the hospital itself, it seems, but I can tell they aren't anchoring her to this world very well.

"Mum," I sit next to her, pull Shahid onto my knee. "This is Shahid." Abdullah climbs up too, heavy and awkward, his knees and elbows digging into my bruises. "And Abdullah."

She strokes their faces. "So big! You've grown so big." She lapses into sleep then, eyes suddenly closed, face lax, barely seeming to breathe.

Dad appears, having spoken to the nurse.

"She's not having a good day," he explains, softly. Jan sits on the other side of the bed. Tired of fighting for the space on my thin lap, Abdullah abandons me and heads for Jan's lap instead. He sits and stares into her face.

In the bed, my mother sighs. She shifts restlessly, and moans. The sound is awful. It tears into me, a physical pain.

"Time for more morphine," Dad says, and on cue, a nurse appears in the doorway. She is young, with long, dark hair in a perky pony tail. She smiles blandly around, and speaks chirpily.

"Ok, let's have a look, shall we?" She bustles about, loudly, an invasive presence in the room. "All right love," she says loudly to mum, a patronising, babying tone, as if Mum is deaf.

"My mother can hear quite well," I tell her. She flicks one glance my way, then returns to her perusal of the charts, raising her voice as if I haven't spoken.

"Now, you're not due your regular dose yet. I can give you some tablets for breakthrough."

"She's in a lot of pain," Dad says. "Can't you make her comfortable?"

"The morphine is doing the job."

"But she seems so distressed! Perhaps the doctor..."

"Doctor has seen Mrs Wills already today, and this," she taps the medication chart, "is the pain relief regime prescribed. Your wife is comfortable, and we can't give her too much, it might affect her breathing and level of consciousness."

She bustles out again. As she passes the twins, now squatting on the floor over their colouring books, I catch the look on her face. I wish I hadn't.

Hours have passed, Mum sleeping all the while. Dad takes us home at last. The boys fall asleep in the car. The house smells pungent, like it always has, a thick atmosphere of cooking smells and old cigarette smoke, but now there is also faint tang of bodily fluids, of a sick person. I tuck the twins into makeshift beds on the "best" sofa in the front room. I want to just lie down and let go, let it all go, let it all go, but Dad and Jan are in the back room, expectant. And I have a lot of questions.

Leaving the boys, passing down the familiar hall, still with the same jumble of shoes and slippers under the stairs,

Mum's old beige cardigan on the hook by the kitchen door, the carpet covered by a clear plastic runner. As I walk down the hall, I feel it settling on me like a weight, a familiar cloak, everything about my past I thought I had left behind.

"Manda?" Jan sees me in the doorway, her wide, flat, moon face lighting up. Dad has made her supper, fish fingers and beans and toast. A scent from childhood, the searing smell of burnt breadcrumbs and hot beans, sugary, sweet, savoury.

"Dad." I sit next to him. The sofa is new, I don't recognise it. But it could have arrived any time in the last five years. That's how long it is since I sat here. "Dad, how long has she been this bad?" I ask, as soon as Jan stops chattering and goes back to her beans.

"It's just the last two days," he says. The lines on his face are deep, like folds worn in a piece of paper, kept in a pocket of time, unfolded occasionally to review what has been written there. "I don't know, Mand, I don't know. They told us she would be ok, that the surgery and the drugs would help, would give her more time. And then suddenly, she's like that, sleeping all the time, but when she wakes, she's in pain. I don't know. I just don't know."

I put my hand on his.

"I'm sorry, Dad."

"I know. And I'm glad you came home. She's been asking for you, every day."

"Where's Karen?" Karen, the sister I forget that I have. We haven't spoken to each other in ten years, or more.

"At work. She'll be back tomorrow. They're letting her take some time off, a day here, a day there."

"Mum's staying in the hospital," Jan pipes up.

"Yes love, the doctors and nurses are looking after her."

"Mum might come home soon."

184

"I don't think so, love, not yet."

"You didn't bring the other boy, Mahmood?" Dad sips his tea.

"No. Muhammed said he was too young. That he had to stay."

"Right."

I close my eyes. Mahmood. He must be missing me. I can feel his weight on my lap, the piping tones of his tiny voice, the blank surfaces of his unfathomable eyes. His face, always so serious, so stern sometimes that it seems I spend all my time trying to make him smile. I should phone. But I'm too tired.

"I'm going to bed, Dad, Jan, I'm too tired to think straight."

"Ok, love. Do you…do you need anything?"

"No, just sleep."

Alone, the twins asleep, I listen to the distant traffic, and try to pray. But the words won't come, and I'm too tired to remember which direction Mecca is.

Sitting by her bedside, I watch Mum's restless wandering between sleep and consciousness. When alert, she talks, sometimes. She talks about my childhood, her childhood, her other children. She pats my hand, looks into my eyes. I wonder who she sees there. When she sleeps, she tosses restlessly, or frowns, or grips my hand tightly. I read to her. Jan likes the stories, and complains when I have to stop. Karen, my angry, older sister, ignores me as much as possible. I can't stay as long as I would like by my mother's bedside each day, because the boys get bored quickly, and when I am not there, Karen takes over. She doesn't read, she talks, or simply sits, not touching our mother. Just sharing the same space.

185

"Manda?" It's Mum. She has been asleep for a long time today. They increased the morphine.

"Mum, I'm here."

Her eyes meet mine. She looks at me, at the headscarf. Closes her eyes again. "It's ok, Mand, it's ok."

"Yes mum, you're going to be fine."

She shakes her head. Sighs. Tries to shift herself on the bed.

"No," she says, calmly. "No, I'm not. But it's ok. Don't be sad." Her face says what her mouth does not. A look of love, unconditional and strong. "Don't be sad for me. You take care of yourself, do you understand me? Look after yourself, and the children. The children…beautiful boys." She pauses, as if gathering her strength. "I'm proud of you, Mand. You've done well for yourself. Don't be sad now."

She turns her face away. The machines feeding her pain medication and fluids whirr into the relative quiet. I watch the rise and fall of her chest.

"She's sleeping again?" Dad appears, cradling yet another plastic cup of tea.

"Yes, Dad. She spoke a little, then went back to sleep."

"Why don't you take the boys home for a few hours. You've been here all day."

"I think I will." It's tiring, watching my mother suffer. My legs ache, sore from sitting on hard chairs all day.

"Take the boys home," Dad says, gently. "And get some rest, get them some dinner. Put them to bed. You can come back later, if you like, when I bring Jan home."

I nod. Stand. Lean over the cold, chrome bed rails and kiss the woman in the bed, the woman who no longer looks like my mother. I stroke her cheek. Illness has drained her of her fire and vitality, the drive and single-mindedness that kept me away from her for so many years, before I left this country. She is empty now, stripped of everything that I think of when I remember her, the rigid, steely curls of her once-weekly wash and set, the pink or blue overalls, the beige cardigan. The set of her jaw, the proud attitude of her whole body, standing, always standing, or moving, bent on some task or other. Never so still, like this.

"I love you, Mum. See you soon."

It feels good to walk outside, to leave the smells, the noises, the pressing despair of the ward, but the wide, high sky seems too big, too grey, too heavy to stay up. We catch the bus outside the hospital. Same bus smell, crowded with people. A woman in a full *burqa* laughs at a joke Shahid makes, the same one he has been telling his brother for the last week or so. "Your sons are beautiful," she says in Arabic. I don't know what to say to her.

Abdullah runs down the pavement, chasing a cabbage white butterfly. Shahid chases his brother. They have both adjusted well, despite the lack of language. They haven't asked after their father once.

I wrestle with the front door lock, old and stiff.

The phone rings.

"Hello?"

"Amanda, it's Dad."

"She's gone, hasn't she?"

"Right after you left. I held her hand. It was just me and her."

"Oh, Dad."

"I know, love. But it was peaceful. It was calm, and quiet, and no fuss."

His voice fades. I stand, holding the phone, not hearing him, not hearing the boys in the back room, not hearing the traffic noise coming through the still open front door. It's hard to think. Am I still breathing?

My mother is dead. Straightaway, I miss her, I want to talk to her. I want to ask her what to do next. What should I do now, Mum? I'm counting off my time here in days. The funeral will be soon, this week, surely. Then there will be no reason not to go back.

I have an open return ticket. All I have to do is phone up and arrange a flight. Going back would be easy. I want to go back. I want to see my son.

But it would be easy to stay. I could find a flat, find a school for the boys, find a job for me, and start my new life. Surely my teaching experience would count for something? And my family would be nearby. I could start again.

Without Mahmood. Without my precious boy, the boy I couldn't let die.

Jan loves the boys. And Dad would help out.

Dad's not getting any younger. And the boys don't even speak English, not really.

But they would, in time.

Mum, why aren't you here to tell me what I should do?

Since when did I listen to her advice? Everything she told me to do, I did the opposite. That's guidance, of a sort.

In the night, on the hard, narrow camp bed that is much too short for me, I feel an ache in my body, in my breasts, as if I have milk to feed my baby. My womb contracts. I feel empty. Empty and bereft.

The rain and wind are lashing against the window. I keep the curtains drawn. Even with the nets, I feel exposed. The headscarf helps, but I feel cold, cold through to my bones, and the wind is whistling in the chimney behind the gas fire.

This was always the "best" room. It was a valley thing, I think, harking back to the days when people had parlours and kitchens, and the parlour was kept for company, the kitchen for daily life. This was the room where the Christmas tree stood, every year the same tree, silver plastic, filling the window with a riot of mismatched baubles that grew, year on year, in no particular style or order. This was the room where birthday presents were laid out, and Easter eggs. This was the room where we sat to discuss me going to university, and my mother told me it just wasn't possible.

"Amanda, you're sixteen now. You're old enough to get a job. I was working at sixteen, wouldn't take a penny from my parents. And there was only me. We've got Jan to look after."

I was thin and gangly even then, too tall for a girl, not soft enough. I had no idea what to do with my life. I had no boyfriend and what friends I had at school were all staying on for A levels.

"But I want to get my A levels. Maybe I could get a Saturday job."

She shook her head at me. "It wouldn't be enough. We can barely manage as it is. Another wage coming in would mean a better life for all of us, especially Jan. Your father and I aren't getting any younger. What's going to happen when we're gone? Karen's got a husband now, and kiddies, so Jan's going to need you to look after her. You need steady work. Get yourself a house, some security."

I hated her then. I hated her overall with the poppers at the side and the front pocket, faded pink and flowery. I hated the shapeless cardigan and the worn out slippers and the firm set of her mouth as she laid out how my life would be. I didn't want a job in a shop or factory, a mortgage, responsibility, burden. My friends were all talking of university, freedom, futures that would take them far away from this narrow, grey-black slice of forgotten hopes and dead industry. Karen had got out, got married, got a life, but I didn't want the endless emptiness of the nine to five, kids, a two week break each year in the sun, and arguments at Christmas over which in-laws to visit first. Karen's choices were not my choices.

I hated her more when she came home bright and smiling, two weeks before the end of my O levels, happy to inform me that she had found a job for me. Her old friend from school had a daughter who was a manager in the chicken factory three miles away, and there was a job waiting for me the week after my last exam.

"The chicken factory!" I exploded when she told me. The smile on her face turned instantly to that flat, firm, pressed-lips look that brooked no argument.

"Yes, the chicken factory, and you'll take it and be glad of it. Most people would bite my hand off for that job, especially someone straight out of school. Pamela remembers you, and since you've done so well in school she thinks you could do well there, work your way up to manager quickly."

I couldn't look at her. "Mum, I can't do it. I just can't. Could you have picked a more soul-destroying job?"

"This is what comes of reading too much. I told your father no good would come of you always having your nose stuck in a book, instead of being out with your friends and doing what normal teenagers do. It's not healthy. Soul-destroying! It's a job, with a steady wage and prospects! You want something for your soul, join a Church!"

She stood, hands on hips, her hair in curlers, furious at me. The fact that I was so much taller than her didn't help as she had to look up at me. Still, there was no escaping her wrath.

"I'm sorry, it's just… I wanted to do something with my life, I wanted it to mean something."

"No you bloody don't, you just want to swan about for another five years pretending to study and not getting work or taking responsibility. I worked from the age of sixteen, and so did your father. Are you saying our lives don't mean anything? That the way we live, the way your sister lives, isn't good enough for you?"

"No." I gave in. There was no point. "No, Mum. Thanks for finding me a job."

"It's about time you showed some gratitude, young lady. Having children and a family, keeping a clean house, that means something. Bringing your sister up, taking care of her, that means something, and don't you forget it. Now, go upstairs and fetch your sister's bag for club. Then you can do the dishes."

Funeral day. Dad is tired and his suit is old and a bit too tight. Jan stands beside him with red eyes. She has cried an awful lot, more than any of us. In her black dress and shoes, she looks like a child in her mother's clothes. The twins wear dark trousers, shirts, and jackets. Dad paid for them.

I pin the headscarf more soundly, watching myself in the hall mirror.

"Do you have to?"

Karen, of course. Only she would actually say something like that.

I try to ignore her. Anger rises to my throat, constricts my airway, lies on my tongue like a weight.

"People will stare, people will notice. It will ruin everything. You'll make a show. What would Mum say?"

Pretty much what Karen is saying. Or maybe not. But I can't take it off, I can't. I pull on a black cardigan, and say nothing.

191

Black-dressed people in black cars, men in black suits and sombre faces, half the street and all the family, most of whom I have forgotten. It seems that I should know them, though. Shahid and Abdullah seem to shrink back at the cross displayed above the coffin. I see myself written in the faces around me, but not them. Every eye is on us as we take our places, in the front row of chairs. We stand for the hymn, and Karen prods me, noticing my silence.

"Sing!" she hisses, shoving the hymn book at me.

"I can't!"

"It's your mother's funeral."

I say nothing. The boys are wide eyed. The vicar who christened all of us sisters says a few words. Karen delivers the eulogy. The music starts. The coffin is obscured by a navy blue curtain, the noise of its motor audible as at last it covers the alcove.

It is over. I try not to look at the smoke as we drive to the wake. I can't find any tears.


"Mama, when are we going home?" Shahid demands. The quiet is giving way to loud conversation. The back room of the Home Guard club, white bread sandwiches and crisps and pasties and finger food. Auntie May tries to get Abdullah to take a sausage roll.

"Haraam!" I whisper, to soften the blow of denying him as I take the sausage roll away. How would he know? He has never seen a pork product before coming here.

"Mama!" Shahid tugs on my arm again. "When are we going home?" The conversation around us dies as his voice rises, the sound of the Arabic cutting through the jumble of English.

"Shush, Shahid. I don't know. I haven't decided."

"I'm cold." He complains.

"I know." I know. I'm cold too, and the kindly voices are offset by the searching, questioning looks. No one says anything about my brown-skinned children, but no one has to.

People step up and offer Dad their condolences, cousins of some sort.

"That's Tony," hisses Karen. "You used to play with him when you were little."

"He didn't recognise me."

"Oh, he did. He just doesn't know what to say to you."

"Don't be ridiculous! Not everyone has a problem with me."

"Wake up Amanda! There's no one here who doesn't have a problem with you. Where have you been these last three years, while Mum's been sick? What have you been doing while we've been looking after Mum, watching her get worse and worse, and never talking about it, just keeping on, smiling, keeping cheerful, keeping Jan happy; Dad working himself into the ground to look after both of them? And me, I've had to take a pay cut, and work less hours, and that's left me and my kids going without! And where have you been?"

"Karen, I didn't even know until a few weeks ago."

"Yeah, that's right, Dad and Mum both, always protecting you! Just because you're younger than me. Always the same, protecting you, leaving me to deal with everything by myself."

"I would have helped…Karen—"

"Jake left me!" She is getting louder and more shrill with every passing minute. "Jake left me, six months ago. After I lost my promotion, after the money stopped coming in, the mortgage needed paying, the kids always needed stuff. And I was looking after Mum all the time…"

"Jake's a complete shit if he leaves you because your mother is dying."

"Jake got tired of always being left on his own. He found someone else. He's living with her now."

"That's not my fault, Kar—"

"You weren't there! You were never there! And she was worrying about you, and pining after your half-caste children, the grandchildren she couldn't see."

"Girls, girls, don't fight." Dad intervening like when we were kids, or really, when I was a kid and she was an angry, frustrated teenager relegated to babysitting her sisters, the baby, and the "mong". I remember the teasing. Dad the peacemaker. Karen turns her back on me.

"I'm taking the boys home now, Dad," I say gently. "Do you want me to take Jan back too?"

We both look at her. She clings to Dad's hand, her eyes red.

"Jan, do you want to go home with Amanda?"

"You coming too, Dad?"

"No, not yet."

"I'll stay with you."

I marshal the boys out, through the beer fumes and cigarette smoke. No one speaks to us, or says goodbye. A crowd starts to form around Dad and Karen and Jan, a sympathetic flock, dark birds, feasting on their grief.

I'm dreaming. I know I'm dreaming, but I can't wake up. I'm back in the Kingdom, in the big bed in the family house, and Muhammed is on top of me, pinning me down, his forearm across my throat, his weight on my windpipe, his body pushing mine into the soft mattress, like he always used to. And I'm not fighting, I'm letting him, and worse, I'm aroused, and he's all over me, and I can't stop him, and

I don't want to. And I welcome it, the pain, the sensation, the feeling. I don't ask him to stop.

It doesn't stop, not at all, it gets worse and worse, and I really can't breathe now, and even when I start thrashing and gasping he doesn't stop. I can't draw breath.

"No!"

Catapulted into consciousness, I lie, one hand on my throat, rigid with terror. It's as if he's really here. The sensation won't stop, a lump in my throat. In my dream, I was dying. I knew I was dreaming, but it still felt like dying.

"What shall I do for tea, Dad?"

"Oh, make anything you like. Something the boys would like."

I make *jareesh,* with rice instead of cracked wheat, and chicken soup, and flat bread. The spices aren't quite right, but there's enough in the cupboard to approximate some of the flavours. The smells filter through the house. It feels good, shaping the dough, stirring and chopping and mixing. The boys watch *Scooby Doo* on the TV.

Dad eats the food absently, sitting in front of the TV. The twins eat more than they have done since we arrived. They sit on the carpet, a towel spread out, bowls in front of them, much more comfortable now. Jan eats slowly, making the bug-eyed face she does when she's not quite sure of something, when she has to deal with something new. But she eats the rice happily and doesn't complain.

Now I'm sitting, I have an appetite for once. The seasoning isn't quite right, the soup is too bland, but it tastes good.

Other things taste good to me now, and smell good. Scents have awoken my senses. Fish and chips, hot salt and vinegar smell. Fresh baked bread in the supermarket –

making my mouth water for the taste, for the texture, crisp outside, soft and melting in my mouth. And bacon, of course, bacon frying. Of course I don't eat it. But the smell… I am alive in more ways than I remember being for a long time.

Not since before Muhammed. And then he came and a door opened up for me. Allah, maybe, opening the way.

Eating this food, that almost tastes like home, watching my boys eat. Grains of rice separate on my tongue, sticky, almost sweet.

"Dad?"

"Hm?" He looks up at me. He has aged so much in the last weeks. He's sad. But he has to keep going, he has to get up in the morning, and after forty-five years together, he has to be mother and father to Jan now, because she still needs him so much.

"Dad, will you be ok with Jan now?"

"What?" He looks around. "Oh, yes Mand, don't worry, me and Jan will be fine."

"I could, maybe I could stay on, you know, help out."

He looks at me. "You've got your own family, love, little Mahmood back in Saudi Arabia. And you've got your job over there, and your friends. We miss you, we all miss you, but it's always good to get the letters, and the photos."

"But if I could get Mahmood, come back…"

"Well, I suppose we'd manage, but what would Muhammed do here? Would he let you come back for good?"

"I don't know." Of course not. But if I didn't go back…

"Mama, when will we go home?" Shahid asks again, as he does every day.

"Soon, my love."

"I want to tell Baba about the trees, and the sea, and the grass."

"Yes love, when we get back."

"I'm cold." Abdullah is tired. His eyes are dull. We're playing snap on the floor in the front room. Shahid is winning.

"Mama, when will—"

"Shahid, let's just play the game."

## *Thaqal*

This time, I know what I am going into. This time, I've made the decision myself, alone. As we stand to leave the plane, I pull on black gloves, check the fit of the veil, then pick up the hand luggage and usher the boys in front of me. A slow, halting snake, too many bodies too close around me, the aisles too narrow. Heat and smell and light, the dusty dryness of desert air, mixed with hot tarmac and metal. The nylon of the scarf sticks to my forehead, sweat collects and soaks into my clothes. Ya, Allah, I had forgotten the heat! Still, I persevere, across the tarmac, down the hot, stifling tunnel, and once inside, the welcome air conditioning chills my damp skin.

I pass through customs, the boys talking non-stop. Where is Baba? Will he be waiting, Mama? Where is Baba? Mama, mama, will we be home soon?

When we emerge with our bags, I look around, peering through the cloth at the men in white, their red and white *schmaars,* their glittering dark eyes.

"Umm-Shahid!" It is my brother in law, Abdelaziz.

Shahid breaks from my arms as I emerge from the crowd and runs past the barrier, straight towards his uncle.

"Uncle, Uncle!" I follow, Abdullah clinging to my hand, his eyes huge, and something inside me, some tight band, relaxes slightly, as I see my brother-in-law. I follow with the trolley.

He greets me in the usual way, not looking at my eyes, nodding, and taking the bags from me. I check the bags as Abdelaziz goes through the paperwork with the officials. He takes the trolley, and loads the bags into his truck. It is huge, shiny, with big wheels. We pile into the cab. The seats are hot, too hot, and the boys shriek and clamber all over me, laughing, tiredness forgotten.

Abdelaziz doesn't speak to me on the drive until I can ask him, "Where is Muhammed?"

"He is working, I think," Abdelaziz says. "My mother asked me to come and bring you home."

"That's very kind of you, thank you. How is Mahmood? If we could just go and pick up Mahmood, I would be very grateful if you could take us home then."

He doesn't answer. Riyadh's familiar mix of desert and city slips by, the men in their white *thobes* on the streets, the odd black shape, here and there, a woman. Something stirs in me. I draw my veil closer over my face as we slow at a junction, as a group of young men stare in through the window. Shahid is chatting to his uncle about the trip, Abdullah joining in from time to time. I am uneasy. Where is Muhammed? Where is Mahmood? Where is my son?

"How is Mahmood?" I ask again.

"He is well, my mother says."

"Good, I can't wait to see him." I close my eyes. Outside the light is too bright, the reflections of the white and orange and sand-coloured stucco, and the frosted windows, almost blinding. The boys settle against me, little hot bodies, their breathing slowing. They are relaxed, more relaxed, I think, than they have been since we left. Or maybe I'm just seeing what I want to see, to justify my decision.

Khala is there, in the women's salon, when we arrive. Abdelaziz brings the cases in. He says the plastic might start to melt in the sun. Mahmood is playing on the rug. He seems bigger, and for a minute, a long moment, like a stranger, someone else's baby. But when I throw off the big cloak, his smile is all for me.

"Mama!" He reaches his arms up, and I catch him up into my own arms. For a moment, nothing else is real, only the feel of him, my little stranger. The boy I couldn't let go.

Because I am a guest today, Gadria brings coffee and dates on a tray. My ears are ringing with jet lag, and everything feels dull and far away. Khala is urging me to stay, because no one knows where Muhammed is. I try to insist. At last, Khala brings Mahmood's things and puts them with my bags in the hall. Then it is time to pray. The voice of the first *muezzin* rings out, and the echoing cry begins from the other mosques, until it seems the walls are singing the call to prayer. I feel a pricking of tears at the corners of my eyes, a lump in my throat, as the call goes on, and on. *Allah hu Akbar*. God is great.

Everything is familiar here. Afternoon prayers. A meal is served. The men eat, then the women. They have prepared *saliq*, lamb with milk and rice, and the flavours burst on my tongue. The mint tea refreshes me like nothing else can. I nod and smile, and express thanks, and answer the questions that come after the meal. Yes, my family are well. Yes, it is sad to lose my mother, but I was glad to spend some time with her before she died. Yes my father was sad to see me leave, but he knew I would be looked after by my family here.

At last, Abdelaziz is loading our bags back into the truck. I have heard the family news, who is getting married, the people has done what, when. I still can't keep track of all the relations and relationships, but I pretend that I know who she is referring to. There is still no mention of Muhammed.

Abdelaziz drives us home. Mahmood nestles into my lap. I hold him there, bracing myself against the dashboard as Abdelaziz zooms in and out of traffic, slamming on his brakes, accelerating, swerving with no warning.

"Has Muhammed been working a lot?" I ask my brother-in-law.

"I suppose so," he mutters. "I am sure he will be back soon, he will want to see his children."

"Right. Can we stop at the supermarket, please? I need to buy food." It is afternoon, and the malls will be shut until after the *asr* prayers.

"I can't take the time, I have to get back."

The flat is dark, dank, and stuffy. The air-con has been off for at least a few days. I wonder where Muhammed has been. Abdelaziz leaves the bags in the family room, then stands a moment in the doorway.

"What is it?"

He looks as if he is about to say something. Then he turns, and leaves.

With him gone, I am galvanised into action. First I call Grace. She sends her maid and driver to get shopping for me. I turn on the air conditioning, turn on the tv, and settle Mahmood and the boys on the low divan and cushions in the family room. The twins pull their cars out of the toybox and start playing. Mahmood complains at being set down, so I take him with me as I put the kettle on, and rifle through the cupboards. Something has gone off in the fridge. I clean it out, throw away the stinking mess. The boys are all hungry, and tired, so I pull out the ingredients for *fatir* and quickly mix the dough up. Mahmood whines to go back to his brothers, so I set him back down and then make myself tea and start shaping and cooking the *fatir*, the hot metal of the bottom of the wok, the oil smells, and then the toasty, barley flour aroma, all feeling familiar. I put the bread on a large plate, with some dates, and take it in to the boys.

A knock on the door. It's Grace's driver, with bags of shopping for me. I smile when I see the things in the bags. Grace is generous, and thoughtful. There is everything I could need, and a quick note.

"Amanda, welcome home. Call if you need anything else. I will come and see you soon."

I fold it up and slip it into the pocket of my skirt. I can feel it there as I move around the kitchen, putting food away, putting the chicken pieces into the large pan to fry, making a large pan of *tabbouleh*, and *haysa al-tumreya*, the dip that goes with dates. Now that I am home, I expect lots of visitors, from the family, and also from my friends. I check everything is ready, enough coffee, the cardamom ready, the pots. Enough dates. A large amount of food, for unexpected guests. Tea. *Laban* for the children. If it doesn't get eaten today, it will tomorrow.

As I work, the note from Grace rustles in my pocket. I clean the front room, the room where Muhammed and the men will sit. I clean the entrance hall, the bathrooms, and the bedrooms. I put laundry into the machine, unpack the cases and bags, put things away. Time ticks on. Mahmood is sleepy, and I turn off the tv put all three boys to bed.

A knock on the door.

"Kath!"

"Hi Amanda, no, I won't come in, just wanted to say hello, and welcome you back."

"Thanks."

She hugs me briefly, gently. "Are you ok?"

"Oh, yes, you know."

"Sad, yes, I know. Well, I won't keep you, you must be exhausted. Let me know if there's anything you need."

"Thanks, but my friend sent over some shopping, so I'm ok for now."

"That's good. Well, I'll let you get on. Pop over for coffee or tea tomorrow?"

"Yes, thanks, I will."

"Bye then."

Night falls. The food in the kitchen grows colder. The room grows darker, but I don't switch on the lights. In the darkening room, I hear the sounds of the night, traffic, men in the street, muffled noises coming from next door.

Darkness. Night like a thick cloak, an *abaya* that covers and contains the whole world. Dusty air, and the underglow of the city lights. It's all just a haze through the frosted glass. I shed my clothes like shedding a skin, layers of self, falling away. Goosebumps rise on my arms and legs in the cold, pumping, air-conditioned air. My boys are fast asleep, all of them. I want to sleep. I want to lie down and let go, let go of the parts of myself. The *abaya* is gone. My western clothing falls to the floor. Naked, I stand, and feel the edges of my being, the cold of the floor tiles, the rough weave of the rug, the places where my skin meets the air.

I can't stand up any more. I can't stay awake. Crawl into bed, pull over the cotton sheet. I can't relax. My body is rigid, expectant. Eyes open, staring into the shadowed darkness. The night ticks by. Muhammed does not come.

The chicken factory was every bit as awful as I anticipated. I thought I knew what it felt like to be tired before I started there, but I really had no idea. I was up at six the first day, making my packed lunch of white bread and cheese sandwiches, crisps, and an apple, and getting ready. I caught the bus to the factory and joined the line of workers. They were all women, mostly middle aged with a few older and a few younger. Hard-faced women, with lips worn thin and colourless from years of biting back anger and disappointment, with short hair coloured or tinted, or longer, bleached-blonde hair in ponytails. They greeted each other with easy camaraderie, the basest of valleys accents filling the air.

"Oi Barb! Saw you down the bingo last night! You wanna watch youself, that Paki from the garage 'ad 'is eye on you!"

"All right Claire? 'Ow's your mam then? She out of 'ospital yet?"

"Aye, I tol' the bitch, she wannoo watch 'erself 'cos I'll be round there with my fist in her cowin' face!"

One separated herself from the crowd to approach me. "You're Amanda, yeah?"

"Yes."

"Your mam an' me was friends in school. So, I'm Pamela. I'm manager of the day shift. Come with me and I'll show you the ropes, get you started."

"Ok, thanks."

Pamela was about five feet tall, and almost as wide, with steel grey hair cut very short, and a ruddy, coarse face. I recognised the features of someone who smoked and drank heavily. She was smoking as we approached the building, a great squat concrete monstrosity, stained and old, with few windows, all frosted. I could already smell an unpleasant odour, the combination of something unpleasant, like a sewer, and cooking chicken.

We entered a side door, and Pamela led me into a changing room, like a school locker room, with battered lockers and racks to hang clothes on. I was directed to change, and given white overalls, a hair net, hat, and white wellies. Pam then showed me where the toilets were.

"You need the bog, you raise your 'and. A superviser'll come and she'll let you know if you can go. We get fifteen minutes in the mornin', and thirty minutes for dinner. When you come off the floor, you takes everything off, washes your 'ands, and goes to the bog if you need to, or whatever. When you go back 'en, you washes your 'ands again and puts it all back on again. We clear?"

I could only murmur assent. Large double doors opened into the factory proper, what Pam called, the floor, and as

204

a loud hooter sounded, a gaggle of women spilled noisily through them, laughing and talking to each other and the new arrivals. Then I was caught up in the tide of women moving into the factory, and the stench hit me fully in the face. I thought I would gag, vomit, right there. It was thick, cloying, greasy, and vile, and immediately I felt dirty and greasy myself. Pam led me to a "line" and showed me how the frozen chicken halves came out of the blast freezer, through a chute, and fell into a hopper for me to pack. Then she told the woman next to me to keep an eye on me, and was gone.

And so the horror began. There were not enough gloves for even half the workers, and I learned quickly that there was a kind of informal but rigidly enforced pecking order which governed who got gloves, who worked where, and who went to the toilet. The frozen halves of chicken were bitingly cold and rock hard, with sharp, nasty bony edges that cut my hands. Within half an hour my hands were raw, cold, and bruised, and I was aching from bending over the hopper. I was too tall for this. By lunchtime I had had one chance to pee and a brief break in which I had bought, but not had time to drink, some plastic-tasting coffee from the vending machine.

To give my hands a rest after lunch, Pam put me on "Chinese chicken". A vast vat, the size of a small car, was wheeled out from some mysterious back room, filled to the brim with chicken wings that were covered in a thick, sticky, dark red sauce. I had to reach in to the vat and transfer these into bags, using a scoop, ensuring that each was the right weight. The stuff was vile, and still warm, and soon the sauce was all over me, up to my elbows, and stinging in the cuts and grazes on my hands. Time ticked by slowly as I hurried to keep up with the pace, only half listening to the

205

gossip of the other workers. My arms ached, my back ached, and soon my head ached and reeled from the work.

By the end of the day my feet felt as if they had been beaten with sticks, my hair and skin were thick with grease, and I felt like I would never get the stench of the place from my nose. I went to bed when I got home, after a long hot shower, unable to eat, too tired to think, knowing that I had to get up and do it all again the next day, and unable to look at the grim satisfaction on my mother's face at the result of my first day's work.

# *Sā-ilīn*

"Amanda." Grace greets me as I open the door. Behind her a car waits a moment longer, then pulls away.

"Where are the children?"

"At my husband's sister's house for the day." Grace sweeps into the apartment and into the sitting room. She removes her veil and headscarf, and the cloaking *abaya*. I take them from her, silk cool in my hands, her perfume rising from the fabric. For a moment, I am overwhelmed. This scent, it is Grace, everything that I think of when I think of her – bright laughing eyes, that unashamed earthiness, juxtaposed with innate grace, style…and compassion. It is as if I am holding her in my hands.

I turn, and place the soft piles of fabric on the coat hooks in the entranceway. The small rituals of tea-making occupy me for a while, and I hear Mahmood's burbling as he regales Grace with his half-formed ramblings. She laughs with him, and their voices blend, and for a moment, I am smiling too. Something of the smile must linger in my face as I bring the tea in – Grace looks up at me and says, "You look better."

"Thanks."

She starts in straightaway.

"So, have you heard the gossip?"

"What gossip?" I take my tea, and Mahmood crawls up my leg and onto my lap. I cuddle him into my body, and ignore his wrigglings.

"Well, Nura has found another teacher, Danya, a Canadian woman. She has been in the Kingdom six months. She's married to the brother of Nura's cousin's wife, and she has no children. She's lovely. I'm having another one of my parties next week, so you'll meet her then."

"That's good. What else has been happening?"

"Well, not much. Tell me about you."

I stay silent, sipping my tea.

"Amanda, what is it? Was it awful?"

"No, not really."

"I must admit, I'm glad to see you. I wasn't sure…"

"I know. I wasn't sure either."

I nod. "I had no real choice."

She watches my expression for a moment, then realisation dawns.

"You're pregnant again."

"Yes, yet again." I watch her face, trying to divine her feelings, but she is more guarded than normal.

"I expect you're glad to be home though, back in your own place."

I ponder this. "Yes, I suppose I am. It does feel like my own place, here. I mean, it's not like Muhammed has anything to do with it, really. I decorated it, I do all the cleaning, I spend the most time here."

"And the boys are back at school already?"

"Yes, they left quite happily this morning with their father."

"How has Muhammed been, since you got back?"

"It's hard to say. He got in late last night, or early this morning, while I was asleep. He didn't say much to me at breakfast, and then he was gone with the boys."

Hands on my body, rolling me over, breaking into a dream of large, empty rooms in strangely familiar houses, running from room to room, looking for something. His hands, hot on my skin, greedy, grasping, and his body, between my legs, opening them, his hot, hard penis probing at my flesh until he enters. The pushing, the thrusting, hands on my shoulders, bearing down on me, panting, grunting, his forearm across my throat now. I turned my head. His face came close to mine, panting his rank breath into my mouth. I turned my head the other way, he followed me, staring at me intently, inches from me. I turned my head back, and he followed again, relentless. He wanted me there, present, in the moment. He wanted to see my reaction. I was pinned, helpless, and I felt as if I couldn't draw breath, because when I did, I inhaled the foul emanations from his mouth, his flesh, his alien body. Invasion. Possession.

I am already possessed. His child has burrowed into the red fleshy fertile ground of my womb, sucking out life and sustenance, a demanding, greedy thing that will consume me from the inside out. And here, his father, devouring me from the outside in, flesh in flesh, his in mine, and there will be no escape, not ever.

Grace watches me. Can she read my thoughts? Sometimes, sometimes she seems so close to me, that I wonder if she can. She is under my skin, or else, perhaps when she is around it is as if I have no skin, as if we share the same outer skin and only inside do we differ. She is me, or me as I could have been.

Ahmed, Muhammed's brother, comes to dinner. Muhammed greets him with dates and coffee. He is a family member, but still the men eat first, and the older boys eat with them. I serve *al kabsa, fitr*, soup and salad. Coffee, tea, and no home brew. I hear raised voices, and then the slam of the front door. Ahmed appears in the kitchen. I hide my shock and surprise.

"Muhammed has gone out," he says, not meeting my eyes.

"Right."

"He has not been showing up to work, not for some weeks now."

"Oh."

"How long has he been this bad?"

I can't answer him. It has been coming on so slowly, over such a long period of time, I just don't know.

"It's been getting worse and worse," I admit, not looking at my brother-in-law, who is, after all, so similar to Muhammed, with those same flinty eyes, the unassailable core.

"Is he even bringing home any money now?"

This astute observation surprises and unnerves me. Is this how Ahmed communicates with his own wife now? Almost like an equal?

"Hardly any," I admit, eyes downcast. Uncertainty and fear rise in my chest.

"And the children see him like that often?"

"Yes." What can I say? Should I describe the countless times I have tried to reason with him, to slow him down, to stop him? We both know it would make no difference.

"You are pregnant again, my mother tells me."

I nod. As if in response, the tiny life inside me moves, a flutter like a little bird.

Ahmed stays silent, for a few moments, looking at me directly.

"I just told him that if he doesn't get himself under control, stop drinking and taking drugs, I will adopt his children," he says, finally.

"What?" My hands are still, resting on the cream countertop, and I can hear my heart beating.

"The boys need a father, one who will look after them properly. They need guidance, care, proper family life."

"You can't do that."

210

"I can. If the father does not provide for his children, it is the responsibility of the other men in his family. My wife has had only daughters."

"But what about me?" I didn't mean to say it aloud. What would happen to me? Would I become his second wife, the lowest status woman in the house again?"

"You.... would not be needed."

My hands clench the side of the worktop. I feel nausea and a rushing anger. I look him full in the face. "These are my children. I provide for them. I look after them. You will not get your hands on them."

He stares back. "You will have no choice."

"Over my dead body."

Ahmed turns and leaves the room. I follow him out to where the boys are playing in the family room. He looks at them for a moment, then at me. Then he leaves without another word.

So, the stakes have been raised, and yet another man thinks he holds all the cards.

# *Jihād*

Alone, too much time alone now. The twins are self-occupied, less demanding, and Mahmood is their shadow. It gives me more time, longer stolen moments. I sit in a shaded corner of the family room, while they play a game with Mahmood on the rug.

The sublime feeling of opening a book for the first time. A simple paperback, crisp-edged, the spine unbroken. The clean shine of the cover, the colours. The smell of the paper. The image on the cover, slashed red lips, starched white wings, red gloved hands.

The eyes. Distant.

I had the book sent through the post. I don't know why it wasn't stopped at customs. Maybe it was, but there is no bare flesh to black out.

Here, in my hand, it is heavy with promise. It is a delight. *The Handmaid's Tale*. Along with *Emma, Romeo and Juliet*, and the poetry of Keats, these are my texts for the Open University course in English that Grace encouraged me to start. The course materials have arrived, Muhammed hasn't noticed. He says little to me these days, and is out most of the time. I haven't confronted him about his work, because I don't want to suffer the consequences. There's nothing I could do about it anyway. Still, it hurts that he doesn't confide in me.

I no longer want a degree in Philosophy. I never really did. I wanted to go to university to try to find out what I wanted out of my life, but the answers weren't there. Instead, I found Islam, and Muhammed found me. But now I know what I want to do. I want to teach. One day, I want to teach in a British school. Grace's idea, again. Grace with her sideways smile, her warmth, her way of looking at the world as a series of infinite possibilities. She believes in me. Which means, I suppose, that I believe in me too. That something like this might be possible.

The book sits, untouched, in the family room, for days. It shines like a secret treasure. Today, I open it, taste the first few words. Let them sit on my tongue, whispered aloud. English words. North American, really. I imagine them in Grace's voice. From that moment on it is Grace who narrates this tale inside my mind.

"You must do this, Amanda," Grace murmurs in my ear, a living memory as I close the book. "You must do this for yourself. If you wish it so, it will happen, and this is the first step. Do the courses you need, while you are here. Take a distance learning degree. Become the woman you want to be. You know that you can do anything you set your mind to."

Yes, I believe her. But how ironic, that this should be the first set book that I read. A book about women, veiled and regulated, relegated to specific roles in society. Here, I would be wearing red one moment, blue the next, green a lot of the time. I have to read this in small bites, like nuggets of gold stolen from the long dark of the mine that is my life. I won't show this to Muhammed. I don't want to let him know how much it means to me. Hidden among the books and papers I use for teaching, it will be camouflaged, and he will never need to know.

"What's this?" Mum was stern and her voice loud as she brandished the envelope in my face.

"What?" I was folded limply over the table, exhausted. Three weeks had passed since the start of my job in the factory, and I was no nearer to coping with the sheer, dull, relentlessness of it all, the stink, the pain from frozen meat, and the ache in my legs, feet and back.

213

"You've applied to go to college."

"Yes, to do some A levels."

"What did I tell you? Your father and me won't support you to do A levels."

"I know. I'm saving up. There's some money, so this woman in the careers office said, and I'm going to find a part-time job."

"No." She threw the letter onto the table and walked away.

I picked it up.

"Fine, I'll do it in the evenings then."

"What, and who's going to help with Jan then?" she was shouting from the living room.

I followed her in. "Look, Mum, you wanted me to have a job, you wanted me to be bringing money in. Why can't I go to college as well."

"It's too much for you, you'll never manage."

"Don't tell me what I can and can't do," I retorted. "This is what I want."

"Oh, Amanda," she said softly, all concerned now. "I know you like your books but you won't cope, it's too much. You're young, you should be out with your friends, you should have a boyfriend, a social life. When I was your age I was out every Friday and Saturday night. Forget this nonsense. You'll never get to university. It's not for the likes of you and me."

"I won't forget it."

"You're not going to college."

"You can't stop me."

And so it went on. Then fate decided for me. That summer I was laid off after five weeks, and couldn't find another job with no skills and very little experience. All the best jobs had already gone to other school leavers. Rather than have me sitting around the house doing nothing, my mother assented and I went off to study at the local college. I found a job waitressing and washing up in a local pub restaurant, Friday and Saturday nights and Sunday lunchtime. So much for the social life.

Monsoon season. Hot and humid. Sweat all over me, stinging in my eyes, in the scratches and cuts on my buttocks. My head aches from pressure. Pressure from outside, the atmosphere, the low, boiling clouds that occlude the usually bleached blue sky. Pressure from within, constantly pushing myself to do what needs to be done. The children are tired and fractious; the heat affects even them. When the rains come, it will be cool for a short while, and the *wadis* might run with water, for a day, maybe two. The desert will swallow the water, and the brief bright desert flowers will bloom and then swiftly die.

Muhammed is spoiling for a fight. His face is a thundercloud; the children cast him cautious glances from under their heavy eyelids. He occupies a chair in the entrance hall. Every time I pass back and forth, preparing the meal, doing housework, I have to pass him.

He makes comments, goading me with criticisms and questions that are just this side of accusations. He talks about retribution, shame, and his reputation. He murmurs darkly about his sons.

There will be an argument soon. I pray he'll wait until I put the children down for their afternoon sleep. I'm trying to ignore him, though the sighs and sniffs keep on coming.

As soon as one of the boys says something, he jumps on them.

"Mama, my robot can fly," Shahid races across the flat, holding the plastic toy aloft.

215

"Shahid, don't be stupid!" Muhammed says. "Robots don't fly."

Shahid's face closes down immediately, becoming heavy and blank, guarded. He is crushed, a butterfly caught in joyous flight by his father's fist. Poor Shahid.

Muhammed challenges me, silently. He is still goading me, daring me to leap to Shahid's defence.

"Come on Shahid, why don't you play in the sitting room. Don't get in Baba's way."

Abdullah follows his twin, then Mahmood toddles after them. I put my hand on my belly, on the baby growing inside me.

"Fucking hell, I'm at work all day, and when I come home, I want to see my sons!" Muhammed roars.

The soft chattering of the boys stills entirely. I turn off the rice and then hurry to settle the children down in the family room, and spread out the cloths and rugs ready for the meal.

The meal is a tense one. Muhammed is silent and bad-tempered. He eats rapidly, angrily. The boys eat timidly. I wait in the kitchen, and when they are done, I clear the big platter away. I can eat nothing. My stomach is contracted, my throat tight. I am too afraid to even try to swallow.

The book sits on the pile in the corner of the room. Perhaps he has noticed it. Perhaps this is the reason for the bad mood. Perhaps something has happened today. Not that it really matters. The fight will happen anyway. Except, can you call it a fight? The word implies two combatants. On this day, as on so many others, he will get angry, and I won't fight back.

I store the uneaten rice and vegetables and wash up the dishes. None of the boys resist going to bed. They stretch out on their beds and close their eyes. The loud hum of the air conditioner masks the noise from outside. I close the door.

Muhammed's hands are on me the moment I step into the hallway. I don't know why he holds off until we are alone, unless it's because he's afraid the twins will tell his mother, sometime, that Baba hits Mama, and makes her fall down. Would it make a difference? I don't know. But the fist that makes contact with my face makes little sound, and the explosion of pain is entirely silent.

"Here." Kath from next door hands me some iced tea. "And here." She presses an ice pack against my cheek.

"Thanks."

"Where is he now?"

"Out, with his friend, in the truck. I have no idea what he's doing. Sometimes he comes back with money in his pocket. But I don't know how he gets it. I don't ask."

"Mm." Misha appears with the youngest child on her hip, and a plate of dates and almonds. I shake my head. My jaw is too tender to chew. The iced tea is good.

"I fell over," I try to say as Kath probes my face gently with her fingers, assessing the damage.

"I don't think it's broken, but you should get an X ray, just to be sure."

"No, no, I'm fine."

She looks at me for a long time. "Amanda, the walls in these flats are very thin. Please, I'm not stupid or deaf. Now, where else are you hurt?"

I want to tell her. There is a sharp, deep pain in my side, when I move, when I speak, when I draw breath. He has cracked a rib again, I think. But I can't say anything. She would want to look at me, to examine me. I can't let her see the pattern of bruises across my chest, abdomen, legs

217

and groin. My hand rests on my belly, and I shake my head. "Just a few bruises. I'm fine." Miraculously, the baby is still alive, moving a little inside me.

The tea is sweet and cool. I listen out for sounds from my flat. The doors to both flats are open, opposite each other. If the boys wake, I should hear them.

"Omar will be home soon," Kath warns me, as I finish my tea. "Do you want him to take a look?"

"No, thank you."

"Amanda, why don't you try talking to him, or even speaking to his mother?"

"It doesn't happen often, not like that."

"All the same…"

"His mother believes he has the right to chastise me. It's in the Qu'ran, that a man has the right to discipline his wife, if she shames him or challenges him, or challenges his authority and status. He can beat her whenever he likes to make her virtuous."

"Not to this extent."

"I know. But it's not usually like this."

"Even so, you should get treatment. Is there no one who could help?"

Misha reappears, looks pointedly at the very English clock on the shelf.

"No matter, Amanda, we're here for you. You can come here if you need to."

"Thank you."

Footsteps in the hall. I pull my veil over my face. Omar, the doctor, is home.

"Thank you for the tea, I say, rising swiftly. I cross the hallway, and stop inside my front door. Not a sound.

I retreat into the smaller family room, and curl my long legs up under me, ignoring the bruises. The boys are asleep, the housework is done. The book nestles in my lap, and I open it, and step inside.

"Get up, get up, get up now!" Muhammed slams into the flat, into the bedroom, shouting at me, yelling, roaring. "Get out of bed! Get up, get the children up, we have to move, we have to move now."

I am up and on my feet without knowing how I got there. Cold toes on cold tiles as I run to the bathroom, and vomit, over and over again, dizzy and sweating.

"Abdullah, Shahid, get up, get dressed, now."

"What the hell time is it?" I ask, staring around at the night dark windows.

"I don't know, it doesn't matter! Come on, get dressed, dress yourself, start packing, we have to move."

Muhammed is wild eyed, his hair sticking out, his *ghutra* and skullcap gone, his *thobe* crumpled and dirty. I smell alcohol and the sweet-sour reek of marijuana. As I stumble back to the bedroom, my heart stops. He is waving a gun.

It's a handgun, absurdly iconic, a Smith and Wesson like in the American films. A revolver. It is dark metal, shiny, black, and it makes no sense to me, but it terrifies me. Fear is a stab in the belly, and I hurry, throw on an *abaya*, slip my feet into shoes.

"We have to go, we have to go!" Muhammed is mad and dangerous, yelling in the middle of the central hall, waving the gun, shrieking. "Pack your things."

I run from room to room, panicking. The twins emerge, looking sleepy and frightened.

"Come on boys, it's a game of chase," I manage to say, herding them back into their room. "Here, take these bags, and put everything in that you can find." Mahmood looks over the edge of his bed at me. "You too, Mahmood,

219

start getting your toys and putting them here for us to pack."

"Stop wasting time!" Muhammed yells at me. "Get packed. Don't waste time on toys! We have to go, we have to leave this flat, take what you can, we're not coming back."

I run back to the bedroom, seize the suitcases from under the bed, and start throwing clothes in as fast as I can. I can hear him pacing and gibbering in the hall. What has he taken, what has he done? I have no breath to ask these questions, and I fear the answers. Run, grab, pack, I finish with clothes and shoes, and run to the kitchen, dashing back and forth with dried food and goods, pots and pans. There is too much, too much, I can't take it all.

"Forget about the food, forget about everything, we have to go!" Muhammed has hold of my arm, and is dragging me towards the door.

"No! Let go!" I run back to the boys' room. Shaking pillow cases off the pillows, I stuff their clothes into them as fast as I can, trying not to look at the terror on their faces. They have seen the gun in their father's hand.

"Come on boys, let's get moving." I turn to the door. "Muhammed, stop behaving like an idiot, and come and get these cases and bags. Take them down to the truck."

Unbelievably, he does as I ask, seizing the bags and one large case and running out into the landing and down the stairs. I bundle up the boys' bedding, and then grab more toys and books and games, shoving them into a duvet cover for transport. In our bedroom again, I glance around the room, then dash to the family room. My books. My notes. I pile them into the duvet cover as well, and grab the photographs and all the family papers, kept in a cardboard box file. The bathroom! I take what I can, and Muhammed finds me there. He upends his bucket of home brew down the toilet.

"Now, Amanda! We have to go, there isn't any time."

I snatch up Mahmood and the duvet cover full of things, and stagger down the stairs. I put Mahmood on the front seat of the truck. "Stay there, love, just stay there." He is crying, eyes huge and filled with fear. "It's ok, just stay there."

Back in the flat, I try to grab more things, but Muhammed takes hold of me again. "Come on boys," he yells at the twins, who each emerge, carrying toys. "We're leaving."

"Baba, what's happening?" Shahid dares to ask, and Muhammed fetches him a backhanded slap across the face.

"Stop wailing and act like a man!" Muhammed yells at him.

"Jesus Christ, Muhammed, he's only five!" I yell at their father, and that shocks the boys more than the slap. "Keep your hands off him."

"Shut up and get in the truck, or I'll leave you behind!" Muhammed's voice has dropped to a menacing snarl. The gun is in his hand again, and he points it at me. "Now!"

I grab the twins and run, pelting down the stairs and out into the hot, humid night. Mahmood is sitting in the truck, crying. We throw the last few bags and pillow cases into the back, and I climb in, pulling Mahmood onto my lap, pulling Shahid against me, patting Abdullah's shoulder. "It's ok, Mama and Baba are just playing a game."

Muhammed scrambles in, and before he has even closed the door, guns the engine and peels away, screeching of tyres on tarmac, lurching of the car. I'm fumbling for the seat belts, trying to buckle the boys in, one arm on the dashboard, and Mahmood is clinging to my front like a monkey, and Shahid takes the seatbelt and buckles it around himself and his twin.

The traffic is better this time of the morning. It's not Ramadan, so the streets are not crowded.

"Where are we going?" I dare to ask, after a few minutes.

"My mother's house," Muhammed replies, as if I should have known that. Of course.

"Why, Muhammed, what's gone on? What's going on?"

"I was out with Majid, we were driving around town, driving my truck." His words are tumbling over each other, out of his mouth, like a dam bursting. I look at his eyes, the sweat on his skin, and think, he has taken something, that's why he's like this.

"We were driving past the mall, and a car with two men in overtook us, cut in, and hit the bumper of the truck. So we chased them, through town, we followed them in the car, and we were yelling at them through the window, and they were yelling back at us, and then Majid said something to me, I don't know. And then I shot one of them. The passenger. I shot him, and I saw the bullet go through the glass, and through the seat, and hit him. Blood everywhere. So I turned around and came home. Majid leapt out about half way, said he'd get home on his own."

"You were in this truck?"

"Yes," he says, speeding up again, "I've got to get it off the road, hide it, and I have to make sure the police can't find me." And my heart in my mouth, as he veers around corners and slams on his brakes to avoid hitting pedestrians and other cars, and roadside barriers, and everything else around us is turning into a blur, and I can't breathe, but if I faint, who will hold onto Mahmood and stop him going through the windscreen next time. Hold on Amanda, hold on. I close my eyes and brace myself against the roof of the

222

car and the dashboard, and I pray, Allah, Allah, please help us, please save us.

At last we are at his father's house, screaming brakes, lurching to a stop. He runs from the truck, opens the gates, and drives the truck inside, into the car port. Already lights are coming on in the house.

"Out, get out," Muhammed yells at me as he races to shut the high gates. I clamber out, wearing my pajamas under my *abaya*, the children in their nightclothes too, and as I reach it, the front door opens, and Baba is there, and Khala, jabbering away at me in rapid Arabic.

"I can't understand you!" I say, loudly, but it is ok, now, because Khala takes Mahmood from me and ushers the twins inside, and my father-in-law goes out to help Muhammed unload the truck. I hear them talking furiously, and I catch something about police, truck, trouble. Then I am inside, and Khala is fussing at me.

"I don't know," I tell her, "he just said we had to leave the flat. So we did."

She is not happy. But she takes the boys up to one of the bedrooms, and settles them all in one big bed. They are wide awake and frightened. Khala fusses out of the room. "Come," she says, without looking back at me. "Let them sleep."

"Mama," Abdullah says quietly, "don't go."

"It's ok, I'll stay a while," I smile at him. "Let's have a story, shall we?"

"Yes, please Mama," says Shahid.

"Once upon a time, there was a man named Ali," I say, trying to remember the story from my childhood. "He was a poor man, and he lived in a big town. One day a djinn came to him, and told him about a great treasure that was hidden away, in a great cave. He told Ali to remember a word, a special word, that would lead him to the treasure."

223

I can't remember the story, not at all, though I heard it as a child. I don't know what made me start on this one. But I can make it up, string it together, I'm sure.

"Ali went to work for a man who wanted some errands run. He took a camel out into the desert, and got lost, and the camel ran away. Soon it got dark. From a distance, he saw a fire and a camp, and cautiously approached, but as he drew near, he felt nervous, and wondered why the men were out in the desert, when they were not herders, and had few camels, and no goats or sheep."

Mahmood is closing his eyes, slowly, and Abdullah's body has relaxed already. Shahid is still tense, alert, and watchful.

"Ali was very frightened, because as he listened, he heard that the men were robbers, thieves, and had stolen treasure and hidden it in a cave out in the desert. It is a magic cave, and can only be opened by a magic word. Ali thinks, this must be the treasure that the djinn told me about. So he follows the thieves, all through the next day, until they reach the cave, which had a door of red rock. But the thieves cannot remember the magic word to enter the cave, and so they are frustrated. One of them notices Ali's footsteps in the sand, following them through the desert, and then finds him, hiding behind a sand dune. The thief finds Ali, and drags him back to the gang, and takes out his sword to kill Ali, but Ali cries, 'Stop! Do not kill me. I know the magic word to get into your cave.'

"'Tell us, and we will let you live.'

"'I am not as stupid as that,' declared Ali. 'I will open the cave for you, and then you will get your treasure, and you will give me whatever I want. But I will not tell you the word, because then you will kill me. I have to make sure you have good reason to keep me alive.'"

Shahid's eyes are closing. Mahmood is already asleep.

Abdullah is almost asleep, though his fingers are still holding onto my hand.

"And so Ali remembered the word the djinn had told him, and he went up to the door, and said the word quietly, so that the thieves could not hear him. And the cave was full of treasure, gold, and jewels, and money, and rich carpets and rugs. Ali was overwhelmed by the great amount of treasure. And he took for himself one of the camels of the thieves, and loaded it with as much treasure as he could, and he filled his pockets with gold coins, and hung great necklaces of gold and jewels around his neck, and put a gold crown on his head. And he hung chains of gold around the neck of the camel, and wrapped many treasures in a great carpet, and carried it on his own back. And Ali, who had been a beggar and a poor man, all his life, thought with joy and thanks that he was free now, and would never be hungry again, or homeless, or unable to make his way in the world. The djinn had set him free. He escaped from the thieves, and disappeared across the desert, into a town where no one knew him, and started a new life, taking his treasure with him. And he was always generous to beggars, and made many, many acts of charity."

They are all asleep now, their eyes tightly shut, in that way of children, as if sleep has sealed all the secret doors to the treasure house of their minds, and some benevolent spirit watches over them as they wander far in dreams of treasure and freedom.

Breakfast. The old routines come back to me. I am making *laban* and *fitr,* and *ful medames*, and sweet tea, and Gadria is here with me, and Khala, and Layla is helping the boys get dressed, delighted to have her cousins here again, so she can play at auntie. Muhammed was up early.

"Amanda," Layla says, when I go upstairs to check on the boys, "What happened? Why did Muhammed bring you back here to stay?"

I'm not about to lie to her, but I can't tell her everything. "I think he was involved in some incident with the car. Some kind of argument, maybe? I don't know, maybe he wants us to spend more time with his family? I'm not sure, perhaps you should ask him."

That shuts her up. Khala appears, and as Layla strips Mahmood's pyjamas off, she starts talking over him, saying the blessing against evil spirits. I lose patience, and take over getting Mahmood dressed.

"Mama, I liked the story last night," Mahmood says. I smile at him, and he puts his arms around my neck. I hold his little body against me for a moment.

After breakfast, Muhammed's brother Ahmed takes the boys to school in his car. As soon as Khala has gone out shopping, I call Grace.

"He did what?" Even the sound of her voice is an inexpressible comfort, the slow, soft vowels, the familiarity.

"He shot some guy."

"Amanda, you shouldn't be saying stuff like this over the phone, you know they listen in."

"I don't care."

"You will if he is sentenced to death, and you're left without a husband!"

I hadn't thought of that. Freedom from him would not be freedom for me. Fear rises in my throat again. "I don't know what's going to happen. I don't think he'll let us go back to the flat."

"What about all your furniture and everything?"

"I'm going to talk to the family about it. Maybe his brother can help him get it."

"Come over today or tomorrow," Grace suggests, "so we can talk properly"

"I'll try. He won't use the truck, so we don't have a car."

"I'll send mine. Just tell me when."

"Thanks."

"Will you still be coming to work next week?"

"Yes, I'm sure… I'll have to sort out getting there, but yes."

"Good. Good. That will get you out of the house."

Muhammed appears, and I say goodbye to Grace and put down the phone.

"Where is it?" I demand, as he straightens his *ghutra* and glares at me. His eyes are bleary, his skin an odd pasty grey colour. I notice his hands are shaking. "Tell me, where have you put that gun?"

"It's nothing to you, woman," he says, dismissively.

"It's got everything to do with me," I hiss, "because if the boys find it, what happens then? You should have told me you had a gun."

He turns his back on me. I reach out to take his arm, to make him look at me. I have never been so frightened as I was last night. I am still reeling from it all. "And another thing, how long will we be here? Are you going to find us another place?"

Big mistake. He swings his arm out of the way, and backhands me across the face, the same as he did to Shahid in the night, but harder. I'm knocked to the floor, and I roll, cradling my belly to protect it.

He's gone when I look up. It will be a miracle if this child survives to term, I think. I don't know how I feel about it.

"Oh Grace, I've only been there two days and already I'm going crazy."

Grace smiles as she lifts the teapot and pours me more tea. "Eat something, Amanda, one of these cakes, or some of the sweet rolls. You look like you're wasting away."

"I can't eat, I'm too stressed."

"You can eat. You need to feed yourself, and your little passenger."

She looks so wistful that it makes me laugh. She's wearing a black chiffon silk headscarf that frames her face loosely, edged in satin ribbon that seems to reflect the blue of her eyes.

"Come on, eat something, or I'll treat you like I do my children, when they refuse to eat their dinners."

"What?" I find myself laughing with her as she purses her lips, picks up one of the sweet rolls, and breaks it into bite size pieces.

"Grace, honestly, I don't… I can't…"

Then she lifts the bread to my lips, leaning in, and I am enveloped in her light, sweet scent, so close I can see the green flecks in her eyes, and the curving bow of her lips, rich and full. Her soft fingers and the doughy bread, covered in powdered sugar, are teasing at my lips, and then with her other hand she strokes my cheek.

"Come now, my little one, eat for Mommy." Her closeness is intoxicating. Unable to help myself, I gasp at a rush of heat, at her body so close to me, her hand on my face. I open my mouth. Slowly she slides the sweet bread into my mouth, then strokes my cheek again.

"There now, isn't that good?"

The sweetness makes my jaws ache, and saliva run into my mouth. "Yes," I whisper. She looks at me curiously, then lays her soft, cool cheek against mine. "Come on Amanda, you have to survive, you have to be strong. Don't let him beat you down."

228

My arms are around her then, and I'm pulling her towards me. She hugs me, hard, and my hands move of their own accord, reaching, touching the silky blonde strands of hair, caressing her face, holding on to her.

Then she pulls away, a small, sweet smile on her face.

"There, now eat the rest of that, and drink your tea, and I know you'll feel better."

I sit, and eat, obediently, one piece after another. The bread goes down easily. I take another roll, and eat that as well. Then the hot, dark tea.

"Thank you."

"Better?"

"Yes, much better." I pause. The heat from the tea seems to flow through my limbs, and into my brain as well. "Oh, no!"

"What's up?"

"Kath and Mishal. I never had a chance to say goodbye to them."

"Ring them up."

"I don't have their number. And I can't go back. Muhammed is convinced they are watching the flat, waiting for one of us to turn up. I can't risk it. If he's arrested…"

I think of Mishal, and Kath, and all the children, running around that little flat. I think of the times they opened their door to me, and made me tea, and coffee, and kept the kids occupied while they tended to my bruises.

Grace finishes her tea and sets down the cup.

"Now, are you coming to the party next week? I am inviting all of my female relatives, and all of my friends. Will you come?"

"Yes."

"I've been covering your classes while you've been away," Grace rises and fetches a notebook, showing me the work she has been doing, the exercises she has set. I relax. Let myself rest. Listen to her soothing voice.

When I wake, she is smiling at me, holding up the teapot. "Wake up, sleeping beauty."

"What happened?"

"You dozed off, probably as a result of my scintillating conversation," she teases, filling a clean cup with tea. "I let you sleep for an hour or so."

"Oh! I've got to stop doing this."

"It was sweet. Though, did you know you talk in your sleep?"

"Oh no, what did I say?"

"Not much. Something about Karen."

"Oh, great. Must have been a nightmare. She's my older sister, but we don't have anything to do with each other unless we have to. I don't speak to her."

"Your own sister?"

"Yes, she always was jealous of me, and resented my choices, I think. She's very straight-laced, you know, everything has a plan. School, college, pick up a husband along the way, have two point four children, etc, etc."

"And she's divorced?"

"Yeah, while my mum was ill her husband started playing away. She blamed me for it!"

Grace shakes her head. Her sympathy for me is almost painful. Harder yet is getting up and going home, when Muhammed appears, driving his father's car, to collect me.

## *Mustaqarr*

"Push, Amanda, push!"

The voice of the midwife is an anchor, holding me to my pain-racked body.

"I can't!" I groan, through gritted teeth.

Pain and pressure and the heaving, aching power of it all.

The baby is born on a roar, rushing into the midwife's hands as if eager to greet the world. It screams as soon as it feels the shock of cold air, a howling, indignant cry. What is it like, to hear for the first time, and the first thing you hear is your own crying?

"Is it ok?"

"Yes, yes, it's a boy, he's fine."

A quick labour this. I fall back on the bed, thankful. Another boy. Muhammed will be pleased. His family will be pleased. Another boy. Thank Allah.

"Here, you must feed him now." I wake from a half-doze to stare at the wide eyes of my son. He is a wizened little thing, frowning up at me.

"No, no, I'm going to bottle feed," I tell the midwife. "Please, bring him a bottle."

I can hear the disapproval in every step as she hurries away. Do midwives ever walk slowly? Even off duty, do they bustle and march, in the supermarket, or at home?

My baby. He takes the bottle well. I have not torn, there are no stitches, only the lax, jelly-like skin of my belly, white like cold rice.

The baby is taken outside, to his father, to have the words spoken in his ear, the chewed date placed on his tongue. In seven days, if he lives, his head will be shaved, and he will be circumcised.

231

"Lots of gold this time, eh?" I say to him, stroking the thick shock of black hair on his head. "Lots of gold."

Sweat on my skin, cooling, the air conditioning is on high. Sweat and blood pooling between my thighs, a cooling, sticky mass, itching where it touches my skin. Iron and ocean smell, blood and things kept hidden, wet and dark, mysteries of the depths of the female sea.

No mystery here, the aftermath of pain and cramping, the veiled midwife, the noises from outside. No screams and howls, no crying and desperate begging for release. I remember those sounds, the suffering women when I had the twins. But not here, not now. While I was in the waiting area, I saw a Saudi woman in labour. Only the beads of sweat breaking out between her eyebrows betrayed her bodily struggle.

"Amanda?"

I know who it is before I open my eyes. That scent, that voice, the surging joy inside me. It could only be Grace.

"My dear, congratulations!"

"*Mashallah,*" I reply. She embraces me gently, touches cheek to cheek. I almost shrink from her, my scrubbed, battered body against her perfumed, perfect self.

"A boy then."

"Yes."

"How are you feeling?"

"Annoyed. I want to go home."

"Heavens, why?"

"I want to be in my own home, with my boys, not here…"

"Amanda, love, whatever for? You can't do anything, and it would just mean your mother-in-law or one of your sisters having to stay with you."

232

"But I'd be home."

"I understand. But you really are better off here, where you can rest."

"Rest? Oh yeah, being woken at five a.m. every day, disturbed by other people's screaming babies, not to mention the midwives."

"You'll be home soon enough."

"I suppose so."

"And I'm here now, and I can stay all afternoon. The children are with my mother-in-law, so I can stay as long as you want me to."

She settles in a chair beside me, lays her hand gently on mine. I curl my fingers around hers, feeling the roughened skin of my fingers against the warm velvet of hers. Feeling the skin, and the flesh and blood and bone under the skin. Feeling the spirit, the energy that seems to emanate from her.

The baby sleeps on in his little crib. The sounds of the ward surround me, the ebb and flow of its particular tide. My eyes close.

My hand in hers. Her hand in mine.

Sleep, not a blanket but a ship, sailing slowly out into a sea of darkness and forgetting. My hand and hers, on the tiller. Sailing without fear towards an unknowable horizon.

Everything shifting, from dream to waking to sleep again.


"A strong boy," Muhammed says, carefully, in English. I shift the baby into the crook of my arm.

"Yes, he seems like a real fighter. He's a lot like Shahid was."

Is that a faint smile on his face? I echo it. Another one like Shahid? Another handful, as my mother would say.

Shahid is, at this very moment, having an impressively loud argument with his grandmother about playing football outside with some boys from upstairs.

"Oh, let him go if he wants to," I say loudly over the both of them. "They'll be fine in the courtyard."

Shahid immediately dashes out, ignoring Khala's ongoing protestations.

The new flat is in a different street, further away from school. Muhammed found it quickly. I think his father gave him the money for the year's rent. It is bigger than the other, and on the ground floor of the building. There is a large room off the hall for the men, a bigger sitting room for the women, and a dining room between the men's room and the kitchen. There are also four bedrooms. The kitchen is bigger, and lighter than in the last place. Muhammed is working for the telephone company. He used to work for them, before he came out to Britain. I don't know how long it will last. But for the time being, it is enough. Most of my furniture was left behind at the old flat. But we can manage.

"You shouldn't let him, he'll get too hot."

"They play outside during school," I say, to pacify her, but not caring, really. My house, my rules. "Just let him be. He'll come in when he gets too hot."

Abdullah rushes in, to check if he can join his brother outside. "Go, go!" I smile. "Have fun. Don't leave the courtyard."

"I won't, Mama," he assures me, beaming, and dashes off, his trainers squeaking on the tiles in the hall.

Muhammed disappears to join the men in the front room. Yusuf sleeps soundly, his shaved head against the pillow. When I changed him, I noted he was healing well, and I left off the little plastic cup from the circumcision site. All he does is feed and sleep. He hardly cries.

Day and night, light and dark, noise and quiet. Only the heat is constant, searing or simply bearable. No wind to give relief, because a breeze means dust and stinging eyes, and not putting laundry outside to dry. Routine, one day running into the next. Prayers and breakfast, laundry and feeding the baby. Cook the meal, visit the mall and the souk, visit the supermarket, visit Grace and Muhammed's family. Play with the boys, serve food, prayers, prayers, family. Conversations spiralling around the same news, the same concerns. Children, marriage, family, children. Who is doing well, who is not, who is getting married, who is still looking. Family connections, tribal ties, good matches, bad matches, run-ins with the law. Muhammed's brother Ali in prison again, Muhammed's job, Layla's wedding, the Americans, the Royal Family, prayers, prayers, children to bed, my body stripped bare for his scrutiny, his hands, his flesh on my flesh, piercing me, possession, more, more, again, the endless fucking, morning, noon and night. Yusuf sleeps in his cot as I turn my head and hold my breath, hold in the pain and the deadness of no pain, not so much anymore. Blow from a fist, a hand, soft, he's too soft, my fault, always my fault. Sour smell of skin up close, too close, crinkled curly hair, sour salty smell, acrid whiff of urine, and the taste of him, soft curd texture of limp flesh in my mouth, the sucking and the pumping, encouraging, tongue probing and teasing, salty curdled milk taste, filling my mouth, flesh and what comes out of it, don't gag, mustn't gag, just breathe, take a breath. It will pass.

Morning and night and morning again. Heavy sleep and light, dreams and shadows and blurred faces, blurred shapes, sounds muffled by the all-encompassing veil, sight

235

limited by the closed doors and blurred windows. Just light and dark and shadows. And Grace.

Daylight or shadows, early or late, early most likely. Timing is important, because of the children, and the husbands. Familiar ritual of tea and talk, this is how we always begin. My place or hers, does it matter? I know them both well, the edges and the spaces, the soft contours of her huge, American sofa, the firm solidity of the plush floor cushions in my sitting room. The wall that is her backdrop is plain, pale, as if in a photograph, and she is in sharp focus. Eyes wide, so close now, pupils dilated, is that my breathing or hers, my hand on hers, my body or her body, the rising and falling, the gentle landscape, the smiling and the sighing. Her hands or mine, cupping, caressing, chasing each other in the race to map new territory.

This is hunger, and thirst. This is the desert, before the rain. And the flowers that come after.


"You know, it may be a cliché, but they do grow up fast." Grace, sitting in her room, smiles down at the *thobe* she is folding on her lap. "This used to fit Gaffar, and now Ali has outgrown it!"

"I know what you mean," I pick up the next garment from the pile of clean laundry and hand it to her. Our fingers meet in the exchange. "All that Shahid and Abdullah do is eat and grow."

"You're looking better these days," Grace says, putting the last white *thobe* on the pile in the basket.

"Thanks. Forgive me for saying it, but you look a little tense. Not your usual self."

"Well…" to my surprise, she starts to cry.

I am at her side in an instant, cradling and holding her

the way she usually does for me, one hand on her back, the other stroking her silken hair.

"What's wrong? It's not like you to cry." Grace's composure is usually absolute.

Her hand grips my wrist, not hard, but firmly. After a few moments, or is it a long, greening spring day, she releases me, and wipes her eyes.

"I'm sorry, I shouldn't, but, well, you won't understand, probably, you've not got girls, yet. But Hala is... I took her to get fitted for a woman's *abaya*, and to pick out scarves and veils."

"How old is she now?"

"Nine, nearly ten."

"I thought so. Surely..."

"Her grandmother says it is time. As soon as they show any sign of maturity. And I didn't think she would start so soon. So...she's my little girl, and suddenly she has to dress and behave like a woman. It doesn't seem right."

"Grace, I don't know, I mean, are you surprised by this? You knew it was going to happen, sooner or later."

"I know, I know, but I didn't realise..." she takes a sip of her tea. Her composure is returning, but slowly. "It's different with boys, it's not such a...marked transition. It seems like they are always moving in that direction, always in the process of becoming a man, right from the moment they are born."

Yes, yes, she is so right. From the very first moment.

"But this, it seems so sudden. And it's too soon, much too soon. I thought I'd have another couple of years before..."

"It must be hard for you." Empty words, but I have to say something.

"And her grandmother had already started talking about

marriage, making arrangements, looking for a good match." The tears resurface. Fear in her eyes, and a kind of grief. She has lost something.

Stop crying, please, Grace, please stop. You can't know what it does to me, how it hurts me, to see you so sad.

"I'm just being silly," she says, visibly pulling herself together. "I'll be ok in a minute."

I let go, sit back, as she straightens up and moves away from me. Cold, my arms are cold now.

"The worst thing is, she's really excited about it," Grace half-laughs. "Oh, why do they have to grow up?"

"I don't know about you, but I don't want mine to stay babies forever!" I glance guiltily at Yusuf who, as usual, is sleeping soundly in his pushchair. He is a fat little thing, placid and happy, ready to be amused by anything and everything around him.

"Oh, I would," Grace looks at him too. There is such tenderness in her voice, it makes me pause.

"No, they are lovely as babies, but so demanding!"

"Does that ever change?"

A shadow across my mind, a dark thing, the colour of a fresh bruise. "No, I suppose not."

"Not until we can marry them off, and they become some other woman's sun, moon, and responsibility!"

"Which could take a long, long time!"

Laughter. Oh, I love it when she laughs. I can't help joining in.

The doorbell rings. "Oh, that will be Elena, she said she might call today."

"Oh, lovely." I hate Elena, her patronising tone, her possessiveness, the exaggerated intimacy with Grace, as if they have known each other for ever. Just because Elena's husband works in the oil business, "He's in oil sweetie, just like our Grace's man," and because they're both American. Grace never criticises her, she's too nice. I don't know how she can stand it.

I compose myself, modelling my posture on Grace's, legs aligned, skirt falling neatly, casual pose on the sofa, next to Grace's seat, at home.

Elena breezes in. "Oh hi honey, hey there! And how are you? And the baby, such a darling, so good. He looks so well."

"Hello Elena, how are you?"

"Well, Grace, quite the party." Elena collapses on the sofa where Grace was sitting previously. "I'd love some coffee, if you have some." She takes off her headscarf and flings it aside with a flourish. "Dear Lord, glad to get that off! Can't bear the thing, really, such a pain in the you know what!"

Something stirs in me, bitter and black like coffee left to brew too long. "I hardly notice it anymore," I say, moving away from her. "Grace, can I help you with the coffee?"

"Oh, yes, thanks."

"Back in a minute." I hurry out. "Here, let me take the tray." I arrange the cups. "Are you ok now?"

She smiles at me. Her eyes are a little red; otherwise, no tell-tale signs mar her perfect features. "I'm fine. But…" she flicks a glance towards the door.

"I know. Not a word."

As we enter the room, me with the coffee, Grace with the big plate of biscuits and cakes, together, Elena looks from Grace to me and back again. One eyebrow creeps up slightly, and the crease between her flinty little eyes deepens.

What is she seeing? Whatever it is, I want it to be real.

It was a bright summer when I moved to the shared house in the town. All my life I'd lived down in the thick of things, on the lower slopes of the steep valley sides, crowded in with row upon row of houses, family piled on family, with no privacy and little escape from the neighbours who saw everything and reported back. Moving elsewhere was a shock to everyone, including me, but it was Jane who put me up to it.

The first year of college, of A levels, was easy, but home was harder and harder, and the increase in my hours to four nights and two weekend lunches a week still wasn't enough for my family. My mother acted as if I had betrayed her by not finding a full time job with "prospects".

Jane was an older woman, late thirties, late returning to education but doing A levels to try to better herself. She had three children, all grown up and left home, and a husband who left too, the moment the youngest had flown the nest. She was the only one I really spoke to in my classes. We started talking when paired together to analyse Keats' 'Ode on a Grecian Urn', where she mocked the words with a jaded sagacity.

"I know it's supposed to be an oxymoron – unravished bride of quietness – but I think it's crap. Brides don't get ravished. They submit."

I laughed. I had grown my hair longer and dyed it black, and taken to wearing long black skirts and Dr Martens boots, with baggy shirts and jumpers. Jane wore jeans and cowboy boots and plain shirts, and her hair was short and spiky. We were an odd pair.

"I think it's a symbol of the passage of time, and how time changes everyone."

"Yeah, a lament for the loss of girlish femininity, more like. The urn is the woman who remains beautiful because she is never ravished."

"I don't get it." I toyed with my biro, the end chewed beyond recognition.

"It's just the way that society, that men, see women. It's ok when they're young and beautiful, and virginal, but as soon as they're used, they're spoiled, and nothing can put them back the way they were."

"That's horrible. It's not like that really."

"You are naïve, aren't you?" Jane looked at me closely. "How old are you, eighteen, nineteen?"

"Seventeen."

"Hmph, you look older. So, you have no idea what it's really like. You probably swallow all that garbage they feed you about marriage, and motherhood."

"Not really," I felt defensive. "If I did I'd be working and looking for a husband, like my sister did, not doing A levels against my parents' wishes."

That made her pause. She creased her wide brow in thought, blue eyes like ice. "Well, ok then, that's a positive sign."

"A sign of what."

"That you've got half a brain, at least."

I didn't know if I liked Jane or not. But she seemed to take a liking to me, and soon we were having coffee together each day, eating lunch together. She deplored my lack of appetite, accusing me of dieting, and was disgusted with me for doing so. I defended my utter lack of interest in food and instead challenged her about wearing men's shirts and being so bloody critical of everyone. We fell into easy disagreement, a camaraderie based on difference rather than commonality. I loved to listen to her talk, holding forth on politics – somewhere far left of feminist – and religion – a dirty word, whilst I wished I had half the words or eloquence that she displayed.

"How come you're only doing A levels now? The way you talk you'd think you were a lecturer or something?" I dared to ask over a plate of limp salad and a rubbery jacket potato in the college canteen.

"Oh, well, it's the old story. I got married at sixteen, thought I knew my own mind, nice boy, nice man, really. We'd been friends since primary school. He went to work for his father as an apprentice carpenter, ended up with his own firm. I had kids and brought them up. Life was straightforward. Three boys I had. I thought that was it, that I was living a good life. There was money in the bank, holidays twice a year, new clothes for me when I needed them, the boys well looked after. But I was bored. Once they were all in school I joined the library, started reading. Before I knew it I was reading more than just romances and Westerns. I picked up Virginia Woolf, and the world began to change.

"I got to thirty before I realised none of them felt any obligation to wash a plate or pick up their own dirty clothes, no matter how many times I told them to. When my youngest, Gary, turned fourteen, I finally saw myself through their eyes. I was there to do the dishes, wash the clothes, cook the dinner, do the shopping, anything they needed. Brian, my husband, wanted sex twice a week – Tuesday night and Friday night. I didn't even have to participate. I was nothing. I knew my neighbours, all wives and mothers, and they were the same, but I knew that nothing I did would last, would go on beyond me. So I said to myself, I'm a woman and I have a story to tell. I made up my mind to be an author, like Virginia Woolf, Charlotte Bronte, all them.

"I thought me and Brian, we had something. I thought that all those years of being together meant something. Turns out he was just there for the boys. He'd been carrying on with another woman for the last eight years. He left me as soon as Gary went off to uni in Birmingham.

"I watched the three of them leave for university, one after the other. Geoff, he went to London – economics. George, he was the artistic one, he went to Cardiff. Got himself a boyfriend now. And Gary, he went into law. So I thought, I'm going to uni too, going to get myself some A levels and then I'm going. Brian gave me the house – somewhere for the boys to come home to, see. I've got enough from the divorce to live on, just about, till I get a degree. Then I'll get a job.

"The thing is, this family thing, it's a lie, really. Three kids and I hardly see them except once in a blue moon with a bag of dirty washing and empty pockets. I wish I'd known earlier that there was something else I could be."

"Good for you," I said. "I'm not going to end up like that."

"Well, girls now, your age, you have the choice. More than I did back then."

It was after that conversation that she urged me to move into the shared student house where she lived. There was a spare room, she said, small, yes, but the rent was cheaper. I could manage it on my wages. My parents didn't object. One less to feed, one less to worry about. I was leaving and becoming independent. It was the best choice for all of us.

## *Mutakallif*

"Stop!"

Muhammed pauses, mid slap, looking almost comical with a surprised expression on his face.

"Just fucking stop, Muhammed. Stop hitting me."

"Don't talk back to me, woman!" he thunders.

"Stop hitting me then, and stop yelling. You'll wake the baby. "

He raises his fist again. "There's no need!" I yell, standing up to my full height. He hates that. "Whatever it is you want, tell me, and I'll do it. If you want me to let you fuck me, fine. If you want me to use my mouth, ok. If you want to tie me up and hold me down, go ahead. Just stop hitting me!"

The next blow is a fist, heavy, hard and calculated. Blackness, a minute, or more, maybe. Winded, on the floor, I gasp for air.

"You bastard," I growl at him, pulling myself first to my knees, then to my feet. "What is wrong with you? Why do you have to do this?"

"Just be quiet!" he hisses at me. "Shut up."

"Stop hitting me then."

Wham! I didn't see that one coming, and I'm lifted off my feet by the force of it. On top of me, he forces my face into the carpet with one hand, lifts my skirt with the other, exposing my backside, my anus and vagina, open and waiting, and I struggle to support my weight and his on my spread knees.

"You can fuck me as hard as you like," I mumble, inhaling dust and carpet, "but it won't change anything. I won't say no to you. But fucking me into the floor still won't make you a man."

244

An explosion of pain, then darkness, and then I wake to find him rolling me over, his hands feeling my abdomen.

"You're pregnant again?"

"Looks like it."

"Why didn't you tell me? Have you been to the doctor?"

"No."

"Who have you told?"

"No one.

Slap. "Liar! Who have you told?" Slap. "Why didn't you tell me?" Slap. "Is it mine?" Slap.

"Don't you dare!" I wrench myself away from him, cover myself, ignoring the hard, protruding and insistent bulk of my belly. "Of course it's yours. I haven't been near another man."

"How soon?" He stands, shakily I note.

"I think I conceived almost as soon as I stopped bleeding, after Yusuf was born."

"You haven't…"

"Not once."

He pulls me to him, those bloody iron fingers biting into my arms. "Why have you kept this secret?"

Stink of rum and cigarettes and that bloody *meswak* he chews to hide the alcohol.

"I haven't. I didn't think about it. I sort of knew, a few weeks ago, but…"

How can I explain it to him? I can't even explain it to myself. Maybe, I thought, maybe if I didn't acknowledge it, it wouldn't be real. Maybe if I ignored it, it would go away.

"I wasn't sure. And I've been so busy, I didn't really want to think about it."

He thrusts me away. When I look around, he's gone. I hear the telltale noise of the closet door, then, after a few more minutes, the slam of the front door.

Good. He's gone. A few breaths, and I'm calm. Cold compress, first, for my jaw. Not that anyone outside the family would see it. Not that it matters. But I don't want the boys to see, to start asking questions. Already I think they see and hear too much. Lamplight, the hum of the air conditioner, quiet, boys all asleep.

Time to face what I've been avoiding. Time to let myself acknowledge it.

Pregnant.

Again.

I can't do this again, the waiting and the worrying. I can't care about this one. I can't think about it.

Yusuf is a fat seven months old, with the appetite of a cart horse. Muhammed is drinking more than ever, turning up to work drunk. Will he lose his job? As far as I can tell, that's pretty much what happened last time. Not that anyone told me, as such. Everyone assumes that I know what he does when he's not here, when he's not working, what he does between home and work and work and home. I don't know! How could I? I thought it was like that with all of them. Then I see Fatima's husband hurrying in from work to see her, love in his eyes, and telling her about his day. I overhear business discussions, Baba involving Khala in all of his business worries, and taking her advice. Only since I've been able to follow the Arabic have I been able to see, to really understand, so much more of what's happening around me. Suddenly the world opens up, and I hear how Fatima talks to her children, hear Khala's advice to her, pick up on her pride in her sons (at least the ones that can hold down a job and stay out of prison).

A whole world, and they all assumed I knew.

There is a movement, there, inside me. A baby. A curled and partly formed thing, not a baby yet. Give it another month and it might have a chance of surviving. Don't think of that. No hope, no fear. What will be, will be. *Inshallah.* Is this it? Is this, finally, what it means to be a Muslim? This is submission, yes, to God or fate or whatever it is that says this one will live, this one will die, this one will torment you first with weeks of uncertainty, fear and doubt.

Cold spots on my chest. Despite the plastic bag, the ice is melting, dripping. Teardrop splashes on the blue silk of my blouse.

What is he doing? My mind comes back to it, like a tongue to a sore tooth. What is he doing this time? When will he be back, and in what state? I won't let him make us move again, they can arrest him, take him away. My wages will pay the rent. Except that's never going to happen, is it? Not with his brother waiting in the wings.

A trapped moth, beating against the lampshade. Someone told me it isn't the light that attracts them, it's the deepest, darkest shadow, the one that lies directly behind the light.

Slam! I wish he wouldn't slam the door! And now the baby is crying.

Abdullah appears in his Spiderman pyjamas that my Dad sent him. "Mama?"

"It's ok, love, go back to bed." He looks pale and upset, on the verge of tears.

"I heard shouting again."

"I know. I'm sorry, sweetheart, I really am. Mama and Baba were having a disagreement. We shouldn't have been shouting, I know."

"Why do you argue with Baba so much?"

"I don't know. Let's not talk about it now. Let's get you back to bed."

"Ok."

Back to bed, a kiss and a hug, then tuck him in. Shahid is sleeping fast. Mahmood is lying on his back, looking up at me with wide eyes.

"Sleep, my love," I say to him, dropping a kiss onto his forehead. The baby has gone back to sleep. I would love to be like that. Immune to it.

Grace sits in my sitting room, relaxed, her bare feet curled up underneath her as she reclines, singing softly to Yusuf, leaning against me on the sofa. I lean against the arm of the sofa, feeling her body against mine, reading my book. In it a veiled woman seeks comfort in the arms of a forbidden lover. I mark the page in pencil, make a note in the notebook on my knee. Grace raises her head and looks at me. She smiles. I smile back.

A tear drops onto the page. Then another. Her hand appears, strokes my cheek.

"Don't cry."

"I'm not crying."

"Don't lie to me. Why are you crying?"

"It's the book, that's all." *Don't stop touching me Grace, please don't. It's the only thing that feels real.* Her lips bend softly into a slight smile. I could watch her lips for hours; they are so mobile, so expressive. All the more criminal to cover her face every day. Or maybe not. Maybe it's better that I am the only one who sees this smile. Or that I can pretend I am.

I go back to my book. She shifts slightly against me. Yusuf is falling asleep. Her head on my shoulder now, and her breathing deepening. I lay aside books and pencil, and stretch slightly. My hand finds hers, and accepts the brief touch of reassurance.

The shadows deepen, and the baby sleeps on.

Muhammed and Jane and Greg and Phil and me. It wasn't like I imagined it. It worked though, well enough. Muhammed was doing business studies, Jane and I were doing arts, Greg was studying music and Phil was doing a catering course. They were strangers to me. I saw them in the kitchen, on the way to and from the bathroom, or in the small living room which was dark, cold and sparsely furnished. I was on my own, with no one telling me what to do, when to get up, what to eat, when to be home. I was seventeen but I looked older. I had never had a boyfriend, never even kissed a boy. I don't know why. I was a bookworm. I studied philosophy, English Literature and Religious Studies. I wrote essays on Marxism, existentialism, feminism and faith. I washed my clothes by hand in the kitchen sink and ate pot noodles and peanut butter sandwiches, and drank cheap beer from the bargain shop. I thought I was grown up. If only I'd known how far that was from the truth.

Bang!

Why does he have to make so much noise? Not that I can sleep. The baby inside me likes to be awake at night. The minute I lie down, he starts: kicks, great somersaults, some limb or other poking out. Hiccups that go on for hours.

Awkward now, to accommodate Muhammed. He stands beside the bed, naked, his beard bushier than normal. Onto my knees then. Ignore the insistent jabbing from a foot or elbow. Is this baby trying to fight its way out?

I hate it when he holds my head like that. I hate the taste of him.

Wake up! Sleep like a man holding me under the surface of a dream. Drowning. Wake up, I have to wake up. Head

249

pounding, I'm dizzy, this baby is so big! Hard to balance this weight. I need to pee. Can't hold it. Hot stream running down my leg as I race to the bathroom. Shower, quickly, before the boys wake. Clothes – even my maternity dresses are tight. Haven't been this big since the twins. Too big. Not due for another month. Damn, can't see or reach to put my knickers on. Hook them up to my knee with one foot, catch with my fingers, then pull up.

Does he have to snore like that? I wish I didn't have to sleep in the same bed as him.

Breakfast. Forget about prayers, I'm not kneeling down again. *ful medames*, easy to do. Coffee, but not for me now, the smell turns my stomach. For him. Tea for me, strong and bitter. Slice lemons into it, to make it sour – that tastes good. Metallic taste in my mouth, every day, only tea will relieve it. Boys to school. That's next.

"Come on boys, get up!" I have Yusuf in one arm; with the other, I put out clean clothes, strip back the bedclothes. "Come on, rise and shine, time to get up."

Open curtains, let in some light. "Come on Shahid! Get out of bed!"

Help Mahmood, pass him clean clothes. My boys are growing up. The twins look more alike than ever.

"Breakfast is almost ready." Last word as I leave the room. Change the baby. He hardly cries, just looks at me with laughing eyes. Everything is an adventure, a delight.

Toast, *ful medames*, orange juice. Check the boys' school bags, homework…

Muhammed emerges. "Do you need shopping today?"

"No, Grace is coming to pick me up, I'll go with her."

"You should stay home, in your condition."

"I don't want to be stuck indoors all day, every day. Grace is happy to take me out."

"I am telling you to stay home."

"You're going to work?"

"Yes."

"So what difference does it make? I want to do my own shopping."

"You'll do as I say. Stay home."

We're both shouting now. The boys stop eating. Huge eyes, worried faces. Frozen in their seats they look from one to the other of us.

"Eat your food!" he thunders at them. All three obey, slowly and woodenly. Tears are running down Abdullah's face; I can see he's having trouble swallowing.

"Come on now, boys," I say, soothing, coaxing. "Let's finish breakfast."

"Stop spoiling them!" Muhammed yells at me. Take a breath, Amanda, stay in control.

"Muhammed, they need a good breakfast before school, and none of them can eat properly with you yelling and shouting."

Slap! I wasn't expecting it, but the bulk of my belly acts like a counterweight, keeping me in my chair.

"Mama!" Abdullah is out of his seat, leaping to my defence.

"No!" I garble, through a face suddenly numb. Blood in my mouth, iron tang, nausea.

"No, I'm fine," I say, blotting my lips on a tea-towel.

"Sit down!" Muhammed orders. I try not to flinch. He comes close behind me, breathing heavily. Please, not in front of the boys. I close my eyes. Please, no.

Electric tension, waiting, when will the blow fall?

"Hurry up," Muhammed says, leaving abruptly. I stand, and start clearing the dishes. There is a ringing in my ears. My jaw aches, but the blow is not as hard as it could have been. My neck aches too, from the recoil.

Clean up, clean up, start the dishes, start the laundry.

"Mama?" Mahmood is behind me.

"Are you ready for school?"

"Mama, are you ok?"

"Yes, my love, I'm fine."

"You shouldn't make Baba so angry."

"I know."

"Why does he hit you?"

"Because…" what can I say to him. I can't say "because it's in the Qu'ran" because I don't really believe that Allah, or the Prophet, would truly sanction such violence by a man against his wife.

"I don't know. He doesn't mean to frighten you."

"I don't like it when you argue."

"Then I'll try not to argue with him again," I say, holding him to me briefly.

"Come on now," I herd him out to join his brothers, then pick up Yusuf and balance him on my hip.

Quiet. The noise of Muhammed's truck fades into the distance. Close the door.

Wait, Amanda, wait. Don't rush to the phone straight away. He might come back. He does come back, sometimes, to surprise me. To catch me out.

"Come on, baby boy," I take Yusuf through to the family room, and set him down on the floor cushions. "You stay there for a bit."

Quickly, quickly, clean up, wash dishes, put the laundry on, tidy the boys' rooms, make the beds. Sweep the floors, hoover the rugs, get the washing out. I wish I was at work, but Muhammed has forbidden that too, since I got so big.

Dare I ring her now? It's been an hour. He should be at work by now.

"Grace?"

"Hey, Amanda, how are you today?"

"Oh, well, not brilliant. Muhammed has forbidden me to go shopping with you later."

"Oh no, honey, that's just bad luck. Well, it can't be helped. How about you give me a list, and I'll bring it over after school."

"Thanks."

"Well, why don't you just have an easy day today, get some rest, enjoy time with that baby of yours."

"I suppose."

"I'll come by later then. Now, what's your list?"

Chicken. Vegetables. Spices. Tea. Milk. Lemons. Coffee. Oh, and a ticket out of here, please, if you can find one.

Please, Grace, find me a way out.

## Ikrām

In the dream I'm running from room to room in a great, sprawling house, opening door after door, ushering my boys in front of me. I have Yusuf in a sling on my back, and I back out of the doors, looking behind, always looking behind. They're coming, they're coming, I have to protect my boys, but I can't run fast enough, carrying the baby, and I have to shield them. There are guns, and I have to stand between my boys and the bullets. Room after room, searching, for what? A hiding place, a refuge, somewhere they won't think to look. Hide boys, hide in here, how about this cupboard, no, too flimsy, the door swings wide and won't lock, here, behind this door, or here, a tiny, shadowed loft space.

Hide now! Duck down, pull the door closed. Don't breathe, don't make a sound. Still now, please baby, be still, don't cry, don't cry, please! Be quiet, be still, don't let them find us! Don't let them find us! Don't let them hurt my babies. The door is wrenched open, light, faces, the jeering laughter of men, and gunshots, loud and hard, shattering the silence. The bullets enter my body as I shield my son, hot, fast passage through skin and flesh, pain chasing the penetration, I'm sorry, boys, I'm sorry, I couldn't save you, I couldn't keep you safe.

# *Hanīf*

The omnipresent heat, my constant companion. No rest, no surcease just this relentless reality.

"UmmShahid?"

I turn. A pain stabs through my right arm, from the elbow towards the wrist, an echo of the grip and twist of his hands in the hours before dawn. In the shadows of the women's salon, Fatima stands, beckoning me in that Saudi way, the hand turned palm down, fingers curling back towards her.

There are no men in the house tonight: they are all at a party for Tariq, Layla's husband to be. In the dining room, rugs and blankets cover the floor. Two strange older women, and a hot, sweet smell.

Layla looks…shocked. She is wearing a dress of red silk, and her hair is up in combs, and the sweet smell in the room combines with the smell of sandalwood smoke. She looks pale but her face is pinkish and shiny. The two women are painting her palms and the soles of her feet with henna. From the bowl another scent rises, hot and herbal, with an acrid tang.

"UmmShahid," Layla smiles at me, but it is a shaky smile.

"What's happened?" I ask Fatima, who looks at me in confusion. "Is Layla ok?"

"Yes, yes, it is the same for all of us, yes? The sugaring."

This is what she says. The sugaring. But I wonder if I have made a mistake – it's such an odd statement, out of context.

"I don't understand." I follow Fatima to seat myself amongst the women in the room.

"What do you not understand?" asks Asha, one of

Fatima's cousins, in English. She is young, beautifully made up, and her English is excellent.

"What do you mean by sugaring?"

I know that look, the one they exchange so often, always, as now, when I show my ignorance and my alien nature.

"Sugaring – removing the hair from the body."

"I beg your pardon?"

Asha smiles. "The women here, Umm Adam and Umm Ali, they are preparing Layla for her wedding night. They use balls of hot, melted sugar, and they roll them like this," she demonstrates with her hands, "all over the body, over the skin, and the hair is removed."

"Oh."

Both women look perplexed. "But, you have not done this?"

"Um, no, never."

They nod. "But you do not remove the hair?" Fatima asks quietly.

"Well, yes, but…"

"You shave, yes?" Asha interrupts.

"Well, yes, I do, but…do you mean the whole body?" I look at Layla, who is sitting now motionless, staring at the henna on her hands.

Fatima shrugs. Again I sense from her a deep, abiding disapproval of me, and this evidence of the untamed nature of my body only seems to reinforce her opinion.

"Do you they take all of the hair, from everywhere?" I ask Asha.

"From below the eyebrows down," she smiles.

"Oh."

"Amanda, come, sit," Asha says. The circle of women around Layla opens to accept me, to include me. Discussion of hair styles, make-up, the duties of a wife.

Khala hands me hot, spiced coffee. Fatima makes more space for me.

Layla sits, her face still reddish and slightly swollen, and I imagine mine to be the same. Each woman is giving her advice, some gem of wisdom or guidance for married life.

"And Amanda?" Asha asks. "What would you tell Layla, to prepare her to be a good wife?"

I remember what my mother told me after I married Muhammed, when I told her about the pregnancy. "Marriage is like a job, you have to work at it every day. And never go to bed angry."

"And learn how he likes his rice!" Khala adds.

"And what his favourite meal is." Fatima says.

"And what sweets he likes," adds Asha.

"And give him a *mushwak* every day!" I finish, and there is general laughter.

It's like a hen party, I suppose, with the bride the centre of attention, and her friends and family around, giving her advice, teasing her a little. But there is no alcohol, no lewd jokes, or sexual innuendo, or at least, none that I can understand.

Layla is dressed in wedding clothes that have been hung in sandalwood smoke, and she in turn is draped and hung with gold. More gold will be added, I'm told, by her husband, during the wedding itself. We arrive at the venue in the car. Veiled and covered, we hurry into the room, and at the inner door, *abaya*s and veils taken from us. The women are unveiled as peacocks in their gowns and jewels, and gold and glitter, and perfect make-up and hair styled gloriously. I feel dowdy in my plain, long cream dress and jacket. Khala bought me this outfit for the wedding, she insisted that I be well dressed. Now, I see I am barely well dressed enough. But my hair is styled, and make-up professionally done. And I am taller than most of them, which is an advantage.

A room full of women, a panoply of beauty and style, and noise and conversation. At the table with some of the family, I wonder where Layla is. Coffee is served, and there are little bowls of Arabic sweets on every table. I feel sick and nervous, and I don't know why. I sip coffee, and wish it was tea. I miss the children, because then I could distract myself from my own thoughts. The hum of conversation is like a rising tide.

And then silence.

The bride enters. She is glorious in her dress, in her gold, her shy eyes are radiant. She is ready, I can see she is ready. This is all that she wants.

As she slowly makes her way across the room, the admiration of the women is all hers.

And she stops, and her friends rush to give her gifts, and more drinks are served, and finger foods. And music begins, music on the drums that they play here, and the women start to dance. Around the room sit the old women, the grandmothers, with their black headscarves firmly in place, holding court, and the tides of women and girls rise and break around them, and the eddies draw the multicoloured waves back towards the dancefloor, and the bride on her seat, and it's almost time. Veiled again, Layla is taken away to be married, and the women dance, and I dance as well, with Fatima and Asha and Gadria, and I watch the tides swirling around Khala, and I think, this, this is how it should have been for me, this is what she wanted for me. Khala's eyes meet mine, briefly, and in that one, briefest of instants, we understand each other.

This is a woman's blessing, this sacred union. This means a woman is valued, protected, cherished by the family and

258

by the tribe. The protection extends to her children, and she need never be alone or afraid again. This is the story they tell about marriage, in every word and gesture, every look, says that her place is here, and she is safe.

Like every story I've read about women, it's only half the truth.

Jane kept odd hours, out doing one thing or another, volunteering at a women's refuge, working part time at a bookshop, and drinking in bars and clubs. One night she persuaded me to go with her to her feminist book group. We had both read *Oranges are not the Only Fruit*, which was the focus of that week's discussion. She said it would be good for me to "meet some real women." I had had a lean week that week – the electric and gas bills had come due and I had only a few pounds left for shopping. There would be free food at the book group, so I went with her.

At the end of the evening, Jane ended up in a heated conversation with another woman about some banned book they were trying to get from America, and I left to walk home alone. It was late, one of those heavy, cold December evenings when the clouds are low and menacing, orange in the upglow from the street lamps. The broken paving slabs were treacherous, and I stumbled even though I hadn't been drinking. I remember the taste of salty crisps in my mouth, and the smell from an Indian takeaway, and noise from the busier street behind me. The man who attacked me was as tall as me, but broader, smelling of beer and sweat, and he had a fat, pasty face covered in stubble. It was the stubble that hurt when he tried to kiss me. I fought him, I screamed at him, but he forced me into a dark garden and raped me. It hurt, but not as much as the hand that held me down or the bump on my head from hitting the ground. When he was done he ran away.

Muhammed found me as I staggered home, my skirt torn and dirty, dirt in my hair. He helped me home. I didn't tell anyone what had happened. I stayed in my room for three weeks, not coming out, not going to classes, just hiding. Every time I tried to go out I saw men, men, men, bigger and heavier than me, just waiting to hurt me.

Four months later I delivered a tiny, dead baby on a tide of pain and nausea. I hadn't even realised I was pregnant. I mourned for it, the poor little thing, but I told no one. There was nothing to tell.

# *Zurrīyat*

Day and night and day again, prayers and cooking and washing, ironing, shopping, inside, outside, the sun like a fire on my head, the air dry, wet season, dry season, and dust blowing in from the open doors. Boys running in and out, my boys, big dark eyes with lengthening limbs, wanting this, wanting that, new toys, new clothes, can I go to my friend's house, can we visit Khala, when is Baba coming home, when is dinner Mama? Bruises and bumps and torn clothes, and time to clean up now, we're going to visit Fatima, going to visit Abdullah, going to visit…

Streets at night and by day, in and out of shaded rooms, hot tea, sweet coffee, spiced food, my boys, my boys, homework and school and home again, and the never ending round of dishes and cooking and clearing up and wondering, where is Muhammed? And in the dark at night, the blows that fall like rain, no tears now, I hardly feel the pain. Pain is all bundled up now into one great cocooned ball, deep inside me.

Babies come, babies go, my babies grow, other babies on my lap, smile, yes, so beautiful, so good, congratulations. And the fleshy belly growing again, and out come the maternity clothes again, a great white moon waxing to full, and the hospital again, but she's born in the corridor on the way to the maternity ward, a delicate scrap of a girl child with a dusting of dark hair and the biggest, darkest eyes of any of them. She cries before she's fully born, calling out to me before her limbs have left my body, and I pull her up and onto my chest, and stroke her face, and thank her for being born, and I'm crying, my baby, my baby, my little one, I didn't care, I thought I didn't care, I thought it wouldn't matter, but it does, it does, and I love her, already,

261

far too much. Aisha, they've called her, but in my mind I give her another name, a name that means love and safety, a name for the woman she ought to be.

*Grace.*

# *Wahyun*

"I have to go." I stand in Grace's lounge, unable to believe I'm finally saying this aloud.

"What?" Grace looks around. "But you've only just got here." Then she sees my eyes. "Good God, Amanda, what has happened?"

I know what I look like. My eyes are burned holes in my head, my face is pale, and I'm shaking, just a tremor, but it runs through my whole body.

"Sit down, love, sit down." I can't move. She stands and takes hold of me, moving me bodily to the sofa. "Sit. Let me get you a drink."

I take the glass, heavy in my hand, and then remember that for Americans, a "drink" is a shot of something strong. "Shit!" I gasp, after knocking it back. It burns. It stings. I can feel it. Through the numbness that has possessed me, I can feel it.

"What happened, honey?" she says softly. My cheeks are burning from the rush of alcohol hitting my empty stomach.

"I…I…" I can't say it. I can't. But I have to. I need her help, and more. I'll need more than one person to help me now.

"I need your help. I need to get myself and the children out of the country."

"What happened?"

My brain returns to it, again, the kitchen, the shadows around the kitchen table, darkness outside and my children, terrified, seated obediently around the table. Their father, drunk, slurring his words, spinning the barrel of the revolver, and laughing. Pointing the gun at Mahmood's head, and pulling the trigger, and laughing. And the boys, frozen in their seats, looking at him in horror, but not daring to move, not knowing what Baba might do next. The world falling away from me, the sky falling in, everything stopping, no, no, no, not my children, not my boys, not now, not after all that I have been through, please Allah, don't let me lose my children!

Her hand to her mouth, Grace reacts as I expected her to. But there are tears in her eyes. *Don't cry now, Grace. Don't cry.* I can't. I must not. I have too much to do.

"Where's the baby?" She says then, looking around.

"I left her with Khala for the afternoon. I couldn't cope. I haven't been able to sleep for two days now. I had my father-in-law drop me off."

"Oh, Amanda!" She puts her arms around me. I wish I could feel this like I felt the hit of bourbon. But the numbness persists.

"Look, I have to get us out of here. As soon as possible. I just don't know how."

"Ok, ok, let me think. We can do this. You just need a plausible excuse."

"Right."

"So, so…" I can almost hear her mind turning over. "What are we going to need?"

"Money."

"Money, ok. So, that's the first thing. Let's work on that. I'll check the price of flights. Then you're going to need money the other end, too. How much do you think?"

"Grace, it's been eight years. I don't know how much things cost."

"Ok, so whatever we come up with, let's double it."

"We'll need rent, money for clothes, for food, bills, for travel."

"I'd say at least two thousand pounds."

"Better make that four, then." She sits back and regards me frankly. "I don't know how…"

"I'm going back to work as soon as I've got Aisha onto the bottle. Talk to Nura for me?"

"Oh, yes, she'll take you back."

"I'll save as much from that as I can…then…well, I'll skim off what I can from the housekeeping."

"Right, I'll look into flights."

"Don't tell anyone else, yet. Let's get things moving first."

"Ok. But our friends, they will want to help too."

"I know."

The room spins, suddenly. A tight band holding me together has relaxed.

"Grace…!"

"Ok, Amanda, I've got you. Lie down here, that's right, just put your feet up. You can sleep now, you can rest."

"But the children…"

"I'll wake you in time, don't worry. Sleep now."

My head is in her lap, her cool fingers stroking my brow. Then I am falling, flying, swooping away into blackness.

"How much so far?" Grace asks, bouncing Aisha on her knee. Aisha looks at her with huge, chocolate brown eyes. She is beautiful, my daughter.

"About three thousand Riyals," I say quietly, glancing at the door.

"A good start then."

"Yes."

"And the plans?"

"Danya's cousin lives in England. She says he can find us a place to stay."

"Ok."

A noise outside the door, we both look up.

"Is she feeding well still?" Grace says loudly. It could be one of the boys, or Muhammed, or one of his family.

"Yes, very well," I stand, open the door, look out into the hall. No one.

"So I have a message from the school. Nura says come back to work when you're ready."

"Great, I'll call her soon. I think I could come back next week. I need to start earning again."

"It will go quicker if you do."


"What is this?"

I spin around at the sound of Muhammed's voice, fear taking my breath. At the look on his face, the washing basket I am carrying slips from my nerveless fingers. He is clutching the brown envelope full of money.

"What is this?" he says again, brandishing the money. "Why are you hiding money from me?"

I can't think of an answer. I close my eyes. When I open them, he is right there, his face almost touching mine.

"It's to…buy presents for the children," I gabble as he grabs me and shakes me.

"Why?"

"I'm working now, I wanted to save some money. The twins are growing so fast, I thought of getting them new bikes, maybe, or…" My excuses sound feeble in my own ears.

He slaps me. "Never lie to me. Never! You cannot hide from me. You cannot hide anything! Whatever secrets you have, I will find them out!"

Weakness claims my legs, as he continues to shake me, shake my whole body, like a rag, a piece of cloth. "I will find out!" he growls into my face. He lets go, and I stagger against the kitchen counter. "I am watching you. Every day, all the time, remember, I am watching."

He leaves. He has the envelope. All the money. It's gone. I'll have to start again.

It was late, a darkening night hugged close around the house. I heard the front door open and close. I stretched tired muscles, and stacked the books neatly beside the single bed. It was a small bed, too small for my long legs – my feet hung over the edge when I lay fully stretched. Instead I curled up under the duvet, missing the accustomed bulk of blankets. As a child their weight and density were the epitome of comfort and security. Night time warmth generated from winter shivers. Cold feet on cold linoleum, the rasp of wool and flannelette.

Sleep hovered around me, but my feet were cold, and the bed was narrow and I couldn't get comfortable. In my constant state of isolation, I spent hours in this bed, hiding from the world. Muhammed occasionally came to talk to me, Jane would pop in with a cup of tea, but otherwise I remained cocooned, hidden, as if I could lie in some state of suspended animation until the world turned and changed and became safe for me again.

The noise of the door opening was a gentle "snick". I looked over the edge of the quilt to see Muhammed framed in the doorway, the light from the landing throwing his face into shadow. He was tall, but not broad – slender, rather.

"What's the matter?"

He advanced, closed the door behind him, and was on me in an instant. A surprising weight, and his breath close to mine, his lips on mine, his mouth pressing so hard, forcing my lips apart. I smelled alcohol and cigarettes and garlic, and started to gag. He continued, crushing my lips with his, breathing into my mouth.

"No!" I struggled, writhing under the grip of his arms on

mine, but he held tighter, pressing his body against me, pinning me to the bed. Turning my head to the side broke the contact, but his hands were on me, pulling at the T-shirt and boxers I wore to bed, fingers tearing at my skin.

"Stop! Muhammed, stop!" I shouted as soon as I could draw a breath. Then his hand was over my mouth, smelling of fresh soap.

"This is what you want," he said to me, his teeth gritted with the effort of restraining my flailing arms and legs.

At once, the fight went out of me. My face turned to the wall, I felt him lift my T-shirt, maul my breasts, feel teeth on my skin, and the hot hardness of his erection against my stomach. I didn't want him to do this. But I couldn't stop him. His hand stayed on my mouth. His other hand forced open my legs. There was no fight in me now. His fingers again, painful, and then he entered me. I sensed every millimetre of his length as he penetrated me, as he thrust against my dryness, as his hipbones ground into mine. I felt the sweaty length of his torso, his breath on my face, the painful grip of his fingers on my tender jaw.

Then his hands released me, as he concentrated on the act.

*Stop*, I said into my mind. No sound left my mouth. *Stop. Please, stop.* But why would he stop? I had not stopped him. I had not said clearly enough, I do not want you. I didn't break the silence, the silence of assent.

He ejaculated with a slight groan. The sign of his climax was the sudden, spreading coolness inside me. Unlike the last time, when I was numb with fear, this time I was aware of every sensation. The fullness of his penis waned.

"You have tempted me since I first saw you," he whispered in my ear, breathing heavily. "I have not been able to resist you. I could see you wanted me by the way you looked at me."

No, I wanted to say, no, I didn't want you, not like this. This is not me. This has nothing to do with me.

"You are so attractive to me, Amanda. I have wanted you so much." He smiled as he levered himself off my body. Cold air hit my skin. I wanted to move, to cover myself. My body remained unresponsive. After the flood of sensation came the numbness. The door closed behind him.

No sleep came. Unmoved, I could not escape what had just happened. My mind replayed every second, over and over. My body responded, warming and chilling with each repetition. His fingers were on me still, bruising, tearing, pinching. His teeth were at my breast, his penis pierced my body and claimed it. This was what my body was made for. This was what a woman was for. A stickiness oozed from my vagina, pooled on the sheet, turned cold beneath me.

And then, as the sleepless night faded into dawn, I felt it, like the ringing of a high-pitched, distant bell. They say some women know immediately, but I never believed that. Until then. Somewhere, deep inside me, the single-minded sperm of a single-minded man met the submissive, receptive egg, which also allowed itself to be penetrated. That is, after all, the purpose of this one cell, its sole purpose. The act of violation was repeated microscopically inside me, with consequences that would repeat themselves forever.

# Bayān

Grace shakes her head at me. "Where had you hidden it?"

"In the twins' room, under the dresser. I have no idea how he found it."

"He must have suspected something. He must have been looking for it."

"I suppose so. But how... Oh, I don't know, Grace, I don't know if I can start again. And where will I hide the money?"

"I'll help. We'll all help."

"Thank you."

"Amanda, we have to do this. I'm afraid for you, afraid how far he'll go. Afraid that one day he just won't stop."

Silence. What can I say? Some part of me is warmed by these words, and my mind registers her concern. But I can't let myself feel what I should feel, or I would be too afraid to even get out of bed in the morning.

Don't acknowledge the fear. Put it aside. Don't look at Grace, don't let her see how you feel.

Grace's house, her sitting room, all pale golds and creams, white rugs. She's redecorated. It's very stylish. The scent of cinnamon and coffee, the subtle perfume that she wears, the muted light – sensory overload. This is real.

"Don't lose hope," she says to me.

The door bell rings. "That will be Sheena." Grace waits for the maid to answer the door. Then Sheena enters, her bare feet sinking into the thick rug, a plump, short woman shedding a shimmering silk *abaya* to reveal a pale blue blouse and skin tight black jeans. The gold at her throat and wrists catches the sunlight. Her hips roll as she crosses the room.

"Sheena, you remember Amanda?"

"Yes," Sheena answers in almost perfect English. "It's good to see you again."

"I'll see to more coffee," Grace smiles.

"No dates, thank you," Sheena replies to Grace's query.

"Perhaps something savoury, or some biscuits,"

"Yes, that would be nice."

"Oh, I forgot, Sheena, I got some American peanut butter."

Sheena's face lights up. "I went to university in America," she confides to me. "I loved the food, and I was hooked on peanut butter! Grace keeps me supplied now I'm home."

"What did you study?"

"Oh, Arts. I was there five years, got a BA and then an MFA. California. Berkeley. I did enjoy it. I spent a year in the UK too, working on community arts projects."

"But you came back."

"Yes, of course, my family are all here. And my husband. Though, compared to other women, I'm lucky, because he was happy for me to go.

"You were married before you went?"

"Oh, yes, and he knew all along that I planned to go away, he was happy with it. It meant we wouldn't start a family till later, and he was happier with that."

"Do you work now?" I accept a coffee from the maid. Grace reappears with a small bag, heavy with its contents, and hands it to Sheena. She smiles, like a child given a present.

"Now? Oh, I write things for women's magazines – I studied fashion journalism for a while, and so I do a little here and there. I'd like to write more radical stuff but this is the best I can do for the moment."

The maid retreats. Grace settles herself, a darker shadow in dark cream linen, against the coffee-cream sofa. "Now, Amanda, I've told Sheena a little bit about your situation."

Sheena smiles, just a small smile. "Don't worry," she touches my hand lightly. Her fingertips are warm. "It's a terrible situation really, and in any other country, we could take action quickly. If this were America, I'd have you in a women's refuge as fast as you could say restraining order."

"Sheena worked as a volunteer at a women's shelter," Grace explains. "She understands…"

"Yes," Sheena interrupts, "but we don't have any such luxuries here. The only way that I can see is to simply get you and the children out, either back to the UK, or to the USA, where you can get the help you need. I have some contacts in the US, but getting a visa will be more complicated than just going home to the UK. But in the US, you could more easily disappear."

"Muhammed's family, some of them live in the US." I muse. "So there aren't any women's shelters here?" Stupid question, really.

"You won't find a need for them. This kind of thing is usually dealt with within families. And you know, your husband is unusual. I'm not saying it doesn't happen here, but women usually support each other." She looks at Grace.

"And we can support you, now. But usually, if all else fails, a woman can go back to her mother's home. But you can't do that."

"And even if one of us took you in," Grace adds, "the law would support Muhammed's case. Or that of his brother. We couldn't hide you forever. And he would have the right to his children."

"So," Sheena sets down her coffee cup. "The best thing we can do is help keep you and the children safe until you've saved up enough to get out."

"He found the money." I have to say it.

"Oh. All of it?"

"Yes."

"You kept it all in one place?"

"Sheena!" Grace flashes her a look.

"Sorry, sorry, right, well, it's a setback, but it's not the end of the world. We just have to think again."

She sits, staring into the distance. I notice the subtle highlights in her hair, the texture of it, thick and glossy, the care with which it has been cut and styled.

"Ok, this is what we'll do. Grace will keep some money for you, as will I. And some of our other friends, ones we can trust. I know some women who will want to help you."

"How will we stay in contact?" Grace asks. "We can't use the phones."

"Muhammed works for the phone company," I explain. "He has this…thing, like a big thick phone in a huge block." I show the size with my hands. "It's used to listen in… It's a government thing, they have people who listen… but he brought one home to show me, and he's kept it. So I know that he's listening and checking up on me."

"We'll use a code," Sheena says. She is so decisive, so dynamic. "You'll be, oh, auntie's present. That's it! And the money will be… rice! We'll refer to it as rice. A thousand riyals will be a bag of rice."

"Ok."

Fatigue, a blanket of fatigue, on the tide of pain that rises and ebbs, hour by hour. I want to feel this, the kindness of women, the proffered strength. If I am to feel anything, I would feel the warmth that this represents. But the pain obliterates everything else for a while. I want to sleep. I want to lie down here, on Grace's beautiful sofa, put my head in her lap, and sleep. Sleep. But maybe it's not a good idea. If I sleep, will I ever want to wake up?

Jane stopped talking to me when I told her I was going to marry Muhammed. She moved in with one of her women friends before the wedding, before I had a chance to explain. Not that I could. I counted the weeks of the pregnancy and prayed that this baby would live, that I would have a chance to do it right. I looked on Muhammed with new eyes. He had saved me. When he said it was meant to be, somehow, it seemed right, that there was some purpose in life, and he had come into mine to fulfil it.

On the day of the wedding Jane came into my room while I was getting dressed. For a moment I thought things would be ok. She said nothing, but helped me brush my hair and put it up.

"Thanks." I looked at myself in the mirror, too tall still, too gangling, awkward and lean. I looked nothing like a bride. The dress was a simple, black one that hugged my shape, but my breasts were too small to fill the bodice properly and it hung from my shoulders loosely.

Jane watched me as I put on earrings. Then she spoke.

"Amanda, don't do it."

"What?" I turned to face her.

"I know you don't want to hear this, but I'm your friend, and I can't let you go through with this."

"Can't let me? Jane, it's up to me. I turned eighteen three weeks ago. I make the decisions."

"Amanda, please. I know you are pregnant, and that's why you're doing this, but there are other options. You don't know him, not really. You haven't told your parents, you've just gone ahead and done this. You don't need to. You can live with him for a while, see how things go. Or not, really, you don't have to go with him. *I* can help you bring the baby up, if you want, we could find a place. You don't have to do it. You don't even have to have the baby if you don't want to."

"Don't start, Jane, with all that women's right to choose stuff. I know what I want. *This* is what I want, for me, for the baby, ok?"

She seized my shoulders and shook me, only a little, but I shoved her away. "Don't! Just don't! You don't know what's best for me, Jane, so don't pretend you do."

"Oh Amanda... I've known Muhammed longer than you have. He's a man, and he's from another culture, and you're about to dive into all of that and you haven't got a bloody clue what you're letting yourself in for."

I took a breath, let it out, and picked up my bag. "Jane, I know you care about me, but this is my choice. What do I have to do to convince you?"

"You're giving up everything, your life, your home, your future..."

"Jane! This baby is my life, and Muhammed is going to give us a home and a future."

"You don't love him."

"I don't hate him. He's good to me. He's kind and tender and he wants to take care of me."

"But you're giving up everything..."

"I don't see it like that. What am I giving up? A levels? A chance to get into uni? For what? I don't have a future now, I'm pregnant. And I can't get rid of it, I just can't. So I'm going to marry Muhammed and get away from this place, and live a real life, instead of existing on pipe dreams."

"You're making a mistake."

"Well, I don't see it that way."

"I won't stick around and watch this"

And then she was gone.

Food, washing, ironing. School and home, waking and sleeping, prayers and shopping and home. The family for a meal.

"Have you enough lemons?" Khala asks as I make the *kabsa*.

"Yes," I say. Her brusqueness is solicitude, I know now. She is proud of me. She smiles at me often. I have given her five grandchildren, and while Muhammed goes off the rails, the children are well looked after. "And three chickens."

My rooms are filled with people. Abdullah is visiting from America. His wife Jahira is here, and their five children. Jahira is with the youngest three in the family room, and the oldest two boys are with the men.

The baby is in a sling on my hip, her bright eyes watching everything that I do. The chicken is cooking, a rich, meaty, sweetly spiced smell. Khala manages the coffee and dates, Gadria chops the salad. We move around each other, with each other, the dance well practiced now, more of a ritual than a domestic act, each contributing to the final product.

"Here." I pass Gadria the peppers. In return, she passes me the salt and the spices that I ground earlier in the mortar. I season the chicken again, chop onion for the soup. Khala has already made the dumplings. All is in order.

Times like this, I feel like I could stay. Maybe I should stay. Maybe Muhammed will change, or grow tired of hitting me. The boys are growing up and soon they will be old enough to stand up to him. Abdullah and Shahid are already almost five feet tall, and they're barely ten.

But how can I stay? Muhammed is on best behaviour while his family are here, but later, when they are gone, when the children are worn out, I wonder what he will do to me. I daren't take my eyes off them when he is around, now. Or when he's not. I don't even know where he keeps his guns – what if one of the boys finds out? I should try to find them. He's doing a good job of diverting attention from his bandaged thumb, where he shot off part of his nail last week. I don't know how it happened. I daren't ask.

What if…?

My hands shake, and the knife slips, almost cutting me. I can't think that, I can't think that.

I am not enough of a martyr for that, and I couldn't do it to my children.

"Layla's baby is doing well," Khala smiles as she returns to the kitchen after serving the coffee.

"She seems very happy. Married life suits her."

Even now we can sometimes run up against it, the innate difference. Both Khala and Gadria look at me, as if to say, what else would a woman do?

"Tariq is a good man," I add, turning up the heat under the soup.

"Yes, he is," Gadria agrees. "I can't wait to get married."

"Yes, little sister, but you should enjoy being young, and free," I say.

"I'm old enough now," Gadria retorts. Watching her, I know exactly what it is she's ready for – love, passion, sex. All of it. There is only one way out in her mind. What is it like, to grow up in this world, from a girl to a woman, and have only one option for all those churning hormones and the burning, unnameable passions?

My baby girl. As if in response to the change of mental direction, she wakes and starts to cry, that delicate, mewling cry.

"She's hungry," I announce unnecessarily.

"Give her to Jahira, she'll feed her," Khala says.

"No, I'll feed her myself." My breasts ache in response.

"Keep an eye on the chicken," I tell Gadria, turning the heat down under the soup before hurrying to the sitting room. Aisha is hungry at the breast, a greedy guzzler, feeding often. She reminds me of the twins. Yusuf toddles over and claims a portion of my lap, jabbering at me. He is followed by Saadi, Jahira's second youngest, a fat little boy of two, clutching a toy dinosaur in his chubby fingers.

"No, I think we might just move there permanently." Jahira says, in her American-accented English. Layla nods, but she looks sad. I know that Jahira has switched to English for my benefit.

"So will you sell the house here?"

"I think so."

"Khala will miss the pool."

"And the satellite tv!" Layla laughs. "But we wouldn't be able to see you so often!"

"You could visit."

"That would be nice."

"And you, Amanda, if you could manage it. It would do you good, I think, to come out and see us. Have a change of scenery."

Does it show on my face then? Is it that obvious?

"I would like that. I'd like it a lot."

"I'll talk to Abdullah about it."

That means that Abdullah will talk to Muhammed. Would he ever let us go? Could we afford it? Possibilities, hope, yearning for something, for one moment of insanity I want to open the windows, throw them open, and look outside.

No, no, he would ask for my money, and I wouldn't be able to save for our escape. I can't afford to get side-tracked.

"Maybe when the little ones are older," I say, looking down at the curve of Aisha's skull, the light fuzz of hair, paler than the boys'.

"We'll plan on it!" Jahira smiles. I like my sister-in-law. She brings me paperbacks whenever she visits, knowing how much I love to read. This time, she brought a dozen from the bestseller rack at the airport. They sit in a neat pile near my chair, a feast, waiting to be devoured. But I will have to hide them from Muhammed.

"Are you going back to work when this one is weaned?" Jahira asks.

"Yes, two days a week."

"I know how you feel, work gets to be a habit."

"How about you?"

"Oh, I have maternity leave, then I'll put these ones in daycare on campus, and go back half-time for a year or two."

"They made you permanent then?" At last I understand why they are planning to stay on in America.

"Yes. Both of us are tenured now."

"Congratulations."

"Thanks." She sips her coffee. "Have you ever thought about going back to school?"

University, she means university.

"No, not really. Though I've done some courses by correspondence."

"Well, that's a start. You should think about it. I think every woman needs something in her life besides husband and children."

It's well meant but anger rises inside me. She has no idea. It's hardly an option for me, in my situation. But the thought of it...studying...fulfilling that long held dream. For a moment I think of Jane, and her plan of becoming a writer. Did she do it? I wonder sometimes what became of her. It wasn't too late for her, maybe it isn't for me.

279

Yusuf makes a face, and my knee suddenly gets warmer. A pungent aroma confirms my suspicions.

"Come on, let's get you changed," I say, looking down to find Aisha fast asleep. I lay her down on the mat and pick him up. In the bathroom, I clean him up, hardly noticing the stench. This is my reality. This is my life. To give birth to child after child until…until what? Until I can't do it any more. And then, what is there for me?

# *Fawāq*

"So, the total so far is two thousand, eight hundred and seventy pounds," Sheena says, stretching her legs and wiggling her toes. She looks gleeful.

"That's a lot." I try to be happy. Grateful. Women I don't even know have been adding to the pot, slipping Sheena a few hundred riyals here, a few there. I have been passing money to Grace. And now I'm back at work, Nura is saving a third of my pay every week. It just doesn't feel like enough.

"I just don't know how we're going to manage it," I say it aloud. I have too many fears.

"Look, let's just try."

"So we have the fares…"

"Yes, we have the fares. And enough to get us into a B&B for a few weeks. But I need more. And first, we have to get him to let us out of the Kingdom."

"Ok. I think we could start planning now. By the time we get flights organised and everything in place, you should have enough."

Sinking feeling, a lurch, not butterflies, but worse, a hot-cold spasm the entire length of my body. Can I breathe?

Is this real? Is it really going to happen?

"How soon?"

"How soon can you get the letter sent?"

"Soon. A month?"

Sheena looks at the list in her hand. "Make it sooner, if you can."

Sheena tears the list into tiny, little pieces. I look down at Aisha, sleeping deeply in my lap. She's a small child, delicate, looking more like a five month old than a great girl of eight months.

"So, this is it?"

"I guess so." Grace smiles, but she looks sad.
"Ok."

"Muhammed, I've had a letter from my father," I say, holding out the paper and envelope. He takes them, examines the postmark.

"What is it about?"

"He wants us to visit. It's his sixty-fifth birthday – he's having a huge family reunion. He really wants us to come."

He makes a noncommittal noise, and I return to the kitchen. My heart is pounding, and my hands shake. I have to make him think I don't mind, either way.

"I don't think this is a good idea," he says from the doorway, waving the letter at me. "Aisha is too young."

I hold back, refrain from telling him that she is older than the twins were when we brought them out here.

"Oh well, never mind," I carry on chopping tomatoes. Red skin splits, parts under the pressure of my knife; red juice bursts forth, pooling beneath the ruptured flesh, framing the exposed innards. "I'll write and explain. Don't worry about it. Will Gadria be coming today with your parents?"

"Yes, I think so."

He leaves the letter on the worktop. Good.

Gadria and Khala come straight to the kitchen.

"Oh, I'm glad you came," I say, and Khala immediately takes over making the coffee. "Thank you."

She stirs and pours, Gadria takes over the vegetables, and I put the cracked wheat into a big dish and add seasoning.

Gadria notices the letter on the counter. "A letter from your family?"

"From my father."

"Ah."

282

"He will be sixty-five soon. It's an important event, in my culture. All the family will visit him for a celebration."

"Family is important." Khala says, fussing with the spices.

"Yes, it is."

"So," Gadria picks up the onions and tomatoes and drops them into the frying pan, "will you go to visit him?"

"Oh, no, Muhammed says we can't. But that's ok, it's a long journey."

"You should go," Khala says. She pours the coffee into the final pot, sets up the tray, and whisks out of the room. I turn the chicken pieces over in the pan and Gadria talks about her wedding.

"We should go to your father's party." Muhammed says.

I pause in the act of setting out the breakfast. "Oh."

"Yes. Family is important. Khala says she will help with the fares."

"That's nice of her. As long as you're sure."

"Yes, we should go."

How much pressure did his mother put on him? All these years and I've finally figured out how to pull his strings. Now, when it's almost too late.

"I shall book the tickets, then," Muhammed says.

"Good, I'm sure Dad will be pleased. And pleased to see you again, as well."

Grunt.

It is enough. My mind races, and I bend low over the dough in my hands to hide my expression.

If he's coming too, that's plan B.

"So, plan B then!" Sheena nods, tight lipped.

Grace nods too. "I have the numbers for you." She hands me a slip of paper.

"I can't take this, what if he finds it?"

"I've disguised the numbers with family names, see?"

"But he might ring them. And then he'd know we'd gone to Women's Aid. It's too risky. I'll...I'll memorise them."

"Once you're there, you ring the number as soon as you can, and explain. They'll help you to get away."

"I can't believe this is happening."

Grace takes me aside as Sheena bustles off to the bathroom. "Are you sure about this?" she asks in a low voice.

"Yes. Very sure."

"There are so many things that could go wrong."

"Don't you think I know that? I can hardly eat or sleep these days, thinking about what might happen. But I have to take the chance."

"Amanda... What if...oh, I don't know, what if they won't take you to the shelter with all of the children? Sheena said that can sometimes happen."

"Then I'll find another way."

It hurts to see the love in her eyes. I can't let myself feel anything for her now. I can't let myself feel anything that might hold me back.

"Grace, it will work out. It has to. And I'll get word to you, somehow, to let you know I'm ok."

"I will miss you," her voice is so small, I can barely hear her. "You're the best friend I ever had."

"I'll miss you too." Time stops. Her arms around me. I can have this one moment, I can allow myself this. I can savour her sweet scent, the soft, petal-fragile skin of her face. "But I have no future here." And I can't be like you, and let my daughter grow up thinking that there is only one path open to her. I can't.

"Can you change some money for the trip, Muhammed?"

"No, not yet. I'll do it at the airport."

"The rates are higher at the airport. Can't you do it at the bank here?"

"Stop bothering me, woman. I'll do it at the airport."

"I just want to get everything ready for our trip, and the money…"

Slap! "Shut your mouth. Or we won't go."

"Ok, you hold hands, and Yusuf, you hold on to the pushchair. Now, stay close."

I don't really need to warn them. The airport is a crush.

"That's right, this way." I guide my gaggle of children after their father. No time for a last look at the blinding white of the sky, the sandy coloured buildings. No time to regret.

"What's taking so long?" I ask Muhammed.

"They are checking the passports."

"I know, but why is it taking so long?" The children are fractious. My heart is pounding, and I'm starting to feel breathless.

"Keep quiet, woman!"

"I'm sorry. It's the stress, you know, managing the children."

He goes to the desk. Voices are raised. When he returns, he thrusts the passports at me. "Come!"

He is heading back towards the entrance. I jog to catch up, the children running beside me, the pushchair bouncing.

"What's going on?" Shahid demands of his father.

"We're not going."

"Why?" I blurt out. Stupid. He slaps me, and I feel my teeth cut my lip. Taste of blood in my mouth.

"Shut up. Get the children to the car."

285

Deep night darkens the shadows behind the closed doors of the apartment.

"I should never have married a Western woman."

Slap.

"This is all your fault."

Slap.

"You have shamed me. Nothing has been right since I brought you here."

Slap.

Don't think, don't think, don't think about what he is doing to me now, what his hands and his fist are doing, the stretching and the pain, and the violence. Don't think about what he might be using, now, instead of his own body.

Don't cry out.

Don't wake the children.

The pain is suddenly awful. I feel a gush of blood. Something snaps inside me, like an overstretched elastic band. He doesn't stop. Then he is on top of me, holding me down, fucking me. Something is broken inside me, and it hurts.

Blood, always blood, more and more.

Let go now, let go. Let me go.

# *Halīm*

"Amanda."

"Amanda."

"Amanda, wake up! Wake up now!"

I can't open my eyes. They are glued together.

"Wake up, Amanda, please."

"Grace?"

"Oh, thank Allah," she says, her voice thick. Grace is crying? She shouldn't be crying. I open my eyes. Grace is veiled, but tears leak from her eyes, which are red-rimmed and bloodshot.

"Oh God, I thought he'd killed you!" she sobs. "Can you hear me? Say something."

"Grace. What…?"

"You're in the hospital. Women's surgical ward. They… You had an operation."

"What?"

"It was Abdullah. You should be proud of that boy. He found you lying in a pool of blood. He couldn't wake you, so he rang his grandmother, who called an ambulance. Then he rang me."

"What…" My throat is sore, my voice hoarse. "What… operation?"

"A vaginal repair," says another voice. I swivel my heavy head. A woman in a white doctor's coat over full *burqa*. "Good to see you awake." Her English is soft, she sounds Irish.

"What happened?"

"We repaired multiple deep lacerations to the vagina and introitus, and one recto-vaginal tear. We removed a foreign object from the vagina. You had a general anaesthetic. You've also had three units of blood. You are being given

287

intravenous antibiotics to prevent infection. How's the pain?"

"Ok."

"Ring for a nurse when you need more pain relief," she draws closer to me. "Have you been sexually assaulted?" She murmurs.

"It was my husband."

Silence.

"I'm sorry."


"How are you?"

"Why is it you always end up needing to ask me that?" I gesture to Grace to take a seat. Khala appears with coffee and dates.

"Thank you," Grace says. Her voice is like ice. Then she turns her back on her.

I know Grace is angry. I would be too in her position, angry at my mother-in-law for letting this happen.

"She doesn't know," I tell Grace when Khala leaves the room. "He told them it was another miscarriage."

"What…? But you're going to tell them, right?"

"No." I almost smile at her look of outrage. "What good would it do? His brother has already threatened to take my children away. This would make things worse."

"But…"

"I'm healing fast. And apparently he hasn't damaged my womb. I can still have children."

## Qalb Salīm

"How much more do you need?"

"Oh Sheena, it's hopeless. He won't let us go."

"You said he'd sorted the legal thing."

"Yes, he paid the fine. I'd need another thousand, at least. More like two."

"We'll find the money."

"It's impossible."

"Nothing's impossible. We have to try again."

Hot and humid, air thick as soup in my lungs, the rainy season must be near

"How much?"

"A little over two thousand."

"Grace, you shouldn't have." I stand at the edge of the park, shrouded, watching the children playing.

"Yes, I should. I don't want to lose you, Amanda. I'll miss you, miss you terribly, but I can be content knowing you're alive, somewhere in the world. Alive and unhurt." She presses the package into my hand.

"So, what's the occasion this time?" she asks.

"My sister's wedding."

"That's handy."

"It's still four months away. Anything could go wrong."

"We have to make sure it doesn't."

I am dreaming. I know I am dreaming. I stand in the desert, after the rains. It is dark, with a full moon riding high over rocky hills and dunes. The sand is still warm on my feet, though the air about me is cool, almost cold. Or like the memory of cold. Flowers bloom around me, all monotone shades. Leached of colour, the desert is a lunar landscape, barren save for these pale imitations of life.

I know that there is something here I need to find. Somewhere under the sand. I have been searching for it all my life, and here in the dead desert, I must find it, now, or be forever wanting.

Running, I am running, barefoot over shifting shadowed sands, reaching out for something beyond reach. I crest one high dune after another, scrambling down steep inclines, over stones and sand, and around me the shadows deepen.

Darkness and shadows and the leftover heat of the day. Who is following? Who is coming? I must run, I must find what I seek and I must find it now, now, now, now, before they catch me.

Wake up, Amanda.

Aisha lets out small, mewling cries, telling me she wants feeding. "A daughter!" Khala said to me when she saw her, and there was a peculiar kind of pride, or pleasure, in her voice.

*Come, my little one. Let's start the day together.* Already the sun is bright outside, and when I open the curtains in the sitting room, I blink at the light.

It's a long time since I wanted to see out.

"Amanda." Muhammed stands in the doorway. "I need clean clothes."

"On the airer, in the kitchen. I ironed them last night." Piles and piles of white, cream and grey, one thobe after another, his and the twins. I should have dreamed of ghosts, or snow, not deserts and shadows.

No time to sit and commune with the baby. My bones ache as I stand in the kitchen, my legs ache, as if I had been running all night.

The *kabsa* from yesterday will be good for lunch. Where is Shahid's schoolbag? Sweet, sugary bread, toast, cereal, set the table. Breakfast is the meal most like home.

Coffee, standing at the sink like every morning, washing up, the boys eating, Aisha in her high chair.

"Muhammed?"

He looks at me. The opaque brown-black of his eyes, unfathomable. Is now a good time? Is any time a good time?

"My sister is getting married again."

"Mm."

Well, it's a response. "Yes, in May. And she's invited us, all of us, to the wedding."

"Mm."

"Well, I thought I'd let you know. She'd like us to go, and it would be good for the children. Aisha will be almost two by then, and…"

"I'll think about it. Maybe it would be possible."

"Thank you."

The practiced blank face, yes, I can wear this face for as long as I have to.

"What if he says no again?" I say to Grace. She stretches her legs and crosses her ankles. The staff room is quiet.

"Then we try again, and again. What about enlisting your father's help?"

"I don't want him to know."

"Amanda, why do you have to take care of everyone?"

"I don't know."

"When are you going to take care of yourself?"

Noon prayers are over, and the streets are filling again. The car stops outside, and I open the door swiftly.

"Here's half." I hand Sheena the money.

"That's great. I'll change what I've got sometime this week."

"How?"

"Kifah's husband works at the airport. And he gets a good exchange rate. Her cousin is going to the UK soon. Kifah will say it's for her."

"But…" There are too many things that could go wrong.

"Her cousin is in on our secret too. Try not to worry. You're not the first woman we've tried to help."

"Does it always work out?"

She doesn't answer me. I'm scared. Fear tastes like blood and vomit and petrol. Fear and the taste of it, every day. Fear of being found out.

Fear of what will happen if…


"Fatima, this is a surprise!" I step aside to let my sister-in-law in. "Where are the children?"

"With my mother."

"Oh." Why has she come alone, without the usual family entourage?

"Coffee?"

"Yes please." She follows me to the kitchen. As she removes her headscarf, I see that she has had highlights put into her long, glossy hair. "Your hair looks nice."

"Thank you."

Coffee made, no dates, thank you, we sit in the sitting room.

"The boys are at school." She nods. "Yusuf is upstairs, having a nap with his sister. He loves to sleep."

She nods again. "Amanda, I've come because I feel that someone should speak to you."

"Go on."

"My brothers, and my father, have been talking about

Muhammed." She looks at me. Of course, I must know what she is talking about.

"You need to explain." Someone needs to say it out loud.

"His behaviour. His drinking. He is taking drugs too, yes?"

"I think so."

"Surely you would know?"

"How?" I hear myself say. "How, exactly? He doesn't exactly walk in and say, oh, by the way, I've done a few lines of coke today, on top of the booze! What he does with his time is his business – he's made that very clear to me. And I don't ask questions."

"Well, maybe you should."

"I beg your pardon?"

"We are all shocked by his behaviour, the way he seems to miss so much work, and, well, the stories, and the arrests… Perhaps things are different in Britain, but here, well, when a man is…womanising and drinking, people start asking questions about his home life."

I'm standing, suddenly, unaware of how I got here. "You think it's me? Me? My fault?"

"Please, don't shout, you'll wake the children."

"Fatima, after all this time, do you really think he is the way he is because I encourage him?"

"No, no, nothing like that. But, you didn't grow up here, and you're a good mother, but being a good wife is probably different for you…"

"So you think I'm not being a proper wife." For once, as I raise my head and look at her, I let the mask slip, let her see me, really see me.

She looks aghast, because at last the façade has cracked, dissolved, and even she, proud and oh so sure, can see the anguish.

"In what way, exactly? Do I feed and clothe his children, keep a clean house, make food, behave with proper deference, wear modest clothes?"

She nods, tried to speak, but the flow has become a rushing wave, picking up speed and inexorable momentum.

"Do I visit his family, make sure my children spend time with their uncles and cousins, eat with the women and not complain?"

She nods again.

"And now you suggest that he is the way he is because I am not a proper wife? Perhaps you are thinking of the things that go on between a husband and his wife, behind closed doors?" My voice cracks on the last words, and I take a breath.

"I...I..." I am beating my fist on my chest. "I have done everything, everything! Everything he has asked of me, I've done it. No matter what it is, no matter how hard, or... degrading, I've done it."

"Maybe...with you working..."

"If I didn't work there would be no money to feed the children some weeks" I spit at her.

"But...Amanda, please, I am talking to you as a woman, as your sister..."

"Do you mean sex?" I laugh. "Oh, yes, of course, that's it." My fingers are on the veil ripping it from my head, and then on the buttons of my blouse, until it, too, drops to the floor. She gasps.

I know what she sees. Finger marks on my neck, bruises on my ribs, and the bitemarks on my right breast.

"I never say no to him." My voice is quieter now. "I never say no, Fatima. Even when he is too drunk to...even then, I do what has to be done. And this is what he does to me in return."

"Why…?"

"I don't know. Maybe because he doesn't know how to love a woman. Maybe because he hates his life. And before you say any more, please, listen to me. I don't want your family to know. All these years I've been here, and you've never known. I've been beaten, raped and strangled, and you never knew! I've been a good wife, a good mother. I've learned the language, behaved as I should. And I've lain on the floor as he kicked me and wondered if I'll live to see the sun come up. So, no doubt by the time you get home you will have rearranged reality to your own satisfaction, and somehow twisted it to make everything my fault, but I know it's not."

"I did not know things were so bad," she says. "Please, cover yourself."

My fingers shake as I do up the buttons on the blouse, tuck the scarf around my face. I drink the coffee, hot and black. It scalds my throat.

"Amanda, you must understand my concern, especially for the children."

"Why do you think I'm still here?"

"But this is not acceptable. Something must be done."

"Your brother Ahmed has offered to adopt them. In fact, he told me he would take them off me if Muhammed carried on like this."

"Perhaps it would be for the best."

"Oh, no! You are not taking my children from me. Why do you think I've stayed, all these years, putting up with all of this, if not for them? Fatima, you're a mother, surely you can't feel that would be the right thing to do?"

"Children need their parents," she says. "But…" She sips her coffee. "I'll talk to my mother. Our father will speak to him. Try to get him to…well, you know. But if things don't change, I think it may come to that."

295

"No. If Ahmed takes them, he won't let me see them again. Perhaps if you could…"

"It's not up to me."

"I see."

"I will talk to my mother," she says. She embraces me gently.

"Thank you."

"So my father says that I have to be there and sign the papers." I don't look at Muhammed over the breakfast table.

"How much is the insurance?"

"Around twenty thousand pounds, but it's shared three ways, so I'll get around seven thousand."

"Not much then."

"Well, it's still money. And he says he'll pay for the tickets home if we can make it to my sister's wedding."

"Ungh."

"We wouldn't have to stay long. Two weeks maximum."

"Tell your father to send money for the tickets." Muhammed stands over me. He smells of alcohol. His eyes are bleary.

"Oh, ok. That's great."

"But I'm not coming. I can't leave work. And I will be helping my brother out with his business soon, as well. You must go. You can take the children. Tell him to send enough for all of us, though. In case I can come. But you should go. You should go to your sister's wedding and see your father about this money."

"Here are the tickets," Grace hands me an envelope. "Sheena got them with cash."

"Good."

"This could be it."

"I hope so, this time."

"My father sent me the tickets."

Muhammed looks up from the television. "I thought he was sending money."

"He said he would, but I think he got a better deal buying them himself. He is sending some more money soon, to cover our expenses. "

"You should have asked for money!"

I'm ready, feet planted, body braced. Slap! There it is. Slap, slap!

"Baba!" Shahid leaps to his feet. Muhammed backhands him swiftly, but not as hard as he hits me.

"Leave it," I tell my son, who has tears of fury and pain on his face. "I'm fine."

"Tell me when the money arrives." He turns back to the television.

"Grace."

"Amanda." She steps inside, closes the door, and enfolds me closely in a flower-scented embrace. Her hands on my back, my face in her neck, my hands clinging to her.

Time to say goodbye. There is no time, no long, lingering farewell. Just the two of us, held close for a prolonged moment.

"Don't cry," she whispers. But tears flow down her cheeks too.

"He might say no again," I say. "I might be back tomorrow night."

"No, this is it. I can feel it."

"I feel it too."

"Oh, Amanda, I hope everything works out for you."

"Grace..." My voice breaks, and for a moment, I can't breathe. I cling to her more tightly. There aren't words enough, in any language, to articulate all that she has meant to me, all that she has done for me. She has been a gentle hand after stinging blows, a calm centre in the storm-tossed sea that is my life. The children have kept me breathing, functioning. Grace has kept me sane.

"Grace. Oh, Grace."

"Hush, I know, I know."

All the pain and fear and anguish disappear for a while, dissolve and vanish, and the heat of the desert is tempered by the memory of other times, other places, and of how tenderness feels. I imprint her face upon my memory, along with the stop-motion capture of every single second of our last moments.

At last, she steps away. "Here is the last of the money."

"Thank you."

She picks up the bag. A stray curl escapes from her headscarf, and I feel myself smiling through the tears that are starting again.

"Well, goodbye then. Write to me, if you can. Let me know how you are."

"Goodbye, Grace. Thank you for...for everything."

She shakes her head, her eyes on mine, staring at me as if trying to memorise my face too. Then she flips the veil into place, and disappears, leaving behind, not her smile, like the Cheshire cat, but her beautiful eyes, framed by a shroud of blackness.

# *Ma'rūf*

"UmmShahid, just in time, you can help put out the dinner." Khala greets me with her thin smile as I enter the house, kicking off my sandals. I hang up the *abaya* in the hall, and hurry into the kitchen.

"Abdelaziz is here," Fatima smiles. "And Layla."

"Wow. What's going on?"

"Well, you are going away."

"It's only for two weeks," I protest, picking up the big platter of lamb and cracked wheat.

"Yes, but it's a great adventure for the children," Layla appears. "Here, let me help with that."

"Ok."

We lay out the meal. In the kitchen, I can hear my boys in the men's room, chattering away.

"I'm going to bring you back Big Ben, Baba," yells Mahmood at his Grandfather.

"I will bring you lots of pictures," Shahid says. His grandfather has given each of the boys a camera for the trip.

I am numb now. I look at the women: Khala, tiny and wizened and never still; Fatima, superior and beautiful; Layla, young and happy, so happy, to be married; Gadria, with her lush body and a knowing smile on her face.

"Make sure you don't stay too long," she says. "Make sure you are back in time for my wedding!"

I pick up Aisha who has toddled into the kitchen. She is heavy. "Mama," she smiles at me, all chubby cheeks and big, brown eyes.

"Come on, let's get you changed," I tell her, noticing a certain odour.

Fatima follows me into the bathroom. "I spoke to my mother. She spoke to my father. He spoke to my brothers.

I think maybe, that Muhammed might…calm down now. But we shall see."

She looks at me, not unkindly, for a long moment.

"I've done all I can, Amanda. But I must ask you to tell me if you ever think he would hurt the children. They would be better off with Ahmed if that was the case."

"I know."

"Good."

"Say goodbye to your grandparents, children," I say, holding Aisha on my hip as I slide my feet into my sandals.

"See you soon, my sons," Khala hugs them in turn. "Be good. Hurry back and tell me all the stories about your trip."

I look at her, and she looks up at me. Layla smiles, and Fatima nods farewell. I veil myself, then take a last look at the house, through the dark mist that clouds my vision. It smells of spices, and incense, and home.

I step outside, the bangles jingling on my wrists, my boys crowding around me. A brief flash of heat, the sun beating down on me, then into the car, my children crawling over me like monkeys. Muhammed roars away and the house disappears in the dusty sunlight.

"The tea is cold," Muhammed complains. We are home, at last, in the family room. He slaps me.

"The tea is cold, Mama," says Yusuf. Then he raises his hand, and hits me hard on the leg.

"Don't do that!" Shahid grasps his hand.

"Why not? Baba does."

300

# *Hawā*

Bright sun, a blinding disk high above me, and heat that defies belief. After all these years, a decade, here in this place, still the sun can steal the life from me when I step outside. Hot pavements, too hot, even through my shoes, and every surface too hot to touch. Inside the great tent of black fabric my breath is rank with fear, and sweat stands on every surface of my skin. It trickles into my eyes, stinging, and soaks the edge of the headscarf at my temples. Around me, men in white, with their red and white checked scarves, hurry past, sometimes accompanied by black shapes, formless, shadows against the impossible light.

Like the sun, the movement is relentless, moving forward in time, herding my children before me, four boys in white *thobes* and headdresses, and a plump baby girl in a pushchair. The only uncovered female face for miles around, perhaps. Here in the Kingdom, the solidarity of women lies in our mutual anonymity. The secret lives of women connect us all. There is understanding without recognition, commonality without communion.

At the airport, hand luggage on my shoulder. Tension. My neck is stiff. The sedative I put in Aisha's morning juice is taking effect – she's sleepy and quiet in the pushchair. The boys are calm. Yusuf trots by my side, holding onto the pushchair. His *kufiyyah* is awry as usual. Eyes huge, taking it all in. And my older boys stride like little men, talking with their father, looking around at the airport with interest, but unafraid. Mahmood is quiet, walking beside Abdullah, but Shahid still hasn't stopped talking.

I should be panicking. The clenched fist in my stomach is ice. All feeling is frozen there. Even fear.

It will happen. It will happen now. Muhammed stands at the check-in desk. I remember the last time, how worried I was that he wouldn't sign the paper. He shows the marriage licence. He shows our passports. The official asks him a question; he answers rapidly, comfortably. Last night he moved quickly too, his fists a blur as he beat me, his breath fast, in and out, mimicking the movements of his body possessing mine.

I am the silent watcher, the faceless pillar of black. The boys cluster around me. Mahmood has his eyes on his father. He is watchful too. All this time, I've wondered if he knew. Now it is obvious. His eyes never leave his father. I can feel the tension in his body, echoing my own. At nine, he's starting to shoot up. Sometimes, when I turn my head, the way he moves…it's his father all over again. More so than Shahid or Abdullah, my twins, who look like each other, who belong to each other first and foremost. Like they shared their father's essence between them, diluted it. It's still there, though. They are all Arab. They are being treated like men now, my twins, who are showing some signs of starting to mature. The family expect them to be in the men's room at family gatherings, the special province of the men, and they eat now before I do, waited on by the women. Mahmood is also accepted there, and he follows his older brothers in whatever they do.

Yusuf starts to droop.

"Sit on the front of the pushchair, then," I tell him. He does. His sister laughs, kicking her feet.

Muhammed beckons me over. "This is my wife."

Please don't ask me to do anything. I've been holding it together so long. I am a walking wounded soldier, held together by sticking plaster, hope, fear and faith. If this is meant to happen, it's meant to happen. Please don't ask anything else of me. The *niqab* is a blessing. No one can see my face. I keep my head down, as I should.

Boarding passes, passports, travel papers, exit visa.

He has signed it.

Seeing the signature, I start to shake. My hands are shaking as I slip the passports into my bag. Does he notice? I couldn't have left the country without this, without his express permission. I was so afraid he would refuse, at the last minute, like last time. I think of all the women, the great web of wives and daughters and mothers who helped me to do this, who hid money for me in their houses, who lied to their husbands for me, who kept my secrets. Women who passed messages amongst themselves, made arrangements, bought us clothes, changed currency. Women who protected me and lied for me and looked out for me, and for Grace. Women who understood what she meant to me. Women who looked after our children so we could spend a last few hours together.

I couldn't bring Grace with me. Even if I could have found a way, she wouldn't have come. Her children come first, and her husband. They always have.

"Come, all of you," I say to the children, pushing the pushchair forward. One step at a time, one foot in front of the other, this is all I can manage. I heft the carry-on bag. I check the boys have their small backpacks.

"Perhaps I should come," Muhammed says at the gate, as I hoist Aisha into my arms, awkwardly, and they take the pushchair away.

"If you want to," I say, glad of the veil, glad he can't see my face. This is the easier way. Even if he comes, nothing will change. It ends today, one way or another. When I lie down to sleep tonight, I will be free.

"If you want to get a ticket, you'd better hurry," I say. "It would be good if you came, managing all the kids on my own…"

"No, I cannot, not really. I told Abdelaziz I would help him with his chauffeur business. And it's only two weeks."

"That's right."

The boys precede me down the long, grey corridor. I am clutching Aisha. Abdullah has the boarding cards. Yusuf is hanging on to the edge of the *abaya*. I turn, once, when Shahid does, to look at Muhammed, watching from the gate. His black eyes are flat, opaque, unfathomable. He nods once at me. I look into his eyes, for the last time. I feel nothing.

Out onto the tarmac, the heat rising in waves, I follow other passengers, mostly men, some women, one other family. Holding it together, clinging to Aisha, one step after another. For one second, before the door of the plane, I look out, at the bleached sky, the baked earth, the heat haze, and dust. The orange-yellow light. The plane door opens, a mouth in the side of a dragon, to carry me away. Carry me away home and let me go. Sun gives way to shadow, and we squeeze into our seats, the four boys in their own seats, Aisha on my lap. That was the other reason Muhammed wouldn't come. The cost. I am thankful for such a large family. I am grateful for my boys, who watch me nervously as we settle in.

Aisha sleeps most of the way. I worry that I gave her too much of the sedative, but it's too late now. Airline food. The boys sleep. I cannot even close my eyes. I sit, one hand on Aisha's plump leg, the other on my bag. The pain, my constant companion, localises in the bruises on my thighs, back and arms. He beat me with his belt last night, every part of me that wouldn't show. He bound my wrists to the bed, and raped me. I can call it that now. I didn't say yes to him. He never noticed. He never asked. He just took. And I didn't want it, not last night, not for a long time. I didn't want him. His foul breath, the fat, sweaty weight of him, his lumpy, doughy skin on mine. His pale, flabby backside pumping and pumping. The rancid oily smell of his hair. No, I didn't fight. Fighting is dangerous. Never fight back. Never give him an excuse. But just because I let him doesn't mean I said yes.

By the time he woke, I was showered, dressed, and ready for the journey. He undressed me again, and did it to me again, on the edge of the bed, him standing, me with my legs balanced on the floor. When he finally stopped I thought, is that the last time?

Now, now I remember, the first time, the time when I did say no, but he went ahead and did it anyway. I remember the realisation that I was pregnant, his kindness, his solicitude, sitting in a kitchen in a small town in Wales, telling me he would marry me. I didn't have anything else to hold on to. He held out a lifeline, and I took it.

How could I have known? I was wrong. It wasn't him that saved me. Islam was my lifeline, the submission to the will of Allah. The sweet, inner silence of prayer, the regularity of ritual, the calm at the centre of everything. The inevitability of the pregnancy, the marriage, the birth of the twins. Everything meant to be. *Inshallah.* The welcoming embrace of his family, a great circle, and the society of women, in our secret, private places, taking care of ourselves and each other.

In the pocket of my skirt, folded into an envelope, are letters from Grace. They are the last tangible proof that she existed, that she was a part of my life. I couldn't leave them behind. The first, from just after my last trip home, full of day to day trivia, gentle affection, soft words and kindnesses. The notes she left for me, at school. The letter from Mecca, the year she did *hajj*. And the note she gave me last week, with the details of the flat in Plymouth.

But we're not going to Plymouth. We're not going home to Wales, either. As hard as we have tried to keep it all a secret, I know we have left a trail, and that Muhammed will find us, if we go to any place that he knows of. I have my own plan.

The cold hits me as soon as the plane lands. The flight was delayed, and it is late morning, a cold, wet morning. Must it always rain? We hurry to the safety of the terminal, the boys quiet, Yusuf demanding to know the English words for everything he sees, trotting along beside Shahid who is holding his hand. Aisha is more alert now. Abdullah carries her on his shoulders, his knowing eyes watchful, always following me. He's too clever, that one, but even he doesn't know, yet. Not that he would tell, not on purpose. He has seen too much to deny me my escape. Mahmood trails behind Shahid, still trying to keep up with his big brothers.

In the toilets at the airport, while we are waiting for the bags, I take it off at last. The headscarf and veil. Ten years. For ten years I have worn this every time I go outside. I take it off, and my face emerges, a pale, old face, lined and weary, with huge, scared eyes, long, greying hair, and a thin neck. I change my clothes, and leave behind the hunched, awkward shadow that was Amanda. I change Yusuf and Aisha into warmer clothes, then throw the *abaya*, veil and headscarf into the bin. I leave behind the letters, in the pocket of the *abaya*. I leave Grace behind me, everything about her, everything that she was to me, all the feelings, the secrets, the unsaid words. I leave behind prayers five times a day, and the heartbreakingly beautiful sound of the *muezzin*, and *kabsa,* and Arabic coffee and dates. I leave behind the beatings and the fear and the prayers that I can live long enough to see my children safe. I turn instead to the future where I face every single aspect of my life alone, ready at last to fight.

The rope burns and bruises on my forearms stand out as I rejoin my sons, who are staring at me as if they have never seen me before. I feel as naked as I must look to them, with my hair down about my face, my faded jeans and t-shirt, too loose on my worn out body, but still revealing my shape.

"It's time to change," I say to the three older boys, when we have collected the suitcases. They file into the gents. When they emerge, they look different, in their jeans and jumpers.

Grey skies, drizzly rain like mist, cold air and wet pavements. Outside crowds are milling around. I follow the signs, pushing the pushchair ahead of me, dragging the suitcase, and veer away from the taxi rank. I don't want to leave a trail. I pay for the train tickets in cash, and then join the crowds on the platform, disappearing into the melée, my children and I, losing ourselves amongst the throng. I can't go home, I don't have one. I can't go back, not this time, not ever. I have shed my name, my identity, my religion, but my faith is still there, my belief in something, in a future, a real future, for all of us.

I trust in Allah, though I will never call myself a Muslim again. I trust this is the right road, the right path, for me and my babies. If so, He will keep us safe, and my husband and his family will never find us, and my friends in the Kingdom will not suffer for their part in helping us escape. My sons will grow up safe and well and recover from the horror, and my daughter will never have to wear the veil, unless one day she chooses to. And my body and my breath and the words of my mouth and the work of my hands will be my own again.

*Inshallah.*

# Glossary of Arabic Words used as Titles

*Baraa* – Innocent

*Sabr* – Endurance

*Falaq* – Dawn

*Mukhtalif* – Differing, discordant

*Bil-gaibi* – Unseen

*Qaul* – Saying, word, theory, doctrine

*Hāsib* – A violent tornado which brings a shower of debris

*Maknūn* – well guarded, concealed from exposure, kept close

*Munkar* – uncommon, unusual, unaccustomed

*Bāl* – Condition of the heart or mind

*Zikrun* – Remembrance, memorial

*Thaqal* – Weight, something weighty, weighed down by something

*Sā-ilīn* – those who seek or those who ask

*Jihād* – The fight

*Mustaqarr* – A time limit, or a place of rest or quiescence

*Mutakallif* – A man who pretends to things that are not true

*Hanīf* – one who is true

*Zurrīyat* – progeny, offspring, family

*Wahyun* – Inspiration (divine)

*Bayān* – The ability to understand and to explain; power of expression

*Fawāq* – Delay

*Halīm* – Forbearing

*Qalb Salīm* – A heart that is pure

*Ma'rūf* – What is commonly known and accepted, the good

*Hawā* – To set, or to rise, like the sun or moon

*Inshallah* – as God wills it

## *About the Author*

 **Alys Einion** has been writing since the age of seven. She has been a nurse, midwife, and is now a lecturer at Swansea University. She has also worked as a chef, and still loves cooking mouth-watering vegan food.

She has a PhD. in Creative Writing and is passionate about writing, and about promoting women's health and wellbeing through her work. She lives with her partner in the South Wales valleys, as well as two cats, two dogs, a teenage son, and two grown up stepsons.

*You can find Alys at:*
@alyseinion
www.alyseinion.wordpress.com
www.onceuponamidwife.wordpress.com

# More from Honno

*Short stories; Classics; Autobiography; Fiction*

Founded in 1986 to publish the best of women's writing, Honno publishes a wide range of titles from Welsh women.

**In a Foreign Country** *Hilary Shepherd*

Anne is in Ghana for the first time. Her father, Dick, has been working up country for an NGO since his daughter was a small child. They no longer really know each other. Anne is forced to confront her future and her failings in the brutal glare of the African sun.

ISBN: 9781906784621
£8.99

**Left and Leaving** *Jo Verity*

Gil and Vivien have nothing in common but London and proximity, and responsibilities they don't want, but out of tragedy something unexpected grows.

*"Humane and subtle, a keenly observed exploration of the way we live now…
I am amazed that Verity's work is still such a secret. A great read"*
Stephen May

ISBN: 9781906784980
£8.99

### About Elin *Jackie Davies*

Elin Pritchard, ex-firebrand, is back home
for her brother's funeral. Returning brings
all sorts of emotions to the fore, memories
good and bad, her own and those of the
community she left behind.

*"…unsettling and evocative"*
*"…a deeply moving novel from a new Welsh
talent."*
Cambrian News

ISBN: 9781870206891
£6.99

### Dear Mummy, Welcome *Bethany Hallett*

Despite a successful City career, there is a
void in Beth's life, a void that only a child
can fill. Newly on her own, she is
confronted with the inevitability of a
childless future and so embarks on a
journey to adopt the child she has always
longed for.

Poignant, honest and intimate, *Dear
Mummy, Welcome* is the true story of one
woman's fight against the odds, and a little
girl'sjourney to find a mother.

ISBN: 9781906784300
£8.99

All Honno titles can be ordered online at
**www.honno.co.uk**
twitter.com/honno
facebook.com/honnopress

**Jill** *Amy Dillwyn, ed.Kirsti Bohata*

Jill is an unconventional heroine – a lady who disguises herself as a maid and runs away to London. Life above and below stairs is portrayed with irreverent wit in this fast-paced story. But at the centre of the novel is Jill's unfolding love for her mistress.

"*Jill's experiences are told in a style of quiet power, and with a dry, almost grim, humour.*" The Academy

ISBN: 9781906784942
£10.99

**Here We Stand** *Ed. Helena Earnshaw & Angharad Penrhyn Jones*

A fascinating and unique anthology about contemporary women campaigners and how they were changed by the process of changing the world.

'*A beautiful and necessary book full of passion, humour, encouragement, information and hope. This is the kind of writing that saves lives.*'
A.L. Kennedy

ISBN: 9781909983021
£10.99

All Honno titles can be ordered online at
**www.honno.co.uk**
twitter.com/honno
facebook.com/honnopress

# ABOUT HONNO

Honno Welsh Women's Press was set up in 1986 by a group of women who felt strongly that women in Wales needed wider opportunities to see their writing in print and to become involved in the publishing process. Our aim is to develop the writing talents of women in Wales, give them new and exciting opportunities to see their work published and often to give them their first 'break' as a writer.

Honno is registered as a community co-operative. Any profit that Honno makes is invested in the publishing programme. Women from Wales and around the world have expressed their support for Honno. Each supporter has a vote at the Annual General Meeting.

For more information and to buy our publications, please write to Honno at the address below, or visit our website: www.honno.co.uk

Honno
Unit 14, Creative Units
Aberystwyth Arts Centre
Aberystwyth
Ceredigion
SY23 3GL

### Honno Friends

We are very grateful for the support of the Honno Friends: Jane Aaron, Annette Ecuyere, Janet Henderson, Beryl Thomas, Gwyneth Tyson Roberts. For more information on how you can become a Honno Friend, see: http://www.honno.co.uk/friends.php